Shug's Place

A Novel-in-Stories

BY
Bob Strother

MINT HILL BOOKS
MAIN STREET RAG PUBLISHING COMPANY
CHARLOTTE, NORTH CAROLINA

Copyright © 2013 Bob Strother

Cover Photo and Design by Anne M. Hicks

Author Photo courtesy of Cameron Clark,
www.cameronkellystudio.com

Acknowledgments:
"By Any Other Name" first appeared in *Scattered, Smothered, and Covered* by Bob Strother, published by Main Street Rag Publishing Company, 2011.

Library of Congress Control Number: 2012953891

ISBN: 978-1-58848-410-5

Produced in the United States of America

Mint Hill Books
Main Street Rag Publishing Company
PO Box 690100
Charlotte, NC 28227-7001
www.MainStreetRag.com

*This book is dedicated to my grandchildren,
Brody, Owen, Harper, and Darby,
whose smiles light up my life.*

Special Thanks

I would like to thank my editor, Anne M. Hicks, for her ongoing support and encouragement, and my publisher, M. Scott Douglass, for providing me this opportunity. Also Susan M. Boyer, Sarah Cureton, David Burnsworth, and John and Marcia Migacz, who read and critiqued early versions of these stories, and a special thank you to John, whose idea it was to turn a simple piece of short fiction into this novel-in-stories. Finally, my continuing love and affection go to my wife, Vicki, my First Reader and favorite muse, for her unending support, wisdom, and patience.

Contents

By Any Other Name 1
The Legacy: Beginnings, March 15, 1906 18
Hide and Seek 20
The Legacy: Out in Left Field, September 6, 1912 41
Forgive Us Our Sins 44
The Legacy: Pride and Patriotism, March 19, 1917 71
Where Smiling Bastards Lie 73
The Legacy: The Blind Pig, April 12, 1922 104
A Good Day in Hell 107
The Legacy: No Good Deed, October 7, 1935 130
Old Soldiers 134
The Legacy: Billy and the Brown Bomber,
November 14, 1944 158
Blood Uncles 162
The Legacy: Dancing at the Den, September 22, 1955 181
Could'a, Would'a, Should'a 184
The Legacy: Billy Wilson Returns, July 26, 1967 196
Plausible Lies 200
The Legacy: Long Time Gone, February 15, 1973 227
Bird with a Wing Down 231
The Legacy: Feels Like Home, October 18, 1981 257
Kill Me Softly 261
All's Well 289

The characters and events in this book are fictitious. Any similarity to real persons, living or dead, is coincidental and not intended by the author.

By Any Other Name

The drifts had built to three feet in some places and snow clung to the big plate glass window in a shimmering array of silver-white patterns. It was almost five o'clock in the afternoon and the light was going fast.

Shug put on a fresh pot of coffee and slid onto a battered oak stool next to the cash register. He wore his brown hair pulled back in a short ponytail, his way of eschewing the trendy perms of the 1980s. Sun-etched crinkle lines at the corners of his eyes made him appear slightly older than his thirty-five years. He finished counting the register change and did a quick inventory of the back bar supplies and coolers.

"Hey, Leon."

"Yo," came the reply from the combination office and storage room located at the rear of the bar.

"We could use another case of Molson's."

"Comin' up."

Leon worked first shift at the Buick-Olds-Pontiac plant in Southfield, a few miles north of Detroit proper, and moonlighted nights and weekends with Shug, doubling as bartender and, when needed, bouncer. The latter wasn't often because Leon could intimidate the rowdiest of customers. He looked a lot like the actor who played Shaft, only bigger, and he'd spent four years in the Marines with a Force-Recon unit. His toothy smile could be engaging or scary as hell, according to the situation, and his dialect varied from educated to "street" depending on his mood. He slept five hours a night and ran five miles every day.

Shug took the case of beer from Leon and slid back the brushed-chrome top of the cooler. At first, he thought the blast of frigid air he felt came from the unit, then realized someone had opened the front door to the bar.

The girl hung there in the open doorway, snow in her hair, eyes roaming over the mostly unoccupied booths and tables. Shug thought she was cute in a wet, Rat Terrier sort of way.

"Close it!" Leon yelled. He turned to Shug and mouthed the word, "Hooker."

Shug took a longer look. She was somewhere between sixteen and twenty-two, with frizzy brown hair and way too much make-up. She wore a white, fake-fur coat that stopped at the waist, a tight black skirt barely covering her stock in trade, and strappy heels that practically guaranteed she'd bust her ass on the icy street outside.

She looked over at Shug and Leon and said, "Huh?"

Leon pointed to the open door behind her. "The door," he repeated. "Close it."

She did and then turned back to the men. "I'm sorry. I wasn't sure if you were open yet."

"Oh, we're open all right," Shug said, waving a hand at the nearly empty room. The retirees had cleared out, gone to wherever they went for their five o'clock suppers and early bedtimes, and it was too early for the influx of office workers. "We're just going broke."

She walked to the bar, looking awkward in her high heels, and slipped onto one of the leather-backed swivel stools. "I'll have a rum and Coke." She dug into her purse and pulled out a pack of Virginia Slims.

Shug leaned over the bar on his elbows. "How old are you?"

She held her cigarette up and he lit it for her with a match from one of the small gold-foil boxes dotting the length of the mahogany and Formica bar. Leon rolled his eyes and disappeared into the back.

She blew a plume of smoke toward the ceiling. "Twenty-one."

"I.D.?"

She snorted a laugh. "Oh sure, I got I.D."

"How about a cup of coffee instead?"

"What are you, my daddy?"

"No, honey, I own this place. And if it's okay with you, I'd like to keep my liquor license."

She picked up the matchbox and looked at the lettering embossed on the foil. "You're Shug?"

"Uh-huh." He placed a cup and saucer on the bar and poured coffee for her.

"How'd you get a name like Shug?"

"My mother called me Shug—short for Sugar—when I was a kid. It stuck."

"Oh." She took another drag on the cigarette. "So, Shug, are you a sweet guy?"

He grinned. "Sometimes. What's your name?"

"Rose." A corner of her mouth turned up. "Roselyn, actually, but I like Rose better." She gulped down a third of the coffee and slid off the stool. "I gotta start work now. Thanks for the coffee."

"What? You're not gonna pay?" He watched the color rise in her cheeks as she began to fumble in her purse. "Rose?"

She looked up at him.

"Rose, I'm kidding. Coffee's on the house. Anytime." He glanced around the room again and shrugged. "Hell, I'm going broke anyway."

She gave him a grateful grin. "Thanks, Shug."

He called after her as she pulled the door shut behind her. "Don't bust your ass on the ice."

Jeffery "Shug" Barnes had served four hitches in the First Air Cav, including a thirteen-month tour in Viet Nam. In 1979, he invested his reenlistment bonuses in Apple computer stock. When he mustered out in the fall of 1981, he had enough money to make the down payment on a small neighborhood bar not far from Tiger Stadium in Central Detroit.

Shug's Place drew a steady group of regulars. Not exceptionally profitable, it still provided a modest but comfortable living for

Shug and his long-haired, feline live-in, Midnight. If asked, Shug could not have said for certain whether Midnight was male or female. There existed between the two a certain measure of respect and a mutual appreciation for privacy. Neither was going to comb through the furry parts of the other over such inconsequential and irrelevant information.

Unlike Leon, Shug slept as much as possible and didn't walk, let alone run, anywhere he could drive his two-year-old '85 Oldsmobile 442. Thus far, his indolence hadn't overtaken his metabolism, but he'd recently begun a careful scrutiny of his waistline.

Rose came in again the next night and the next, and before long, Shug came to look forward to her visits. Over the course of a couple of weeks, he learned she was eighteen years old, had graduated from high school in eastern Kentucky, and she'd come north with a boyfriend who'd found work in one of the Ford factories.

"So, where's the boyfriend now?" Shug asked.

"He didn't like the cold." She checked to make sure Leon was in the back and whispered, "And he didn't like working around so many blacks, you know? One day, he just decided he was going back to Pikeville and he left the next morning."

"And you didn't go with him."

She shook her head. "There was no work there for me. I'd rather do what I'm doing than live off welfare."

"How'd you get started?"

"Hooking?" She smiled at him. "I didn't, not at first. As a matter of fact, I went down to the Ford factory where Billy—that was his name, my boyfriend—worked, and asked for his job."

"They gave it to you?"

"No, but they gave me another one. And that's what I did for four months. Then I got laid off." She smoothed the fabric of her skirt. "That's when I met Silko. He took me in, turned me out, and here I am."

She checked the cheap Timex on her wrist and gave him a playful wink. "Speaking of which, I should be going to work now. Keep my seat warm, Shug. I'll see you tomorrow."

Shug watched her disappear through the doorway.

Leon eased up next to him and leaned on the bar. "You about ready to let her start working the place?"

"As far as I'm concerned, she's not a hooker in here, Leon. She's a customer."

"Yeah, I can see where her free coffees are having a real positive impact on the cash flow." Leon shook his head and began wiping down the bar.

Rose didn't show up the next night, or for two nights after that. On the fourth day, she came in sporting a split lip and a yellowing discoloration under one eye.

Shug lit her cigarette and studied her face. "Rough customer?"

"Nah, it was Silko." She touched a tentative finger to her lip and winced. "He found a letter my older sister sent me. Janet works on a horse farm north of Lexington. She wanted me to come back to Kentucky. Said she'd get me on at the farm."

"And Silko didn't like that, huh?"

"There was a bus ticket in the envelope. He just about went crazy when he saw it. Said I was his money girl and I wasn't never leaving him."

"Sounds like a good reason to head south to me."

"You weren't there. You didn't see his eyes." She shivered. "He said he'd kill me if I tried to leave."

"What, to set an example for the other girls?"

She nodded. "I heard some stories…"

Her voice trailed off, and Shug noticed her hands were trembling. She looked down at her lap for a minute. When she looked at him again, her eyes were moist. "I don't know what to do, Shug."

"Look, Rose, do yourself a favor and get the hell out of Detroit."

A tear rolled down her cheek, and she stifled a small sob. "I don't even have money for another bus ticket. He took it all."

The office crowd was starting to drift in. Shug moved down the bar, poured a couple of drinks, and came back to where she sat. "Tomorrow," he said. "Don't bring anything except what you absolutely need. I'll have a ticket for you. I'll even drive you to the bus station."

She pulled a small compact from her purse and used a bar napkin to wipe under her eyes. "I don't know, Shug. I'm scared."

"Think about it at least."

"Okay," she promised. "I'll think about it."

The following evening, she came into the bar carrying a small suitcase and wearing a long, gray wool coat. The heavy makeup she usually wore was gone. She looked at Shug and took a deep breath. "I'm ready. Let's do it."

Shug went into the back and spoke to Leon. "Cover the front for half an hour, okay?"

Leon looked out to where Rose waited by the bar, a frown on his face. "Man, you shouldn't be gettin' mixed up with this."

"Just do it, Leon. Please?"

"You the boss."

Rose chattered nervously on the way to the station. She told Shug how her sister had always loved horses, how she'd worked for one of the farm vets after high school and later was hired by Kensington Stables in Paris, Kentucky.

"She's gonna freak out when she sees me."

"You haven't told her you were coming?"

She shook her head. "I'll call her from the road. Right now, I just want to get out of here."

They turned into the parking lot at six-fifteen. It was near freezing outside, and dark. The lights of the bus station seemed a cozy haven amid scattered clumps of snow and ice. Shug pulled into a parking slot just outside the front doors.

"C'mon," he said. "I'll wait with you until the bus leaves."

She placed a hand on his arm. "No, it's okay. You need to get back to the bar."

"But—"

"I'm a big girl, Shug. Don't worry. I'll get on the right bus."
He smiled at her and handed over the ticket. "Good luck, Rose."
She leaned over and hugged him. "Thanks, Shug. Thanks for everything."
Shug rolled his window down and watched as she waved from the station doorway. He returned the wave, backed out of the space, and pulled out onto the street. He never noticed the black Cadillac Seville that had followed them from the bar.

It was going on nine o'clock in the morning when Shug woke to a continuous pounding on his front door. He pulled on a robe, padded across the living room, and yanked the door open. "What the hell?"

The man who stood there wore a camel-hair coat and a darker brown snap-brim hat. He was trim, late forties, with hard-looking eyes. "Are you Jeffery Barnes?"

"Yeah."

"I'm Detective Frank Owens, Detroit Homicide." He flipped open the badge holder on his belt and put one hand on the door frame. "Mind if I come in?"

Shug stepped away from the door, and Owens stepped inside. He did a quick scan of the room. "Nice place."

"What's going on?"

"You know a hooker name of Rose?"

Shug felt his chest tighten up. "I know a young woman named Rose. What happened? Is she all right?"

"No. She's dead. One of the girls that works the area around the bus station on Sixteenth Street took a john out back for a blowjob and found her there about eight o'clock last night." Owens scratched at the back of his neck. "The girl said she'd seen this Rose around but didn't know her last name or anything. I wondered if you might."

Shug slumped down onto the living room sofa. "It's Hargraves. Roselyn Hargraves." He rubbed his face hard with his hands. "How'd you know to come to me?"

Owens pulled a gold foil matchbox from his pocket. "She was carrying this. I pulled up your liquor license and found your address."

They rode together to the morgue. On the way, Shug filled Owens in as much as he could.

"She was from Pikeville, Kentucky, but I don't know what family might still be there. She's got a sister works in a town called Paris, north of Lexington, I think."

"All right," Owens said. "We'll check with the local cops and try to find the next of kin."

"She was going back home." Shug said. "Her pimp, a guy called Silko, beat her up the other day. She said he threatened to kill her if she tried to leave."

Owens pulled into a parking space in front of a nondescript three-story building. He took a small pad from his breast pocket and scribbled a few notes in it. "Sounds like a real nice fellow. I'll look into it."

Inside, Shug identified the badly beaten body. According to Owens, death was due to multiple blunt force trauma. A weapon of some sort had been used, but nothing was found at the scene.

"Thanks for coming down," Owens said. "I'll get somebody to drive you back."

"This Silko guy, will you let me know what you come up with?"

Owens hesitated. "I'm not sure that's—"

"She was only eighteen," Shug said. "A good kid. She was going *home*."

"Okay, okay. Give me a day or so. I'll call you."

Leon leaned against the bar and wiped his big hands on a towel. "I'm real sorry about your friend, man."

Shug shook his head. "It was my fault, Leon."

"Uh-uh. You were just trying to help. Wasn't nobody's fault but the sonofabitch killed her."

The telephone rang and Leon picked it up. "It's for you. Detective Owens."

Shug took the receiver. "Hey, thanks for calling. What's up?"

The muffled metallic sounds of an electric typewriter came through the phone, then Owens' tired voice. "Nothing's up. Silko's got two of his girls saying they were together all night that night, and we've got no evidence to the contrary."

"But—"

"I know, I *know*, goddamnit. Look, what can I do? The man has an alibi. I know it stinks, but what the hell can I do?"

The line went dead in Shug's hand.

The woman came in a couple of days later, around three in the afternoon. Shug was alone in the bar except for two retirees hunched over beer and pretzels in a back corner booth. There was an outdoorsy look about her and color in her cheeks that said she'd been spending time under a warmer sun.

Shug left his paperwork on the back bar and met her as she slid onto a stool. He gave her a perfunctory smile. "What can I get you?"

"I'm looking for Shug Barnes."

He looked at her a little more closely. She was a brunette in her late twenties, not pretty, but not a dog either. She wore blue jeans and a suede, hip-length coat lined with cream-colored wool.

"That would be me."

She held out a hand. "I'm Janet Hargraves. My little sister wrote me about you."

"Rose? You're Rose's sister?" Shug took the offered hand. Her grip was firm and brief, her palm callused.

She nodded. "I appreciate your help in letting us know what happened. Detective Owens told me where to find you. He's helping me make arrangements to take Rose's body back home."

He let out a long breath. "Miss Hargraves, I—"

"Call me Janet, please."

"Janet, I hadn't known her long, but she seemed like a sweet kid. She'd come in for coffee, we'd talk, and…" He shrugged. What more could he say?

"Mister Barnes, I was several years older than Rose, but in our own way, we were quite close. I was already gone when she left high school and came up here with her boyfriend. If I'd still been there, I would never have let her go. She told me when they split. She told me about her job at Ford. And then a couple of weeks ago, she said she'd gone to work for you."

Shug stood without moving for a moment as her words soaked in. "Well, I just ... I mean, she'd just started."

She held up a hand. "I know now that's not true. Detective Owens told me that she had been working as a prostitute." She gave him a sincere smile. "But thanks for what I think you were going to say. Anyway, I'm a big girl and a survivor. Rose was a survivor, too. She may have been selling her body, but she wasn't a whore. Not to me, anyway."

Shug slid a napkin over in front of her. "I'll drink to that, Janet. How about you?"

"You got any Kentucky bourbon?"

He reached under the bar and pulled out a bottle of Maker's Mark. "How do you like it?"

"Neat. Water back."

He poured and they touched glasses. "To Rose," he said.

"To Rose."

It was after eight o'clock when Janet returned to Shug's Place. Leon was tending bar while Shug was finishing a cheeseburger plate from the restaurant two doors down. She looked like she needed another bourbon, maybe a double.

"What's wrong?" Shug asked.

"I went to see Detective Owens again. He told me about Rose's pimp, Silko, what you'd said about him, about his alibi. And he showed me the crime scene photos." She hugged herself and shuddered. Then her face went hard. "You think Silko killed her?"

Shug nodded. "I think so."

"But the police can't do anything."

"That's what they say."

She stared at Shug for a long moment. "Can you get me a gun?"

He shook his head. "That's crazy. You can't do something like that. Hell, you couldn't even find this guy, let alone—"

"I'll find a way. One way or the other, I'll find him, and I'll make him pay for what he did to Rose. If you won't help me, I'll do it by myself." She brushed angrily at a tear and slid off the stool. "Excuse me."

Shug watched as Janet disappeared into the ladies' room, Rose's words ringing in his ears. *Keep my seat warm, Shug.* He remembered the way she'd hugged him in the car: *Thanks, Shug. Thanks for everything.* Goddamn it, he should have gone inside no matter what she'd said. He should have waited with her and made sure she got on that bus.

Janet came back from the restroom and slipped into her coat.

"Take it back off," he said. "Let's talk."

Half an hour later, he took Leon to one side. "You know this Silko guy?"

"I know *of* him."

"Can you find out where he lives?"

Leon nodded. "What you plannin' here?" He looked beyond Shug to Janet, who was still at the bar.

"We're going to find Silko and rough him up. Make him pay for what he did to Rose."

"Rough him up? You're going to *rough this dude up?* Shug, you don't know what the hell you're doing, man." He glanced at Janet again. "She talk you into this?"

"No, she wanted to kill him, but I wouldn't go along with that. Now, will you help us find him or not?"

Leon took a breath and let it out. "Let me make a few calls."

The bar closed at one o'clock. Shug, Janet, and Leon sat together at a small table in the back.

"The man lives off Woodward, about fifteen minutes north of here." Leon slid a scrap of paper with an address over to Janet, who looked at it and passed it to Shug. "His usual habit, he checks on the girls between one and two o'clock, heads for home, relaxes a bit."

"Will he have anybody with him?" Shug asked.

"No." Leon smiled. "He wants some fun with the girls, he has an afternoon delight before they go to work. Likes 'em fresh, or so I was told."

Shug checked his watch. "That gives us about thirty minutes plus driving time." He looked over at Janet. "Are you sure you want to do this?"

"Absolutely."

He walked out to the front and pulled a baseball bat from under the counter. He ran a hand over the smooth wood grain and noted the Louisville Slugger trademark. *How very ironic*, he thought, *made in Kentucky*. "Let's go then. We get there early, we can watch the house, make sure he's alone."

Leon got up from the table and pulled on his heavy parka.

"Where you going?" Shug asked.

"I'm going with you crazy white folk. Otherwise, you get yourself killed, what am I gonna do nights and weekends?" He took a Taurus .380 automatic from his jacket pocket and checked the chamber.

Shug gave him a look.

"That baseball bat is fine," Leon said, "if the man stand still and let you hit him with it. This here is what make him stand still."

"You always carry that?"

Leon shrugged. "This is Detroit, ain't it?"

A black Cadillac Seville turned into the asphalt drive at ten minutes before two. From Shug's Olds, they watched as a man got out and entered the single-story, painted brick house. First one, then two lights went on inside.

Two minutes later, the trio approached the house. Janet waited in front of the door while Shug and Leon positioned themselves against the wall on either side of her. Shug nodded at her, and she rang the bell.

The porch light came on a few seconds later and there was a sucking sound as the front door pulled open against the exterior storm door.

"I am so sorry to bother you," Janet said. "It's my car." She gestured toward the street with one hand. "It quit on me, and, well, I wondered if I could use your phone, or maybe you could call—"

The storm door swung open, and Leon was on the man before he could react, pressing the Taurus into his forehead and backing him into the front room.

"What the fuck? What you doin', man? This is my home."

Leon smacked him across the face with the barrel of the gun. "Yeah, and this is what you call your home invasion, motherfucker."

Janet came around to Leon's left. Shug stood just behind and to Leon's right. He tapped the baseball bat gently on the floor.

Silko wore a black satin robe with burgundy trim. He was tall and thin, his shaved head gleaming in the light from a table lamp. He looked at Shug, the bat, then back to Leon. "This gotta be a mistake, brother. I don't know you, do I?"

Shug propped the bat on his shoulder and walked over to where Silko stood. "That's right, you don't know us, but you knew somebody we knew. Do you remember Rose?" He swung the bat hard into the side of Silko's left knee.

The house shook when Silko hit the floor. He screamed and grabbed his leg.

Shug handed the bat to Janet.

She stood over the man now writhing on the floor. "He asked if you remembered Rose. Do you? She was my sister, you son of a bitch."

Silko rose up on one elbow.

Janet held the bat in both hands and lifted it high above her head.

"Wait!" Silko shouted.

The Louisville Slugger connected between his neck and his shoulder, and this time there was an audible crunch. Silko screamed again and rolled over on his stomach. Her next swing caught him square on the spine just below the base of his neck. He made a guttural, choking sound deep in his throat and his head slumped to the floor.

Janet drew back quickly for another blow, but Shug caught the bat's handle with his hand. "Janet." She struggled, trying to wrench the weapon away from him. "Janet! No! I said no killing." Her eyes were wild, her face a complex mask of hurt and rage. He gripped the bat tighter and said, more softly, "Janet?" He felt her relax her grip and watched as tears streamed wetly down her cheeks. She let go of the wooden handle and her shoulders slumped. Shug put one arm around her and pulled her away from the unconscious man.

Leon used the toe of his boot to roll Silko onto his back. The man's shoulders were pressed back on the floor and his head and neck were at an odd angle from the rest of his torso. Leon stood there for a moment looking down at him. "Well, he ain't dead. At least not yet. His chest is moving." He turned to Shug. "If you folks are through, I suggest we get the hell out."

Shug gave Janet's shoulder a gentle squeeze and followed Leon to the door. He turned off the porch light and checked the street. "Janet?"

She stood looking down at what was left of Silko. "Yeah, I'm coming." She followed the other two out and pulled the door closed behind her.

Shug dropped Leon back at the bar to pick up his car, and Janet at her hotel.

"Well," she said, "Rose and I will be on the train tomorrow morning, going home." She reached over and squeezed his arm. "I'll always remember you, Shug."

He could feel the strength in her hand, and he had a split-second image of the bat arcing down.

She gestured out the windshield. "If you ever get tired of all this, Kentucky can always use another good bourbon pourer."

He could still see her in the rearview as he turned left on Grand and headed for home.

Shug woke once again to a persistent pounding on his door. He looked at the greenish-white numbers on the bedside clock: 11:36 a.m. He pulled on his robe and struggled to the door.

Owens stood waiting, hands in the pockets of his coat. "I thought you'd want to know about this."

Shug felt a flutter inside his chest. He hoped it didn't show. "About what?"

"Can we talk inside?"

"Sure." Shug went into the kitchen and started a pot of coffee.

Owens followed him and leaned against the refrigerator. "It's about Silko."

Shug kept his back turned. "Yeah? What about him?"

"One of his girls found him at his home this morning. He was fucked up pretty bad."

The cat wandered into the kitchen, sniffed at his empty food bowl, and leapt onto the table. He looked at Owens for a few seconds, then dismissed him.

Shug picked up the bowl, filled it with dry food from a box on the counter, and set it down on the table. He and Owens watched silently as the cat began to eat. Crunching noises filled the room.

"So what happened to him?" Shug checked on the coffee and got out two mugs from an overhead cabinet. "Cream and sugar?"

"Just black, please. Oh, it's quite a story he's telling. Seems a salt and pepper team busted in on him—two men, one black, one white, and a white chick. Worked him over real good with a ball bat. He's mostly paralyzed from the neck down. The ER doc wasn't sure if it's permanent or not. Anyway, he must have been unconscious for hours after the beating. Didn't come around good until he got to the hospital."

Shug poured the coffee and handed a mug to Owens.

Owens blew on the coffee for a few seconds before taking a sip. "But that's not the worst part."

Shug's mug stopped halfway to his lips. "Huh?"

"They emasculated him."

The corner of Shug's mouth twitched almost imperceptibly. "Well, I imagine getting pounded with a bat could do that to a guy."

Owens shook his head. "No, I mean they cut his nuts out."

A tingling sensation began in Shug's shoulders. *What the hell?* "They castrated him? Cut his nuts off?"

"Well, to be precise, he was 'gelded.'" Owens took another sip from the mug. "This is really good coffee. Yeah, the ER doc says they made two slits in the scrotum, pulled out the jewels and *snip-snip*. Hell of a thing, huh?"

Shug stared down at his coffee, nodding slowly. "Hell of a thing."

Owens chuckled. "Maybe they were a surgical team."

"Yeah, maybe." Shug walked over to the kitchen window and looked out at the bare branches of an elm in his side yard.

"I don't guess you'd know anything about any of this, would you?"

Shug turned and faced Owens. "Sorry. I can't help you."

"Where were you last night?"

"Got back here a little after we closed, one-thirty or so, went to bed, woke up to you pounding on my door."

"Any way I can corroborate that?"

"You can ask the cat."

Owens stared at the cat. The cat stared back. Owens blinked first.

"By the way, Shug—is it okay if I call you Shug?"

Shug nodded.

"While we were at Silko's house, we just happened to find a silver-handled cane, with what might be traces of blood still on it. We'll check it out. I'll let you know what we find." He sat the mug down next to the cat's food dish. "Well, I guess Miss

Hargraves is on her way back to Kentucky by now. Seemed like a nice lady."

"Yeah. She did." He followed Owens to the front door.

"Watch yourself, Shug."

"I will. Thanks."

Owens called back two weeks later. The evidence found at Silko's house was positive for Rose's blood type. They were looking for whatever else they could find.

"Might be enough to convict," Owens said, "when and if it ever goes to trial. Or maybe he'll cop a plea, or whatever. Nobody's really pushing all that hard because it turns out the paralysis is permanent. For sure, he's not going anywhere."

That afternoon, Shug opened the bar's front door and scooped up the handful of envelopes resting inside below the mail slot. Behind the bar, he fanned them out, keeping the bills and tossing the junk mail. Near the bottom, he found a manila-colored business envelope with a Kensington Stables return address.

There was no note inside. Instead, pressed between two squares of cardboard was a single red rose. It was dry and fragile-looking, and a couple of the petals had come off, but it was mostly intact. He brought it up to his nose and thought he could still smell just the tiniest bit of fragrance. He walked over to the back bar and laid it down next to a half-full bottle of Maker's Mark.

She wasn't a hooker anymore, he thought, *or a whore, or prostitute, or any of the other things she might have once been called. No, now she was just a rose again—a sweet, uncomplicated Kentucky girl who'd finally found her way home.*

The Legacy: Beginnings
March 15, 1906

Three men stood on a rise of land that sloped gradually to the murky waters of the Detroit River. They couldn't see the river from their vantage point, but its smell was unmistakable, its moisture evident in the low-lying fog that swirled around their legs as they began to walk.

"We'll start here—" said John Lee Burgess, gesturing toward the sparsely populated tract of land to his right, then rapidly pacing off sixty yards as the other two hurried along behind him, "—and finish up here." Burgess paused to clip and fire up a Cuban cigar. "As I vision it, we'll have a pharmacy, a haberdashery, a grocery, and a bar." He looked around at the nearby rows of shabby houses and tenements. "A bar for certain. The residents in this area are mostly of Irish descent, and God knows, they have unquenchable thirsts for alcohol."

Burgess studied the faces of his two companions. His gaze was that of someone used to getting exactly what he wanted. That was to be expected. In addition to his real estate interests, he was owner of Burgess Industries, the largest manufacturer of railroad cars in the eastern half of the country and one of the city's major employers.

"I don't know, Mister Burgess," said the older of the two. "I can't see a haberdasher making a living in these surroundings. I mean, these people can barely—"

Burgess plucked the cigar from his mouth. "Sweet Jesus, Arthur, if not a haberdasher, I'll build a laundry or some such thing. We're already being overrun by the Chinese. We might as well give them something to do." He tucked the cigar back into the corner of his mouth. "I'm not asking your advice on what to build, Mister Mayor. I'm asking for the land."

Arthur Armstrong turned to his companion, a nattily dressed man in his thirties. "Can we do that, Seagraves? I mean—" He pointed toward the ramshackle structures dotting the area in question. "—people are living there."

"Yes, sir," the younger man said. "The Fifth Amendment gives us the right to take the land for public purposes."

Armstrong contemplated his shoes for a moment, then took a deep breath and nodded. "All right, Mister Burgess, I'll see to it right away. And you'll have the land at a fair price. But throwing these folks out of their homes will probably make me lose the Irish vote in the next election."

Burgess clapped the mayor on the shoulder. "Nonsense, Arthur. The ones left will thank you for the services we'll provide, especially the bar. It's guaranteed."

The men made their way back to where Burgess's gleaming 1905 Olds automobile waited at the corner of Labrosse and Trumbull Streets.

"I suppose you're right," Mayor Armstrong said. "Still, I can't help feeling badly about evicting those poor people."

Burgess gave the man a patient look usually reserved for some of the erstwhile but incompetent family members in his employ. "Arthur, with the tax revenue the city will get from this development, you'll forget all about it." As they climbed into the car, he added, "Hell, they probably don't vote anyway."

Construction of the development was completed in early December of that same year. Two weeks before Christmas, Douglas Hanahan, an Irish immigrant and proud owner of Hanahan's A Little Bit O' Ireland, hosted a small party for his new colleagues on the block and their employees. John Burgess himself stopped by the bar for a few minutes on his way to a political affair at the country club. While there, he was toasted twice, heartily, before begging off to honor his civic responsibilities.

Hide and Seek

Eve spotted him in the Tiger Stadium parking lot, a distorted reflection in a windshield, twenty yards back, yellow slicker, dark blue baseball cap pulled down to hide the eyes. If she hadn't briefly lost the sense of where her own car was, she might never have noticed him. But when she stopped to get her bearings, he stopped, too. Probably just coincidence, but *probably* wasn't good enough. She kept walking, past her car, out of the parking lot onto Trumbull Street headed south. He stayed a steady half-block behind. At the intersection of Trumbull and Labrosse, she stopped for a traffic light and cast a furtive glance over her shoulder. Her pursuer, if indeed he was a pursuer, had paused and appeared to be studying a street sign a half-block behind. Eve wished she were more familiar with the neighborhood, thinking she might be able to double back and get to her car.

The traffic light changed to green. *What to do?* Eve looked left, then right where a glowing, orange-red neon bar sign caught her eye. She hurried along the sidewalk and ducked into the bar's offset doorway. Cautiously, she peeked around the edge of the brick facade. The man came into view, stopped, looked down the street in her direction, and lit a cigarette. It was no mistake. He was following her. Her heart rate slammed into high gear. Reaching behind her, she found the doorknob and eased backward through the doorway.

Once inside, she turned and did a quick scan of the interior. A long, mahogany bar dominated the left side of the room. Booths with burgundy leather seats lined the right wall, and a half-dozen lacquered wooden tables filled the space in between. From a vintage jukebox on the far wall, Fleetwood Mac's "Little Lies" competed with the noisy chatter of a couple dozen Detroit Tigers' fans. A cloud of cigarette smoke hung just below the ceiling. She turned to the plate glass window just right of the door, straining to see up the sidewalk.

Nothing yet.

Shug Barnes had just loaded a tray with two pitchers of draft Budweiser and a half-dozen frosted mugs when the woman came in through the doorway. No, she hadn't just come in, she'd backed in, affording him a pleasant view of her nicely shaped backside. He hoisted the tray one-handed, weaved through the crowd, and made it to the long table in the center of the room without spilling a drop. When he returned to the bar, she was staring out the big front window, her face close enough to fog the glass. Thirty-something, he guessed but couldn't tell much more from that angle. Her pristine New Balance running shoes and designer jeans said she didn't belong in a working-class place like his. Straight, chestnut-brown hair shimmered in the bar's muted lighting and fell to just below her shoulders.

She turned from the window and caught him staring.

The man in the yellow slicker would be at the bar in seconds. Run? Or hide? Hide won, and she looked for anything that would point her toward the ladies' room. Her eyes swept the room to no avail. Where was it? The bartender was looking at her, and she strode quickly in his direction.

"Restroom?"

He pointed to his left. "Just right of the jukebox. There's a little alcove—"

She hurried past the Rock-Ola and disappeared into the almost invisible restroom niche. She locked the door, went into the stall, and relieved herself—sitting on the toilet until her pounding heart ceased thudding in her ears. Washing up, she studied her reflection in the mirror over the sink. As she often did, Eve wondered who the person was staring back at her.

She gathered her courage, left the bathroom, and stood just inside the alcove doorway. The room was about two-thirds full of patrons, most wearing Tigers baseball caps or shiny orange and blue warm-up jackets. There was no evidence of her pursuer. She stepped out a little further until she could see the bar. Two men and one couple perched on stools. Again, she saw no one she recognized, and if her suspicion was correct, she'd damn sure know him. Eric Farber had been a recurring nightmare for more than a decade.

She walked out past the jukebox. The bartender was behind the long black bar, talking with the couple. He was about her age, maybe a little older, with a nice jaw line and brown hair pulled back in a ponytail. He smiled when she sat down, and his cobalt eyes twinkled.

Shug watched as the woman climbed onto a barstool. She looked as good from the front as she did from the back: luminous green eyes, prominent cheekbones, and a straight, slender nose. He tossed a cardboard coaster down in front of her.

"Evening," he said. "What can I get for you?"

"A draft Miller will be fine."

He'd figured her for a wine drinker, but he drew the beer and set a brimming glass down on the coaster. "I don't think I've seen you in here before. New to the neighborhood?"

She shook her head and lifted the glass, her hand trembling slightly. "No, I have a place up near Mount Clemons. I just came down for the game."

"I live for the Tigers," he said, grinning.

"You must live hard then." Her eyes darted about the room, flitting every few seconds to the big window next to the doorway. Shug wondered if she was meeting someone.

He chuckled. "No, I mean I live for the Tigers' home games. I always do a great business after a home game, win or lose."

"Oh." She downed about a third of the beer and then glanced around the room. "Yeah, I can see that. We either drink to celebrate or to drown our sorrow. But we beat the Pirates tonight. Maybe there's hope yet."

He nodded, thinking she must be either an incurable optimist or truly out of it. The Tigers were eighteen games out of first place and had a winning percentage of just under four hundred.

She was smiling—a forced smile, he thought, because it didn't reach her eyes. *Was she waiting for a reply?* He matched her smile with one of his own. "There's always hope."

Eve had nearly finished her second beer when it occurred to her that she should slow down. If Farber was still out there somewhere, she would need her wits about her. It was possible he hadn't actually seen her come into the bar. If he'd come inside to check, she'd been in the bathroom. But where was he now? Waiting in a doorway, watching for her? She hadn't stopped by her car, so he probably didn't know what she was driving. Still, he'd found her somehow. But how? And how was she going to get back to her car?

Too many questions. The alcohol and her barely controlled panic made it hard to think. A popcorn machine started up at the other end of the long bar, and in a minute the air was suffused with the not unpleasant aromas of hot popcorn and cigarette smoke. She wished now she hadn't quit smoking. She could use a cigarette. After a minute, she downed the last of the beer, mentally said *fuck it*, and signaled for another. The bartender brought over a fresh draft and a basket of the still-steaming popcorn.

"Thanks," she said. "What's your name?"

"Shug," he looked her directly in the eyes and flashed that smile again. "What's yours?"

As tense as she was, she felt something flip deep down in her belly.

"Eve." The word was out before she realized what she'd done. *Damn it!* She wasn't concentrating. "I mean … Evelyn." Where had they gone, those skills she'd so painstakingly acquired over the long years of running? She'd become too complacent.

He extended his hand to her. She took it. His grip was warm and strong.

"Well, Eve Evelyn..." he grinned, a crooked, lopsided grin, and for a moment, she could almost picture him as a young boy, "...it's nice to meet you."

Someone in one of the booths called out to him then, and he went back to filling orders.

Shug noticed the light come on in the back room and stepped in to find Leon wiping his face with a damp paper towel. He'd called in earlier in the day to say he'd be late.

"Sorry I took so long," Leon said. "My nephew just got out the Navy, and Roberta threatened to skin me alive if I didn't stay for supper and help celebrate."

Shug chuckled. Leon's sister, Roberta, a widow before her time, was determined to maintain as full and healthy a family unit as she could. That included cooking Sunday lunches of chicken or pot roast, sweet corn, and whatever other fresh vegetables she found at the Farmer's Market west of town. Leon was a regular at his sister's table, else he'd incur her wrath. Shug had a standing invitation as well but seldom rose early enough to make it.

Leon stole a glance past Shug out into the larger room. "Looks like a happy crowd tonight. I guess the Tigers must have won, huh?"

"Uh-huh—six-three. You didn't watch the game on TV?"

"Nah, I was too busy listening to my nephew lie to his momma about what all he did or didn't do in the Navy." Leon cocked his chin toward the end of the bar closest to the restrooms. "Who's the looker?"

Shug shrugged. "Name's either Eve or Evelyn. I'm not sure which."

Leon raised an eyebrow and grunted. "She looks too high-toned to be drinking here. Probably, she don't want to give her real name."

"Yeah, probably. I'm going down to Mack's Grill for a cheeseburger. You want me to bring you anything?"

"No, man, I ate too much already. Besides, Mack don't have nothing healthy. You eat that shit Mack cooks up, you're gonna get fat and slow."

"Just watch the bar, Leon. I'll be back in a few minutes."

Leon smiled. "You the boss, Boss."

Shug left the back room and walked over to the woman. Her elbows were propped on the bar top and she was staring at the third draft Miller she'd hardly touched. The green eyes were more alert than they'd been a few minutes ago, and worry lines creased her forehead. Mentally, he ran through a few of his flirting gambits, then decided on something practical. "I'm getting a cheeseburger from the diner next door. Can I get something for you?"

She rested her chin in one hand. "Can you get me change for the cigarette machine? I'm starting smoking again. I just decided."

Shug took three dollars from the bills in front of her on the bar and brought back change. He watched as she slid carefully off the stool and disappeared into the alcove housing the restrooms and cigarette machine. He waited a minute, but she didn't come right back. He went to Mack's.

When Eve came out of the restroom, Shug had been replaced by a huge black man with sinewy muscles and a Fu Manchu moustache. He reminded her of a Black Panther she'd known a long time ago—a lifetime ago.

She glanced out the window. It was darker than pitch outside, going on eleven-thirty, and she still hadn't seen any evidence of Farber, if that's who it was. He couldn't still be waiting somewhere outside, could he? If it *was* him, he would wait forever. The beer in her stomach began to turn sour.

The bar's front door swung open, and Shug came back in carrying a grease-stained paper bag. He winked and sat down across from her on a stool behind the bar. When he opened the bag, the smell of food didn't make her sick like she imagined it would. It made her ravenous. And it gave her an idea.

Shug saw the way she was looking at his fried onion rings and held one out to her. She snatched it from his fingers and bit into it greedily. Grease coated her full lips, and she licked it off with the tip of her tongue.

"Oh God," she moaned, "that's so good."

Shug stared at her as she ate the other half and felt himself becoming aroused. He pushed the cardboard take-out plate closer. "Please, have some more."

At a little after midnight, he pulled Leon to one side and gestured toward the woman with his head. "Her car wouldn't start. I'm going to drive her home. Can you handle things here and close up for me?"

Leon glanced at his wristwatch and blinked slowly at Shug. "Where she stayin' it'd take you that long to drive her home? Grand Rapids?"

"Come on, man. She promised to make me breakfast."

"Yeah, I can tell she likes eating with you, 'specially them onion rings." Leon gave him a toothy grin. "Say, you don't even eat breakfast, do you? Sleeping till noon and all?"

The bar owner shrugged. "Hey, I'm flexible."

Leon shook his head and glanced at the woman again. "Yeah? Well, with that one, something tells me you better be."

Eve looked quickly around as Shug led her to his car and held the door for her. She saw nothing unusual, no shadows lurking in doorways or behind trash cans, and almost entertained the idea that she'd been wrong about being followed. It was pleasant to think that way, but her instincts had become too ingrained to be put off easily.

Traffic had thinned considerably as they drove through downtown, and the city lights shimmered in the hazy, moisture-laden air. The throaty pipes on the Olds 442 almost lulled Eve to sleep while they motored north on Interstate 94 toward Mount Clemons and the small, remote house she'd been renting for the past eighteen months. She leaned her head back against the seat and closed her eyes, remembering when she looked at the place with the rental agent. Plain, white-framed, and laid out

Shug's Place

shotgun-style, the house was unremarkable in most ways but met her basic needs. She'd felt safe there. Until today, she'd almost been able to convince herself that it was finally over. Now, she recognized the old, familiar grip of despondency she'd felt so many times before in so many other places, her would-be refuges. It would never be over, she knew now. Not as long as Farber was alive. Now she would have to move on again. Find a new identity, a new—

She jumped when a hand closed over her own. "Oh!"

"Sorry. Didn't mean to frighten you," Shug said. "We're coming up on Mount Clemons. I'll need directions."

"Just take Exit 237, then left. The house is several miles out." She studied Shug's face in the dim reflection from the car's dashboard lights. *Strong profile*, she thought. *Not exactly handsome, but there was something in his eyes...*

As he drove, she mused about her suggestion at the bar: *Take me home and I'll make you breakfast*. Not really a promise of anything more than that, but certainly full of implications. Was she up for a roll in the hay in exchange for a safe ride home? It had been a while for her. After tonight, it might be a long time again. The more she thought about it now, the more the idea appealed.

The Olds' pipes changed from an understated roar to a soft purr as they pulled off onto the exit ramp. The light pollution was less here, and above them in the night sky, stars sparkled like diamonds on black felt.

"Go right on Highway Ninety-Seven. I'll tell you where to turn in. It's pretty remote."

"Yes, ma'am." He half-turned in her direction and smiled. "Anywhere you say."

The smile reawakened whatever it was that had flipped in her belly back at the bar. Something warm and tingly. *Yeah*, she decided, *this was sounding better all the time.*

Traffic was light after they left the interstate. Eric Farber hung further back, keeping a vehicle between his battered Ford van and the Olds muscle car whenever possible. Farber didn't think he'd lose them, but the possibility kept him alert, his senses keen. This was as close as he'd been. He thought of the excitement he'd felt earlier as he followed her through the parking lot at the baseball stadium.

He was pretty sure she'd made him on the street, but that was all right, too. He wanted her to feel the fear, the panic of knowing that her time of atonement was close at hand. The guy with her was a complication he could just as well do without, but he didn't want to wait. No, if he waited, she might find a way to disappear again. She was good at vanishing.

Farber slowed as the Olds made a right turn off the highway onto a narrow strip of dirt and gravel. He continued past the intersection, cut his lights, and pulled over on the shoulder. The Olds' taillights shone brightly through the sparse foliage, and he watched as the car slowed then stopped after about a hundred yards. The car lights went off, and moments later the soft yellow glow of house lights came on. He eased back onto the road and clocked over a mile and a half from the turnout in both directions. He saw no other houses or lights. Satisfied, he did a u-turn and made his way back to the driveway, cutting his lights again as he approached.

He turned in and parked about fifty yards from the house. After unscrewing the van's dome light, he wiped sweat from his forehead, pulled the baseball cap down tight to his head, and exited the van. He crept close enough to get a feel for the house and grounds. The drive opened into a moonlit clearing about forty yards square, surrounded on three sides by a mix of pines and hardwoods. The house was a single-story white frame with a large porch extending across the front. A separate, one-car garage stood behind and to the right of the house, twenty yards from the main structure. Beyond that was what appeared to be a barn. Stepping carefully, he did a complete circuit of the clearing, noting along the way a smaller, enclosed porch at the rear of the house.

From his secluded vantage point, Farber caught glimpses of movement behind the lighted windows. As he watched, the curtains were drawn across the windows in the front room. He remained still for a few minutes, savoring the thrill of the capture, then moved silently back to the van to begin his preparations.

Evelyn, or whatever her name might be, brought Shug a glass of merlot. Not his usual drink, but then, this was not his usual evening. Most nights, Shug closed up between midnight and two o'clock, depending on the crowd, went home, and slept until noon. Alone, except for the cat, who might or might not opt to exercise his assumed right of bed privilege.

"I hope wine is all right," she said. "I don't go into the city that often, and the stores around here mostly sell beer and wine."

"It's fine," he said, taking a sip of the burgundy liquid. "I tend bar, after all. I drink almost anything." Shug looked around the room. They were in the front living room, just off a long hallway that led out onto the front porch. Next to the windows stood two easels and a rolling cart filled with brushes, paints, and cloths stained every color of the rainbow. Mounted canvases, some clean and others filled with subdued, earth-toned hues were stacked against the walls. Shug thought they were probably landscapes but decided to study them more closely before commenting. A 50's-vintage sofa, end table, and coffee table were the room's only furniture. On the wall opposite the windows, a door led into what seemed be a bedroom. When he turned back to her, she was watching him. "You're an artist," he said, more a statement than a question.

She smiled. "I'm a painter. I think you might have to be dead before you can truly call yourself an artist."

Shug set his wine down on the coffee table and ran a forefinger along her eyebrow, down one smooth, prominent cheekbone, and under her chin. She lifted her face and parted her lips slightly. He decided to go for the closer. "I like people who create beauty," he said. "The world needs more people like you."

Her eyes went moist then—he wasn't sure why but figured it wasn't the time for questions—and she reached for him. They kissed. The softness of her body melted into the hard lines of his, and Shug was lost in a jumble of sensations that were new and familiar at the same time. Then she took his hand and led him into her bedroom.

They undressed slowly, carefully exploring each new revelation. She had the body of a runner, with small breasts, gently flaring hips and sleek firm thighs. She nuzzled against his chest and laughed when the soft sandy hair tickled her nose. Shug lay down on his back on the bed pulling her with him. She bent down, brushed his lips with hers, and reached for the bedside lamp.

At that instant, the bedroom door burst off its hinges in a concussive, deafening blast of bright light and thunder. Shug felt himself lifted into the air. A half-second later, he landed on the floor, tangled with Evelyn and the bed linens. The room filled with thick, gray smoke and the pungent smell of explosive. His first sense was that he was surrounded by a complete and utter silence. He looked at Evelyn, trying frantically to free herself of the confines of the bed clothes. Her face was distorted, and her mouth was open. It took him a moment to realize she was screaming. He pulled her close and held her tightly until she quit struggling. Even then, every muscle in her body felt coiled like a steel spring.

It was a beautiful explosion, Farber thought, *almost a lost art these days, using dynamite. Fitting, though, in this case. Live by the sword...*

Farber breathed in deeply and savored the acrid fragrance floating back to him on the breeze. The porch had collapsed in on itself, and a ragged, ten-foot-wide hole smoldered in the front of the house where the double windows had been. He had purposefully waited until they went into the bedroom. He didn't want to kill her. Not yet.

They would be recovering about now, getting their senses about them again. Just now, the guy with Eve would be thinking he'd picked a hell of a one-night stand. The man moved to his second staging area. "Well, my friends," he whispered, "just wait. You haven't seen anything yet."

"What the living hell was that?" Shug shouted. He could barely hear himself over the ringing assailing his ears. "Propane tank?"

She shook her head against his chest and trembled violently in his arms. "Oh God, oh God, I'm so sorry! So very sorry! It's my fault. I should have never—"

The house shuddered with a second explosion, and Evelyn screamed again and twisted away from him, scrabbling to find her clothing amid the bed linens and scattered debris.

And then, Shug was back in Viet Nam—a hilly outpost near Khe Sanh, incoming mortar rounds shattering the humid night air around him. Survival instincts he thought he'd lost coursed back through his body like an electric charge. He grabbed Evelyn by the shoulders and shook her hard. "Look at me! Look at me! Tell me what the hell is going on!"

She stared at him, fear dancing like tiny flames in her eyes. When she spoke, her lips trembled. "There's a man. He was following me earlier. He wants to kill me."

Absurdly, the line from *Casablanca* shot through Shug's brain: *Of all the gin joints, in all the towns.* He grabbed for his own clothes and tossed jeans and a blouse toward Evelyn, who sat hugging herself on the floor. "Get dressed. Hurry!"

Shug dressed quickly and low crawled to the blown-out doorway that opened onto the living room. That room was a disaster. He scrabbled to the hallway door and checked the narrow corridor running from the front of the house to the back. The second explosion had been at the back of the house, its impact diminished somewhat by the solid wall of an intervening room. Midway down the hall, on the right side of the house, was a bathroom. He turned back just as Evelyn finished pulling on her New Balances.

"The bathroom off the hall—is there a window to the outside?"

She shook her head. "No. It backs up to a closet in one of the rooms on that side."

Staying low, he dragged the mattress off the bed and into the hallway. "C'mon—into the bathroom!" He pulled the mattress in behind them and propped it as best he could against the open bathroom door. Standing, he could just see over the top and into the hallway. In the bathroom they were relatively safe from another explosion. They were also trapped like rats if the bomber decided to bring it inside. Just then, the lights went out. Decision time.

Shug whispered, "Do you have a weapon—a handgun, rifle, anything—in the house?"

She answered in a small, uneven voice. "No, not here. I have a handgun, but I left it in my car."

He pulled the mattress to one side and reached out for her in the dark. "Well then, let's get the hell out of here."

They moved cautiously across the hallway and back into the bedroom. Shug opened one of the room's two west-facing windows. No screens on the window. *Good.* He'd parked the Olds on the east side of the house and figured the bomber would want to keep the car in view. He studied the black void outside as his eyes adjusted to the darkness. He bent close and whispered into Evelyn's ear, "How far to the trees from the house?"

"I don't know. Thirty feet?"

He could barely see her beside him. He hoped the bomber would have the same problem. He whispered again. "I'm going out the window, and I'm going to make a run for the trees. If I make it without getting shot or blown to pieces, follow me. Stay low and move fast. Got it?"

Her voice was calmer now. "Got it."

He eased one leg over the window sill and felt her hand on his arm.

"Shug?"

"What?"

"Thank you—"

"Save it. Just do what I tell you to do." He ducked out the window and slid to the ground, stayed motionless for a second, then moved quickly and quietly across the side yard into the trees. Seconds later, Evelyn crawled through the opening, fell to her knees, recovered, and ran toward him. He pulled her down beside him; they sat motionless for a full minute. He saw nothing and heard only his own breathing.

Shug scanned the area. To his left, he had a full view of the east side of the house and the front and one side of the barn and small garage. To the right, beyond the wrecked porch, he could see the rear half of the Olds. He figured the bomber had stationed himself somewhere on the east side of the house, probably in or near the tree line. He'd have a sight zone of everything but the area immediately west of the house. Was he armed? Probably. He'd have a clear shot if they tried to make the car—same if they went for the barn or garage. He pulled Evelyn close and whispered again in her ear. He felt her pulse racing in her neck.

Farber waited patiently five yards back in the trees and scrub. He lay prone, propped on his elbows, a contraband M-14 carbine held tenderly in his hands. His finger rested lightly on the trigger. He had not killed with a gun before, and the thought of it excited him. It would never have the sound and fury of an explosion, but he sensed the act would have more of an air of intimacy. His thumb caressed the stock of the weapon. *Smooth, like a woman's thigh.* He felt his eagerness growing.

Eve watched as Shug moved quietly back into the woods to begin his slow circle of the barn and garage. After a few feet, she could no longer make out his form. He was a good man, she believed, but good might not be enough, not against pure evil—the devil in the flesh—bent on bloody revenge.

In the dark, waiting, her thoughts drifted back fifteen years, just over half a life ago. She'd been a fresh-faced college girl: exuberant, idealistic, and stupid. Bitterness, depression, and anger at her own simple-minded, youthful hubris swept over her. Tears welled up in her eyes; she brushed them away with a swipe of her hand. She couldn't let a good man die because of that stupidity—not again. She checked the sky. The quarter moon was mostly hidden by thick clouds. She crawled slowly out of the trees and toward the front corner of the house.

Shug said a silent thank you to Mother Nature for recent rains. The wet leaves and pine needles made it easier for him to move quietly through the undergrowth. He was a hundred or so feet back into the trees, moving in a wide arc toward the east. Scattered breaks in the tree line gave him a rough sense of his progress. It was slow going, and he wasn't sure what he would do when he reached his destination, but at least he was moving.

Farber couldn't be certain but thought he saw movement at the corner of the destroyed porch. He narrowed his eyes and tried not to blink. He waited. *There!* He saw it again. He gripped the rifle more firmly and tried to slow his breathing, to keep his heart from thudding in his chest.

He inched the barrel of his weapon slightly to the left. *Give yourself a field of fire.* It was maybe thirty feet from the porch to the car. *Don't rush.* He'd have a few seconds to bring them down. Wouldn't have to be a kill shot even—not right away. There'd be time for that. He wanted time with her, wanted to relish the moment.

And if they made it to the car? Well, that would be okay, too, but he preferred to feel the rifle buck in his hands, to see the impact of the slug tearing into flesh and bone.

Shug was fifteen feet away, crawling, when his knee came down on a brittle twig. The man on the ground spun, struggling for position, swinging the barrel of the rifle in Shug's direction. Shug leapt to his feet and lunged forward, screaming at the top of his lungs. At the last second, he threw himself through the air. He got under the barrel but it caught him on the side of the head as he crashed into the man. He rolled to one side, stunned, white-hot stars sparking behind his eyes, trying awkwardly to regain his footing.

The other man was on his feet in an instant, drawing the butt of the rifle back, ready to smash it against Shug's head.

"No!" Evelyn cried, rounding the corner of the porch at a dead run.

The man shouldered the rifle again, swinging it in her direction.

Shug slammed his foot into the side of the bomber's knee. The rifle pitched forward and the man staggered sideways clutching his leg.

Evelyn slid to a halt, wide-eyed and breathless, and snatched up the rifle. Shug was leaning against a tree for support, holding a hand to the side of his head. Evelyn looked at the rifle, then at the man in the yellow slicker less than ten feet away. She raised the weapon to her own shoulder.

The man stared back at her, and then, incongruously, laughed out loud. "Go ahead, Eve. Kill me if you can." He took a step toward her. "Or have you forgotten all your training?" He took another step, then lunged for the rifle.

In her haste, Evelyn jerked the trigger. The round meant for the man's chest caught his left bicep instead. He spun around, yelped once, and wobbled backward, laughing again.

"Not good enough, bitch! Not this time." He turned and ran. Evelyn fired again as he cleared the Olds 442—and missed. She tracked him down the gravel driveway and fired six more times in rapid succession. The last round knocked him to the ground, but he rolled and came up on his knees. Struggling to his feet again, he quickly disappeared into the darkness.

After a moment, Evelyn dropped the rifle in the dirt and sank to her knees. Shug came over and knelt beside her. They heard a car engine turn over, a spray of gravel hitting the vehicle's undercarriage, and, a few seconds later, the squeal of rubber as the bomber reached the paved highway.

Shug let out a long sigh and ran his hand over the side of his face. His fingers came back smudged with blood. "Who the hell was that anyway?"

"I guess you deserve to know." She rose from the ground and gestured toward what was left of the house. "But let me get something first."

He leaned on the Olds' front fender while she went inside. The moon was back, and he surveyed the front porch damage for the first time. Three of the four columns that had supported the roof lay amid the wreckage like Roman ruins. The roof itself was scattered about the front yard in varying-sized clumps of lumber and shingles. A ragged, soot-blackened hole gaped in the front wall of the house where the living room window had been. *Where the paintings had been*, Shug remembered. He wondered if any were left intact.

Evelyn came out a few minutes later carrying a green duffle bag over one shoulder. Under her other arm, she clutched a flat package wrapped in brown paper and tied off with string. She put them in the back of the car and collapsed into the passenger seat.

Shug got in on the driver's side and slipped the key into the ignition. "All set?"

She nodded but then grabbed his arm. "No! Wait!"

"What?" he said.

"Just take the key out. *Please.*"

He did as she climbed out of the car and came around to the driver side door. "Got a flashlight?"

"Nope."

"Then get out of the car. I'll have to do this by feel."

Three minutes later, she rolled out from under the vehicle with a cylinder-shaped object the size of a football. "Here, grab this."

Shug took the package and turned it gingerly in his hands. Five sticks of TNT strapped together with duct tape. One long wire protruded from a metal device at the end. He stared at her.

"It was wired to the ignition." She half-smiled in the wan moonlight and brushed dirt from her clothes. "I should have guessed right away. He was always very thorough."

Shug felt his knees go weak. He wasn't sure if it was from sheer exhaustion or from the realization he'd almost been blown to bits—again. He frowned, tried to keep his hand from trembling, and handed the package back to her.

She removed the detonating device and tossed it and the explosive toward the remains of the porch. "Let's go, Shug. I'll tell you all about it on the way back to Detroit."

A few minutes later, they pulled in at an all-night convenience store for coffee and to use the restrooms. Then, as they rolled up the entrance ramp to Interstate 94, she began her story. "Do you know about Weatherman?"

"The weatherman?"

"Not the guys on TV. I mean the radical activist group back in the late sixties and early seventies. Weatherman, or the Weather Underground, or, if you must, the Weathermen."

Shug nodded. "Sure, I've heard of them, an anti-war group active when I was in Viet Nam."

"Anti-racist and pro-socialist, too." She stared out the side window. "We were going to start a social revolution."

She was quiet for a minute, taking small sips from the cardboard coffee cup. Shug waited for her to start again.

"I was attending the University of Illinois, an art major, feeling very bohemian at the time. I joined Weatherman in 1969, after they took over the Students for a Democratic Society. For a month, we trained like mercenaries—weapons, explosives, survival techniques. Later that year, we bombed a bunch of police cars. That guy, the one we tangled with tonight, was the leader of our little guerilla group. His name is Eric Farber."

Shug peered at her in the dim glow of the dash lights. Her face was devoid of all expression. "Why does he want to kill you?"

She sighed. "I never wanted to kill anyone. The cars we bombed were all empty, until one night when Eric wired dynamite to one car's ignition. I didn't know he had done it. A police officer was killed."

She crumpled the empty coffee container in her hands and let it drop to the floorboard. "He changed after that. He'd read about Weatherman chapters in other parts of the country becoming more violent, and he wanted to do something really dramatic. He hooked us up with one of the national leaders of the group, and we left Chicago and went to Detroit for a"—she did quote marks with her fingers—"strategic act of sabotage."

"Why Detroit?" Shug asked.

She shrugged. "I don't know. But the police were hot on our trail in Chicago. They found our bomb factory just after we left. Anyway, the plan in Detroit turned out to be bombing a police station ... with people inside." She covered her face with her hands. "I didn't want anyone else to die."

She went silent again, and once more, Shug gave her time. They were just approaching the outskirts of the city.

"I called the police, reported the plan anonymously, and disappeared. Eric and the others were surprised by the cops at the Detroit weapons cache, and one of the Weatherman members was shot and killed. Eric and a couple more got away."

"And they figured you were the one who'd dropped the dime on them?" Shug asked.

She nodded. "I was the only one of our group not there when the police showed up. I ran then, afraid of the police, afraid of him. I've been running ever since."

"He called you Eve."

"Yeah, and I slipped and said it at the bar. I guess seeing him after all that time brought everything back again. A long time ago, my name was Eve Campbell. Since then, I've been many people, had many names, seen many places."

"How'd you manage to stay hidden?"

"Weatherman was a national group. Hundreds, probably thousands of members. We trained, we networked, and we learned ways to stay underground."

"But this guy, Eric, found you."

"He's gotten close a couple of times before, actually. Never like this, though."

Shug took the exit for Tiger Stadium and, a few minutes later, turned into its almost empty parking lot.

"There." She pointed at a cream-colored Dodge sedan under a mercury vapor lamp. There were no other vehicles in the vicinity. "Do you think he might be waiting somewhere, watching the car?"

"I don't know how bad he was hit," Shug said. "But I think he'll need to deal with the bleeding somehow. You've probably got a little time." He pulled up next to the Dodge, got out, and peered through the windows.

Eve pulled the duffel from the back seat and tossed it into the trunk of her car. She came back and stood facing him. "I don't know what to say, Shug. You were a life saver."

"I could say the same about you."

"Hardly that," she said. Her face became serious. "You know, in the beginning, I thought I was doing something worthwhile, something that would make for a better society."

"I'm sure you had reasons for doing what you did."

Eve sighed. "Reasons get forgotten. What you actually do stays with you forever."

"But you did do a good thing," Shug said. "You probably saved a lot of lives with that telephone call."

"Maybe. I don't know." She wiped moisture from the corner of her eye, then reached up and put her hand on Shug's chest. "I want you to know something. Last night, when I asked for a ride home, I was using you. But then, later on when we were in the bedroom, that was for real. I really wanted you."

She leaned in and kissed him lightly, then harder. After a moment, she pulled away and reached for the door handle of the Dodge.

"Eve?"

She turned back to look at him.

"Better check under the car."

He waited while she did, then stood there in the darkness moments later and watched her tail lights disappear in the distance.

The sun had just breached the horizon when Shug turned into his driveway and shut off the engine of the Olds. He rubbed his tired eyes and had reached into the back for his jacket when he noticed the package still lying on the back seat. Eve had forgotten it—or maybe not.

Before she'd left for parts unknown, he'd asked if she needed money. She'd told him no, that a friend from her underground days owned a gallery in New York City and that she earned a comfortable living selling her work. Not a renowned artist yet, but a commercially viable painter with a bit of a following. Under an assumed name, of course.

Shug climbed wearily from the car, trudged up the steps, and fumbled for the door key. Once inside, he stripped the string and paper from around the wood-framed canvas. It was a semi-abstract piece filled with creams, tans, soft yellows, and sables that made him think of low hills beyond a meadow.

He got out a hammer and nail from the closet and hung the painting over his TV. The cat watched from the sofa. "You like?" Shug asked. The cat blinked once then hopped down, sidled into the kitchen, and sat waiting beside its empty food bowl.

Leon came in at seven forty-five that evening and hung his Tigers cap on a rack beside the bar. He took one look at Shug and let out a low whistle. "Huh! You look like you been up all night. And what happened to that ear? That pretty lady roll you? Or did y'all just have some rough sex?"

Shug said nothing.

"Yes, sir," Leon continued. "You done been rode hard and put away wet, as we used to say out west."

Shug snorted. "When the hell were you ever out west?"

"West Pacific, 1969. Little place called the Nam. Believe you were there once, too. Let's see now, when was that?"

Shug stretched and rotated his neck. Bones and cartilage ground together and sounded a lot like the popcorn machine in the corner. "Last night, I think."

The Legacy: Out in Left Field
September 6, 1912

With less than a week to go in the regular season, the Tigers were ranked third in the American League, sporting eighty-five wins and sixty-four losses, and were on the verge of drawing four-hundred thousand fans for the season. It had been a good year, if not a great one, and the fans and players alike could afford to be hopeful for their pennant prospects in 1913. Not everyone was happy, though. Tony Mancuso, left fielder for the Tigers and in his second year up from the minor leagues, was anything but—even after an impressive nine to two win over the Chicago White Sox.

"I don't get it," he said to third baseman Chick Simmons as they left Navin Field following the game. "Here I am, batting over four hundred on the season, and Cobb gets all the glory."

"Yeah," Chick said. "It's lousy luck, your being on the team with a celebrity, but you have to admit, he brings in the crowds."

"Huh! 'Best he could do tonight was a double in five at-bats."

Chick grinned. "But he spiked the White Sox second baseman. For the fans, that's almost as good as a home run."

At the intersection of Michigan Avenue and Trumbull, Mancuso paused. "Let's go get us a beer. There's an Irish place I know just a couple of blocks down Trumbull."

Five minutes later, the two men rounded the corner onto Labrosse and stepped inside Hanahan's A Little Bit O' Ireland. The bar was packed with people, most of whom Mancuso knew as Tigers fans.

An older man with wispy white hair and a face flushed red with alcohol jostled his way through the crowd. "Tony! Good game tonight, son, though I wish you'd saved that home run and the three-bagger for a night when we needed 'em."

Right, Mancuso thought. *Like I can pick my hits.*

"And how about that Ty Cobb?" The old man continued. "Who-ee! I didn't know baseball was such a blood sport."

Mancuso glanced at Simmons and rolled his eyes, then shouldered his way to the bar, leaving the oldster still chortling at his own joke. At the bar, the two men ordered beers and shots of Irish whiskey.

An hour later, a small pyramid of shot glasses sat stacked on the bar in front of Mancuso. Simmons put a hand on his teammate's shoulder. "I've got to go, Tony, and you probably should, too. We've got another game tomorrow."

Mancuso stared at Simmons through whiskey-glazed eyes. "It doesn't matter, does it? I mean, Cobb'll win it for us, right?" His gaze wandered slowly around the room. "Just ask anybody. They'll tell you."

"I'll see you tomorrow," Simmons said and made his way out through the crowd.

"Condescending son of a bitch," Mancuso mumbled. His head ached, his neck felt stiff, and he was seeing double. He backed away from the bar and stumbled toward the door. A short, wiry man grabbed Mancuso's arm and said, "Hey, you play for the Tigers, right? You think you could get me Ty Cobb's autograph on a baseball?"

Mancuso wanted to smash the man in the face. Instead, he shrugged off the man's grip and lurched into the street. *Sons of bitches,* he thought, steadying himself against a lamppost. *All of 'em—condescending sons of bitches.*

Mancuso arrived home after midnight and found his wife, Esther, perched on the edge of the sofa, twisting a handkerchief in her hands.

"How was the game, Tony?" she asked, working the handkerchief like a rosary. "Did you play well?"

"Where's my supper?" Mancuso growled. His anger had subsided on the way home, but remerged at the sight of the piteous creature cowering under his glare.

"It's on the table," Esther said. "I wrapped it in waxed paper. I was going to reheat it, but I didn't know when—"

"You couldn't keep it warm?" He stomped into the tiny kitchen, snatched the plate from the table, and stormed back to the living room. "You're *worthless!*" he shouted again and threw the plate of food at his wife.

"I'm sorry," Esther cried, scrabbling at the remains of the meal scattered over her dress and the sofa. "I'll make a new plate. I'll—"

Mancuso undid his belt buckle and slid the leather strap from his trouser loops. "I'll show you sorry, you—"

"Daddy, stop!"

Mancuso turned to see his eleven-year-old son standing at the door to his bedroom, a baseball bat clenched in his fists. The boy's legs trembled, and tears streamed down his cheeks.

"You little shit," Mancuso hissed. "You think you can take a bat to me? I'll knock you over the left field fence." He lunged at the boy even as the bat arched through the air. The next thing Mancuso knew, he was falling—twisting in the air, landing hard on his right side. Then everything went dark. When he awoke the following morning, still on the living room floor, his wife and son were nowhere to be found, and his elbow was swollen to the size of a grapefruit.

Later that day, Mancuso fielded a line-drive from the Philadelphia Athletics' catcher, Lou Harvey, and attempted to throw out the runner from first at third base. The throw fell short and rolled to a stop fifteen feet shy of Simmons' outstretched glove. The runner scored, Mancuso was replaced with a rookie fielder from Hoboken, and the Athletics won the game five to four.

The Tigers' 1912 season ended on the 10th of September. After the game, Chick Simmons and the famous Ty Cobb stopped in for a beer at Hanahan's bar. Already hailed as a hero, Cobb bought a round of drinks for the house.

Tony Mancuso never played baseball again.

Forgive Us Our Sins

Cathy Richards gnawed her fingernail until she tasted blood. It had been seven weeks since her last monthly period. She sighed heavily and peered through the windshield at the rectangular slab of darkness outlining the alleyway entrance. Sully had been gone for more than ten minutes. Waiting always made her nervous. The missed period made her more anxious than usual.

She rummaged in the pocket of her jacket and found the plastic vial of cocaine. Now she would begin the familiar debate, already knowing somewhere deep within herself how it was going to turn out. The coke would take the edge off her anxiety and give her a more positive perspective about things—her future, for example. On the other hand, she was probably pregnant.

She checked her watch again: fifteen minutes and counting. She could actually feel the cords in her neck tightening up with each passing minute. "Ah, fuck it." Cathy tapped a small dollop of coke into her palm and snorted. Taking a deep breath, she waited for the rush to hit, then did the other nostril.

Where the hell was Sully? She checked the deserted street and popped the door on the Camaro. Thirty seconds later, she waded into the early morning gloom of the alley. Feeling her way along the rough surface of the wall, she found the jimmied back door to the bar. Looking inside was like peering into the blackness of a cave.

"Sully?"

She stepped over the threshold and tried again. "Sully?"

"What!"

A penlight illuminated her oval face and momentarily blinded her.

"I was worried. What's taking so long?"

"Jesus, Cathy, you scared the shit outta me. Do not, I repeat, do not creep up on me like that." Sully knelt, placing the penlight on the floor, and began shoveling bills and change from a small floor safe into a cloth sack. "I had a little trouble with the punch. This asshole's safe is better than most."

"Hurry, please, Sully. I'm really nervous tonight."

"Relax, babe." He stood and flicked off the light. "We're good to go."

Cathy surveyed the narrow brick corridor before they stepped out. She saw nothing except the dark silhouette of a trash dumpster and, beyond that, the orange nose of the Camaro framed in the alley entranceway.

"It was a light haul," Sully said as they walked hurriedly toward the street. "Probably less than five hundred."

Cathy hugged herself, feeling better the closer she got to the car. "I'm just glad to get out of here." But then she slowed and touched his arm. "You know that all-night diner over on Fourteenth? Can we stop for coffee and a slice of pie? There's something important I need to tell—"

From somewhere behind her, Cathy heard a noise. Soft, like the scraping of a shoe on concrete. In that moment, she felt a jolt of fear-laced adrenalin that far surpassed the best coke rush she'd ever had.

A metallic double-click preceded the blast that lifted Cathy off her feet. Twin concussive explosions, a split second apart, filled the narrow alley. Then her face hit the alley floor, and she tasted blood once again. Sully lay three feet to her left. She tried reaching out to him but couldn't make her arm move. Her last thought was that she'd never get to hold her baby.

Shug's Place was crowded. It reminded him of a Tigers' crowd. Lots of blue, except there were no baseball caps, only the unmistakable navy blue uniforms worn by the Detroit Police Department's Patrol Division.

Shug kept the coffee flowing while he waited for the detectives to show. He'd been awakened that morning by a 5:00 a.m. telephone call from a desk sergeant in the third precinct and had arrived at the bar a half hour later to a beehive of activity. It was going on eight o'clock now and, despite the caffeine, Shug was feeling the effects of too little sleep.

At eight-fifteen, Detective Frank Owens pushed his way through the collection of officers and crime scene techs and sat down at the bar. He wore a mocha-colored suit, white shirt, and a brown-and-blue paisley tie. "Hello, Shug. Long time no see."

Shug nodded and gave the man a tired smile. "Coffee, Detective Owens?"

"Make it black. And make it Frank, too."

Shug poured coffee and placed the mug down in front of the detective. "Frank it is, then. Can you tell me what the hell's going on? Nobody will talk to me."

"Sure. You were burgled."

"That much I gathered." He shifted his gaze to the doorway leading to the back room and storage area. Inside, the safe door hung open and was covered with a charcoal glaze of fingerprint dust. "What about the rest of it?"

Owens shook his head. "Not my case. I just came by when I heard it was your place. Thought I'd take the time to say hello, ask about the cat."

A grin tugged at the corners of Shug's mouth. "The cat's fine. I'll tell him you asked." Movement at the door caught his eye.

Owens looked back over his shoulder. The woman stopped just inside the doorway and glanced around the bar. Curly, shoulder-length black hair framed a square face softened by a wide, sensuous mouth.

She spotted Owens, smiled, and walked over to the bar. "Morning, Frank."

Owens stood. "Darcy, this is Shug Barnes, owner of this delightful establishment. Shug, meet Detective Darcy Raintree. She caught the case."

They shook hands over the bar. Shug wished he'd taken the time to shower and shave before he left the house.

"Would you like some coffee?" Shug asked.

"Sure," she said, climbing onto the stool next to Owens.

He poured the coffee, then studied her movements as she added cream and stirred in two packets of sweetener.

"What's it look like in the alley?" Owens asked.

Raintree stopped stirring and looked from Owens to Shug and then back to Owens. "Not at all pretty."

"Detective Raintree," Shug said, "can you tell me what happened?"

"I can tell you what I think happened, but we won't know for sure until we finish up the forensics and run some prints."

Shug nodded. "Okay."

She took a sip of the coffee, and then added another pack of sweetener. "Sometime, say between midnight and four in the morning, someone broke into your bar, punched the safe, and left with four hundred and eighty-nine dollars and sixty-three cents."

"How do you—"

She held up a hand. "Let me finish. They—a man and a woman—were in the alley, presumably on their way to an orange '83 Camaro parked on the street nearby." She glanced over at Owens. "They were shotgunned from behind. My guess is someone was waiting for them behind the dumpster."

Shug rubbed his face, feeling the scratch of day-old stubble. "But how did you know how much money was taken?"

"We found it in the alley, so robbery probably wasn't the shooter's motive." Her eyes locked onto Shug's. "Just for the record, Mister Barnes, where were you between twelve and four?"

"At home asleep."

"Can anyone corroborate your story?"

"I live alone."

"Don't forget the cat," Owens offered, his eyes showing amusement.

Raintree turned quizzically in his direction.

"Darcy, I can't say for sure, but I don't think Shug is the kind of guy..." Owens' expression changed from amused to cop-blank. "...who'd ever take the law into his own hands. That right, Shug?"

Shug nodded, trying to get a read on the man's face, but seeing nothing. "Yeah, right."

Detective Raintree took a last sip of her coffee and stood. "I'm going to check with the techs. Mister Barnes, if you don't mind hanging around, I may have some questions later."

"I'll be here," Shug said. He and Owens watched her walk away.

"Attractive lady," Shug said. "Doesn't look much like a cop."

"Attractive, sharp, and ambitious." Owens glanced at the back bar mirror, adjusted the knot of his tie, and eased down off the barstool. "Take it easy, Shug."

Shug called Leon and asked if he could come in early.

Leon showed up at two o'clock. He remained silent as he heard the whole story, then shook his head slowly. "Like they say, man, crime don't pay." The big black man used a thumb and forefinger to absently trace the sides of his mustache. "But you're lucky to get the money back. Maybe you oughta invest it in an alarm system."

"Maybe." Shug let out a long breath. "Look, I've been here since five-thirty this morning. The cops were here until almost lunchtime. Got the back door taken care of after they left. I'm beat, man. I'm going home."

"That's another thing," Leon said. "You spend way too many hours behind that bar. You need to get out more. You lookin' paler than usual."

"Hire somebody, you mean?"

"Yeah. You're doing all right, aren't you, making a profit?"

"Some," Shug said. He worked the bar, on average, ten to twelve hours a day, six days a week. Seven if the Tigers were playing at home on Sunday. Over six and a half years, he'd put away close to a hundred grand. It sounded like a lot of money, but another employee, even a part-timer, would cut into the profits.

"What would I do with the time off? I don't have any hobbies."

"You could develop some." Leon leaned one elbow on the bar. "You could actually go see the Tigers play 'stead of always watchin' 'em on TV. Start an exercise program. Get back in shape. Find a girlfriend." He grinned and tapped a finger on top of the bar. "Like, what about the one was in here a few months back? You know, the one in those tight designer jeans? Promised to make you breakfast?"

Shug frowned and shrugged. "She took off. And for your information, I'm in shape."

Leon arched his eyebrows and looked Shug up and down. "Well..."

A couple of the regular patrons pushed through the door. Welcoming the interruption, Shug met them at their table with a bowl of fresh popcorn.

Later that evening, at his modest home in Sterling Heights, he stripped down to his boxers, examining himself in the bedroom mirror. He tightened his stomach muscles ... relaxed ... tightened ... relaxed. *Not bad*, he thought, *for thirty-five*. Still, he might want to cut back some on the cheeseburgers from Mack's.

Detective Darcy Raintree called the bar at four o'clock the following afternoon. "I've got some information on the couple killed in the alley. I thought I'd drop by and see if anything clicks with you."

"Sure, just come when you're ready. I'll be here."

She showed up at a quarter past five, wearing gray slacks and a navy blazer over a white blouse. She sat down on a stool at the bar, which was otherwise empty. The other patrons, mostly retirees who used the pub for a social outing before going home to dinner, were scattered among the lacquer-topped tables and booths.

"Coffee?" Shug asked.

"How about a white wine?" She checked her wristwatch. "I'm off duty, more or less."

Shug slid open the under-bar cooler and found a nice California Chablis. As he poured, she toyed with one of the gold-foil matchboxes that dotted the top of the bar.

"The guy was Sully Hughes, thirty-one years old, lived up in Waterford. No police record, other than a couple of traffic violations, but we ran the prints against some other B and Es and got several hits. He'd been lucky—until last night."

"The name doesn't ring a bell with me."

"The woman's name was Cathy Richards. She was twenty-eight, no record, had a pay stub from Woolworth's." Raintree took a laminated driver's license from her purse and slid it across the bar. "This is, or rather, was her."

Shug picked it up. The photo showed an attractive redhead with dark eyebrows. She was smiling. "Doesn't look much like a burglar."

"You can never tell," she said, then tried the wine. "Hmmm, that's good."

He leaned forward and braced his elbows on top of the bar, bringing his face level with hers. A subtle fragrance filled his nostrils, soft and light, like a spring breeze. *Nice.*

"The guy was clean," Raintree continued, "No ID on him. She carried hers in her pocket, along with a little vial of toot. We ran her prints, too, but got nothing—not here or anywhere else. My guess is that she was waiting in the car, got anxious, maybe met Hughes in the alley as he was leaving."

"Bad choice."

"Yeah, most likely one among many."

"Less than five hundred bucks."

She nodded, took another sip of wine. "She was pregnant."

Shug wasn't sure how to respond to that. Finally, he said, "That's a shame."

She gave him a thin smile. He thought the detective looked sad. Pretty, but sad. She finished the wine and he watched her throat as she swallowed. It was a nice, slender throat. He glanced at her hands. No jewelry.

"Well," she said, "I guess I'll be on my way." She retrieved her purse from an adjacent bar stool and pulled out a small billfold. "I enjoyed the wine. How much do I owe you?"

"It's on the house."

She put a five-dollar bill on the bar. "Sorry, I can't do that. Regulations, you know."

As he made change at the register, Shug realized he didn't want Detective Raintree, *Darcy*, to go. He could ask her out for dinner, or maybe a movie on Sunday, unless...

She was standing, looping her purse strap over one shoulder.

He checked the Tigers' schedule taped to the side of the cash register. They were in town Sunday, a twilight double-header against Philadelphia. *Damn!* He'd have to keep the place open all day and well into the night.

He went back to the bar and handed her change from the five. "Will you let me know if you find out more about the case?"

She hesitated for a moment, then nodded slowly. "I guess I can do that." She still held the change in her hand.

He hoped she wouldn't leave a tip. If she left a tip, he was just another bartender, another of the many crime victims she must deal with every week. Suddenly, his mouth was moving. "Do you ever go watch the Tigers play?"

"What?"

"The Tigers. You ever go to the games?"

A puzzled expression came over her face. "Yeah, I mean, I guess so. Sometimes."

"Would you like to go this Sunday? With me, I mean."

Detective Raintree opened her mouth as if she were about to laugh, but didn't. Instead, she cocked her head to one side, shrugged, and said, "I guess that'd be all right. Sure. What time?"

"I'll call you," Shug said, breathing a sigh of relief as she stuffed the change back into her purse.

Leon came in a couple of hours later. "Now let me get this straight," he said. "You want me to work the late game on Sunday and close up afterward, right? By myself, right? So you can have a date." He studied the ceiling for a minute, his mind working. "Hmmm."

"Come on, Leon. You're the one said I should get a—"

Leon interrupted. "You know what it's like when they do a double-header. The crowd'll be drinkin' stadium beer for five or six hours, then come in here to piss on the restroom wall and order shots."

"I'll pay time and a half."

"I don't know, man. That crowd..." Leon shook his head and walked over to the plate glass window that looked out onto Labrosse Street. He stood there for a minute, watching the traffic.

"How 'bout this?" Leon offered. "My sister Roberta's boy just recently got outta the Navy. He's a smart kid, been taking courses at the community college while he's looking for work. What if I get him to come in on Sunday and give me a hand with the crowd while you're out with this cop lady? You pay him half what you pay me, you're still no worse off than time and a half. Sound okay?"

"Yeah, I guess so. Okay."

Leon smiled to himself in the window glass as Shug disappeared into the back room. *Been so long since the man had a real date, he was climbing all over himself,* Leon thought, *but that was all right. In fact, that was just fine.* He ambled over to the telephone and dialed. "Roberta? Hey, girl. Put Devonne on the phone, will you?"

Darcy woke to the jangle of the telephone and checked the illuminated clock display on the nightstand: 3:20 a.m. It couldn't be good news. She threw her legs over the side of the bed and fumbled for the receiver.

"Raintree."

"Ah, Darcy."

The Irish lilt in Sergeant Mike Connolly's voice sounded incongruously warm and bright in the darkness of her bedroom. He had been her mentor as she worked her way up through the Patrol Division, and more recently appeared delighted in her progress as a detective. Nearing retirement now, he had become something of a father figure for Darcy, whose own father had died when she was a teenager. Darcy hadn't seen him that often since he'd begun working the graveyard shift two months ago, but even now, knowing something bad must have gone down, she felt a certain comfort just knowing he was there.

"Sorry to trouble you, darlin', but duty calls. Looks as though we've got another one. I'm in the commercial district, over near the Greyhound Terminal on Fifth Avenue."

She was fully awake now. "Give me half an hour, Mike." She scrambled into her clothes, ran a brush through her hair, and raced out the door.

Arriving twenty-three minutes later, Darcy found Sergeant Connolly and officers from two additional patrol units protecting the scene. Headlights from the three patrol cruisers formed a triangle of illumination against the rear entrance of a sporting goods store. The big man walked in her direction, his slow, fluid gait reminding her of a cruise ship rolling on the high seas. They met at the edge of the lighted area.

"The ME and Forensics are on the way," Connolly said. "The suddenly departed is over here." Their elongated shadows preceded them to the rear of the store where an inert form lay partly against the exterior wall, within an arm's reach of the half-open door.

Darcy crouched by the body. The man was black, about forty, she guessed, dressed in jeans and a plaid, blood-soaked shirt. His chest was a ragged tangle of flesh and cloth. Blood had pooled in black patches on the ground beneath him. Next to the body was a light-blue duffel bag with *Lunford's Sporting Goods* emblazoned in white letters across its side.

"What's in the bag?"

"Stolen goods, for sure. Just what, I wouldn't know." Connolly squatted beside her and placed a hand on her shoulder. "Thought I'd leave the crime scene investigatin' up to the detective."

"Let me see your flash." Darcy moved around to where the mouth of the bag was drawn partly closed by a drawstring. Using the flashlight and a ballpoint pen, she worked the opening wide enough to see the glint of metal. "Looks like handguns."

"Poor bastard should have loaded up while he was still inside," Connolly observed. "Might have had a fightin' chance."

"Who found the body?"

Connolly jerked a thumb over his shoulder. "Donaldson called it in. Routine patrol pattern. This area's been hit a lot lately. I was over near the interstate, got here a few minutes later."

More headlights smeared across the wall, signaling the arrival of the crime scene van.

"Better clear out," Darcy advised. "You know how picky these guys are."

They rose and started back toward the patrol units as another car pulled in beside the van. A tall, thin man got out and stood surveying the scene with his hands on his hips. What appeared to be a pajama top peeked out from below the light windbreaker he wore. His hair was disheveled and his eyeglasses glinted in the lights from the patrol units. He didn't look happy.

"Looks like the ME's here," she said.

"Yep." Connolly glanced at his watch and grinned. "It's four-oh-three. Don't you know he'll be in a mood."

Shug called the Detroit P.D. Robbery-Homicide Department late in the afternoon on Thursday and asked for Detective Raintree. A gruff, uninterested voice asked him to hold. In the background, he heard the murmur of voices, labored pecking at a typewriter, and an occasional burst of muffled laughter. He waited almost five minutes before Darcy came on the line.

"This is Detective Raintree." She sounded harried and out of breath.

"Hi, it's Shug."

"What?"

"It's Shug Barnes, from the bar. I'm calling about Sunday ... the game?" He listened to background noises again, suddenly feeling very unsure of himself. Had she forgotten who he was?

"Oh, Shug. I'm sorry. It's been a little crazy around here."

He breathed again. "I thought maybe we'd take in the second game, say around seven o'clock. I could pick you up, or we could meet here at the bar and walk over."

"Yeah, well, I'm not real sure of my schedule right now. Can I get back to you?"

"Sure," he said. "I understand." But he didn't, not really. He hung up feeling dismissed and depressed.

His mood lifted considerably when, at ten-thirty that evening, Darcy walked through the door of the bar. His smile was quick and wide.

"Hey!" he said. "I didn't expect to see you."

"I came by to apologize for earlier. I just got off work." She slipped onto a bar stool across from him. "Can I have a glass of wine, please? The Chablis I had before was good."

He poured one for her and another for himself. They touched glasses and she gave him a tired smile.

"Rough day, huh?"

"It's been a rough month." She took a sip, set her glass down on the ebony-colored bar, and studied the wine absently. Shug had seen the look before, in Viet Nam. They'd called it the "thousand-yard stare."

"Anything new with the case?"

She shook her head, drained half the wine, and closed her eyes. After a moment she said, "I'm going home now, Shug."

His heart sank.

She opened her eyes then, pale-blue and serious. "Will you come with me?"

For two seconds, Shug watched the quickening throb of pulse at her throat, not sure he'd heard her right. Then he nodded, turned, and walked quickly toward the back room. "Hey, Leon, I need a favor."

An hour and a half later, she slid off him and into the crook of his arm. The thin sheen of sweat on Shug's chest turned cool but not unpleasantly so. He lay quietly and stroked her arm as their heartbeats slowed in sync.

"Shug?"

"Hmmm?"

"I need to apologize. I used you just now."

"Hey, anytime."

Her forefinger traced a line through the fine hair on his chest. "No, I did. I really used you. I'm not like that, usually. I mean, we hardly know—"

"Don't say it. Anyway, I don't feel used. I feel good." He ran his hand down over her arm, along the smooth curve of her hip, and breathed in the subtle fragrance of her hair.

After a moment, she pressed her body closer. "I feel good, too."

Later, they sat at her tiny kitchen table while Darcy devoured a peanut butter and jelly sandwich and drank a glass of milk. She had on his shirt with the sleeves rolled up. Shug sat shirtless in his jeans, drinking a Diet Pepsi.

"I wanted to head a major case ever since I became a detective," she said. "Now I have one, and it's eating me alive."

"I know it's a homicide," Shug said. "Two people killed and all that, but that doesn't seem so out of the ordinary for Detroit. Seems like there's always something like that in the newspaper."

She used her tongue to retrieve a bead of grape jelly from the corner of her mouth. "It isn't just the one at your place. Yours was the third similar incident in the last couple of weeks. And last night there was another one. All took place between midnight and four in the morning. All were located roughly in the downtown central business district." She paused long enough to take a sip of milk. "Five people killed, all with a shotgun. And all while committing a crime."

Shug nodded. "Burglaries—like the one at my place."

Darcy shook her head. "Only three were burglaries. One was a street robbery. Guy had a fight with his girlfriend, left her place about two-thirty in the morning, and was walking to his car."

"What happened?"

"He was approached by another guy with a knife, demanding all his cash. He tosses his wallet at the guy and takes off running. He's maybe twenty-five yards away when he hears a loud blast, looks back, sees the mugger on the sidewalk and a third party beating feet for the corner. He calls from an all-night diner, reports the crime."

"So what'd he say?"

Darcy shrugged. "He only saw the back of the shooter when he passed under a streetlight—dark clothes, nothing distinctive. Could be anybody. Everybody."

"Your case is the shooter."

She nodded. "We call him Smoothbore down at the station. On account of he uses a shotgun, which, unlike a rifle, is smooth inside the barrel. So far, we've been able to keep it out of the press. Both the name and the link between the cases. That's the good news—the only good news. The bad news is I've got no leads and big pressure to find the guy."

Shug stood, drained the Pepsi can, and placed it on the counter next to the sink. "Wish I could help."

Smiling weakly, her voice scarcely more than a whisper, Darcy said, "You did."

He also wished he could see her mouth and her eyes smile at the same time. He yawned and stretched. "Guess I'd better let you get some sleep, huh? I'll catch a cab back to the bar and pick up my car."

Darcy got up from the table and walked toward the hall leading to the bedroom. As she walked, she unbuttoned Shug's shirt and let it slip from her shoulders. "You could do that if you wanted. Or, I could drop you off there in the morning."

"That'd work, too," he said, smiling and following her down the hallway.

Darcy spent the next morning rereading the reports on each incident, hoping to uncover some obscure fact, some overlooked detail that might suddenly spark an avenue of investigation. By eleven o'clock, the words were blurring together and she still had nothing. She let her chin rest on her chest and closed her eyes.

Her thoughts drifted to the previous evening, a nice distraction. *More like an escape*, said a little voice in her brain. She was paying for it now, hardly able to think clearly. She had almost fallen asleep sitting at her work station when Lieutenant Whitman called from his office doorway.

"Raintree. Got a minute?"

She shook her head to clear it and scrambled across the squad room. Closing the door behind her, she stood in front of the Lieutenant's desk, waiting.

Whitman gestured for her to take a seat. "What do you have? The Chief wants to form a task force if we don't get something by Monday."

"Still nothing." Darcy hated saying it. But not as much as what she was about to add. "I'm not sure where to go next."

The Lieutenant swiveled in his chair, offering her a profile more suited to a college professor than a veteran cop. His reading glasses rested low on the bridge of his nose, and he tapped his chin with a forefinger.

"Motive?"

It came across not so much a question as a suggested topic for discussion. She took a breath. "Guy's got a hard-on for criminals." She'd learned not to mince her words. Not with the men in her squad, and especially not with the lieutenant. Early in her career, Mike Connolly had told her: *You need to throw in a 'hell' or a 'damn' or worse every once in a while, darlin', just to let the good old boys know you're one of them.*

"And why do you think that is?" Whitman asked.

"I don't know. Maybe he's like McGruff. Pissed off and wants to take a bite out of crime."

Whitman nodded and swiveled back to face Darcy. "Or maybe he's seen too many Charles Bronson movies and wants to play vigilante." His eyebrows formed twin arches in his wrinkled forehead. "Maybe he was burgled, or robbed, or assaulted." He let the words hang in the air.

"And if so," she continued the thought, barely able to contain the excitement in her voice, "there should be a record of it somewhere." The Lieutenant smiled warmly at her, clearly pleased.

Her enthusiasm faded quickly as she navigated the two floors and rabbit warren of green-and-gray cubicles separating Robbery-Homicide from the Records Department, contemplating just how to approach her inquiry. How far back should she go? How wide an area should she search? What was she looking for? An injury to the victim, an assault on or murder of a family member? What might spark a personal vendetta of such magnitude? The options were endless, but it was the only lead she had—and the Monday deadline loomed large in her mind. She would *not* lose this case to a task force, even if it meant working day and night.

Darcy pushed through the swinging double doors and stopped in front of a long counter piled high with manila folders and computer printouts. Half the desks she could see were empty. A round clock against the back wall said eleven thirty-two. Staggered lunch schedules, she guessed. After waiting a full two minutes for someone to notice her, she called out, "Excuse me."

A pudgy young man with acne scars and rimless glasses looked up from his computer. "Oh, sorry. I didn't see you there." He slid his chair back and wound his way around the other desks to the counter. A small, black and white plastic badge identified him as H. Tolliver, a civilian employee. "Can I help you?"

She identified herself and said, "I'd like reported homicides, robberies, burglaries, and assaults for the last six months."

He rolled his eyes. "You got a Dodge Ram to haul them back to R-H?"

"Okay, how about just homicides, robberies, and assaults?"

"You'd still need a short-bed Chevy." He chuckled at his own cleverness.

She leaned across the counter and put one hand on his forearm. He swallowed visibly as she drew to within inches of his ear, and color rose in his round, cratered cheeks. "How about if we narrowed the search radius? Say, just in the central business district?"

His head bobbed like it was on a spring.

It was good to be one of the guys, she thought, but a woman needed to be versatile as well.

They agreed on the details of the search, and an eager H. Tolliver promised to have what she needed by mid-afternoon. Darcy had just finished a pre-packaged ham and cheese sandwich and diet cola when he called her back.

"Hey, it's me, Horace Tolliver. I have what you need. That is, I have what you wanted. Already!"

"That's great, Howard. I really appreciate it." She glanced at her watch. It was only twelve forty-five. "How'd you get it all so quickly?"

"Actually, it's Horace," he said. "Anyway, after you left, I got to thinking, and then I remembered that someone else had requested the same data, or almost the same data. I mean the parameters were a little different—we'd used specific street boundaries rather than Census block groups, so I checked the files and—"

"Horace, slow down, please. Who requested the data?"

"Uh, it was a Uniform guy. Let's see, it was ... Mike Connolly. Sergeant Mike Connolly."

"When?"

"Two, three weeks ago, I think. I could check the assistance request file and get back to you if it's important. Say, detective, there's a great movie playing downtown. I was wondering if you'd—"

Horace Tolliver was still talking as Darcy replaced the receiver in its cradle.

"Hey, Shug, I want you to meet my nephew, Devonne Cole." Leon stood with his arm around the shoulders of a slender young man whose fresh face and generous smile inspired instant appeal. *Put the boy in a sailor suit*, Shug thought, *and he'd be recruiting poster material.*

Devonne stuck out his hand. "I'm pleased to meet you, Mister Barnes."

Shug gave the boy's hand a shake. "Call me Shug. Everybody does."

"Thought I'd show Devonne around the place," Leon said. "Make sure he's up to speed for helping out on Sunday."

"Sounds like a plan," Shug said. He looked at Devonne. "You ever work in a bar?"

The boy was lighter-skinned than Leon and clean-shaven, but Shug thought he could see a family resemblance, an image of how Leon might have looked at twenty-two years old, before he muscled up and became scary. The young man's smooth forehead creased into a frown.

"No, sir, I haven't, but I've been in a few. I did a Med cruise on the USS Arlington. I imagine I've been on shore leave in a dozen or more ports." He grinned and glanced up at Leon who, at six-four, had about three inches on his nephew.

Shug chuckled and said, "Well, Devonne, your temporary duty assignment is Shug's Place this Sunday." He narrowed his eyes and turned to Leon. "You sure we can trust a sailor around all our liquid assets?"

Leon's huge arm slid around Devonne's neck like a boa constrictor, and he pulled the young man in tight and high so that his toes just touched the floor. "We can trust him. He seen Uncle Leon's wrath before, ain't you, boy?"

Devonne was laughing, as best he could, and squirming in Leon's grasp. "Yes, sir, Uncle Leon. I have seen it, and I don't particularly care to see it again."

A few minutes later, as Devonne did a slow reconnaissance of the back room, Shug spoke softly to Leon. "He seems like a good kid."

Leon nodded. "He joined the Navy just in the nick of time, I think. In high school, he hung with a rough crowd. Now he's out of the service, he needs to stay busy and make a little money. Not lose his momentum."

"Yeah, well, he's got a good influence in you."

"Huh. You think so? Well, I ain't been around him much these last few years." The big man headed toward the back. "We'll see how he does on Sunday."

Darcy stared at the stack of computer-generated files. Why would Mike have asked for these particular files? She'd come up through the Uniform ranks, seven years on the streets. She knew how things worked. Yet, she couldn't make sense of it all.

The department employed a crime analysis section that tracked crimes, locations, dates, frequencies, and any other patterns that might help predict when and where a crime might be committed. The higher-ranking officers used the information to set goals and identify strategies. Precinct captains deployed their men accordingly. Sergeants supervised patrols; they didn't do crime analysis.

Mike had started third shift patrol duty about two months ago. She'd asked why the late-night shift? He had seniority and could've had any shift he wanted.

He'd laughed. "I started on the streets nearly forty years ago, darlin'. I'll be retirin' soon. I'd like to say I've come full circle. Besides, I get antsy behind a desk, and night sergeants have a lot less paper to shuffle and can spend more time in the unit."

It had seemed perfectly logical to her at the time. She hated desk time herself. What the hell was she thinking? *Mike Connolly, a vigilante? No way. Still...*

Darcy took the stairs down three floors to check the Uniform Division duty roster. Returning to her desk a half hour later, she peeled the cellophane wrapping from a new stack of index cards and began making notes.

> *1) Duty roster shows MC on patrol in area same nights as shootings occurred. Coincidence? MC on patrol most nights.*
> *2) Shootings occurred between midnight and 4:00 am. Most third shift patrols take dinner break at some point during same period. Would be out of patrol unit for some period of time—could account for breaks in radio contact.*
> *3) Sergeants patrol alone, take car home at night. Would explain how shotgun is hidden, transported.*
> *4) MC is a hunter.*

She remembered the day he brought in the newspaper photo from the back pages of the sports section—a smiling Mike Connolly, kneeling, holding up the fanned tail of a huge wild turkey, shotgun propped upright between his arm and thigh. "How 'bout that, darlin'? Your old Uncle Mike has made the *Detroit Free Press*. Always thought I'd make the papers for shootin' somethin'. Never dreamed it'd be a turkey."

Thumbing through her case file, she found the number she wanted and dialed Raymond Monroe, the victim of the street robbery and the only person so far to catch a glimpse of the shooter. When Monroe answered, she identified herself and explained that she was calling to see if he remembered anything new about the man he'd seen running for the corner.

"Nah, it was pretty dark, you know, middle of the night. I couldn't see much."

Darcy pressed. "There's nothing more you remember? His clothing, hair color, height or weight?"

"Well, at first all I saw was a dark shadow running toward the street light on the corner, you know? What do you call it, like in the movies, when the guy comes into the bar through these swinging doors and the sun's at his back and all you can see is this big, black shadow? You know what I mean, right?"

"Yeah," Darcy said. "Back-lit, I think they call it."

"Yeah, that's it. It's like the guy was back-lit, except he was facing away from me, running. Wait, now that you mention it, the guy ran kind of funny. Sort of rolling along, not very fast."

"Like a big guy might run?" Darcy asked. *Like Mike Connolly might run*, she thought, then hated herself for it.

"Well, maybe. But I couldn't say for sure, you know. It was pretty dark. I was pretty scared."

She thanked him and hung up the phone, her emotions churning. The wall clock over the Lieutenant's door told her it was nearly four-thirty. Except for the Records and Uniform Division excursions, she'd been at her desk over nine hours. And she hadn't gotten much sleep the night before. Her thoughts jumbled crazily inside her head: Mike Connolly's big body loping along dark streets with a shotgun cradled in his hands; the possibility of the chief of police yanking the Smoothbore case out from under her; Shug Barnes, naked and warm beside her in the bed. No, as much as she might want to, might *need* to, she couldn't go there, not now, not yet. No distractions.

She could see Lieutenant Whitman's head through the partially drawn blinds of his office window. He was on the phone, leaning back in his chair, receiver in one hand, a sheet of paper in the other. Her police training told her she should probably go talk to him about her suspicions.

But what if she was wrong?

Mike would find out. She knew that for sure. There were no secrets in the department. He'd been her mentor, her *rabbi*, as it was called in police circles. He had looked out for her like a father. She could see his face, one eyebrow arched, a gentle grin spreading from mouth to eyes.

But what if she was right?

Even if she was right, could she do that to him? He was retiring soon. He'd lose his pension, go to prison, very likely die in prison.

The Lieutenant hung up the telephone, rose, and slid into his suit jacket. Darcy watched. He pulled his office door shut behind him and gave her a slight nod when their eyes met. She was still watching as he left the squad room and disappeared down the hall.

Not today, she thought. *I'm not talking to anyone until I find out more*. Right now, she needed sleep, a hot bath, an early dinner, and ten, twelve hours of sleep. She stacked the files on her desk and gathered up her purse and coat. Lieutenant Whitman was in the hallway, still waiting for the elevator. She slipped into the stairwell before he could turn around.

The telephone rang thirteen times before someone picked it up.

"Robbery-Homicide. This is Detective Salvatore."

"Hi, uh, is Detective Raintree there, please?"

"Sorry, she left about fifteen minutes ago. Take a message?"

"No, no message," Shug said, disappointed. "I'll try again tomorrow." He'd wanted to see her, at least to hear her voice. He liked her voice: feminine and smoky at the same time. In fact, he liked everything about her.

His impromptu plans derailed, Shug returned his attention to the bar. Ralph Kovacs, one of the World War II vets with three day's stubble on his cheeks, leaned on the shiny dark surface, empty beer mug in hand.

"What's a fellow got to do to get a draft Bud around here?"

Darcy fluffed her pillow and shifted position for the umpteenth time. It was no use. She had taken a long, steamy bath, had two glasses of wine with a heated-up microwave dinner, and was in bed by eight o'clock. She should have gone right to sleep. Instead, she'd stared up at the invisible ceiling, thoughts as dark as the room itself swirling in her brain. Now, the bedside clock glowed a mocking red twelve forty-five.

Could Mike have done it? Her notes indicated that it was possible. *But not probable*, she told herself. He was a police officer, sworn to uphold the law. What motive would he have for killing people? Her mind drifted back to Cathy Richards. The poor girl had been pregnant. *Pregnant, for God's sake.*

She flung the sheet back and sat up on the side of her bed. A thin sheen of perspiration beaded on her forehead. She would talk to him. Maybe ride with him, have coffee or a snack. She'd talk about the shootings, her trip to the Records Department. He'd laugh and tell her he'd done the same thing. "Just bein' proactive in my waning years, darlin' girl." He'd have an answer for her. Then she'd be free to concentrate on the *real* shooter. She slipped back into the same clothes she'd taken off and left her house at one-ten.

"He's on the streets," the corporal at the desk told her. "Called in for a dinner break about a half hour ago."

"He say where he was eating?"

"Nope, but you might try the Waffle House on Third. That's one of his usual places."

A drive-through of the Waffle House parking lot brought no success. Darcy found herself taking first one street, then another, finally evolving to a rolling grid from the waterfront to the Fisher Freeway, east as far as Interstate 375 and west to the Lodge Freeway. She spotted Connolly's empty patrol unit on Second Avenue at 2:15 a.m. There were no restaurants on the deserted street, just a locksmith, pawn shop, and a few inexpensive retail clothing stores. She cruised past the car to the next intersection, turned right on Richardson, and parked midway down the block next to the alley.

Removing the nine millimeter Glock from her belt, Darcy got out of the car and walked silently to the mouth of the alley. Light from an adjacent street lamp penetrated about thirty feet. The opposite entrance was a small rectangular spot glowing dimly in the distance, its shape broken only by the dark shadows of head-high trash bins scattered down the passageway. She carried the Glock loosely at her side.

"Sergeant Connolly," she called out softly, her voice echoing faintly off the bricks. Then louder, "Mike! Are you in there?" There was nothing but silence for a moment, broken only by the sound of her breathing. Then she heard a vague noise, a kind of scraping sound in the darkness.

"Darcy? Is that you, girl?" She recognized his voice, but it was strained.

"Where are you? Come out, Mike, where I can see you."

"Oh, I can't do that, darlin'. You'll have to come in for me."

"Mike, what are you doing?"

"At the moment, dear, I'm just waitin'. You'd best come on now."

Taking a few steps along the wall, her academy training clicked in again, and she brought her weapon up and held it pointed in front of her chest with both hands. *But he wouldn't hurt me, would he, no matter what?* She lowered the pistol once more. Her mouth felt dry. She could hear herself swallow, a dry clicking sound in her throat.

Half a minute later, forty feet into the alley, she could barely make out the first dumpster. It was angled out into the dark corridor, leaving a narrow strip barely wide enough for her to pass between it and the wall. She crouched low against the brick. "Mike?" Her voice was softer now.

"Other side of this blasted trash dump, Darcy. Hurry, girl. Let's get this done."

What? Get what done? She crept forward, her back to the brick wall, keeping her profile to a minimum against the light behind her. Ten feet from the dumpster, she called out once more. "Mike?"

Another scraping noise. Like fabric on concrete, far right corner, other side of the bin. Darcy moved to her left, each step slow, silent, irreversible. She slipped into the narrow space to the left of the dumpster and stopped two feet from the far edge. Held her breath. Listened. She could hear him breathing. Long, low, ragged breaths.

She made her decision and pivoted around the corner, arms extended, weapon ready.

In the thin light from the alley's far entranceway, Mike Connolly lay slumped back against the bin, his uniform jacket balled up between his thighs. He looked up at her and smiled.

"What took you so long, darlin'? Can't you see I'm fadin' away here?"

She stuffed the Glock back into her holster and knelt beside him. The jacket was soaked with blood. Dark fluid pulsed from under the fabric, pooling below his right leg, then creeping out like fingers toward the low center of the alleyway.

"Mike?" Tears sprang up in her eyes. "What happened?"

"I almost had him, Darcy. 'Almost had the murderin' bastard." He glanced down at his leg. "He got me though, clipped an artery, I think." His face softened then, and he spoke to her in a whisper. "I was waitin' for the angels, Darcy, waitin' for the angels. And here you are, my own special angel, come to take me home."

"Where's your hand-held?" Her voice was urgent now.

Smiling grimly, he said, "In the patrol unit, I'm afraid. Didn't want any tell-tale noise while I was in the hunt." He pressed the balled jacket tighter to his thigh. "This has helped staunch the flow a bit."

"Hold on, Mike." She jumped to her feet and started toward her car. "I'm getting an ambulance."

Darcy got through to the dispatcher at two thirty-three. The ambulance screamed in at two-forty-one along with most of the precinct's available patrol units. Rotating red and blue lights painted the alley like a 1970s discotheque.

They were all too late.

"Five minutes together," Shug shook his head slowly. "Not much time."

"It was enough," Darcy said. "I guess it had to be."

They had chosen not to go to the Tigers' game after all. Darcy had been too upset and wanted to talk. Shug was grateful to be the listener. They sat on his sofa, her leaning back against his shoulder, sock feet crossed and propped on the battered coffee table. Midnight sat stiffly in the living room doorway, warily eyeing the interloper.

Darcy leaned forward and lifted her wine glass from the coffee table. "He was retiring in less than a year. Third shift afforded him the opportunity to patrol. He always liked that." She took a sip of the wine.

Shug remained silent.

"He'd gotten the crime reports, he said, because he never trusted the civilian employees to know the streets. He thought they sat in their glass tower and made observations like scientists studying slides under a microscope. He'd been analyzing the reports for patterns, particular locations or areas that had been repeat targets, things like that. Things a good street cop would look for. He was trying to get inside Smoothbore's mind."

"But you thought…"

"I thought, well, I guess I'd convinced myself he was on some kind of vendetta, trying to take out as many criminals as he could before he retired." She brushed at a tear tracing a shiny line down her cheek. "I was so wrong."

Shug pressed his lips into her hair. It smelled of peaches. "You might have been right, though. You had a responsibility."

She shook her head. "I don't know, maybe." Darcy sat up and turned to face him. "He actually started hunting the guy after the Richards girl was killed, after he found out she'd been pregnant. Said he'd barely missed Smoothbore at the sporting goods store—

had seen what he thought was the guy's van. Apparently, he was right. That's what he was doing in the alley Friday morning. He'd spotted the same van. He was stalking the stalker."

"How does the shooter find his victims?"

"I don't know yet. But I will, sometime soon. I'm going to find this guy, Shug. He killed my friend." Darcy relaxed again, nestling deeper into Shug's shoulder.

"So, how do you feel?" Shug asked.

"I feel guilty as hell." Another tear rolled down her cheek, hung at the line of her jaw for a moment, then became a dark spot on Shug's shirt. "I thought he'd gone bad, Shug. I was ready to shoot him if I had to. He *saw* me with my weapon trained on him."

"It was an honest mistake." He was quiet for a minute, remembering back to another time. A time when maybe if he'd been more attentive—a little more proactive—a young girl, Rose, might still be alive. "I think the dead forgive us our sins. At least, I hope so."

"I hope so, too," she whispered.

"You're going to the funeral?"

She nodded. "Tuesday. A cop funeral. It'll be a big deal." She slid one hand along his leg and squeezed. "Too bad you have to work. I'd like it if you could be with me."

Later, when Darcy was sleeping, Shug got quietly up from the bed and went into the living room. He dialed the bar, and Leon answered.

"How's it going?" Shug asked.

"Well, everybody want to know where you are, like if you died or somethin', 'cause you ain't never *not* here. But, other than that, we're handling things. Devonne hadn't dropped but a couple of trays so far."

Shug grimaced at the thought. "You think he'll do okay?"

"I'm going to set him cleaning up the bathrooms before we close. If he can handle that, I guess he might do all right."

"I'm going to take a little more time off this week, Tuesday, for sure. Maybe Devonne can work the afternoon trade for me, you know, before the rush."

"Yeah. I'll ask him if he's available. Let you know."

Shug hung up the phone and padded naked back to the bedroom.

Darcy lay on her stomach, dark hair splayed out across the pillow. The cat lay close beside her, eyes closed, purring loudly enough for Shug to hear.

Crossing his arms over his chest, he leaned against the doorframe and studied the unlikely scene.

"Huh," he said. "What do you think about that?"

The Legacy: Pride and Patriotism
March 19, 1917

A spark ignited in Douglas Hanahan's eyes as he read the disturbing headlines: *Three American Ships Sunk! One Unwarned, 22 Men Missing.* It was not enough that the Germans had sunk the Lusitania off the coast of his native Ireland, killing nearly two thousand men, women, and children. Now, they had broken their pact about warnings and passenger safeguards. *How could they be so brutal, so ruthless, so—*

"Aye, it's a helluva thing," Tommy Condon said, his shaggy eyebrows nearly touching as he frowned. The old man's face was a contour map of spidery veins and furrows of age. He took another swallow of his beer and glanced at the bar's proprietor over the top of his mug. "If I was a young man again..."

"Well, I'm enlisting tomorrow," young Johnny McCafferty chimed in, hoisting his beer mug for emphasis. "We'll be in the war before you know it, and I'm gonna kick some Kraut ass."

Hanahan nodded. He understood how both men felt; he could feel the outrage building in himself. Like most successful immigrants, he was filled with pride and patriotism. He took any threat to his newly adopted country, and his way of life, very personally. "You're right as rain. If I could, I'd throttle the Kaiser with my own two hands."

Three weeks later, the United States declared war on Germany.

Maggie Hanahan paced nervously in her kitchen. "You're too old to be doing this, Douglas! And what of me and little Patrick? What will we do while you're off in some God-forsaken place, doing God knows what?" She stopped pacing and turned to face her husband, hugging herself as if chilled. Moisture welled up in her eyes. "What of us?"

"Sweet Maggie," Douglas began. "I'm thirty-five years old and fit as a fiddle. What would you have me do? Our friends and neighbors are lining up at the recruiter's office. It's the right thing—the only thing." He put his hands on her shoulders and drew her close. "You and Patrick will be fine. There's money in the bank to tide you over until I get back, and the bar will be here when it's over.

"America has given us a new life, a wonderful life and a wonderful place to raise our children. I must do this; don't you see, Maggie? Else I could never look my friends or myself in the eye again." He squeezed her tightly. "It'll all be just fine, darlin'. There'll be no harm come to me." Douglas smiled down into his wife's tear-stained face. "I'll have the luck of the Irish on my side."

There was a farewell party at A Little Bit O' Ireland on a Saturday night a few weeks later. Douglas, Maggie, and their friends sang Irish folk songs and danced to music from the radio. Toward the end, wives cried, and the men, many already in uniform, clapped each other on the back and toasted Woodrow Wilson for allowing them this exciting and patriotic opportunity. Sunday morning, those who happened to pass by the bar on their way to church took pride in the sign posted in the window: *Gone to fight for America!*

Douglas Hanahan landed in France with the first contingent of American troops on June 26, 1917. On the second of July, he entered a military field hospital where he was diagnosed with pneumonia. He died one week later, never having seen combat.

Later that same year, lobbied by proponents for a sober workforce, the Michigan State Legislature passed the Damon Act prohibiting the sale and consumption of alcoholic beverages.

Maggie and her son, Patrick, held on for nearly sixteen months, using the savings she and Douglas had accumulated in the years since the bar opened. When the money finally ran out, Maggie, like many women of her time, sought work in the war effort. She was rewarded almost immediately, and went to work as a welder in Burgess Industries' railroad yards.

In December of 1919, almost thirteen years to the day after it opened, the building housing Hanahan's A Little Bit O' Ireland was claimed by the City of Detroit for non-payment of taxes.

Where Smiling Bastards Lie

Kim Li stared wide-eyed down the black hole of the gun barrel. Then he felt the cold steel pressed hard against his forehead and squeezed his eyelids tightly shut. Images of his wife and two small children crowded his mind. What would they do when he was gone? How would they live?

The raspy, impatient voice intruded on his thoughts. "I said give me the fucking money!"

This wasn't like the other times. The other times, he'd simply handed over the money and the guys had run. This guy was different. Kim saw it in his eyes, felt it in the hot spit that peppered his face when the guy screamed at him. This guy was psycho. This guy was going to kill him.

Kim opened the cash register.

"Get on the floor! On the floor, you stupid gook!"

The gun barrel lifted momentarily from Kim's forehead, then crashed back across his nose and mouth. He tasted blood and sank to his knees behind the counter. Above him, the man stuffed the pockets of his filthy windbreaker with money from the cash drawer. Kim closed his eyes again and prayed for deliverance.

He felt the gun jammed back against his forehead. "You got a safe?" The man was screaming at him again. "Tell me, you little piece of shit! Tell me or I'll blow your—"

The window behind Kim exploded in a spray of flying glass and a double-boom of thunder. He blinked rapidly and shook his head to clear it. In front of him, the psycho was lying on his back, missing most of his face and neck. Blood bubbled darkly from what was left.

The store owner staggered to his feet and extracted a small shard of glass from the back of his neck. He turned toward the blown-out window of his liquor store just in time to see a light blue van screech away from the curb across the street.

Deliverance, Kim thought. God had sent an angel to deliver him from the murderous clutches of a madman. He knelt once again and said a small prayer of thanks. Then he walked to the telephone in the corner and dialed nine-one-one.

Detective Darcy Raintree watched the diminutive Vietnamese store owner gesturing wildly and speaking animatedly to a reporter from the *Detroit Free Press*. She hoped the reporter wasn't savvy enough to link this shooting to the others. All she needed was for the newspaper to plaster *Serial Killer Strikes Again* in twenty-point caps across the top of the front page. That'd really help her standing in the chief's eyes, probably get her shuffled off to the Community Relations Department. She turned back to Patrol Sergeant John Phillips, the first ranking officer on the scene, and raised a questioning eyebrow.

"Guy thinks God sent an angel to save him," Phillips said. "I, on the other hand, thought this shooter might just be the asshole you're looking for." His jaw took on a hard set. "The one who shot Mike."

"Smoothbore," Darcy said.

Phillips nodded. "This place has been robbed six times in the last year. Anybody who reads the news, they'd know that. If a guy was staking out places where a crime was likely to be committed, this place would have to be pretty high on the list."

Darcy brushed a lock of dark hair from her face and jerked a thumb in the direction of the store owner. "Did he get a look at the shooter?"

"Well, he saw a light-blue van pull away from the curb. He was too shook up to notice much else, what with the scumbag scattered all over his booze." Then Phillips grinned like the Cheshire Cat. "But..."

"But what?"

The sergeant pointed up toward a small black box suspended from the ceiling in the corner of the liquor store. "Mister Li had a security system installed a couple of months ago—closed-circuit TV monitors behind the counter and—" he paused for effect—"on the roof."

Darcy grinned, too. "Then what are we waiting for? Let's get those tapes."

Smoothbore unwrapped a Twinkie, dunked half of it in a glass of milk, and inserted it whole into his mouth. He chewed absently, alternately licking and smacking his lips. An unnoticed dribble ran down his chin, hung there precariously for a moment, then plopped onto the newspaper spread out below him on the kitchen table. He couldn't take his eyes off the front-page headline: *Shotgun Slayings May Be Linked.*

Finally, his achievements had been recognized. Not stuck away somewhere in a two-inch column in the local news section, as had been the case until now. Now, others would be able to witness his becoming, his cleansing. Already, he could feel the *Hand of God* on his shoulder, guiding him in his journey to redemption.

The killer's finger traced the headline one last time, then continued slowly down the page, his lips silently sounding out the words. The words dripped with a sweetness that no cream-filled sponge cake could ever hope to match: *Police representatives declined to confirm that the recent rash of shotgun slayings, including that of Detroit Police Department Patrol Sergeant Michael Connolly, were the work of the same killer. However, certain key similarities are present in...*

Midway down the page, the photograph of a smiling Kim Li appeared. The liquor store owner was shown outside his store, pointing to the shattered window, and was quoted in the article as saying, "God sent an angel to save me." Smoothbore almost wept with gratitude, pressing the heels of his palms hard against his eyes to staunch the tide of tears welling up there. Instead, he repeated reverently the passage from the Bible that had inspired his transformation from an unclean sinner. "And the fourth angel poured out his vial upon the sun, and power was given unto him to scorch men with fire."

Scorch men with fire. And please The Father. Yes, he would please The Father and be welcomed in from the wild with open arms. No longer a blasphemer, he would be washed in the blood and purified by fire—Hellfire and Brimstone: one from each barrel.

Darcy took a bite of her onion ring, chewed, and sighed. "God, does anybody make a better onion ring than Mack?"

"Nope," said Shug. "They're sinful." He caught her hand and directed the remainder of the deep-fried morsel into his own mouth.

Darcy frowned and gave him a mock pout. "Anyway, like I was saying, we got the van on tape and an image of the shooter from the back and side. It's pretty grainy, but we're working with it. Looks like a fairly young guy, kind of heavy."

"What about a license plate number?" Shug asked.

"The angle wasn't right." Her eyes cut to the television mounted in an upper corner behind the bar. "Hey, turn the sound up a little, will you? That's the state attorney general."

Shug reached for the remote and clicked up the volume.

On the screen, a tall, thin man in his mid-fifties faced the camera. He had close-cropped gray hair and an engaging smile. His face grew more serious as the sound came up. "During the past four years, my office has reduced the rate of increase in street crime by nearly thirty percent. That's good, but we must not become complacent. We must not allow someone who will be less vigilant, less committed, to destroy the progress we have made." The man removed his glasses, leaned forward on the podium, and looked directly at the camera. "I pledge to the voters of this great state that, if I am re-elected, I will double my efforts to make Michigan the safest state in the country."

He smiled again as the camera panned to show a modest crowd of supporters, then to a young male reporter with a microphone. "That was the state's two-term attorney general, James Burgess, campaigning in Lansing in one of the year's most hotly contested races. And now, back to…"

Shug lowered the volume and simultaneously filched another onion ring from Darcy's plate. "You know that guy?"

"Only by reputation. He worked for the Flint Police Department for a few years, then went to law school and practiced for a few years before he ran for office. Mike..." Her eyes filled. "Mike said Burgess was a credit-grabber and more politician than cop. I'm not sure what to think. The guy's known for his 'law and order, tough on criminals' stance.'"

"I guess that'd be my stance, too, if I wanted to be the state's top cop."

"Well," Darcy said, "he's not really a cop, not anymore."

Shug yawned and stretched. "Right now, however, my eyes are glazing over from all this political rhetoric. I think I could use some tactile therapy from my own 'top cop.'"

"I like being your top cop," she purred, licking her lips. "But that doesn't mean I always have to be *on* top."

Shug felt the grin sneaking across his face like a thief. "Hey, Leon! Close up for me, okay?"

Michigan Attorney General James Burgess paced back and forth behind his desk. Despite his impressive record and two-term incumbency, his campaign was struggling. With only seven weeks to go until the election, he and his opponent, a well-known trial lawyer from Ann Arbor, were neck and neck in the polls. A loss now would severely hamper Burgess's future political goal for the governorship and, eventually, a seat in the United States Senate.

His young chief of staff, Lowell Seagraves, slouched in a visitor's chair, one leg slung over the chair's arm. The younger man wore an expensive suit, and his blond hair was cut in a conservative style that matched his employer's.

"Randall is a comer," Seagraves said. "He's got an outstanding conviction rate. He's got high-roller backers. He's glib. He's photogenic, not that you aren't, and he—"

"Then why don't you just go to work for the fucker!" Burgess snapped.

"Hey, take it easy, boss. All I'm saying is that you need something big. Something to remind the voters that you—" Seagraves raised his hands and made quote marks in the air— "refuse to tolerate lawlessness in our great state."

Burgess stopped his pacing and slumped into a green leather desk chair. "I'm sorry, Lowell. It's just that the guy gained almost twelve goddamn points in last month's polls. I'm starting to worry."

"Go to your strength."

Burgess rubbed his eyes. He was tired and wished Seagraves would just get to the point. "What are you talking about?"

"Where's the hotbed of crime?"

"Detroit, of course."

Seagraves unfurled a rolled-up copy of the *Detroit Free Press* and placed it on the desk. Below the fold was a full-color photo showing a liquor store with a blown-out, plate-glass window. The paper's headline read: *Shotgun Slayings May Be Linked*, the smaller subhead: *Vigilante At Work in Downtown Detroit?* Seagraves tapped the photo with his finger. "There it is—lawlessness in your face. And I have a source in the police department who tells me that all the killings are almost certainly the work of one person. They even have a name for him down there: *Smoothbore*."

Burgess's eyes narrowed and the corner of his mouth twitched in a brief, half-smile. "All right, then. Let's do something about this vigilante son of a bitch."

Seagraves nodded.

Darcy stopped at her apartment to shower and change clothes before work. She'd meant to come back last night but had ultimately succumbed to the warm feel of Shug's body nestled alongside her own. *There was definitely something about the guy*, she thought, smiling to herself. The answering machine light was blinking as she pushed through the door. She pressed the playback button. The call had come in at seven-thirty that morning.

"Darcy, Lieutenant Whitman here. See me when you get in, and I hope that's soon. I have a little surprise for you." She hoped the irritation apparent in his voice wasn't directed at her.

Darcy hurried through her shower, dressed quickly, and used a patchwork of secondary streets to avoid the inevitable, rush-hour interstate crawl. She knocked on the lieutenant's door at ten minutes before nine. Through the pebbled glass, she could make out two figures inside.

"Come."

Whitman sat tilted back in his swivel chair, hands clasped over his modest pot belly. Sitting with his back to her was a slender man with a good haircut and a nice-but-off-the-rack suit. When he turned, his eyes were quick, giving her a two-second appraisal, then softening to match the smile forming on his lips. He stood and extended a hand.

"Darcy," Whitman said, "meet Joel Melton. He's with the state attorney general's office."

"A pleasure," Melton said. His grip was smooth and practiced.

Whitman gestured for her to take the other chair. "It seems the attorney general has taken an interest in our string of vigilante shootings. Mister Melton's here to act as *liaison*"—he said the word as if it had a slick, oily feel to it—"between our two departments."

Darcy looked from Whitman to Melton and back. "Does that mean I'm not lead on the investigation any longer?"

"Not at all, detective." Melton smiled at her again. "I'm simply here as an observer. Attorney General Burgess wants your office to have the state's full resources at your disposal to help bring this killer to justice. If I can help in any way, as special investigator for the attorney general's office, I'll be available in that capacity."

She was sure those same words had been spoken on numerous other occasions to numerous other hardworking cops just before somebody yanked the chain on the trapdoor. "Okay then," she said, as pleasantly as possible. "What's next?"

The lieutenant leaned forward in his chair. "First thing, Special Investigator Melton is going to spend an hour or so reviewing the files. Afterward, Darcy, you can provide him a full briefing on our progress to date." He glanced up at the electric wall clock centered over his door. "Say, at ten-thirty?" He looked at Melton, who nodded agreement and rose from his seat.

"Ten-thirty, then," the investigator said, heading for the door.

As it closed behind their visitor, Whitman sighed. "We don't need this shit, Darcy."

"I know."

"What kind of progress are you going to talk about at ten-thirty?"

"Damned little, I'm afraid."

"You've got an hour and a half. Go make some. And take Owens with you."

Darcy, Detective Frank Owens, and Special Investigator Melton sat in one of the institutional-green interview rooms located off the Robbery-Homicide bullpen, she with her own file, the two men armed with notepads and pens. She still wasn't sure of the special investigator's intentions, but she had decided to give him the benefit of the doubt, at least for the time being. She glanced at Owens for moral support and began.

"He's young, we think, pretty good size. And he has that kind of rolling gait that large people have when they're in a hurry. Short hair, not shaved, but real close to the scalp."

"How does he conceal the weapon?" Melton asked.

"He's cut down the stock and barrels and he was wearing a jacket or long shirt that hid most of the weapon." She shrugged. "His activity has all been pretty late, not many people on the street. He likes alleys and he seems to know his way around downtown. I guess concealment hasn't been much of a problem."

"What about the vehicle?"

"A late-model Dodge van, probably an '84 or '85. Mike ... Sergeant Connolly, the officer who was killed, saw the van a couple of times. He said it was light blue."

"I'd like a copy of the videotape from the liquor store shooting," Melton said. "I want to see if our guys can come up with anything else."

He hadn't said it in an accusing way, like they'd been slack in their departmental observations. *What could it hurt?* She glanced at Owens, who nodded almost imperceptibly.

"Sure," she said.

Seagraves sat with one hip parked on the corner of his boss's desk, a sly grin working at the corners of his mouth. He did that a bit too often for Burgess's taste—that *I know something you don't know* thing—and it pissed him off. But he'd been pissed off a lot lately, so he decided to let it go this time. Let the man have his fun.

"You look like the cat that ate the canary," Burgess said. "What is it?"

"You're gonna love this," Seagraves said, waving the manila folder he held in his hand. "The videotape we got from Joel of the vigilante. It didn't show much, but..."

"What?"

"We had some stills made. I thought we could use this one for your campaign." He laid the folder down in front of Burgess and opened it. The grainy photo showed the side view of a chunky young man opening the door of a light-colored van. One hand grasped the door of the vehicle; in the other was a chopped-down shotgun. Seagraves pointed to the front bumper of the vehicle. Plastered on the rounded corner was a bumper sticker that read: "Re-elect Burgess Attorney General."

"What do you think? Can we use it?" He snickered, waiting for his employer to join in the joke.

Burgess sat staring at the photograph, rigid in his chair. Tiny beads of perspiration popped out on his forehead.

"Boss?" Seagraves eased off the desk, watching his ashen-faced employer. "Boss, are you all right?"

The red cloud cleared from behind Jim Burgess's eyes, and he realized Seagraves was speaking to him.

"Boss, are you all right?"

Burgess felt his heartbeat reaccelerate as the grainy, slightly out of focus photograph crept maliciously back into his field of vision. His underarms were wet and clammy. His bowels churned.

"Give me a fucking minute!" He closed his eyes and tried to breathe. The breaths came shallow at first but gradually returned to normal. He turned the photograph over and glanced at his chief of staff, who had moved to one of the chairs opposite the desk. Burgess trusted the young man as much as he trusted anyone. Aside from his considerable intelligence, Seagraves was both politically astute and ruthless. More importantly, he was dependent on Burgess for his livelihood—and knew it. "Lowell, did I ever tell you about my son?"

Seagraves shrugged. "I knew you had a son. I assumed he was grown and on his own. Not living around here, anyway."

"All true, but there's more to the story." Burgess slid the photograph an arm's length away from him. "Chris was twelve when his mother died. I did the best I could, raising him alone, trying to make a man of him. Then, when he was a senior in high school, I came home early one day and found him in his bedroom with another young man. They were…" He shifted in his chair and cleared his throat. "They were having oral sex." Burgess paused briefly. "We … we hardly spoke after that. He left home right after graduation. I never tried to stop him."

"How long ago was that?" Seagraves asked.

"Nearly eight years. I'd just begun my first term in office. Chris's leaving was a relief, in a way. I mean, if he'd continued to practice his *preferences* it might have—"

"It might have ruined you politically," Seagraves interjected, nodding. "Have you had any contact with him since?"

Burgess shook his head. "I've not seen him or communicated with him at all since he moved back to Detroit. That was six years ago. But…"

"But what, Boss?"

"He writes to me sometimes. Mostly long, rambling apologies, telling me he's going to make up for his 'sins of the flesh.' The most recent letter showed up a couple of weeks ago. It was different." He opened a desk drawer and rummaged through it, extracting a folded sheet of yellow, lined, three-hole-punched notebook paper. He placed it on top of the photograph and pushed both across the smooth leather desktop.

"Read it."

Seagraves unfolded the paper and began to read.

Father Dear,
I am so happy! It has been years since I felt this kind of euphoria, this sweet relief from the filthy thoughts that have plagued my consciousness for years. I am happy because there is a new person swelling inside me. One who shares your values. One who wants to help you in your quest to rid our streets of the iniquitous. I have become an angel—an avenging angel whose fiery sword strikes at the very heart of evil. I know now that one day soon I will again be your precious son. I will make you proud.

Seagraves finished the letter, and his eyes locked with Burgess's. "So, let me guess. The guy in the photograph is your son."

Burgess nodded. "I don't believe anyone other than me would recognize him now, but yes, I guess he's back."

Seagraves leaned forward, cupped his face with his hands, and said, "Oh, shit."

Shug opened the front door and opened his arms. Darcy came into them, sighed, and rested her head on his shoulder. He asked, "When did you eat last?" It was full dark outside, at least nine o'clock.

Darcy broke off the embrace and sank onto the living-room sofa. She yawned and rubbed her eyes. "I don't know. Breakfast, I guess. A sausage biscuit."

He'd cajoled her into meeting him at his house for dinner. She'd declined at first, saying she was going to grab a quick bite and then cruise the grid where Smoothbore typically operated. In the end, he'd won her over with the promise of hot apple pie and ice cream for dessert.

He set out napkins, glasses, and silverware, and dumped Chinese take-out onto their plates. "Want a beer or some wine?"

She struggled up from the sofa and followed him into the small kitchen dining alcove. "No, I'm going out later."

"I was hoping you might stay over."

Darcy managed a weak smile as she sat down at the kitchen table. "I'm sorry, Shug. It's just that Owens and I spent all day in the squad room pulling together vehicle registrations and license information. Do you know how many people in the Detroit metro area own vans like the one in the videotape? It's like trying to find a needle in a haystack." She took a bite of Egg Fu Yung and chewed thoughtfully for a moment. "Anyway, I need to get outside for a while, roll the windows down, and feel some air in my face."

"I'll go with you."

"Uh-uh. I'm in an unmarked. Can't be letting citizens ride around with me, exposing them to the dangers of the streets."

Shug frowned. "I still don't like the idea of your being out there alone." Darcy glanced up from her food, and he raised his hands in deference to the look she gave him. "Sorry. I didn't mean—"

"I can take care of myself, Shug. I don't need a man to do it for me."

"I know. I know." He swung out of his chair. "I'll put the pie on to heat."

Lowell Seagraves sat with his feet crossed on top of his desk, studying Joel Melton's personnel file. He had hired Melton five years ago, and the investigator had proven to be reliable and competent, if not remarkable. He was several years older than Seagraves, in his mid-forties, and had a son who was a senior in high school.

Lowell drummed a pencil against the file and buzzed for his office assistant. She entered his office a moment later, pencil behind one ear, spiral notebook in hand.

"Cindy, Joel's kid—what's his name?"

"Joshua. Why?"

"Ah, just curious. He's applying to law school, isn't he?"

"Yeah, wants to go to Michigan, but Joel says he doesn't have the grades."

"Okay, thanks." He drummed the file again and waited until Cindy was back at her desk. Then he picked up his phone and dialed the Detroit Police Department.

"Robbery-Homicide, please."

Special Investigator Joel Melton took the call at an empty desk near the Lieutenant's office. He listened intently, spoke little, then sat staring at the phone for several minutes after the call was over. After a while, he walked over to where Darcy and Frank Owens were huddled over a couple of dozen foot-high stacks of computer-generated license and registration records.

"Looks like I'm here for the duration." He shuffled through the green-and-white-striped stacks and finally selected one. "I figure I might as well earn my keep."

"Thought you'd never ask," Owens said.

Darcy nodded. "Thanks, Joel. We need all the help we can get."

Shug completed his circuit of the back room supplies and lay the inventory sheets down on the bar. "Devonne?"

The young black man looked up from the cooler where he was icing down a case of beer. "Yes, sir?"

"Good job on the inventory."

Behind Devonne, Leon smiled covertly. For all the big man's apparent gruffness, Shug could easily tell he was proud of his nephew. And, despite his initial reluctance to bring on another employee, Shug was also proud of the young man's progress and the easy way he had with the clientele. Plus, it gave Shug more time with Darcy.

Leon drew a beer for a customer at the bar, then wandered over to Shug. "You look different, somehow. Are you lettin' your ponytail grow?" he asked with a slight frown.

"A little, yeah. Darcy likes my hair longer."

"Huh!" Leon snorted. "You'd be better off if you'd take some time with your body. Run it a little bit, harden up some. Women don't like soft men."

"I'm not soft." Moved by the power of suggestion, Shug could feel the belt biting into his stomach, and he tightened his abdominals. "I'm in my prime."

Leon shook his head and turned to walk away. "Not for long, you ain't."

Shug said, "I'm thinking of growing a mustache, too."

Leon continued to shake his head and kept on walking.

Shug lay on his back with his eyes closed, feeling Darcy's warm breath on his neck. She slept soundly, curled around him like jasmine on a trellis. Before tonight, it had been two days since he'd seen her—the night they'd had Chinese—and then only briefly. He worried about the hours she'd been putting in, her growing obsession with finding Mike Connolly's killer, and her penchant for riding the streets of Detroit after dark. Turning his head on the pillow, he kissed her lightly on the forehead.

The telephone jangled on the nightstand, and Darcy jerked awake.

Shug turned on the bedside lamp and growled into the receiver. "What?" He listened, sighed, and handed the phone to Darcy, who was already sitting up and wide-eyed.

"All right," she said, after a moment. "I'll be there in fifteen minutes." She bolted from the bed and started pulling on her clothes.

"What's happening?" Shug asked. "Where are you going?"

"It's the van. One of the patrol units spotted a van near an alley off East Jefferson. Looks like it could be *our* van. I'm going to check it out."

"You want me to call Owens or somebody? You'll want backup."

Darcy was already heading out the bedroom doorway into the hall. "I'll radio him from the car."

"Call me as soon as you can!" Shug yelled. He heard the front door slam, then the house went deathly quiet—except for his heart pummeling his ribcage. After ten minutes, convinced sleep would be impossible, he got up and put on a pot of coffee.

Smoothbore waited just inside the mouth of the alley, allowing his eyes to adjust to the darkness. He took a deep breath and exhaled. The air was damp, warm from exhaust fans still venting the day's heat into the alley. "Musty," he whispered, "with an aftertaste of spoiled tomatoes." Smoothbore giggled, fancying himself a connoisseur of downtown alleyways. Then he chided himself for straying to foolishness.

He was a creature of the night, God's angel of darkness, treading the city's lightless passageways, seeking out the purveyors of evil and casting them forever into the fires of Hell.

He started down the alley. It was his first of the night, and he could feel the familiar twinge of excitement pinging in his chest. It might ebb if he reached the far end of the passageway without fulfillment, but he would not be discouraged nor deterred. There were dozens of alleys and dark streets to be walked, maybe even hundreds. God would provide.

He was halfway in when he glimpsed movement: the fleeting shadow of a figure silhouetted against the tiny square of light that marked the far end of the alley. His heart rate quickened and he flattened himself against the roughness of the wall. Of course, it could be nothing, just someone passing by on the street. He waited, ears primed for the slightest sound, heard none. He pushed away from the wall and started forward, his body tense, alert for any sound, any movement or shadow that seemed out of place.

Then Smoothbore's left foot struck the side of a discarded soft drink can. The soft clink was magnified by the hard-surface surroundings. He froze, staring incredulously as the can rolled slowly, maddeningly loud in his ears, toward the slight depression in the center of the alley.

"Police! Freeze!" The disembodied voice came from somewhere up ahead and to his right. A female voice.

Smoothbore panicked, leveled his weapon, and fired blindly into the darkness. Then he turned and ran.

Shug was on his fourth cup of coffee, absently watching a late-night infomercial extolling the benefits of the Nordic Track skier, when the telephone rang. He sprang from his seat.

"Darcy?"

"It's Frank Owens, Shug."

"Hello, Frank. What's—"

"Darcy's been hurt."

"What?" Shug felt bile rising in his throat. "How is she? What happened?"

"She's alive. On the way to Detroit Receiving. I'll meet you there." He clicked off.

Shug rammed himself into jeans, sneakers, and a sweatshirt and raced out the door. Fifteen minutes later, he spied Owens and two uniformed patrolmen smoking cigarettes outside the hospital's emergency entrance. He parked in a space reserved for doctors, leapt over a low boxwood hedge, and sprinted to the ER area.

"How's Darcy?" Shug asked, out of breath.

"She's in the OR," Owens said, tossing his cigarette butt into a concrete ash receptacle. "C'mon, let's walk."

The two men entered the hospital parking complex, and Owens guided Shug to his unmarked police cruiser. He shook another cigarette from the pack and offered it.

"I don't smoke," Shug said.

"Yeah, neither do I." He lit the cigarette anyway.

Shug took a deep breath. "How is she?"

"I don't know yet."

"Then talk to me. Tell me what happened."

Owens took another drag, the smoke rolling out as he talked. "Darcy radioed me from her car. While I was en route, I monitored her radio traffic with the patrol unit that spotted the van. They saw it parked on West Elizabeth over near the Marriott. The unit guys took up a position about a half block behind the van and waited while Darcy worked her way on foot through the alley between Elizabeth and Beach. She was angling for a head-on look at the van that the alley entrance would have given her."

"She should've waited on you," Shug said, shaking his head.

"Yeah, she should've, but she's been a little fixated on this guy since he took out Mike Connolly. Anyway, the guy must've already been in the alley, because the next thing that happens, the patrol cops hear a shotgun blast and see this big dude running out of the alley. Then Darcy appears at the mouth of the alley just as the guy is scrambling into the van. She levels her weapon and gets off at least one round. The patrol car hits the lights and siren; the guy panics and floors it into the alley." Owens took a final drag on his cigarette, its hot ash glowing red-orange in the semi-darkness of the parking garage. "Darcy was in the way," he said. "The son of a bitch clipped her good. We put out an APB, but the guy disappeared."

Shug looked back at the emergency room entrance. At least a dozen more cops had arrived, milling around aimlessly, drinking coffee and smoking. He felt a gentle hand on his shoulder.

"C'mon," Owens said. "Let's go see what the doctors can tell us."

Shug's Place was empty except for the three men standing around the bar. Shug drained the shot glass and shoved it forward for another. "She has a fractured leg, broken collarbone, a severe concussion, and internal injuries."

Leon winced. He leaned on the bar as Devonne poured another shot of Jim Beam. "Ah, man, that's some heavy shit. She gonna be all right?"

Shug breathed in slowly, let it out, and pinched the bridge of his nose. "I guess eventually she'll be all right. Right now, she looks real bad."

Leon slammed his fist down on the bar top. "That motherfucker ought to be made to pay for what he did! Cops didn't get the license number of the van?"

"The plate was smeared with mud. By the time they were close enough to read it, the guy was careening down the alley. One thing, though. While Owens and I were in the room with Darcy, she was awake for a few minutes. She said she was certain it was Smoothbore. In the videotape from the liquor store shooting, a bumper sticker was visible on the front bumper of the van. Darcy said she saw it right before the guy ran into her."

"A bumper sticker?" Leon asked.

"Yeah. It said, 'Re-elect Burgess Attorney General.'"

Devonne spoke for the first time. "That's weird."

Leon straightened and stretched, his biceps straining against the sleeves of his tee shirt. "So, what're the cops doing about getting this asshole?"

"I'm not sure. Owens'll continue to work the case, and there's some state office guy also assigned to it. Doesn't seem like enough, though." Shug stared at the bar's big plate glass window, and his eyes narrowed. "I'm ready to go after the bastard myself, you know?"

Leon nodded.

"That don't seem like it'd be too hard to do." Devonne said.

Both men turned and stared at the young man.

Devonne shrugged. "Late model, light-blue Dodge van. Got a political bumper sticker on it, most likely got a couple of bullet holes in it, maybe a busted windshield. The dude cruises the streets at night like he's some kind of invisible night stalker. Stay out there long enough, you're going to come across him."

"There're beaucoup streets in downtown Detroit," Shug said.

Devonne shrugged again. "I got friends."

Joel Melton spoke softly into the phone. "This whole thing just got a hell of a lot more complicated."

"Tell it," Seagraves said.

"The crazy bastard almost got himself caught last night. He got away but—"

"But what?"

"He ran down one of the detectives, the lead investigator on the case. A very nice lady, name of Darcy Raintree. She's in pretty bad shape."

"Christ!" Seagraves said. "If she croaks, the whole fucking department will be on this thing. How bad is she?"

Melton was quiet for a moment. "I'm not sure, but I think she'll survive. At least, I hope she will."

"Yeah, right. Oh, man, this could really hurt us. How close are they to identifying him?"

Special investigator Melton had a brief vision of himself locked behind steel bars, hearing the familiar clatter of cell doors slamming home. "We've been combing through thousands of license and registration records here at the police department. I've ... uh, *contained* the computer printout sheet with Chris's vehicle registration on it. So, chances are, they won't find him that way. Even if they do, his connection to Burgess wouldn't be that readily apparent, would it?"

"Jesus, Joel, the kid's nutty as a fruitcake. He could say anything. *Anything!* He'd probably ask the arresting officer 'Do you know who my father is?'"

Melton said nothing.

"The best thing," Seagraves said, "would be for the cops to take him out before he has a chance to open his mouth. Come to think of it, maybe the girl getting messed up isn't such a bad thing after all. I mean, if the cops are mad as hell, maybe they'll shoot first and ask questions later."

Melton could picture the chief of staff's dismissive shrug, the shrewd, calculating look on his face. He felt a little sick to his stomach.

"I'll keep you informed," he said and hung up the phone.

Shug pulled the Olds 442 next to the curb and glanced around the crumbling warehouse neighborhood. Scattered up and down the block, rusted metal dumpsters and long-abandoned shipping containers sported a colorful array of gang graffiti. The brick building to Shug's immediate left was three stories tall, set back from the street, and surrounded by a barbed-wire-topped, chain-link fence. There were no signs of life anywhere, but Shug had the uneasy sense he and his crew were not alone. "I'm not at all sure I want to leave my car parked here."

Leon turned to face Devonne, sliding one elbow over the back of the car's front seat. "He's kind of funny about his car, nephew. And I think I just might agree with his assessment of this 'hood.'"

"It's all right, Uncle Leon. Trust me on this." Devonne pointed toward the building and a shadowy inset doorway some twenty yards away. As if on cue, a young black man stepped into the light. He was tall and thin, wearing jeans, a charcoal-colored beret, and matching tee shirt. "That's Ju-Ju. He'll make sure your car's okay while we're inside."

The trio piled out of the Oldsmobile and walked along the cracked sidewalk to a gate the young man had unlocked.

He and Devonne touched clenched fists. "Where you been, bro? It's been awhile."

"In the Navy mostly." As they walked to the building, Devonne gestured toward his two companions. "Now I work for Shug here, at a bar over close to the Tigers' stadium. And this's my Uncle Leon."

Ju-Ju's shiny eyes flicked quickly over Shug and rested for a moment on Leon's highly toned bulk. "Workin' huh? What the future in that?" He opened the heavy metal door, allowed the men to pass through, then resumed his post.

Inside, the two men followed Devonne through a maze of dusty corridors stacked high with wooden crates and rusting machinery of all descriptions. Bare light bulbs hung at intervals from a fifteen-foot ceiling. At the end of one long hallway, they climbed a staircase that led onto a large, square open space. More crates and boxes were stacked against the left- and right-side walls. Directly opposite the opening, a row of grimy windows provided daytime illumination to a modestly furnished living area. The scent of gun oil and solvent was strong in the air.

"Devonne, my *man!*"

Their three heads jerked sharply right in unison, where a thick-chested man in his early forties appeared from behind a stack of metal-reinforced boxes. He had light caramel skin, dark brown hair cut in a flattop, and bristly, week-old stubble. The man's most remarkable feature was one eye clouded over to the point of being opaque. The remaining orb was chocolate-brown and sparkled with amusement as he approached Devonne.

"Hello, Faro, you old pirate," Devonne said as the two embraced.

"*Au contraire*, my young friend. You're the one been riding the high seas most recently." He glanced at Shug and extended his hand. "Mister Barnes, I presume."

The two men clasped hands briefly, then Faro's good eye shifted to Leon. "And you must be Devonne's uncle."

Leon nodded but kept his arms crossed over his chest. "I still ain't sure about this whole thing. I spend considerable time and effort making sure my nephew stays away from some of his pre-Navy ... *associations.*"

The man held Leon's gaze. One corner of his mouth curled up in a lop-sided half-grin. "And I don't blame you. I'd do the same for mine, if I had one. But rest assured, Mister Tweed, I have no plans for Devonne's future. I can see he's in good company."

The staring contest went on for several seconds, then Leon nodded again, almost imperceptibly.

"All right then," Faro said. "Let's talk about the situation." He shepherded the men into the living area where they took seats around a Formica-topped table littered with stained newspapers and gun cleaning materials. "I trust Devonne has told you a little about me and my line of work?"

"You're part Cuban," Leon said. "Your father was in the military. You spent time in the Navy and later fought with mercenary forces in South America. In the early eighties, you came back to the states and set up an illegal, low-level arms supply business."

Faro's face remained expressionless for a moment, then he leaned forward on the table and steepled his fingers under his chin. "Low-level is a relative term, Mister Tweed, but that's a topic for another time. Devonne wants to help you and Mister Barnes find someone who has harmed a friend. I am willing to do that."

"Civic duty?" Leon asked.

When he answered, Faro turned so that he looked directly at Shug. "You may not appreciate what I do for a living, Mister Tweed, but your friend here seeks retribution. Something I'm good at. Most importantly, Devonne asked for my help. That's more than enough for me."

"I don't know about retribution," Shug said. "I just want this son of a bitch put away forever."

"Forever?" Faro asked, the crooked smile playing at his lips once more.

"I didn't necessarily mean—"

"Relax, Mister Barnes. I haven't killed anyone in a long time."

Smoothbore opened his eyes and looked again. It was still right there on the page. So, he hadn't been dreaming or seeing things that weren't there. It was there all right, in print. At the bottom of the page, but still front page. God's work was always newsworthy.

An anonymous police department source had leaked the information. And now he had a name. No longer simply the vigilante killer, the world would soon come to know him as *Smoothbore*. He rolled the word around on his tongue, savoring its flavor, enthralled by its power. He was a power to be reckoned with: Smoothbore, Angel of God, sent by The Father to scorch men with fire.

"Smoothbore," he said and was filled with happiness.

He couldn't have done better if he had thought of it himself.

Joel Melton cracked the door to Darcy's hospital room and did a quick survey. The soft glow of recessed lighting gave the space a sense of warmth incongruous with the still, white-clad figure on the bed. Entering the room quietly, he stood by Darcy's side and took in the array of tubes, monitor cables, and assorted other equipment tethered to her body.

Her head and one side of her face were wrapped in gauze bandages; her left leg was in a cast up to her thigh and suspended from a pulley over the bed. Her right arm was bent and held immobile across her chest by a sling and webbed strapping.

Joel wasn't sure how long he'd been standing there when Darcy turned her head toward him and whispered, "Hi."

His smile came easy despite the anguish he was feeling. "Hi yourself," he said.

"I'm a mess," she said.

Yeah, but only on the outside, Melton thought. *Not like me.* "How do you feel?"

"Broken."

"Is there anything I can do for you? Get for you?" As he watched, a tear formed in the young woman's eye and slid slowly down her cheek.

"No, but thank you for coming to see me," she said, her voice quavering.

Melton turned and started for the door, thinking he had to get out of the room, get some air, just get away.

"Mister Melton ... Joel?"

He stopped and turned.

"There's just one thing," Darcy said. "I have a friend, Shug Barnes. He was here with Frank when they brought me in. He was really upset. I just don't want him to do anything rash. Will you talk to him, kind of keep an eye on him?"

"What, you think he might try to find the guy who did this? I doubt it. He wouldn't have the resources."

"You didn't see how he looked," Darcy said. "And there was something, the way Frank kept looking at him. Like ... I don't know. It was just a feeling."

"Sure," Melton said. "I'll keep an eye on him." He touched her gently on the shoulder.

She was smiling a little when he pulled the door closed behind him.

The voice quality coming over the hand-held radio was surprisingly clear. Shug and Leon were parked on Griswold, almost dead center in the quadrant of downtown Detroit where the shotgun slayings had taken place—Smoothbore's hunting ground. *Killing field was more like it,* Shug thought.

"I have my colleagues stationed at numerous intervals throughout the district," Faro said. "If he shows tonight, someone will see him."

Shug keyed the radio the arms dealer had supplied them. "We're ready. We'll move on your call."

"Excellent. Take heart, gentlemen; tonight the hunter becomes the hunted."

The transmission ended with a soft pop, and Shug placed the radio on the dashboard. A patrol cruiser rolled past and turned left onto Trinity.

"What happens if the cops also have men on every street corner in the district?" Leon asked.

"I don't know," Shug said. "I guess if they make the guy, they'll do what we're doing."

"Which is what?"

Shug sighed. "I'm not sure anymore. I thought I wanted to just catch this guy and turn him over to the cops, but every time I think of Darcy, the way she looked in the hospital..."

"You want to blow this stinkin' mother away."

"Yeah, I guess I do."

"You got the juice runnin' again, like in the Nam."

"Like in the Nam," Shug repeated.

Leon reached for the canvas duffel they'd taken from Faro's warehouse. "Well, c'mon, my brother in arms. Let's check out the firepower our unlikely ally has provided us. Lock and load."

Attorney General Burgess answered the telephone on the fifth ring. "Hello."

"Are you watching the eleven o'clock news?" Seagraves asked.

"No, I'm in bed, for chrissakes. What?"

"Your challenger has just moved to within three points of you in the polls. That's ten points in three weeks."

"You called me at eleven-fifteen to tell me this? It couldn't wait until morning?"

"I'm calling to reiterate that if the situation with your son blows up, we're done for. *Adios*, baby. We can kiss our asses goodbye."

"What *is* the situation?" Burgess asked. "How's the detective doing? The one Chris ran down in the alley."

"Well, our man is on the job, but there's only so much he can do. We've got five weeks until the election. Between now and then, anything can happen. Have you heard from your son again?"

"No," Burgess said.

"Look, I know you're not particularly religious, but if you want to stay in office, we're going to need something. Pray you don't hear from him again, ever. Pray he drops off the face of the earth. Hell, pray for a fucking miracle."

Shug checked the time. Almost one o'clock in the morning. Traffic had thinned considerably. They'd seen a couple more police cruisers, but it wasn't the kind of saturation they'd speculated about. "The bar should be closed and cleaned by now. Devonne's a good kid, Leon. He's taken to the job well."

"I know. But I worry about him falling back in with the likes of this crowd we're dealin' with. That Ju-Ju, he looks twitchy to me, maybe pumped on something."

"Well, yeah, I sure wouldn't want him dating my sister or—"

Headlights lit up the Oldsmobile's rear window. Both men twisted in their seats. Within seconds, Devonne was out of the car and rapping on Leon's window.

"What the hell you doin' here?" Leon rasped, rolling down the glass.

"I had to come." Devonne raised his palms in a placating gesture. "I know. You didn't want me to, but damn, Uncle Leon, you say you got to watch Shug's back. Well, somebody gotta watch *your* back."

"Yeah," Leon said, "but it ain't gonna be—"

The radio burped, and Faro's voice came on. "Mister Barnes, we've acquired our target. He's cruising slowly at the moment, trolling, I imagine. I'm about a block behind him on Montcalm Street."

"You're sure it's the right van?"

"I'm told all the key identifiers are there, including what appears to be a spider-webbed section of windshield just below the roofline on the passenger side. We have the bait ready to go, a *faux* burglary in progress. We just have to wait and see if our fish takes the bait. Hold on a second. I have another transmission coming in."

Faro came back on thirty seconds later, his calm voice just a decibel higher. "My colleague in the alley between Montcalm and West Columbia thinks he's just been spotted. Smoothbore has stopped just beyond the alley entrance. If he enters, Mister Barnes, the trap is set. Are you ready?"

Devonne jerked the car door open and tugged at the seatback. "C'mon, Uncle Leon, lean up. I'm in this thing."

Leon said, "Shit," but made way for his nephew to slide into the back seat.

As the Olds pulled away from the curb and sped toward Montcalm, none of the men noticed the brown Crown Victoria trailing half a block behind.

Shug pulled in behind Faro's Ford Conversion van. The three men piled quickly out of the car and met the arms dealer in the shadowy alcove of an adjacent storefront. A hundred feet north of them, a light-blue Dodge van sat parked at the curb next to the darkened mouth of the alley.

"That's it?" Shug asked.

"That's the one," Faro said. "Our target entered the alley less than a minute ago." Already suited up for light warfare, Faro distributed Kevlar vests to the others. "Weapons ready?"

Shug and Leon nodded and patted the Glock nine-millimeters stuffed into their belts.

"I'm light," Devonne said.

Faro stepped back to the van. A few seconds later, he brought out a Colt Forty-five and handed it grip-first to Devonne. "Remember how to use this?"

Devonne took the weapon and racked the slide. "I remember."

Leon frowned.

"Good'" Faro said, sliding a pistol-grip, pump shotgun from the back of the van and closing the doors. "Ju-Ju's stationed at the other end of the alley. He'll work his way toward us and cut off that avenue of escape. Our mock burglar has parked his vehicle near the rear door of an abandoned retail store about halfway down the alley. He'll most likely stay inside, but he's armed, too, if we need him. And he'll make enough noise to keep our target focused while we close in."

Faro stepped off the curb, then stopped and turned to Shug. "This is your show, Mister Barnes. How do you want to play it?"

Shug's thoughts again flashed to Darcy's hospital room, and he wrestled with his conflicting emotions.

"Quickly, please," Faro said.

"It's his play. If he drops the shotgun, we take him easy, and I'll call Darcy's partner, Frank Owens. If the bastard resists—" Shug's mind summoned up a mental image of Darcy smiling at him over a cup of coffee in the morning, wearing his shirt—"we'll disable him any way we have to."

Faro nodded and spoke softly into his hand-held radio. Turning back to the street, he said, "All right then, let's do it."

The foursome hurried down the sidewalk and turned cautiously into the alleyway, hugging the side shadows, using trash bins and wall recesses for cover. The alley was wider than most, with several loading docks protruding from backdoor delivery areas. A third of the way in, Faro stopped and whispered to the others. "The store is down about thirty more yards. We try to move in much closer, it could get dicey."

Leon and Devonne took cover behind a dumpster while Shug and Faro crept quietly across the alley and crouched at the edge of a loading dock. Shug could barely make out the older man's face in the near darkness. "You think Ju-Ju's where he needs to be?"

Faro nodded.

"Then here goes." Shug took a deep breath and shouted, "You there! In the alley! Throw down the shotgun and step to the center."

They heard a faint sound several yards away and then nothing.

Shug waited a few beats and tried again. "You won't be hurt if you'll just drop the shotgun and step to the center of the alley."

A surprisingly high voice trilled through the early morning quiet. "I will not submit to the unrighteous! I am an angel for the Lord, a sinner transformed, sent to cleanse—"

Leon's voice echoed loudly in the alley. "You hurt one of our friends, motherfucker! You come out now and come out easy, or we sendin' your angel ass straight to Hell."

The flash and boom of the shotgun came as one, and pellets caromed wildly off the trash dumpster and whined off the bricks. Leon stood and squeezed off three shots in quick succession. Faro rose from his crouch and pumped two explosive blasts in the general direction of the disembodied voice. The next sound they heard was the slap of leather on concrete.

"He's running!" Devonne shouted.

Shug dropped to one knee and extended the Glock. Smoothbore's loping silhouette was framed in the light from the far end of the alley. Shug took a breath and let it out, applying slow, even pressure to the trigger.

Suddenly, a smaller silhouette materialized from the shadows. Faro's hand clamped down hard on Shug's shoulder. "Wait!"

As Shug watched, the darkness was shattered by the white-yellow, strobe-like illumination of an automatic pistol, and the alley vibrated with staccato thunder.

In the flickering light, the ponderous figure that had been Smoothbore pirouetted lightly on his toes, hands twirling in the air like a ballerina's.

As echoes of the gunfire faded, the men ran quickly down the alley and gathered around the bloody mess that had been the hunter-turned-prey.

Ju-Ju walked slowly out of the shadows, a still-smoking MAC-10 submachine gun held loosely at his side. He raised the weapon to his lips and blew across the tip of the barrel. "I believe I have *disabled* the motherfucker."

They were quiet for a moment. Then Faro said, "Gentlemen, we'd best be on our way."

Melton watched from the Crown Victoria as the four men got into their vehicles and sped away. He got out, jogged down through the alley, and found Chris Burgess's bullet-racked body lying tangled on the concrete, the infamous shotgun a few feet away. He dug into the corpse's pocket and found the keys to the van. Then he retrieved the shotgun and made it back to Chris's van just as the first sirens sounded in the distance.

Twenty minutes later, after ditching the van and the shotgun separately in other sections of the city, he found a working telephone booth and used it to place a call to Lowell Seagraves.

"It's over," he said.

"What happened?" Seagraves asked, his voice thick with sleep.

"The kid is dead."

"Cops get him?"

"It's a long story and not really relevant. The point is he's not saying anything, and there's no evidence tying him to the vigilante shootings."

"Great! We're in the clear. I'll call Burgess and let him know he can breathe a little easier."

Melton looked down the block. A police cruiser passed through the intersection, lights flashing. "Jesus, Lowell, the guy's son is dead, blown to bits in an alley."

"Yeah," Seagraves said, "and we're off the hook. By the way, Joel, I appreciate your loyalty, your *flexibility* on this thing. I'm sure your kid will enjoy Michigan Law next fall."

Melton was silent for a moment then, "Fuck you, Lowell."

"What? What did you—"

Seagraves was still talking as Melton left the phone swinging on its cord and walked away.

Two days later, the newspapers and TV news shows reported that Chris Burgess, beloved son of State Attorney General James Burgess, had been killed in a senseless and random act of violence in downtown Detroit.

At first, Shug thought she was asleep, lying there with her eyes closed. Her leg was still in the cast, but most of the bandages had been removed from around her head, and the contusions and abrasions had morphed from an angry red to purple-black. He closed the door softly and walked to the side of her bed.

Darcy turned her head on the pillow and opened her eyes. "Hello, Shug."

"Hello, yourself." He covered her hand with his own. It felt cold in his grasp. "How are you feeling?"

"I hurt all over," she said, offering him a brief smile, "but I'm told I'm coming along nicely."

"You're going to be fine. In a few weeks, you'll be good as new."

"Huh," she said. "Good as new. You sound like my mother."

Shug waited, looking down at her, wanting to smother her bruised face with kisses.

"They say I can get out of here in a couple of days."

"I know," Shug said. "I wanted to ... that is, I'd like you to come home with me. I want to take care of you. Now that Devonne's working, I can take more time off. We could—"

"I'm going to my mother's house in Grand Rapids," Darcy interrupted. "She's picking me up on Friday, already made arrangements for me to get into a physical rehab program at the hospital there."

"Oh," Shug said, and then he shrugged. "Well, Grand Rapids isn't that far. I can come and visit every week, if you like. The Tigers' season will be over soon, and I'll have every Sunday off."

Darcy turned her face away from him. "I'm not sure, Shug. I feel broken, inside and out. I think I just need some time to mend. Alone."

You won't be alone, he thought. *Just without me.* "Sure," he said. "I understand. But you know where I am. Anytime you want to see me, day or night, all you have to do is call. I'll be there."

"I know," she said, and a tear slid down her cheek. She gave his hand a gentle squeeze and closed her eyes once more.

He waited a full minute, and when she didn't open her eyes again, he left.

One month later, Shug Barnes sat on a stool at the bar, staring idly at the telephone, a cup of coffee growing cool at his elbow.

Leon stepped over and leaned on the bar's shiny black surface. He spoke low enough that the other customers wouldn't overhear. "How long since you talked to her?"

"Over two weeks."

"She needs some time," Leon said. "That's all. She was hurt pretty bad."

Shug said nothing.

"Females have a delicate psyche," Leon said. "She don't want you feeling sorry for her."

Again, Shug said nothing.

"She ever ask you anything about Smoothbore? Like what's he doing, any more similar shootings, that kind of thing?" Leon asked.

"No."

"Ironic, ain't it? Our serial killer turns out to be the attorney general's son."

Shug finally tore his gaze away from the phone and looked at Leon. "And nobody knows but us."

"And we can't tell." Leon smiled and clicked the TV remote. On the screen, the newly re-elected James Burgess addressed a cheering crowd of followers at his campaign headquarters in Lansing. When the cheering stopped, Burgess put both hands on the podium and his face turned serious.

"No one knows more than I how violence can rip a family apart. As you know, my son—my only son—was killed hardly more than a month ago by street thugs in Detroit. My pledge to each of you tonight is that I will double my efforts to quell street violence in our cities and once again restore law and order to our great state."

Smiling broadly, Burgess lifted both arms and flashed a victory symbol for the cameras.

The screen image switched to the news studio where a tanned anchorman turned to his female counterpart. "Lily, there's been some speculation that the murder of the attorney general's son may have created a sympathy vote that won him the election. Any thoughts on that?"

"Well, David—"

Leon clicked the remote again and the screen died. "Burgess seems pretty happy for a guy just had his son murdered by street thugs, don't he?"

One of the regulars had come up behind him at the bar and spoke, "Them lyin' bastards will smile at anything, say anything, promise you anything, as long as they keep gettin' elected." He set his glass on the bar. "Fill that up for me, will you, big guy?"

Leon drew the beer. As the customer retreated to his table, Leon glanced back at Shug. "You okay, man?"

Shug was staring at the telephone again. "It's not like I'm in love with her or anything."

"Yeah," Leon said, smiling sadly. "Nothin' like that."

The Legacy: The Blind Pig
April 12, 1922

When the Volstead Act was passed in 1920 and Prohibition became the law of the land, bootleggers in Detroit were ready—they'd gotten a jumpstart on much of the nation when Michigan passed a state prohibition on liquor in 1917. What the lawmakers failed to take into account was Detroit's close proximity to the Canadian and Ohio borders. Anyone with a boat could get to Canada. For the others, Toledo, located sixty miles to the south, was more than willing to meet the needs of thirsty Detroiters. Illegal alcohol was easily available to the populace through a network of underground bars known as "speakeasies" or "blind pigs."

Lenny Scanlon's brow gleamed with a fine patina of perspiration. He also felt it snaking down his ribcage, slowly soaking his shirt and the waistband of his trousers. "Trust me, Mister Lewis. It's a steal at that price. All they want is the back taxes. You'd have a piece of the action, of course, for your investment."

George Lewis, a steely eyed veteran of the Detroit crime world—and purportedly one of the members of the City's infamous "Purple Gang"—sat expressionless behind his desk, smoking a Cuban Quintero. "You'd give me a piece of your action, huh? For my investment. How much are we talkin' here?"

Scanlon swallowed hard. "I was thinking maybe twenty-five percent of the profits. That seems fair, don't it?"

Lewis leaned back, plucked the cigar from his mouth, and appeared to study its long white ash. After a moment, he took a long drag and blew a perfect smoke ring.

Scanlon watched the ring float lazily up toward the ceiling. He could smell the acrid stink of his own sweat. *C'mon, I'm dying here*, he thought. Then, *no, don't say that word*. Don't even think it.

Finally, the crime boss leaned forward in his chair. "You're Albert's cousin, right? So, because of that, here's what I'm gonna do. I'll take forty percent of the gross and supply you with all the liquor at a 'family' rate. Me and my friends come by, you'll take care of us." Lewis cocked his head to one side and grinned. The grin made Scanlon think of a hungry wolf. "How's that sound?"

"That's very generous, Mister Lewis, very generous, indeed. Thank you, sir."

"Hey," Lewis said. "That's the kind of guy I am." He reached into a desk drawer and pulled out a stack of banded bills. "You be sure and let me know when you get underway. I like to keep a close eye on my capital ventures."

Two weeks later, Scanlon and his cousin, Albert Simpkins, a low-level gunsel for the Purple Gang, waited nervously for the first customers to arrive. They had scraped the gold-leaf lettering of Douglas Hanahan's A Little Bit O' Ireland from the bar's front window, then boarded it over so no light would escape. The front door was still padlocked, but the rear entrance had only a deadbolt. A small peephole had been installed there to screen the patrons and ensure privacy.

Both men jumped when someone pounded on the rear door. Scanlon walked cautiously over and slid back the metal plate covering the peephole. Four men stood in the gloom of the alley, their features shadowed by almost-identical dark felt fedoras. A chill ran up Scanlon's spine. Finally, one of the men spoke.

"Well, Lenny, aren't you going to invite us in? I've come to check on my investment."

By 1929, there were as many as twenty-five thousand blind pigs in the Detroit area. Local authorities were not only helpless to stop the practice, they were often part of the problem. One such establishment operated across the street from police headquarters. Famous for its potato soup and free lunches, it was frequented by newspaper reporters and police alike.

Lenny operated his bar until Prohibition was repealed in 1933. Legend has it Al Capone himself once stopped by for a drink while in Detroit, apparently to recruit members of the Purple Gang for the St. Valentine's Day Massacre.

A Good Day in Hell

Shug's Place was crowded. The TV meteorologists had forecast a heavy snow that evening, and the office workers had come in early and mixed with the retiree daytime drinkers. Everyone wanted a couple of shots or a few beers before tackling the soon-to-be snow-clogged arteries of downtown Detroit.

Leon Tweed stared idly out the bar's large front window as a gust of late January wind sent pages of a newspaper dancing down Labrosse Street. The phone was crimped between his thick neck and shoulder. He polished bar glasses with a cloth as he talked.

"Now, hold on, Roberta. Slow down a little and—"

It was no use. His older sister was not one to hold on or slow down when she had something on her mind. And what was on her mind this Tuesday afternoon was her daughter, Cassandra.

Leon listened a few minutes more then replied, "All right. I'll see what I can find out. Try not to worry. I'll call you back." He placed the receiver back in its cradle and stood motionless for a moment, thinking about his niece.

Cassie had been a rebellious teenager, busted once for possession of marijuana but released after one of Leon's Detroit PD buddies intervened. Despite spotty grades in high school, she was a second-year drama student at Wayne State when she'd gotten a small part in a made-for-TV movie. She and Roberta had a falling out when Cassie dropped out of school to pursue her acting career. Shortly afterward, Cassie moved out and found a part-time job as a waitress. That was four months ago.

"I need two fresh pitchers of Miller, Uncle Leon."

Leon glanced over as Devonne flipped back a hinged portion of the bar and slipped several glass pitchers into a sink filled with sudsy water. On Leon's left, Shug popped bottle caps and poured shots for drinkers lined up two-deep at the bar. Devonne waited expectantly, drumming his fingers on an empty tray.

"I'm on it," Leon said, hurrying to the beer taps.

Things slowed down around six-thirty, and Shug went in search of food for the three of them. Behind the bar, Leon spoke quietly to his nephew.

"Talk to me about Cassie."

"You spoke to Momma?"

"Yeah. Told me someone called from the restaurant where Cassie works, said she hadn't shown up for her shift in three days."

Nodding, Devonne said, "Right. She called me before I left this morning wanting to know if I'd heard from Cassie. I hadn't. Momma was gonna try all her friends from school, too."

"When did you last hear from your sister?"

"One day last week, Thursday, I think. I saw her at the restaurant, La Grotta, over on Twenty-Third Avenue. I go there sometimes for dinner if I'm not working."

"She seem okay?"

Devonne shrugged. "I guess so. She was a little tired but excited. Said she was trying out for a part in an independent film."

"She tell you any more about it?"

"Nah, she was kind of busy, you know?"

The bar's front door swung open then, and Shug bustled in carrying two large brown paper bags.

"I bring Chinese!" he said, nudging the door shut with his hip.

Leon smiled. Until a few months ago, Shug's main food groups had consisted of cheeseburgers, fries, and onion rings. During the fall, a short but intense love affair with Detroit homicide detective, Darcy Raintree, had ended badly. The Viet Nam veteran-turned-bar-owner had worked through his depression by changing his lifestyle—working out in a local gym, eating less-damaging foods, and spending more time outside the bar. That arrangement had worked in Leon's favor as well. Shug had offered him a half-ownership in the bar, and he'd accepted.

Shug set the bags down and began unloading cartons of food. "You guys hungry or not?"

Leon found paper plates. "By all means, partner, let's eat."

After closing up, Devonne swept the floor and straightened tables while Leon checked inventory. Shug secured the day's cash receipts in the safe and joined Leon at the back bar.

"Where've you been, buddy?" Shug asked.

"Huh?"

"You've had that thousand-yard-stare all evening. What's going on?"

Leon sighed. "Roberta called. My niece hasn't shown up for work in three days. She's worried."

"That would be Cassie, right—the actress?"

"Wants to be one, anyway. She works at it, I guess."

"Maybe she landed a big role," Shug offered. "Decided to chuck the waitressing."

"Yeah, maybe." He hoped Shug was right.

Nine inches of snow piled up overnight. Traffic the next day was light, both on the streets and in Shug's Place. Leon used his free time to make calls. He spoke to Roberta again. There'd been no word from Cassie, and none of her friends from school had heard from her in weeks. The owner of La Grotta told him Cassie was reliable and good with the customers. She'd seemed a bit distracted lately, but he wished his other girls had half her energy. A call to the apartment Leon's niece shared with three other girls went unanswered.

Around three, Leon called John Romney at the Detroit Police Department. Close friends in high school, both had signed up with the Marine Corps after graduation. Leon had become part of a Force Recon unit while Romney went into the Corps' Special Investigative Branch.

"Leon, my man! How's it hangin', bro?"

"I'm cool, John. How are Mary and Daleesha?"

"They're great—my reasons for living. Daleesha turned four on Friday. Say, you need to come for dinner soon. It's been a while since you've seen my baby girl. She misses you, Mary, too."

"I'd like that."

"How's Cassie doing?" Romney interjected. "Layin' off the pot, I hope."

"She hasn't shown up for work in three, no, four days. We can't find her. Roberta's worried. So am I."

"She's what now, twenty?"

"Nineteen."

"Still living at home?"

"Nah, she moved into an apartment with some other girls a while back. She and her mother had a disagreement."

"Look," Romney said. "I'll have someone contact Roberta, get the details. We'll list Cassie as missing."

"How's your record on that, finding the missing ones?" The phone went silent for a moment. "We find some."

Leon said nothing. A long pause ensued.

"Actually, not that good," Romney finally said.

"John, I got to do something. It's been four days. She's still my sister's sweet baby girl, no matter what." Leon waited as seconds ticked by.

"There's a guy I know, Rick Scanlon, a private detective. He's ex-Army, but he's okay, a former MP. I could give him a call if you want, have him contact you."

"He any good?" Leon asked.

"Yeah. He drinks a little, but after Nam, who doesn't? I worked with him a couple of times over there, again some here."

"Have him call me. I'll be here at work until midnight."

"Will do, brother. Let me know how it goes. Semper fi."

S canlon walked into the bar shortly after nine. A dozen customers were scattered among the booths and tables. *Working class types*, he thought, *Detroit's bread and butter.* Behind the counter, a well-muscled black man expertly filled a beer pitcher from the tap. He was tall, about Scanlon's height, but maybe thirty pounds heavier. Scanlon moved over to a bar stool, sat, and unbuttoned his overcoat.

The black guy glanced in Scanlon's direction. "What can I get you?"

"Double whiskey, neat." He waited until he had the drink before speaking again. "You Leon Tweed?"

"Yeah." Tweed gave him a closer look. "Scanlon?"

Scanlon nodded.

"John Romney says you're a good guy."

A grin played on Scanlon's lips. "John doesn't know me that well."

Tweed managed a reciprocal but brief half-smile, extracted a small photo from his wallet, and placed it on the bar.

A young, light-skinned black woman gazed up at Scanlon through smoky eyes. She looked to be in her mid-teens, with shoulder-length hair that curved in under her chin. Very pretty. He took a sip of the drink.

"She ever gone missing before, been in trouble?"

Tweed shook his head. "Busted once for pot, that's all. Basically a good kid. She and her mother didn't see eye to eye on everything, so she moved out, got this evening job, spent her days looking for work as an actress."

"Sounds like a lot of kids," Scanlon said.

"Yeah, but this one's special."

"How's that?"

Tweed bent forward on his elbows, and this time the grin was for real. It reminded Scanlon of the shark in *Jaws*. "Her uncle is Leon Tweed."

Scanlon nodded slowly, then tossed back the whiskey and set the glass down. "Good enough for me."

Scanlon's first stop was La Grotta. He arrived just before closing and ordered an Irish coffee. The waitress was about thirty, friendly enough, but he could tell she was ready for home and a hot bath.

"Will there be anything else? The kitchen's closed already, but I could maybe get you a salad or something."

He dug his investigator's license out and held it up for her to see. "I'm looking for Cassie Sutton. Any idea where she is?"

She shook her head. "She hasn't been here in a few days."

"That's why I'm looking for her. The family's worried. You know her very well?"

"Not really. She's younger than me."

Scanlon studied the woman. She was plain in every way but had a pleasant face. He tried for charming. "What, a couple of years? That shouldn't matter."

She smiled, probably knew he was bullshitting, but she blushed anyway.

"More like five," she said.

Now *he* smiled. She was bullshitting *him*, but he said, "No way."

She tilted her head coquettishly. "Can I get you another drink? Or, I get off in five minutes. You and I could maybe get one together. There's a place just up the street."

Uh-oh. He'd gone too far.

"I'd like that, but I have to work. Cassie, you know?"

The tired look came back. "Sure, I understand." She turned to go, then stopped and came back to the table. "Talk to Angie," she said, pointing to a redhead just pulling on a long khaki-colored raincoat. "She and Cassie were buddies."

He thanked her, left a ten on the table, and caught up with the redhead in the restaurant's entrance foyer. "Angie?"

She looked at him questioningly; he showed her his license. "I'm looking for Cassie Sutton."

"Oh, God," she said. "I've been so worried about her. I can't imagine why she hasn't called."

"You two were close?"

"Yeah, but just here at the restaurant. We didn't socialize otherwise. She was always busy looking for an agent, an audition, or whatever."

"She have any success at it?"

"Uh-huh. She did an ad for a local car dealership. I saw it on TV." She looked at her watch. "I need to go."

Scanlon walked out with her. It hadn't gotten above freezing all day, and a thick white blanket still covered everything. "Where are you parked?"

"Down the street, middle of the block."

He buttoned his coat, and they walked side by side, their footsteps making scrunching noises in the packed snow.

"Did Cassie say anything to you that made you think she wasn't coming back to work?"

"We didn't talk much on Friday night. It was kind of busy."

"Before that?"

"Earlier in the week, she said she'd talked to an independent film guy about some movie that was casting. She seemed pretty excited about it."

"She say who it was?"

"No. Just that she'd seen an ad for it in one of the weekly tabloids."

Angie got into an aging Toyota sedan and kicked over the ignition. Scanlon listened for a moment to the steady purr of the engine. The car must have been eighteen years old. *No wonder the Japanese were kicking Detroit's ass,* he thought.

She cracked the window, and he leaned in. "Who else can I talk to? Who might know about the movie guy?"

"One of Cassie's roommates found the ad and showed it to her. Joan, I think. Maybe she'd know."

Scanlon stood and watched as the Toyota eased cautiously away from the curb and down Twenty-Third Avenue. On the way back to his car, he passed a bar, probably the one the waitress had mentioned. He stopped and went inside. The place was nearly empty. On a television suspended from the ceiling, a sports commentator was hyping Sunday's Super Bowl Twenty-Three—the Forty-Niners versus the Bengals.

Unfortunately, he'd bought season tickets for the Lions, who went four and twelve. He'd stopped going to the games mid-season. Scanlon looked longingly at the whiskey bottles displayed along the wall. He wanted another drink. Instead, he went to the pay phone and dialed one of the numbers Tweed had given him.

A female voice answered on the fifth ring. "Hello."
"May I speak with Joan?"
"This is Joan. Who's this?"
"Rick Scanlon, a private investigator looking for Cassie Sutton. I'd like to come by and talk to you."
"It's kind of late."
"I can be there in twenty minutes. It's important. You want to make sure Cassie's okay, don't you?"
"Well, sure, I ... okay."

Eighteen minutes later, Scanlon pulled his '85 Charger up outside a four-story walk-up on Calumet and was buzzed in on the first ring. He walked up two flights and knocked on the door. The girl who answered looked to be in her early twenties. She was blonde, dressed in tight jeans and a tee shirt, pretty in a hard way. She gave him an appraising look.

"You're the private investigator?"
"Rick Scanlon." He reached for his credentials, but she turned away. "Come on in."
"Don't you want to make sure I'm who I say I am?"
She looked back over her shoulder and shrugged. "I called Cassie's brother. He said his uncle hired you to find Cassie, described you as a big ugly guy."

One corner of her mouth curled a little. Scanlon wondered if it was the beginning of a smile or a sneer. He decided on a smile and stepped into the room, closing the door behind him. She sat down on a threadbare couch and gestured toward an equally distressed upholstered chair.

"When did you see Cassie last?"
"Saturday morning, around eleven, I guess. I'd slept in. I'm a dancer at the Uptown Downtown. Didn't get in until late. She was just leaving when I came out for coffee."
"She say where she was going?"
"No, but she was excited and in a hurry."
"You showed her an ad, some guy casting for a movie. Do you think that's where she went?"

"How'd you know that?"

Scanlon winked at her. "That's what I do, detect things."

"It might have been that. Like I said, she was pretty energized."

"You still have the ad?"

The girl got up and prowled through a stack of magazines and newspapers strewn haphazardly on a nearby table. Scanlon got a good view of hard buns and firmly sculpted leg muscles. He believed the part about her dancing.

She straightened and riffled through the pages of a tabloid. "Here," she said, handing him the folded paper.

The ad was circled in black ink. It said, *Have looks and talent? Dreamland Productions is looking for you! This new independent production company is casting for its latest film endeavor. Call now! Find your dream!* A local number followed.

"Mind if I keep this?"

She shook her head, and he got up to leave.

"Would your other roommates know anything I might need to know?"

"I doubt it," she said. "They work days. Cassie and I barely see them."

Scanlon paused at the door. "Thanks for your help."

"I hope you find Cassie."

"Me, too."

The door was nearly closed when she said, "Hey, Scanlon."

He stopped, looked back. She was standing with her hands on her hips and her chest thrust forward. It was a nice chest.

"You're actually not a bad-looking guy. You could come by the club sometime if you want, have a drink, watch me dance."

He smiled at her and nodded. "I'll keep that in mind."

Descending the stairs, he conjured up an image of Joan naked. Then he mulled over what was wrong with him that he didn't much care how good she might look. He knew the answer, of course, but that was a problem for another day. Speaking of days, he'd had about enough of this one.

He got into his car and drove home.

Thursday morning, he was in the office before nine o'clock. He heard Carla come in and start the coffee maker.

A minute later she stuck her head through his door, looked surprised, and said, "Did I miss Hell freezing over?"

She had long dark hair, large brown eyes, and a body built for holding. She was the reason Scanlon hadn't tipped to Joan's invitation. He was completely in love with Carla. She was also his secretary and married to his one-time best friend.

"What? Can't a guy come in early for a change?"

"On the contrary." She smiled at him sweetly. "I'd like it if you came in early all the time."

She'd seen him at his worst—the drinking, the hangovers from hell. He knew that all too well. And he imagined she knew the reason he drank.

"Well, don't get your hopes up, sweetheart. The weekend's coming up, and I have a date with a fine young thing whose daddy owns an Irish pub."

"You wish," she said. "You want some coffee?"

He nodded.

A few minutes later, they got down to business. Scanlon filled Carla in on Cassie's background and summarized the information he'd gleaned so far.

"You think this ad thing is legit, that she's on location somewhere, on her way to stardom?"

"Who knows?" Scanlon rubbed his forehead. "I should've checked, though, to see if she'd taken anything with her—a suitcase, clothes, toiletries."

"I'll call her roommate. Ask her to check."

"No, I'll do that later. Right now," he said, tapping the newspaper ad with a finger, "I want you to call and chase your dream."

Carla was back in his office ten minutes later. "I have an appointment at two, a place over on Endicott near the Amtrak Station."

"Good. I'll pick you up out front at one-thirty. I'm going with you."

SHUG'S PLACE

They were parked in front of the building, a small storefront in a mostly vacant strip shopping center. A sign in the window read: Dreamland Productions Casting.

Scanlon had found a space in the second row behind a scattering of other vehicles.

He glanced at his watch; they had fifteen minutes. "Doesn't look like much, does it?"

"It might if you have stars in your eyes." Carla pulled down the visor and checked her lipstick. "Who did you talk to after you left the office?"

"I spoke to Cassie's mother and the restaurant owner in person. Nothing new from either of them. Then by phone with two of the other waitresses and Joan, the roommate I talked with last night. Joan checked Cassie's stuff while I waited, said her cosmetics and daily items were still in the bathroom."

"Doesn't sound as if she was planning to be away."

Movement at the storefront caught Scanlon's eye. A plump young woman in her mid-twenties exited the building and got into a nearby car. He checked his watch again: one fifty-five.

"You're on," he said.

Carla winked at him. "See you in the movies."

She came out forty minutes later. The sky had cleared, and a bright afternoon sun warmed the car. Scanlon might have dozed while he waited, but the photo of Cassie kept slipping into his head—the defiant tilt to her chin, the vulnerability she couldn't hide in her eyes.

"So?" Scanlon asked as Carla pulled her door shut.

She shivered. He figured it wasn't from the cold.

"I feel like I've been slimed."

"Tell me."

"Minimal furniture and equipment. Everything has rental store tags. Pictures of actors on the walls and a few obscure movie posters. Very transient setup, if you ask me."

"I am asking you. What else?"

"There were two guys—one sleazeball Caucasian, another probably Hispanic. The white guy did most of the talking. The other one looked at me like I was a piece of meat."

"Filet mignon," Scanlon quipped but got no response.

"I filled out a personal information sheet—the usual stuff—address, telephone, social security number, emergency contacts. Then the white guy asked some questions. What kind of experience did I have, did I have an agent, like that. I fabricated a few modest acting credits, told him I didn't have an agent yet, but I was hopeful. The Hispanic guy kept staring the whole time. I could feel his eyes crawling all over me."

"Do you feel it when I stare at you?" Scanlon said.

She locked eyes with him for a moment then flashed a brief smile. "You want to hear this or not?"

"Yes."

"Since I didn't have any photos available, they made a couple of Polaroids. I thought we were finished, but then the white guy got chatty. Asked about family and friends in the area, would I be free to relocate. I thought that was a bit unusual, but I suppose if I was twenty years old and my mind was in the right place, I'd be thinking Hollywood. Then he looked at the information sheet I'd filled out and said, 'Hey, you didn't give us an emergency contact. Don't you have one?'" She arched an eyebrow.

"Huh. What'd you say?"

"I said no." She glanced back at the storefront. "Just a feeling I had, but…"

"You think they wanted to know if you'd be missed?"

Carla nodded. "After that, they huddled in the corner for a minute, talking low. The Hispanic kept glancing over at me. Then the other guy comes back and tells me I'm a little old for the part they're looking at, but maybe they could use me in something else. He said they'd call."

"And when they do?"

"They'll get the Domino's Pizza a couple of blocks from my house."

Scanlon grinned.

Carla continued. "I asked about shooting locations. They have a set and production facility somewhere else in the city, but he didn't say where. I didn't want to seem too nosy, so I didn't press."

"Anything else?"

"The front door has a deadbolt. I think the back one opens out onto an alley. That one didn't look as formidable."

"Apparently, you read minds as well."

"Yours I do. That's why I'm such a dynamite secretary."

He was back in the parking lot by four forty-five, close enough to see without being seen. His first glimpse of the Dreamland casting crew came a few minutes after five. The taller man was light-haired and thin, the other was short, thickly built, and dark. The short one locked the door, and the two men got into a late-model Ford van and drove away.

Scanlon waited until nearly six. It was dark by then and the remaining occupied storefronts had emptied around five-thirty. He started his car and pulled around behind the building. There were a series of doors opening onto a concrete strip about twenty feet wide with a chain-link fence separating it from an adjacent vacant lot. No lights in back, at least none that were working.

He parked at the side of the building and walked quickly back along the rear wall, counting doors to make sure he had the right one. He doubted the operation had bothered to alarm a temporary office and was prepared to force the door if necessary. As it turned out, he found a rusty hasp for a padlock but no lock. The knob had a simple spring latch. He loided it with a credit card and stepped inside. Mercury vapor bulbs from the front parking area cast enough light for a visual scan of the room.

Carla's description had been accurate. A cloth-covered room divider separated the front waiting area from the main office where he stood. The office area had two desks, a filing cabinet, and a few scattered chairs. A Polaroid camera sat on a folding table near the side wall.

Scanlon flipped on the small penlight he carried and went to the file cabinet. It was cheap, didn't have a lock. He pulled the drawer open and saw rows of alphabetized hanging files. About two-thirds of the files were filled with one or more manila folders with names hand-printed across the index tabs.

The "L" file contained three folders. Carla Lewellen's was in front. He flipped it open, studied the two photos for a few seconds, then slipped them and the information sheet into his pocket. There were five folders in the "C" file, none of them Cassie Cole's.

"Damn!" he muttered. "I was so sure."

He ran through all the files quickly, determined Cassie's information had not been misfiled, and took a deep breath. *What was he missing?* Turning to the desks, he rummaged through the drawers but found nothing of interest. As he swiveled in the chair, his coat sleeve caught the corner of a large desk pad. He swept the penlight over it—a calendar.

Carla's name was listed under Thursday at two o'clock. He went to the previous Saturday's time slots and found "Cole, Cassandra" inked in at four in the afternoon.

His heart leapt. *Bingo.*

Scanlon thought about it. *If she'd been here, where was the file?* Either she hadn't made the appointment, which seemed unlikely given her excitement about the interview, or she had been here and they'd pulled the file. Or—Scanlon felt a chill run up his spine—they never filed it in the first place. *They hadn't wanted a record of her being there.*

He moved hurriedly to the rear door, checked the alley, then ran back to his car. Back in front of the building, he pulled to a stop. Earlier, he'd noticed "For Rent" signs in the windows of several vacant spaces. A quick check told him the same agent leased the entire building. He noted the number and drove to a telephone booth at a nearby convenience store.

The office was closed but a pleasant recorded voice suggested interested parties were welcome to contact the agent at home. *Thank God for the slow commercial real estate market*, Scanlon thought. He dialed the number.

A man answered. "John Taylor."

"My name is Rick Scanlon, Mister Taylor. I have a question about the building on Endicott, near the train station."

"Sure. That area has lots of potential. How can I help you?"

"You rented space to Dreamland Productions?"

There was a short pause on the line, then, "Right, they took possession on the first of January."

"Short-term lease?"

"Month to month. We don't normally lease that way, but the market lately has really—"

"Did you rent them any additional space anywhere else in the city?"

"Are you interested in leasing space on Endicott, Mister ... what did you say your name was?"

Scanlon thought quickly. "Scarborough, Deputy Reece Scarborough with the Wayne County Sheriff's Office. And no, Mister Taylor, I'm not interested in leasing space on Endicott. I am interested in finding a young woman who's missing. I believe you may be able to help. We can do it over the phone or I can come to your home."

"Well, sure, I'd like to help if I can. What did you need again?"

"Did you rent space to Dreamland elsewhere in the city?"

"Yeah, as a matter of fact. Warehouse space just north of the Eastern Market, near the intersection of Willis and Dubois. They rented it to store their production equipment. Said they hoped to do some location shooting around the city."

"Give me the exact address," Scanlon said.

Fifteen minutes later, Scanlon cruised slowly past a squat, two-story brick warehouse located in a crumbling industrial section on Willis Street midway between Dubois and Orleans. He parked near the corner, removed the nine-millimeter Beretta and an extra clip from the car's glove box, and walked back along the dark street.

The building appeared deserted. An eight-foot, chain-link fence surrounded the property, with double gates in front wide enough to permit truck entrance. A windowed office area occupied the street side of the structure with a parking area running along the left. Scanlon checked and found the gates secured with a heavy chain and padlock, apparently locked from the inside. That was promising. On the other hand, there still might be a night watchman. He scanned the area, then leaped and caught the top of the fence. Seconds later, he dropped to the ground inside the fenced perimeter.

He moved along the side parking area until he reached the rear where there was yet more parking space, much of it covered with wooden pallets and piles of scrap metal. Four vehicles were in back, including the van the two men had driven earlier. An elevated concrete loading dock ran the width of the building. Scanlon hoisted himself onto the dock and crept along a rear wall interrupted every ten or twelve yards by large overhead doors made of corrugated metal.

Halfway down, he stopped at a standard-size, smooth metal door. The small eye-level window was blacked out, but a strip of light bled from around the ill-fitting doorjamb. He tried the knob and found it locked. He put an ear to the space between the door and jamb and heard music and muffled voices. A moment later, he heard a laugh and a shout that sounded like, "Oh yeah, baby!"

Scanlon moved away from the door and made his way back along the dock. He wished now he'd brought the portable telephone Carla had purchased recently. Some backup would be nice, Tweed maybe, or Detroit's finest—but the damned phone was so bulky.

Among the scrap metal, he found a steel rod three feet long, an inch thick, and crimped at both ends. If he was lucky, it might work on the front door. Then again, he might be very wrong about Dreamland Productions. He might just get himself shot by a rent-a-cop or arrested.

But he didn't think so.

Scanlon ran his hands along the front doorframe—aluminum, he figured, or something similar. The door itself was glass, framed with the same metal. He inserted the bar between the frame and the door and pushed. There was the brief sound of tearing metal, a soft clunk, and the door popped open. He pulled the Beretta from his belt, flicked the safety off, and stepped inside.

He heard the muffled sounds again: music and an occasional recognizable word or phrase. Using the penlight, he found his way around a curved service counter, past a bank of tiny, windowed office spaces, to a hallway leading toward the rear warehouse space. The sounds grew louder as he neared a set of swinging doors at the end of the passageway. He pushed one open a few inches and looked out through the narrow space.

Rows of shelving jutted out at right angles from along the left interior wall. On the right, a concrete-block wall blocked further view of the warehouse. Scanlon eased the door open wider. The music grew louder, some sort of Latin beat. Three doors were spaced evenly along the right wall. He saw small metal signs above each: two designated restrooms and another read, "Security." The door to the security office was ajar.

He moved carefully across and shined his penlight inside. A desk and chair occupied almost half the space. Farther back, next to the wall, a single-size mattress lay atop a steel bed frame. Takeout food containers littered the floor and desktop, and discarded clothing, a woman's clothes, lay scattered on top of a wool army blanket. He backed out of the room and crept along the wall to where it ended across from the rows of shelves. Bright lights shown from farther in, and a guttural voice said, "That's good ... oh, yeah, that's it, that's the way."

Scanlon crossed the area between the wall and the first row of shelving. Two feet of empty space separated the rows from the side of the building. Using the shelves for cover, he made his way silently toward the lighted portion of the warehouse. A third of the way down, he stopped.

Thirty feet away, behind the restrooms and security office, a makeshift movie studio had been set up. Four stand-mounted lights lit an area roughly the size of a boxing ring. In the center of the light, a naked Cassie Cole was on her hands and knees on a mattress. Two other men sat in director's chairs just beyond the lighted area, and one man manipulated a movie camera mounted on a rolling platform.

Scanlon's stomach churned.

Cassie was facing in his direction, performing oral sex on a kneeling man with his back to Scanlon, while a second man mounted her from the rear. He was the ugliest man Scanlon had ever seen. He was big, powerfully muscled and tall, much bigger than Scanlon himself, and had a face like a skeleton: deep, close-set eyes with skin that seemed stretched too tight across his cheeks.

Scanlon tore his gaze from the orgiastic scene on the mattress and recognized the two seated men as the ones from the casting office. The Hispanic seemed to be directing the action. At a gesture from the director, the camera rolled backward to get a wider angle as both of the naked men accelerated the timing of their thrusts.

Scanlon's fingers tightened on the Beretta's grip as he inched forward along the row of shelving. In his mind, he saw Leon Tweed's face, then Cassie's face in the photograph, young and vulnerable, then Carla's.

The Hispanic gestured again. Skel-face grunted noisily through his finish then grasped Cassie's hair and stood—jerking the girl roughly away from the other man and up on her knees. She appeared dazed and frightened. The cameraman scurried in for a close-up shot as a vicious-looking hunting knife suddenly appeared in the Skel's right hand.

Scanlon froze. *Snuff film! They're going to kill her!*

The knife moved slowly down in front of Cassie's face toward her slender neck.

She screamed.

The Beretta bucked once in Scanlon's hand. The slug caught Big Ugly high in the left shoulder and sent him spinning backward off the mattress. Scanlon raced across the floor with the semi-automatic held chest-high. The cameraman stumbled backward and fell into the other naked guy. The tall white guy from casting came out of his chair with a small revolver in his hand. Scanlon shot him in the throat. The Hispanic slung his chair at Scanlon and scrambled after the tall guy's weapon. One round from the Beretta slammed into his upper back. Another tore a sizeable chunk from the right side of his neck.

Scanlon spun to his left, ducked as a light stand almost took his head off, and shot the other naked man square in the chest. The cameraman was already thirty feet away, at the back of the warehouse, yanking at the door like a madman. Scanlon let the Beretta drop to his side and walked slowly in the man's direction. He stopped six feet away.

"It's a deadbolt," Scanlon said. "You need the key." He raised the gun.

The cameraman half-turned, never taking his hands from the door. "What?"

The slug went in just above the man's right ear and zinged off the metal door when it exited. He was dead before he let go of the knob.

Scanlon let out a long breath, staring absently at the guy he'd just executed. For a moment, it was very quiet, except for the ringing in his ears.

Then he heard footsteps, no, *running feet!*

When he turned, the Skel was fifteen feet away, charging at him full-tilt, the hunting knife raised high over his cadaverous head. It was almost funny, this huge, ugly, naked man running at him with a knife.

Scanlon popped the last two rounds from the magazine into Big Ugly's chest. The body bounced once on the concrete, then was still.

It had all taken less than a minute.

Scanlon's eyes were drawn to the lights. Cassie lay sobbing, curled into a fetal position on the mattress. He walked back to the girl, removed his coat, and placed it gently over her. Then he stood and surveyed the surrounding carnage. A quick search of the Hispanic's pockets turned up what appeared to be a key to the padlocked gate. He slipped it into his own pocket, then helped Cassie into the security office to retrieve her clothing.

While she dressed, Scanlon collected his spent shell casings and ejected the VHS cartridge from the camera. On the floor near where the two guys from casting lay leaking blood, he found a felt-lined box containing a dozen more tapes. They were dated sequentially and labeled by last name and initial. The last four read "C. Cole." He tucked the box under his arm then wiped down any surfaces he might have touched on the way in. Ten minutes later, they were in Scanlon's car, and five minutes after that at a pay phone on Saint Aubin.

Cassie was leaning against the passenger side window when he got back in the car. She wore his trench coat over her clothes but still shivered visibly in the darkness.

He put a hand on her arm. "How're you doing, kid?"

She shook her head.

"I'm taking you home now, to your mother's."

She came off the window and buried her face in his chest. She wasn't sobbing anymore, but he could feel a little hitch in her breathing. He slipped one arm around her shoulders, the other through the steering wheel to start the ignition.

They were going home.

Leon Tweed was meeting them there.

Scanlon spent Friday working in Ann Arbor, following up on an insurance case for Fidelity Mutual. It was after five when he returned to Detroit, and he didn't bother going by the office.

Contrary to what he'd told Carla, he did not have a date with a sweet young thing that weekend. He did, however, go to a bar. Not an Irish pub, as per the same conversation, but a working-class bar he was beginning to like very much, a place where his drinks were now on the house.

In the private detective business, just as in law enforcement, Mondays were no more than chaotic endings to weekends. Husbands and wives went missing, lovers—straight and gay— maimed and defamed each other, property was stolen, failing businesses burned for insurance money. On weekends, the city's residents had more time on their hands—not a good thing.

This Monday was no different. Carla answered calls, screened clients, did research, and paid bills. Scanlon did paperwork all morning, fieldwork in the afternoon, and made it back by four-thirty. Carla followed him into his office and slumped in one of the client chairs.

"Mondays," she sighed. "I'm whipped."

Scanlon studied her from his side of the desk. Even tired, she was the most beautiful thing he'd ever seen. He got up, circled around behind her, and began massaging her shoulders.

"God, that feels good." She tilted her head back and smiled up at him.

He wanted to lean down and kiss her.

"I've been so busy," she said, "I never got a chance to ask you about Cassie Cole."

He gave his response a moment's thought. Carla wouldn't mind. Her eyes were closed, and she was breathing deeply as his hands continued their ministrations.

He'd spent an hour Saturday evening talking with Leon Tweed about Cassie. When Cassie had filled out Dreamland's personal information sheet, she'd left blank the spaces for emergency contacts and next of kin. She had wanted to give the impression she had no encumbrances to her mobility or her much-anticipated rise to stardom. From that point on, it had been a logical progression to the scene in the makeshift studio. The Dreamland casting crew had promised her a part in their film. They'd celebrated with drinks in the storefront office, and the next thing she remembered was waking up in the warehouse. The dream had become a nightmare.

They'd shot her up with something, probably heroin, keeping her drugged and docile until the next night when the filming began. The same routine had been followed every day until Scanlon had arrived and busted up the party. Cassie was suffering from drug withdrawal but was being well cared for at her mother's house in Dearborn Heights. What neither Tweed nor Scanlon could know was how Cassie might be affected by the mental and emotional trauma she'd endured. Scanlon hoped she'd be as strong as she'd appeared in the photo Tweed had shown him.

In Sunday's *Detroit Free Press*, a small article lodged deep in the local news section had read: *Five Found Shot in Warehouse.* A modest cache of drugs had been found on the scene, and the deceased included three men from Bogata, Colombia. A Detroit PD spokesman characterized the incident as "possibly drug-related" and said the investigation was ongoing. No mention was made of the movie set and equipment.

Scanlon had read the article at home while eating Rice Krispies and sipping Irish coffee. He doubted anyone else would bother to read beyond the Super Bowl game-day coverage.

Carla's voice brought him out of his reverie. "I asked about Cassie Sutton. Did you find her? Was she okay?" She looked up at him again.

"I found her. She's okay now, or will be, I hope. She's back home." He paused, knowing Carla was waiting for more, but that was all he was willing to share.

"So," she asked finally, "you had a good day?"

Scanlon gave her shoulders a final squeeze and went back behind his desk. He sat down and looked her in the eyes. "Yeah, a good day."

Carla got up.

"Hey," he said, "why don't we close up shop and grab a drink somewhere?"

She gave him a rueful smile. "I can't, Rick. You know how Denny is. He gets upset if I don't have dinner ready and on the table by six-thirty."

Scanlon knew all too well how Denny was, and it ate at him like a disease. "When are you—"

She closed her eyes and shook her head, cutting him off in mid-sentence.

"Forget it then," he said, a little more gruffly than intended.

Carla left the room and pulled the door closed gently.

Scanlon let out a long breath and stared for a moment at the door. Then he took a folded sheet of paper from his shirt pocket and looked at it. On the paper, he'd scribbled *A. Lundgren* and *P. Oppenheimer*—the two other names he'd found on the videotapes. He wondered briefly about the fates of those young women. He'd kept the last dated tapes for each before destroying the rest. Maybe, when he worked up enough courage, he'd play them. And depending on what he found, he might do some follow-up, but not now.

Now, he wanted a drink.

He opened his bottom desk drawer and lifted out a bottle of Jameson's and a cloudy glass. The amber-colored liquor warmed his soul, what soul he had left. He added another shot to the glass.

He was going to Hell one day at a time.

The Legacy: No Good Deed
October 7, 1935

Gerhard Koch, a former industrialist from Hamburg, Germany, migrated to the United States in 1910 and began work at the Fisher Body Plant in Detroit. In the years following, his technical expertise and vast knowledge of manufacturing efficiencies landed him a place in upper management.

As the Great Depression engulfed the country, automobile manufacturing went into decline. Ultimately, Fisher Body was idled, and the plant turned into a City Municipal Lodging House to serve the homeless.

Out of a job, Koch found himself with time on his hands and enough in savings to allow for a modest but relatively comfortable lifestyle. Prohibition had ended, and, in 1935, he purchased what had once been a "blind pig" near the intersection of Labrosse and Trumbull Streets. When questioned by the former owner as to why anyone would start a business at the height of the Depression, Koch replied, "The City will provide you with food and shelter, even a job selling apples on the street corner. But men still have to drink, and nobody gives away gin and beer."

In preparation for the reopening, Koch set to work restoring the interior: removing the boards from the big front window, sanding and painting the walls, and varnishing the wooden floors. At eight o'clock in the evening on October 7, he was applying a second coat of paint to the work area between the main bar and the back bar. He glanced up when he heard a muffled knocking at the window. A raggedly dressed man stood on the street looking in at him.

"I'm not open yet, my friend. Come back in a couple of weeks."

The man persisted in his knocking, however, and Koch went over and opened the door. "I don't have my stock in yet. Won't be here for several—" He noticed then the woman and two small children, a boy and a girl, standing at the curb. Like the man, they were dressed in ill-fitting clothes and carried tattered cardboard suitcases.

"Sir," the man began. "I see that you're paintin' and wondered if you'd possibly need some help. I'm a painter by trade, but..."

There was no need to say more. The Depression was on, and the family's plight was obvious. Koch was touched. Hundreds, perhaps thousands, walked the streets of Detroit in need of work. He could do nothing for them, but for this one family maybe he could help.

"I can pay you one dollar a day," Koch said. "I'll need help with the floors as well. A week's work, probably no more than that, but you'll be out of the weather. Your family can rest in the back."

The woman began to cry quietly, tears staining her unwashed face.

"Thank you, sir," the man said. "I'll work hard. You won't be sorry."

Over the following week, Koch and John Connolly painted and varnished by day while Connolly's wife and children stood in line for food and clothing. At night, the family slept on the floor in the workroom behind the bar area. On the fifth day, Rachel and the children came back empty-handed from the food kitchen.

"They've run out of food," she said. "There's a sign on the door saying 'Closed Until Further Notice.'"

Connolly's shoulders slumped in despair, but then he managed a smile for the children. "It'll be all right now, loves. We've a few dollars left. We'll get by for a few days." He went over and embraced his wife, then ruffled the children's hair. "Things will get better soon, darlin'. They have to."

Koch bought food for the family's meal that night from the next-door grocery. The next morning he spent on the telephone. Afterward, he brought the family together to detail his new plan.

"Instead of a bar, we will open a restaurant. Our customers will pay what they can afford, or nothing at all."

The Connollys stared at him with amazed expressions.

Koch shrugged, smiling back at them. "This country has been good to me. I have some money, and now I want to repay by helping others. I have ordered a stove, and an oven, and kitchen supplies which we will install in the back. You will all help. There will be a small amount of pay, and all the food you want."

The family stood silently for a moment more. Then Rachel said, "I can cook, Mister Koch. I make a pretty good roast beef."

"So can I, my dear." The smile broadened into a wide grin. "In my native language, Koch means 'cook.'"

Gerhard Koch's Kitchen, as identified by the gold leaf lettering in its front window, served thousands of poverty-stricken Detroiters over the next few years. By the late 1930s, as Hitler's army marched to war in Europe, the United States geared up to provide the tanks and planes for Great Britain and its allies. Factories began to hire again. Men went back to work, and eventually, off to war.

In early 1940, the kitchen was converted back into a bar, and the Kitchen in the window was replaced with *Hofbrauhaus*. By that time, however, anti-German sentiment was on the rise. Patronage fell off sharply, and—sometime during the night of August 8, 1940—a brick was thrown through the bar's window. Koch arrived the following morning to find *Go home, Kraut!* scrawled in white paint across the bar's front door.

Disappointed and embittered, Koch abandoned the bar and moved to a small apartment in Germantown, an immigrant community located between the city's Jefferson and Gratiot Avenue corridors. With most of his savings depleted, he eventually found work in a small brewery providing beer and ale for a number of Detroit's restaurants and drinking establishments.

In 1938, John Connolly became a welder for the Michigan Central Railroad. Thirteen years after that, his daughter, Catherine, married a fine Irish boy by the name of Flannigan, and, a year later, provided John and Rachael with their first grandson. In 1953, their son, Michael, returned home safely from Korea. Shortly thereafter, he passed the examination for becoming a member of the Detroit City Police Department.

Old Soldiers

The man sitting on the park bench was unremarkable in every way. Casually but neatly dressed, he might have been someone's uncle, a brother, perhaps even a young grandfather. He wore a cream-colored straw fedora, protection from the bright sunshine that bathed the city streets and dappled the long, serpentine path through Detroit's Cass Park.

Foot traffic was moderate due to the heat, but there was still an ample supply of sweat-drenched joggers, dog-walkers, and young women pushing strollers. At regular intervals, the nearby zoo's Howler monkeys shattered the quiet of the park with their cacophony, and children would erupt in nervous laughter or grasp at their mother's skirts. The man on the bench smiled at them and nodded knowingly, as if to say, "Aren't kids wonderful?" He was pleasant, non-threatening, safe. Just another of the many middle-aged men and women who passed some leisure time enjoying the ambience of a day in the park.

He was none of these things.

The eyes below the brim of the fedora were watchful and sharp, practiced and confident. At the moment, they followed an older gentlemen who, approaching from the opposite direction, ambled along in no particular hurry, a newspaper folded under one arm. When the old man was some thirty yards away, he settled himself on another shaded bench, unfolded the paper, and began to read.

The man in the straw fedora counted to sixty then rose and strolled slowly along the path, pausing as he approached the bench.

"Good morning, sir. I see you've found a spot of welcome shade. Mind if I join you?"

The older man looked up from his paper, squinted, and adjusted his eyeglasses. "Not at all. Please, sit down. Talking always did beat reading. It'll be a pleasure to talk to someone other than myself."

The man chuckled politely and sat down. He removed his hat and wiped his forehead with a handkerchief. "Thank you very much. Seems few people take the time these days to chat with one another. Even my wife and I barely have five minutes in the morning before she's off and gone on some mission."

The old man nodded, and his eyes turned somber. "Well, you just sat down here, Mister, and you sure didn't ask for it, but let me offer one piece of advice. Make the time, and make her take the time. I wish I'd spent more time talking to my wife. Now she's gone, and there's not a day goes by I don't regret all the things I chose to do over spending time with her."

"Well-spoken, sir," the man in the fedora said. "I'll bear that in mind. Indeed, we should take advantage of all the opportunities we're afforded. Sound advice, and I thank you for it." He offered his hand. "By the way, name's Paul. Paul Allen."

The older man took the hand and shook it. "Jimmy McCafferty here. Nice to meet you."

As often happens after introductions, the men fell silent for a moment. Then Allen shifted his gaze over the other man's shoulder. "Say, what's that over there?"

McCafferty twisted in his seat. "What? Where?"

"Just over there, lying in the mulch at the base of that oak."

McCafferty raised his glasses and peered under them. "Can't tell from here. What do you think it is?"

"Looks like a package to me, sir. What do you say? Should we find out?"

"I suppose. Might be just something a picnicker left behind."

Allen retrieved the package and returned to the bench. The object was small, about the size of a brick, and wrapped in brown paper. "Should I open it?"

McCafferty shrugged. "Guess so. Could be there's something inside with a name or an address on it."

Allen peeled back the wrapper and looked up, his eyes wide.

"What is it?" McCafferty said, straining forward for a look.

"It's money, Jimmy. Lots of money."

A sudden and unlikely breeze popped the tattered window shade like a flag in the wind. Jimmy McCafferty's eyelids fluttered open, and he lifted his chin from his bony chest. The shade settled back into place, the room regaining that orange glow that might, under other circumstances, have been comforting. Jimmy's shirt was soaked through with perspiration but he didn't care. He'd never minded the heat, not even when he served in northern Africa during WWII, kicking Nazi ass.

Children's voices floated up from the street three floors below, and he let his mind wander. As children a long time ago, he and Andy Clausen had played war in the wooded area near his friend's house. Andy'd had fiery red hair and freckles, with eyelashes so light in color they seemed almost non-existent. During the real war years, they had corresponded a time or two, both expressing regret their service had placed them halfway around the globe from each other. Andy had been killed in the Philippines in 1943.

Jimmy wiped sweat from his face with a yellowed handkerchief. *What was it General MacArthur had said? "Old soldiers never die. They just fade away." It was MacArthur, wasn't it? Or maybe someone else said that about him. It didn't matter anyway. It wasn't true. Not for a goddamned minute. There were lots of dead old soldiers, and soon there'd be another.*

A burst of youthful laughter came from the street below, and inevitably, as they had done almost constantly over the last few days, his thoughts turned again to his great grandson. Little Stephen James McCafferty, so named to honor his great grandfather, would turn two in September. The birthday party invitation, showing an impossibly purple monkey holding two balloons, lay open on the coffee table.

Jimmy loved the feel of the boy's arms around his neck. He was so warm. It was like nothing he'd ever felt. Better than a cold beer, maybe even better than sex, though that'd been so long, it was hard to judge. He'd been a good father; at least his children seemed to think so—he and Esther had had three. And the grandchildren had been a treasure.

He turned his head and Esther smiled at him from the framed photograph on top of the television. He took a deep breath and closed his eyes. *Oh God, babe, I wish you'd been here.* If she had been, he would never have been so foolish. But she'd been gone nearly four years, hadn't been there for little Stevie's birth, or for Jimmy's big financial schemes.

Jimmy levered himself up and out of the worn recliner, his knees popping with the effort. He pulled back the window shade, watched the children for a minute, then took Esther's photograph from atop the TV and sat down again. Tears welled up in his eyes as he studied her face, then he clasped the frame to his chest, whispering, "Forgive me, Babe. Please forgive this stupid old fool."

His right hand dropped to the magazine rack beside the recliner and returned with the Colt Forty-five he'd brought back from the war over forty years ago. Jimmy cocked the hammer, put the barrel to his temple, and squeezed the trigger.

Ralph Kovacs tried the telephone once more, letting it ring fifteen times before hanging up. He recovered his change, stepped out of the telephone booth near the zoo entrance, and checked the winding concrete park path in both directions. He was worried. It wasn't like Jimmy to be late. Hell, he was usually the early one.

"Still no answer?" Harold asked, fanning himself with a Tigers' cap.

"No answer," Ralph said.

"Did you let it ring a long time? He might've been on the can."

"No, Harold, I didn't. I just stood in a stifling phone booth that long 'cause I enjoy sweating through my shirt."

"You don't have to get mad at me just because you're worried. Jimmy's probably with his great-grandson. He probably just forgot to meet us. I hear great-grandkids will do that."

Kovacs regarded his friend. Harold was the perennial worrier, not Ralph. If Harold wasn't worried, then he shouldn't be either. Still, Jimmy had been pretty upset a few days ago, and Harold wasn't privy to all that.

"I'm gonna go check on him," Ralph said. "You wait here in case he shows up." He strode off across the park toward Glendale Street.

Ten minutes and four blocks later, Ralph turned into the apartment complex on Lynn Street where Jimmy McCafferty had lived since his wife died. It was a modest grouping of plain, cinderblock, three-story buildings Jimmy laughingly referred to as "der Fuhrer-bunkers." A swimming pool was located in the center of the complex, and usually there were children about, but not today. School had started back the day after Labor Day, and the only thing presently in the pool was a Church's Fried Chicken box, bobbing at the surface.

Ralph climbed the wrought-iron staircase to the top floor and walked down the concrete apron to number thirty-six. The air conditioner, mounted in the single front-facing window, was the only idle one on the third floor. *Maybe Harold was right*, Ralph thought. *Maybe Jimmy's gone to visit his great-grandson.* If he was here, he'd sure be running the AC. Mid-September in Detroit was little different from the dog days of August.

Ralph knocked once, twice, and got no answer. He started to leave, feeling a little better about things, then, as an afterthought, took a few steps back and tried the doorknob.

The door was unlocked.

He stepped inside, into the cramped kitchen, and the stench slapped him in the face. It was one he'd smelled before, in France on the battlefield, an odor that once he'd smelled it, he knew he'd never forget it. He didn't need to go into the other room, but he did anyway. The window was open, the discolored shade flapping lightly in the breeze. Flies had descended on the body.

Shug's Place

"Oh, Jimmy," Ralph said. "It wasn't that bad—not this bad." He knelt beside the body and looked at the framed photograph of Jimmy's wife, still clasped tightly in his friend's hand, splattered with blood. "I hope you're together again." Then he walked into the kitchen and called the Detroit Police Department.

Shug nudged the thermostat down a few degrees and turned to find Devonne staring at him from behind the bar, shaking his head in disbelief. Leon's nephew was enrolled in a marketing class at the community college, something both Shug and Leon had strongly encouraged. Like many good ideas, though, this one had produced unexpected results.

Devonne moved around the side of the bar, walked over, and looked critically at Shug's handiwork. "What's the use of me making all this effort to take classes if you don't let me apply practical applications to academic theory?"

Shug cocked an eyebrow. "Say again?"

"Marketing theory says that if you keep the temperature inside the bar warmer, your customers will drink more beer or whatever you've got that's cold."

"Maybe," Shug said. "But it's almost ninety degrees on the street. If it's too warm inside, the customers will find a cooler bar. Then they'll drink beer there."

"C'mon, Shug," the young man said. "I need to write a paper on Applied Theory. Look, since I started this course, I'm either here working, sitting in the classroom, or at home sleeping. I got nowhere else to test the hypothesis."

Shug couldn't hide his grin. If Devonne kept this up, he'd have to get a dictionary. "Okay, how about this? We'll keep the bar cool enough to attract the customers, then you make sure to keep fresh, salted popcorn at every table. The more popcorn they eat, the more beer they'll drink. It'll be a kind of double hypothesis." He thought for a moment. "Like leading a horse to water and tricking him into drinking."

Devonne's face brightened. "Yeah, I like that. We'll trick 'em into drinking."

As the young man strode purposefully to the popcorn machine, Shug surveyed the bar's afternoon patrons. All were regulars, mostly retirees, along with a few victims of lagging sectors of the economy. They didn't need encouragement to drink, let alone trickery.

A man in one of the booths caught Shug's eye and hoisted his empty beer mug. Ralph Kovacs was a World War II veteran, widower, and sometime security guard at Henry Ford Hospital. He was lean and wiry, with a salt-and-pepper crew cut that shined like gun metal under the hanging lamp above the booth. He was on his third beer already and had eaten no popcorn at all.

Shug acknowledged the silent request with a two-finger salute, then headed for the bar. A minute later, he set a frosty mug of draft beer on the varnished wooden tabletop. "How's the security guard business, Ralph?"

The old man snorted. "Piss poor, if you ask me. I haven't worked in over a month. They only use me when somebody's sick or on vacation, and of late, I guess they're all either extremely healthy or too broke to go to Disneyworld." He drained a third of the beer and licked foam from his upper lip. "Fact is, they think I'm just too damn old. Maybe they're right."

"Are you kidding? I'd trust a guy with your experience over a rookie any day."

"Oh yeah?" Kovac's mouth curled into a wry grin. "How many of us you need? I can get two or three buddies easy—provide Shug's Place with round-the-clock protection."

Both men laughed, and Shug asked, "Speaking of your buddies, where's Jimmy McCafferty? He hasn't been in for a while."

Flinty eyes stared at Shug for a few seconds, then softened. "You didn't hear? Jimmy's dead. Killed himself last week. They had the funeral yesterday."

Shug slid into the booth opposite Kovacs. "I didn't know. What happened?"

"Blew his brains out with an old army Colt. Hell of a mess. I'm the one who found him."

"But why'd he do something like that? He was showing me pictures of his grandson just a couple of weeks ago, proud as he could be."

"Great-grandson, it was." Kovacs took another long pull on the beer, then peered down into the mug for several seconds before answering. "He was ashamed. That's why. He was just too goddamned ashamed to go on living."

Shug watched the older man stare into his beer but said nothing.

Finally, Kovacs glanced up, studied Shug's face for a moment, and leaned closer. "He had this plan, see, where he was gonna provide for his great-grandson's education. There was some insurance money when Jimmy's wife passed away. Ten grand or so after the funeral expenses. It sat in a savings account for years earning diddlysquat. Then, not long ago, he starts thinking about how he could invest that money for little Stevie's college fund."

Kovacs was silent for a moment as Devonne placed a wicker basket of hot popcorn on the table, then he pointed to his nearly empty mug. Devonne glanced at Shug, grinning smugly before turning back toward the bar.

"Anyway," Kovacs continued, "Jimmy didn't trust the stock market—too risky—so he did a little research and found out he could invest in a CD and earn maybe twenty-five grand by the time the kid's ready for college. Thing was, he wasn't sure that was gonna be enough, what with inflation and all."

Shug nodded. "Yeah, who can say what it'll cost fifteen, twenty years from now. But I still don't see—"

"I'm getting to that. Okay, here's the kicker. Two weeks ago, we're sitting here, he's got numbers from half a dozen banks, trying to figure out which deal is best. Okay? Then, last Monday I get a call. It's Jimmy. He's three sheets to the wind, crying like a baby and making no sense at all."

Kovacs paused again as Devonne delivered a fresh draft beer, then resumed his story. "So I go over there, and he tells me how he got conned. 'Lost everything,' he says. 'Every goddamned penny of little Stevie's college fund.'"

"Conned? How'd he get conned?"

The old man shrugged. "I don't know all the details. It was a street con of some kind. You know 'found' money—you help them do something or other with it, then you share in the dough. Like I said, he wasn't making much sense."

"But in the end..."

"In the end, Jimmy was out his ten grand."

Shug was quiet for a minute, picturing Jimmy McCafferty, one of several old soldiers who'd seen action in one WWII theatre or another. They'd sat around trading war stories for as long as he'd owned the bar. But their numbers were dwindling. He felt sorry he hadn't known of Jimmy's passing. Things like that shouldn't go unnoticed.

Kovacs sighed and fiddled absently with the basket of popcorn, picking up first one piece then another and dropping each back on the pile. "I left him there passed out in the chair. It was the last time I saw him before..." His sentence trailed off, and when he spoke again his tone was so low Shug could barely make out the words. "He should have waited, the silly old son of a bitch. We could have worked it out, done something."

Shug reached over and placed a hand on Kovacs' liver-spotted forearm. "I'm sorry, Ralph. I really wish I'd known. I'd have come to the funeral."

Kovacs nodded then turned and stared at the wall. Shug slipped out of the booth and walked back to the bar.

Leon came in at six and took over for Devonne, who had left for an evening class. "What's with all the popcorn?"

"Applied marketing theory," Shug said. "Don't ask."

Leon pursed his lips thoughtfully. "Devonne?"

"Uh-huh, but don't worry, he says it'll increase our profits."

Shug frowned. "You remember Jimmy McCafferty, don't you?"

"Sure. He was in the tank corps, fought in North Africa. If I heard one of his war stories, I must've heard a dozen of 'em."

"He's dead."

Leon frowned. "Say what?"

Shug recounted Ralph Kovacs' story.

When he finished, Leon's eyes blazed. "That pisses me off, man. I mean an old guy like that, served his country. It shouldn't have happened."

"Lots of our regulars are like Jimmy. It could've been any one of them. Still could, for that matter." Shug drummed his fingers on the bar, then got up and went to the phone.

"Who're you calling?"

"The cops."

Detective Frank Owens strolled in a little after seven o'clock and ordered a Dewar's on the rocks. He took a sip and loosened his tie. "Haven't seen you in a while, Shug. How're you doing?"

"Good enough. You?"

"Same old same old," Owens said, sliding a manila folder in Shug's direction. "That was quite a story you told me about the old guy getting conned out of his money."

Shug nodded. "Yeah." He opened the folder and glanced at the top sheet of paper. "So, this comes straight from the Bunco Squad, huh?"

"We don't call it that anymore. Nowadays it's called Economic Crimes. There're some flyers that explain all the most widely used frauds and cons and a list of places and times for department-sponsored seminars on the subject, mostly senior centers and church annexes." He reached for a nearby basket of popcorn and shoveled a handful into his mouth, crunching loudly as Shug flipped through the papers. "You thinking of hosting a seminar?"

"Nah, just posting something in the restrooms. Give the guys something to look at while they're taking a leak."

"Better informed than not," Owens said, grabbing another handful of popped kernels. He chewed thoughtfully for a moment then asked, "You heard anything from Darcy?"

Shug had halfway expected the question. Had, in fact, planned to ask Owens the same thing. Still, it left him with a hollow feeling in his stomach. "Not much." He paused for just a second. "You?"

"Nope. She took several month's medical leave of absence. The lieutenant said she could have more if she needed it, but I haven't heard anything else."

Shug couldn't think of anything else to say and was relieved when a customer signaled for a refill. He took care of the order, and then went into the restrooms to post the flyers. When he came back, Owens was gone, a few dollar bills lying next to the empty popcorn basket. Devonne would have been disappointed that the popcorn hadn't prompted the detective to have more than one drink. So much for applied marketing theory. Or maybe Owens was just more complex than he appeared.

Ralph Kovacs came in around three o'clock the next afternoon with Harold Macmillan, another WWII vet. The two men shared pitchers of beer at a table near the window. When Shug brought a third refill, Kovacs said, "Saw your flyers in the bathroom. Too late for Jimmy, but maybe they'll show the rest of us worthless old husks how to hang onto our money."

"Maybe you should take in one of the seminars," Shug suggested. "Might be interesting."

"Hell, I haven't been in a church since Gracie died. And I'm flat not going to one of those senior centers. They're like a staging area for 'Operation Heaven.'"

Macmillan peered briefly into his shirt pocket then stood and dug into the pockets of his trousers. Unlike Kovacs, Macmillan was overweight and loose-jowled, with folds of flesh that hung from under his chin and disappeared into his shirt collar. He finally extracted a folded scrap of paper and squinted at it. Shug recognized it as having been torn from one of the flyers.

"Says here they're having one on Thursday at the Masonic Temple. That oughta be safe enough." Macmillan looked at Kovacs. "What'a ya say, Ralph?"

"Ahhh, I don't know. Maybe."

Shug had a late-morning appointment with the bar's accounting firm. It was one-thirty when he returned and spotted Kovacs and Macmillan huddled in one of the corner booths. Shortly, they were joined by two other veterans: Cliff Hauser, a marine who'd fought at Tarawa, and Sam Blackbird, a full-blooded Chippewa, who, according to local legend, had taken out two machine gun nests and captured thirteen prisoners at Anzio.

Devonne delivered a fresh pitcher of draft to accommodate the new arrivals and came back to the bar where Shug waited. "I gave 'em two baskets of popcorn with that pitcher. A dollar says they'll order a new pitcher every time the baskets go empty."

"They'll order a fresh pitcher every time the pitcher's empty."

"No, no, see, eating—"

Shug raised a hand. "I get it, Devonne, I get it."

The young man leaned an elbow on the bar and studied the foursome in the booth. "Did you know that the Indians invented popcorn?"

"I never thought about it," Shug said.

"They threw kernels into the fire and told the future by whichever direction they popped."

"Hmmm," Shug said. "You think Sam Blackbird knows that?"

"I got no idea. And, personally, I ain't gonna ask. Sam's kinda scary, you know? He never says anything, just sort of watches you."

Sam was a tall man with penetrating, obsidian eyes, and big. *Like a bear*, Shug thought. After the war, he'd left his tribal home in Michigan's Upper Peninsula and brought his family to Detroit. He'd retired from General Motors in eighty-two.

The last member of the group, Cliff Hauser, was also the newest. He and his wife had come to the city only three years ago to be closer to her remaining family. They lived with his wife's sister in the near-Westside in Woodbridge. Cliff owned his own taxicab but drove only when the mood struck him, mostly to pass the time. Short and compact, with an angular face and a thin gray mustache, he and Leon had taken to each other quickly. When together, the two former marines looked like a salt-and-pepper version of Mutt and Jeff.

"Guess I'll go pay my respects." Shug said. He stepped over to the booth. "Good afternoon, gents. How's everyone?"

Kovacs and Hauser said hello. Sam Blackbird grunted, and Harold Macmillan replied, "Say Shug, me and Ralph went to that seminar at the Masonic Temple yesterday. It was great! They showed us all kinds—"

"How about another pitcher, guys?" Kovacs said. "That sound good, Harold?"

The two men exchanged glances. "Yeah, sure, another round. That'd be good."

"Coming right up. Glad you enjoyed the seminar, Harold." Back at the bar, Shug relayed the order to Devonne and watched with new curiosity as the small conclave resumed its enthusiastic discussion.

Ralph Kovacs sat on Jimmy McCafferty's sofa watching the last round of a Jeopardy re-run. He'd gotten the apartment key from Jimmy's son, who'd been happy to oblige when Ralph offered to pack up a few things for the Salvation Army. He'd also been paying the rent on the place since the beginning of October, using it as a staging ground for the covert operation he and his friends had undertaken. At the sound of the apartment door opening, he pressed the mute button on the television remote. He was pissed. "You're late. Harold's been on the street twenty minutes."

The big Indian closed the door behind him, tossed a library book onto the sofa, and disappeared down the short hallway. A minute later, Kovacs heard the toilet flush, and Sam Blackbird re-entered the room.

"I said you're twenty minutes late."

Blackbird picked up the book and sat down. "Nothing happened, did it? Not last week, not yesterday, not so far today."

"No."

"So, it's no problem. Look, I been spending so much time away from home, my wife thinks I'm having an affair."

"That's not the point, Sam, even if you having an affair were a physical possibility, which it isn't. Something could have happened. Could happen anytime."

Blackbird snorted and opened the book to a dog-eared page. "What are you reading?" Kovacs asked, smiling thinly.

"*Rules of Prey*, by some guy named John Sanford."

"Oh yeah, I read that. It's one of my favorites." He turned back to the television, but he could feel the Indian's eyes on him, watching, waiting. "I thought it was funny that the serial killer would turn out to be—"

"Damn it, Ralph, I knew you were gonna do that. Don't say nothin'. Not another word, you hear? Just because you're pissed, you don't have to ruin my book for me."

Kovacs raised a calming hand. "Okay. Sorry." The two men exchanged flat stares. After a moment, Blackbird leaned forward over the book and began reading.

Kovacs pressed the television remote once more and heard the clackity-clack-clack as Pat Sajak spun the Wheel of Fortune. He smiled to himself. Like any good leader, he had to keep his troops in line, alert and ready to move out on a moment's notice. The smile faded as he glanced covertly at the telephone, willing it to ring. It would ring. He knew it would. Maybe not today, maybe not tomorrow, but sooner or later it would. He just had to be patient. They all had to be patient.

On Tuesday, Harold Macmillan exited the Sunrise Bakery Shoppe with a bear claw in one hand and a tall coffee in the other. At the intersection, he crossed the street and strolled along one of the sidewalks that curved through Cass Park. It was here, according to Ralph, that Jimmy McCafferty had been approached by the con man.

Harold found an unoccupied park bench and sat down. He was wearing his best suit. He hadn't wanted to, because the newspapers had called for a chance of showers, but Ralph had insisted. "You gotta look financially comfortable," he'd said. "Not rich or nothing, just like maybe you got a few bucks in the bank. A retirement account, you know?"

Harold doubted that Jimmy had been wearing a suit or even a necktie. Certainly, Harold had never seen him in one, except at his funeral. But arguments with Ralph seldom went in his favor, so he'd gone along with the idea. Harold glanced absently at his wristwatch—another hour and twenty minutes before he was due to be relieved.

They had settled into a regular pattern of patrols. He, Cliff, and Ralph each pulled two-hour shifts in and around the park. They'd decided to omit Sam from the rotation because of his intimidating size and demeanor. Ralph had said, "Anybody'd try to con that mean-looking sonofabitch, I'm not sure I want to mess with." It was one thing Harold and Ralph had agreed on.

He finished the bear claw and drained the last of the coffee, dropping the empty cup into an open trash bin beside the bench. *Everyone should be so litter-conscious,* he thought, observing the array of fast food containers, bottles, and bags surrounding the receptacle. A sound like a low-flying airplane startled him. He looked up quickly as two teenaged boys in baggy pants and baseball hats careened past his bench on skateboards.

Skateboarding was not allowed in the park. Harold was sure of it. He looked around for a park worker or a patrolman. To his chagrin, all he saw was a young woman pushing a baby carriage, and a pleasant-looking gentleman, perhaps in his late fifties or early sixties, reading a newspaper at a bench fifty yards up on his right. As Harold watched, the man folded his newspaper, rose, and tucked it under one arm. He looked left and right, as though deciding how he might spend the remainder of his morning, then strolled leisurely in Harold's direction.

The man paused on the sidewalk and spoke briefly with the young mother. She laughed cheerfully and moved along. Harold checked his watch once more: an hour and ten minutes left on patrol. He closed his eyes for a moment, hoping he might be able to while away the time dozing in the late morning sun.

"Excuse me."

Harold opened his eyes. The man from the bench stood on the sidewalk just to Harold's right. He was dressed in a dark suit, white shirt, and a burgundy bow-tie. Harold thought he looked a little like Gregory Peck in *To Kill A Mockingbird*.

"Excuse me," the man said again.

"Yes?" Harold replied.

The man pointed to the ground just behind and to the left of the trash bin. "Is that your package?"

Amid the food wrappers and soft drink containers sat what appeared to be a brown-paper grocery sack. Harold observed that the top had been folded over and secured with a strip of masking tape.

"Why, no," Harold replied. "I hadn't noticed it sitting there."

"It doesn't really look like trash," the man said. "I wonder if we should open it?"

Harold's heart began to beat a little faster. "I don't know. What do you think? Should we?"

"I think so. Could be that someone left it behind by mistake. If it's valuable, and if there's some identification inside, we could return it to the owner."

It was *we* now, Harold noted, remembering the seminar. Even he had said it. He'd let himself be dragged into the scheme so easily he'd hardly realized it. He furrowed his brow. "Well, if you really think so."

The man retrieved the sack and sat down, placing the package on the bench between the two of them. "Feels kind of heavy," he said.

Harold nodded, though he had no way of knowing, of course. He glanced about quickly, wishing one of the other fellows was there but knowing all too well he was on his own.

The man smiled. "Would you like to do the honors?"

"No ... I ... you found it. I think you should probably open it."

The man looked Harold directly in the eyes, his kind face brimming with sincerity. "Nonsense. We found it together. But, if you insist..." He pulled off the masking tape and unfolded the top of the sack. The man's face became a mask of surprise. "Oh, my goodness! Oh, my!"

Harold swallowed. His throat felt incredibly dry. "What? What is it?"

The man tilted the sack in Harold's direction. "Money. A great deal of money, I think."

Harold peered into the sack. Stacked neatly inside were what appeared to be rows of fifty-dollar bills, bound in currency bands. Harold tore his eyes away from the money and looked up at his bench partner. The two men stared at each other for a moment and then, almost as one, looked both ways along the sidewalk. No one was anywhere near them.

The man reached inside, removed one of the small bundles, and thumbed through it. "All fifties." He held the bills out for Harold's inspection.

Harold worked the paper band down toward one edge of the stack and riffled through. He'd never seen so many Ulysses S. Grants in his life. "Why, there must be at least twenty bills in here. That's—"

The man eased the money from Harold's hand and tapped the yellow and white strap with his finger. "One thousand dollars. It says so right there."

Harold looked. Indeed, the strap identified the amount as one thousand dollars. "How many more are there?"

The man took a couple more money bundles out, fifty-dollar bills showing beneath their bands, and rustled around inside the sack. "Looks like eighteen, no, nineteen more." He let out a low whistle. "Twenty thousand dollars!"

"Do you see any identification inside?"

The man shook his head.

"What should we do?"

"We could turn it over to the police, I suppose."

"Yes, we could do that."

The man rubbed his chin, apparently deep in thought. "But the chances of them finding the rightful owner are pretty remote, don't you think?"

"You're right. I mean, how would they know? Anyone could say they lost it."

"I have a thought. My brother is an investment counselor. I could call him, see if he has an idea what we should do."

"I don't know," Harold said. "I was just a kid during the Depression, but I'll always remember when the banks closed. I don't trust 'em, never have. I keep my money locked away at home." Harold saw the man's eyes light up at his words. *This wasn't as tough as he thought.*

"Things are different now," the man answered. "Deposits are insured by the government. Besides, we'd only be asking for advice."

"Well, I guess it wouldn't hurt to call."

"Right," the man said, patting Harold's knee and scooping up the sack. "Let's find a phone."

They found an outdoor telephone booth at the corner of Third and Charlotte. Harold waited nearby while the man called his *brother*. Along the way, the man had introduced himself as Charles Johnson, a semi-retired commercial realtor. According to Charles, the commercial market was down, had been down for a while, and "wouldn't it be great if we could share our 'found money?'" Harold had agreed, saying he'd had to dip into his retirement nest egg too often recently, just to get by.

After a couple of minutes, Charles hung up the phone and walked back to Harold. "This is a great plan. John says the law requires us to wait ninety days to see if someone comes forward and can prove the money is theirs. If they don't, it's ours to split. That's ten thousand apiece. Even better, he's offered to invest the money in a three-month certificate of deposit at six percent interest, in both our names, of course. We could actually get more money that way."

Charles' practiced spiel made it all sound so simple. Neat and tidy—when Harold knew the plan was full of holes. How would anyone even be aware they'd found the money? "I don't know," Harold said. "The banks ... I just don't know."

"Hey, remember what I said earlier. It's insured by the government. Tell you what. Just to show you how safe it is, I'll put another ten thousand of my own money in. How's that strike you?"

Harold pursed his lips, appearing deep in thought. "Six percent, huh? That's pretty good, I guess."

"Yeah, it's pretty good, but not as good as it might be."

"What do you mean?"

"If we could come up with at least forty thousand to invest, the interest rate would go up to eight percent. It's a special deal, John says, good only for a few days."

"How much more would we make?"

Charles shrugged. "A couple of thousand, maybe. Certainly more than you had when you sat down in the park this morning." He patted the paper sack tucked under his arm. "What do you say, Harold? Can you invest ten to get back twenty plus?"

Harold grinned sheepishly. "When you put it that way, it sounds like I'd be a fool not to."

Charles grinned, too. "We can go see John as soon as you get your cash ready. He's got an office over on Woodward. I already have my checkbook with me."

"I'll need to call a cab," Harold said. "My apartment's too far to walk."

"Okay if I ride along? We could split the fare, right?"

"Sure," Harold said as he walked back to the pay phone. "We're fifty-fifty partners, all the way."

Kovacs watched from the front window as Cliff Hauser's cab pulled to the curb and Harold and another man stepped out onto the sidewalk. Harold's call had come in at a little before noon, and Kovacs had relayed the location to Hauser for the pickup.

He turned to Sam. "They're here."

Sam snapped his book closed and disappeared down the hallway.

Kovacs glanced at the framed photograph of Esther McCafferty, now cleaned up, then the German Luger resting on top of the television next to it. It was his one souvenir from the war. He picked it up, liking the feel of the weapon in his hand. He had to hand it to the Germans. They knew how to design implements of war. He walked over, stood next to the wall behind the door to Jimmy's apartment, and waited.

Two minutes later, he heard footsteps in the outer hall. Harold's voice carried through the closed door.

"Here we are," Harold said. He was breathing hard from climbing the stairs.

The door swung open. Harold came through first, followed by a trim man in a dark gray suit. Kovacs kicked the apartment door shut, holding the Luger loosely by his side.

The man spun around in surprise. "What the hell?" His eyes found Kovacs' then dropped to the pistol. He lunged for the door and yanked it open.

Cliff Hauser's bony fist caught him squarely on the nose and sent him stumbling backward over the coffee table and onto the sofa. The con man sprawled there wild-eyed, his gaze darting back and forth between his captors. A trickle of blood ran from his nose, which was already starting to swell. The paper sack lay open on the floor in the middle of the room, bound stacks of bills spilling from it.

Cliff moved into the room rubbing his knuckles. "Damn! I haven't hit anybody since my last bar fight in forty-six. I forgot how good it feels."

Kovacs closed the door and leaned against it, gesturing casually with the Luger. "Harold, you see to the money. Cliff, get the duct tape."

Five minutes later, Charles Johnson—who really was Charles Johnson according to the information in his wallet, but of course, with a con man, they weren't taking anything at face value—was trussed tightly and sitting across from Harold at the late Jimmy McCafferty's kitchen table. He sat stiffly, strips of silver duct tape binding his wrists and ankles to the arms and legs of the chair.

Harold stacked the money in front of him. "It's just like they said at the seminar. There's only one stack that's all fifties. The rest have fifties on the outside, dollar bills in between. That would make our take about twenty-two hundred."

"Not enough," Kovacs said. "Not nearly enough." He sat down in a chair on Johnson's left. "So tell me, Charles, or whoever the hell you are, where's the rest of it?"

"I don't know what you're talking about," Johnson said. His nose was red and swollen, and he sounded as if he was suffering from a head cold. "This is crazy. Have you all escaped from some psycho nursing home or something?"

Kovacs smiled grimly. "Does the name Jimmy McCafferty ring a bell with you?"

Johnson blinked rapidly but said nothing.

"This is his apartment, or at least it will be through the end of the month." Kovacs pointed to the photo on top of the television. "That was his wife, Esther. She passed away a few years ago, so all Jimmy had left to live for were his kids and their kids, and, most recently, his great-grandson named Stevie. He was saving for the kid's college fund, and then you came along."

"I told you, I don't know what you're talking about."

Cliff Hauser came over and stood on Johnson's right. "Let me hit him again, Ralph. That nose looks like it would bust wide open."

"Nah, I don't think so. I think it's time to get serious." Ralph turned in his chair and yelled down the hallway. "Hey, Chief!"

The bedroom door crashed open, and Sam stalked into the room shirtless except for a leather vest adorned with rows of white and cobalt-blue beads. He wore black trousers and a black, almost shapeless felt hat with one long, white feather sticking up from the band. Finger-length streaks of red colort rode high on his prominent cheekbones and bisected his face from nose to chin. He took a seat across from Kovacs and turned slowly to glare at Johnson.

"You sure you still don't know nothin'?" Kovacs asked.

Shug's Place

Johnson swallowed and shook his head furiously, his eyes never leaving the big Indian's face.

Sam grinned maniacally and pulled a bone-handled hunting knife from his belt. It gleamed brightly in the overhead light as he leaned over and slit the tape holding Johnson's right wrist.

For a moment, for *just* a moment, Kovacs thought he saw a thin glimmer of hope in the con man's eyes. It faded as Sam took Johnson's hand and forced it out flat on the table top.

"Tape his mouth, Cliff," Sam growled. "Harold, reach over there to the sink and hand me that dish rag. This is gonna get messy."

"You can quit fretting now," Devonne said. "They're back."

Shug looked up from his desk in the back room. "What?"

Devonne was standing in the doorway, wiping his hands on a bar towel. "I said you can quit worrying. Your friends, the old World War Two vets, are back. I'm getting beers and shots for them, but I thought you'd want to know, seein' as how you've been asking about 'em every day for a week."

"Yeah, thanks, Devonne." He got up and went out to the bar. Kovacs, Macmillan, and Sam Blackbird sat at one of the tables near the jukebox. Cliff Hauser was huddled with Leon at the far corner of the bar. Hauser snagged a shot glass of whiskey from the tray as Devonne passed by on his way to the table.

Shug had missed the old guys, and had worried more than a little about them. They were getting on in years, after all. He might not know if something happened to them—*like Jimmy McCafferty*, he thought. As much as he dreaded the thought of someday going to one of their funerals, he for sure didn't want to miss another one. He ducked under the bar and went over to the table.

"I'm glad to see you guys. I thought maybe you'd found another watering hole."

Kovacs gave a wave of dismissal. "Nah, we just been busy, that's all."

Harold's pudgy face brightened. "We were taking care of Jimmy's last wish. You remember, don't you, the college fund?"

"Jesus Christ, Harold!" Kovacs said. "Can't you just for once—" He stopped in mid-sentence and glanced up at Shug. "We pooled our resources, the four of us, and started a little trust fund. It seemed like the least we could do for Jimmy."

"Hey, Shug!" Leon called from behind the bar. "Telephone."

Shug excused himself and picked up the phone at the end of the bar. It was Frank Owens.

"I thought you'd find this interesting," Owens said. "The boys in Economic Crimes got an anonymous phone call yesterday afternoon. Went to a place over on the Westside, one of those motels offering weekly rates, and found these two guys wrapped up in duct tape." Owens chuckled softly. "The guys who responded said they looked like a pair of mummies."

Shug sat down on one of the stools and leaned back against the bar's mahogany edging. He glanced over to see Cliff Hauser leaving Leon and moving to sit at the table with the others.

Owens continued. "Anyway, it turns out these two guys had warrants out for them in about a half-dozen states. Grifters, both of them. And after what you told me the other day, I just figured, well, maybe you'd like to know there's some justice in the world, after all."

"What'll happen to them?"

"We'll send them back to Ohio, or Illinois, or somewhere for trial, I guess. We got nothing on them here."

"Doesn't seem like enough. Not if they were the ones that conned Jimmy McCafferty."

"Well, if it's any consolation, one of the guys had his thumb sawed through down to the bone. Broken nose, too. I understand he was going on and on about some fuckin' Indian chief, all dressed up in war paint, some crazy shit like that."

Shug glanced at Sam Blackbird. He was shoveling popcorn into his mouth like he hadn't eaten in a week.

"What did your guys think about that?"

"Who gives a damn what a con man says? They're not our problem anyway."

"They, uh, find any money?"

"Not a cent. If these guys ever had any of Jimmy's cash, it was long gone."

"Thanks for the call, Frank." Shug dropped the phone into its cradle and walked down to where Leon was still standing, elbows on the bar, studying Cliff Hauser and friends.

"So how's Cliff?" Shug asked.

"Feeling younger and more vital every day, according to him."

"Ralph says they got together and started a college trust fund for Jimmy's great-grandson."

An amused, and, Shug thought, rather condescending look came over Leon's face. "Yeah? That's what Ralph told you?"

"Yeah, that's what he said. Why are you grinning like that? You know something I don't?"

Leon shook his head. "Nope, I don't know nothin', and take my word for it, you probably don't want to either." Leon's eyes flicked out over Shug's shoulder toward the foursome in the booth. "But if you really feel you got to know, ask Sam Blackbird if he's ever worn any of his wife's lipstick."

Leon turned to the back bar just as Sam plopped his weight down on the stool next to Shug. He slid an empty pitcher toward Devonne.

"Fill that up, how about?" Sam growled. Then he turned to Shug. "Damn popcorn makes my throat dry as a desert."

Shug felt trapped in the big man's gaze as surely as if he was wrapped in duct tape. Here was a real, live war hero. What if it *had* been forty years ago? That didn't change anything. Shug could imagine how the German machine gunners at Anzio felt when Sam's warrior frame came charging at them, screaming like an eagle, the fires of Hell reflected in those bright black eyes.

He decided he wouldn't ask about the lipstick. As Leon had said, there were some things he just didn't want to know.

The Legacy: Billy and the Brown Bomber
November 14, 1944

The evening of June 20, 1943, marked the start of three days of rioting in Detroit. It started with fights between black and white teenagers at an integrated amusement park known as Belle Isle, and spread quickly over the entire city. Nine white and twenty-five black residents were killed. Of the latter group, seventeen were killed by police. Over seven hundred people were injured. The chaos was quelled only after six thousand Army troops were called in to patrol the city streets. Nazi-controlled radio seized on the incident for their propaganda machine, calling America, "…a country torn by social injustice, racial hatreds, and the gangsterism of a capitalistic police." The city remained under Army occupation until January of 1944.

James Reason strolled leisurely onto his front porch, slumped into the green-and-white metal glider, and lit a cigarette. The first pink glow of dawn glazed the city's horizon, and the only sound he heard was the chink and jangle of the milk truck making stops along the street. The truck pulled up in front of Reason's house a minute later, and the black deliveryman alighted with two quart bottles of fresh milk.

"Mornin', Mister Reason," the man said. "And it does look like a fine one, don't it?"

"Indeed it does, Mister Tweed. I sometimes envy you these mornings, out and about when the streets are all but empty." He offered a cigarette to Tweed, who declined. "By the way, how's that son of yours doing?"

Shug's Place

The big black man smiled. "Oh, he's just fine—ten months old and growin' like a weed. Won't be able to call him *little* Leon much longer."

As the truck chugged away, Reason gathered up the milk and started back through the front door. The smell of frying eggs and bacon filled his nostrils. He stopped, turned back to the porch, and looked again at the growing light in the sky. *A nice, quiet morning,* he thought. He hoped the rest of the day would be as good.

Shortly after noon, Reason unlocked the front door of the bar on Labrosse Street he had renamed the Tigers' Den. He walked through to the back, flipped the latch, and opened the door leading to the alley. As usual, he found Billy Wilson waiting there, sitting with his back against the cold brick wall of the alley.

"Hey there, Billy."

"Hey yourself, Mister Reason."

A black youth of seventeen, Billy Wilson had moved up from Georgia when his father elected to seek work in Detroit's new, war-energized manufacturing sector. Billy had been one of the casualties of the riots. Caught out on the street during the height of the melee, he was severely beaten by a group of white teenagers and sailors from the nearby Naval Armory. Now a jagged pink scar ran from just above his left eyebrow down across his cheek to the corner of his mouth. When the young man smiled, which was still often, that side of his mouth didn't move.

"Well," Reason said, "come on in out of the cold. Plenty for us to do before we open." Reason had hired Billy three months earlier to help clean and bus tables. There really wasn't enough work to justify the job, but the boy was pleasant, and Reason enjoyed his company.

Watching Billy mop the floors to a gleaming shine, Reason thought again of the previous evening's trouble. *Well, it hadn't really been trouble.* Just a vague sense of unease, the same feeling he'd fought all morning to suppress. He pushed the thought down once more and went about his work.

By mid-evening, the bar was crowded and filled with the hum of excitement. This was no ordinary night. Everyone in the Tigers'

Den—and boxing fans all across the country—awaited the start of the Heavyweight Championship fight between Detroit's own Brown Bomber, Joe Louis, and contender, Johnny Davis. Just before ten o'clock, Reason found the station and turned the radio volume loud enough for all to hear. A hush fell across the room as the bell clanged, and the ring announcer spoke into the microphone. "Ladies and Gentlemen…"

The fight was over almost before it began. Louis KO'd Johnny Davis less than two minutes into the first round. The mood of the bar crowd was mixed, awed elation at Louis's prowess, but disappointment at the brevity of the long-anticipated match. One patron's voice rose above the steady murmur of the crowd. "Ain't that just like a nigger? Not a one of 'em willing to give a man full value for his dollar."

A few customers glanced uneasily in the man's direction. Reason eyed him closely. *I should have known*, he thought. *The man's spoiling for a fight.* Reason had seen him for the first time the night before. He had drunk heavily, glaring at anyone who crossed his path, especially Billy Wilson.

Now, the man rose from his chair, squinting, looking around the room. When his eyes fell on Billy, a nasty grin spread across his face, and he moved to intercept the young man. "How 'bout you, boy?" The man curled his hands into fists and assumed a boxer's stance. "You want to go a few rounds, see if you can give the customers their money's worth?"

Billy's eyes widened with fear. "No, sir," he said. "I don't fight."

"Sure you do." The man laughed and pointed at Billy's face. "Not real good, maybe, but—"

Reason tapped twice on the man's shoulder. When he turned, the bar owner caught him with two short left jabs to the nose and a hard right cross that landed high on his right cheek. The man dropped to the floor like a stone.

"A man has the right," Reason told the hushed crowd, "and the responsibility to protect his employees and his place of business. Now, I would be most appreciative if a couple of you men would drag this gentleman out and roll him into the gutter where he belongs."

The Tigers' Den had closed for the evening, and Reason and Billy were finishing up the last of their chores when Billy spoke up. "I didn't know you could fight like that, Mister Reason."

Reason wrung out the bar rag and hung it on a hook to dry. "Just a little Golden Gloves a few years ago. I wasn't all that good."

They worked quietly for a minute more, then Billy said, "That Joe Lewis, he's a pretty good fighter, I guess?"

Smiling at the young man's naiveté, Reason said, "He KO'd the German, Max Schmeling, in '38 and made all of America proud. They say he's the best fighter that ever lived, son."

"The Brown Bomber," Billy said. "That's not bad for a colored man, to be the best *anything*." He leaned against the bar. "How long did it take him to knock Mister Davis out?"

"Oh, about a minute and a half, I guess."

Billy gave his employer that crooked grin. "He might be the best there is, Mister Reason, but tonight, I'd have to say you were a whole lot faster."

Blood Uncles

The weather had warmed up nicely. Unfortunately, the Tigers had not, losing to the Oakland Athletics in the first of a three-game home stand. Twelve games into the season, and they were four and eight.

Devonne clicked off the television and walked to the storage area doorway. His uncle stood near the back, clipboard in hand, checking an incoming liquor delivery. "Crowd'll be in soon," Devonne said. "The game's over."

Leon scratched his signature on the manifest, handed it to the delivery guy waiting just outside, then locked the alley door. "They be drinkin' to celebrate?"

"No, sir. They'll be drowning their sorrows."

Leon produced a smile that widened the corners of his bushy moustache. "Well, either way, it'll be a good night for us."

Devonne nodded. Friday nights were almost always busy. Add an afternoon baseball game to the mix, and the results were highly predictable; it would be a hectic but profitable evening.

The telephone rang behind him. He stepped back to the bar. "Shug's Place."

"Can I speak to Devonne Cole?"

It had been over four years since he'd heard that voice, but Devonne recognized it in an instant. The man's name was Luther Johnson, but, on the streets, he'd been known as "Big Dog."

Devonne glanced toward the storage area door. Leon hadn't yet emerged. His uncle had taken a special interest in him since he'd been discharged from the Navy, and wouldn't think well of Devonne's having contact with what he'd consider undesirable past associations. "What's shakin', Big?"

"My, my, my," Luther said. "I guess all that salt water didn't completely wash away your memories from the 'hood."

"Not you, Luther. I wouldn't forget you."

"That's good, Devonne 'cause I got a big favor to ask and ain't nobody but you can help." The line went silent for a moment, and then Luther said, "You do remember about favors, don't you?"

Devonne remembered well. He'd been fifteen when he became a fringe member of the Kings, a black street gang that started in Chicago and spread to Detroit in the early 1980s. Luther "Big Dog" Johnson had been one of the hardcore members.

The gang operated like a small feudal system. The older, hardcore members were warlords controlling sections of closely guarded turf. They dealt the drugs and were usually the shooters. The younger and more numerous "associates" brought in extra money from small-time criminal activities.

When Devonne turned eighteen, he'd had the chance to move up. He probably would have, too, except for Big Dog.

"I remember," Devonne said.

"Good," Luther replied. "I need to see you tonight, as soon as you can, man. I'm in real trouble."

The door to the bar swung open, and Shug rushed in carrying a canvas gym bag. "Get ready, guys. There's a line of thirsty Tiger fans out there about half a block long. They're headed this way."

Devonne hesitated. He owed Big Dog, maybe more than he cared to admit, but he felt a sense of responsibility to Shug, who'd hired him, and to his uncle, who now owned a half-interest in the place. "I can't leave now, Luther. I got to work 'til midnight."

"Soon as you get off, then. You remember where I stay, don't you?"

"Yeah, I—"

"And hurry, little brother, hurry."

The phone went dead in Devonne's hand just as the first of the crowd piled through the door of the bar.

Weekend cleanups always took longer, and it was one o'clock when Devonne pulled up across the street from Luther's house. Like many areas of Detroit, most houses on this block had fallen victim to abandonment, burning, or demolition. Luther's place stood alone near the corner, its yard and the now-vacant surrounding lots overgrown with scrub trees and knee-high weeds.

Devonne locked his car and crossed the street. A shaft of light from the front window illuminated the crumbling front porch where he and Big Dog had once sat exchanging reefer-induced philosophies. He had been cocksure of himself at the time and ready to go hardcore. Luther, his self-appointed mentor, had other ideas.

"You been three years in," Luther had said, "and ain't never been busted. So, you either real lucky, or you real smart. But once you come in with me and the others, luck and smarts only gonna carry you so far." He had turned to stare directly into Devonne's eyes. "Then you gonna end up dead."

"You're not dead," he'd protested.

Big Dog had taken another hit on the joint. His voice came out high and tight. "Shit, man, it's just a matter of time."

Now, Devonne knocked lightly on Luther's front door. "Luther? You there?"

He got no answer, knocked again, waited, then went to the window and looked in. The living room was empty. He tried the door. It was unlocked. He stepped inside. "Luther?"

Light from the living room leaked down a short hallway that led further into the house. Devonne followed the hall past a small kitchen and a bathroom to a closed door in the rear. He cracked the door and caught a faint trace of cordite and the unmistakable smell of blood. He gave the door a push and it swung wide.

Luther lay on his side near the unmade bed. Dark red stains colored his upper body and had spread along the rug on either side of him.

"Luther!" Devonne knelt and eased the man over on his back, feeling for a pulse in his throat. It was there but weak. "Luther," he said again.

Luther blinked rapidly a few times, and then his eyes focused on Devonne's face. "Devonne, my man. I knew you'd come. I—" He was suddenly seized with a series of wracking coughs.

"I'm calling nine-one-one," Devonne said, starting to rise. Luther's hand closed on his wrist with surprising strength. "Ain't time for that. No use, either. Just stay with me, little brother, stay with me for a minute."

Devonne sank back to his knees. "Who did this?"

"Ol' Big Dog should'a known better. Like I told you a long time ago, once you in, you in for life, however long or short that might be." Luther grimaced and coughed again, producing a fine pink spray that settled back over his face and neck. "But I heard about you, how you did good in the Navy and came back and got yourself a job. Even heard you was in school, and I thought…"

For a moment, there was no sound except for Luther's labored breathing. Then he smiled wanly. "I got me a little girl, almost four years old, stays with my sister. I was hopin'—" Luther grimaced and coughed again, and a thin trickle of blood ran from the corner of his mouth. His grip on Devonne's wrist tightened— "Call Ju-Ju!" —then relaxed.

"Luther?" Devonne felt for the pulse again but found nothing. Big Dog was gone.

Fifteen minutes later, Devonne sat in his car in the parking lot of an A&Z Mart. A girl in tight jeans and a Redwings jacket had commandeered the outside pay phone. He waited with both hands on the steering wheel, remembering a hot August afternoon in nineteen eighty-three.

Luther had sat with his wrists resting on the steering wheel, pointing through the windshield of his Lincoln at the US Navy recruiting office. "That's your ticket out, little brother. Now go in there and sign the papers, or I'll save us all a lot of time and trouble and pop a cap in your ass right here."

Devonne hadn't known why this hardened gang member felt so strongly about getting him out of the life and out of the gang's reach. Even now, he didn't know. But he was beginning to realize the enormity of the change in direction his life had taken at Big Dog's insistence. He blinked back a tear.

The girl hung up the phone and went inside the A&Z. Devonne got out and dropped a quarter in the slot. The number was another part of his past he hadn't totally left behind. It rang six times.

A sleepy voice answered. "Yeah?"

"Ju-Ju? This is Devonne."

"Hey, bro. What's up?"

"We need to talk."

"We talkin' now."

Devonne paused for a second, a picture in his head: Luther lying on the bedroom floor, eyes pleading, the desperate grip he had on Devonne's wrist. Someone had to pay. "And I need a gun."

"Well, then, meet me at the place."

A half hour later, Devonne pulled up in front of a nondescript warehouse on Detroit's Southside. A little over a year before, he'd brought his uncle and Shug Barnes here to seek a favor from old friends. Now, he was back. But, this time, alone.

He cut the lights and waited for his eyes to adjust to the dark. The engine was still ticking when he was startled by a knock on the driver's-side window. Ju-Ju knelt by the car, smiling, having materialized silently from out of the shadows. Devonne cracked the window.

"You goin' soft, brother," Ju-Ju said. "Done lost your edge."

"Big Dog's dead." Devonne responded. "I need my edge back quick."

"Uh-huh. I'm sorry to hear that, but I ain't surprised. C'mon, follow me."

Ju-Ju unlocked the gate in the barbwire-topped, chain-link fence, and Devonne followed him to the building's rear entrance. Inside, the odor of wood crating and gun oil permeated the air. Ju-Ju cut on a dim overhead light, revealing a small office that had probably once been used for accepting deliveries. He pulled out a chair and sat down. "So, ol' Big Dog's gone, huh?"

Devonne nodded, finding a chair for himself. "Just before he died, he told me to call you."

It was Ju-Ju's turn to nod. "Yeah, I guess he would do that. We used to hang some, you know, me and him?"

"I remember." Ju-Ju and Luther had both been part of the gang's nucleus—often a bubbling cauldron of bitter rivalries among the members. Ju-Ju was brash and volatile where Luther was reflective and logical, but for some reason they had become friends. The commingling of their natures had served to keep both men in the forefront of the gang's leadership, and alive. There were only three acceptable ways to leave the gang: get killed, go to prison—usually only a temporary hiatus—or move up to a higher level of criminal activity. Ju-Ju had achieved the latter when he became part of the illegal arms supply operation run by the ex-mercenary, Faro.

"We'd get together and talk," Ju-Ju said. "Maybe do a little reefer now and then. That's how he found out you come back from the Navy, got a job and all. Big Dog was real proud of how you turned out, kind of like he was your uncle or something."

"He said he had a little girl."

"Yeah, that'd be Necie. Her momma was a skin-popper who went mainline and OD'd in a bathroom stall. Luther's sister took the girl in, but I ain't sure she's much better than the momma, if you know what I'm saying." Ju-Ju paused to light a cigarette and blow a stream of smoke toward the warehouse's high ceiling. "He figured you owed him a favor, on account of his gettin' you outta the Kings and into the Navy."

"And that was what? Did he tell you?"

"Uh-huh. He wanted you to take her."

Devonne blinked. "Take her? His daughter?"

Ju-Ju nodded. "Take her, as in, you know, take her out of the 'hood, give her a better life."

"But why would he want me, or anyone else, to take his own daughter anywhere? I mean, wouldn't he want to be with her?"

The cigarette smoke curled up around Ju-Ju's head in an unlikely halo. "Luther knew he wasn't going to be around to look out for her no more. You see, Luther went over to the other side.

He was snitchin' on gang activities to somebody from Detroit's finest. The homies found out and, well..."

Devonne was quiet for a moment. "Why'd he do something like that?"

Ju-Ju shrugged. "Don't know. Maybe he lost his stomach for it all after Necie's momma died, or maybe he just got tired, wanted something else." Ju-Ju ground the cigarette butt out on the floor. "He wanted to get into one of those protection programs for informants, get him and Necie into a little white house in Omaha or some other uncool place. I told him 'shit, man, you ain't big time enough to get yourself moved across town.' But he never listened to me. Now he's dead, and you're here looking for a gun."

"Right," Devonne said.

"What you gonna do, get your own head blown off 'cause of what they did to Luther? He crossed the line, man. He knew the risks."

"He was right, though. I owe him a favor."

Ju-Ju stood and folded his arms over his chest. "Not this, you don't. It wasn't this he wanted from you. All he wanted was for you to—"

Devonne stood, too, and locked eyes with his former gang buddy. "I can't be some little girl's daddy, Ju-Ju, but I can pay my debt to Big Dog the only way I know how. It's all I can do. Now, about that gun, you gonna help me or not?"

Leon woke to the ringing of the phone and glanced at his bedside clock. It was just after two-thirty in the morning. "Yeah?" He growled.

"This is Ju-Ju. You remember who I am?"

"I remember. You're Faro's boy."

"I ain't nobody's boy, bro, but we can let that slide for now 'cause I got something to tell you that you need to know."

Leon swung his legs over the side of the bed and rubbed his eyes. "What's that?"

Leon listened intently as Ju-Ju told him of Luther Johnson's friendship with Devonne, how Big Dog had gotten the young man to enlist in the Navy, and, ultimately, all that had happened earlier in the evening.

"So, what's your interest in this?" Leon asked.

"I got no interest. It's just I already lost one friend tonight. I don't need to lose two."

"What're you telling me?"

"Devonne left here with a gun, bro. He's looking for payback."

Shug Barnes lay awake in his bed staring up into the darkness. The phone had rung earlier, just as he'd arrived home after closing the bar. He'd answered, and there'd been just silence on the line. It happened every so often, and he was sure it happened to everyone on occasion; it was just that he couldn't help wondering about the caller, hoping that one day he'd say hello and Darcy would say hello back.

He shifted positions again, disrupting the rumbling purr emanating from his feline bed companion, Midnight. "Sorry, pal," he said. When the phone rang again moments later, Shug leapt from the bed and answered in the middle of the second ring.

"Hello." He waited.

"Sorry to bother you, partner," Leon said. "I need somebody to watch my back."

"It might as well be me, then. I'm awake anyway."

Devonne cruised the street slowly, straining to see house numbers on the poorly lighted, nearly empty avenue. He'd circled the block twice without any luck and was beginning to wonder if Ju-Ju had purposefully given him an address he wouldn't be able to find. Then, reaching over and laying a hand on the Beretta 93R in the passenger seat, he dismissed that notion. If Ju-Ju had really wanted to stop him, it would have been easier just to refuse his request for a weapon.

Deciding he'd have to walk the street to distinguish the house numbers, he pulled in near an alley that ran the length of the block and cut the ignition. He cranked the window down, hearing a barking dog somewhere in the night and the faint roar of freeway traffic. Alone on the dark side street, he thought for the first time that evening about what he was doing.

Risking it all—his job, his clean record, his future, his life. For what, some kind of gang code of honor? He was through with all that, wasn't he? Then Devonne remembered the look on Luther's face after he had emerged from the recruiting office waving the signed enlistment papers.

"C'mon, little brother," Luther had said. "Let's go get us some supper. Might be the last chance you'll have for some Mexican in a long, long time."

Devonne reached over and picked up the Beretta. It felt cool and smooth in his hands. "Ah, fuck it," he said, getting out of the car.

He passed five dark houses before he found twenty-one-thirteen. The street light at the corner wasn't working, and he might still have been unable to find the right house had the numbers not been painted on the curb in black on white. The darkness served his purpose, though. The gun had come complete with a folding forward grip and detachable shoulder stock. It provided great firepower but was difficult to hide wearing warm weather clothing.

He studied the house from the sidewalk, crouching near a hedge that divided the property from the adjacent yard. It was a modest one-story brick bungalow with a large front porch and twin strips of concrete running alongside the hedge, serving as a driveway. As with the other houses he had passed, this one had no lights showing.

The house belonged to one Delbert Jones, street name "Slick." While not one of the Kings' leaders, he was a veteran, a hardcore member. According to Ju-Ju, Slick would have been the shooter, or at least one of the shooters, who had taken out Luther.

"Sometimes, I hear things," Ju-Ju had said. "I keep in touch with a few of the homeboys. They tell me some things."

Thinking back on it, Devonne figured it was probably Ju-Ju who'd tipped Big Dog that he'd been made as an informant. He couldn't interfere with the planned execution, but he could warn his friend.

Well, whatever role Slick had played earlier in the evening, Devonne was about to find out. He crept up along the driveway next to the side of the house. Near the rear, a window looked out over the drive. Closer inspection showed flickering blue light bleeding through a narrow seam where the shade met the window. From inside, Devonne heard the muted sounds of a television.

He hunkered down next to the side of the house and tried to think. *Maybe you should have done that before now, Kojak. Here you are in the middle of the fuckin' night, squatting in some stone killer's driveway with a machine pistol in your hands. What are you gonna do—start blasting through the window?*

The adrenalin rush he'd had earlier had faded, leaving him with a bit more logic and a lot more questions than he had answers to. Did he really want to kill this guy? *Could* he do it? He thought he could do it in the heat of battle, but now? Besides, he had no way to get inside the house without attracting attention. Maybe it was time to regroup, think it over, get some sleep if he could. He rose slowly and started back down the drive. He was just even with the end of the front porch when he heard the gravelly whisper from just above and to his right side.

"Hold up right there, homes, 'less you want to die in my driveway."

Devonne stopped cold. Behind him he heard the sounds of the man stepping down off the porch and then felt the muzzle of a gun barrel between his shoulder blades. The man yanked the Beretta from Devonne's hand.

"Well, look'a here. Don't see many of these around the 'hood. You must have some friends in high places. Maybe we'll talk about that inside."

The gun barrel bored into Devonne's back, and he stumbled forward toward the steps that led up to the porch.

"Open that door and step in," the man said.

As Devonne stepped through the entranceway, Delbert Jones slammed his weapon into the side of the young man's head, knocking him to the floor. Devonne struggled up onto his hands and knees and caught a steel-toed boot in the midsection. He left the floor for a split second, landing on his side against the bottom of a nearby couch. He felt a piercing sharp pain in his right side. His head drooped toward the floor, and when it did, blood from the head wound trickled down into his right eye.

Jones crossed to an end table next to the couch and turned on a small table lamp. Then he knelt, grabbed a handful of Devonne's hair, and twisted his face up toward the light. "Two minutes, nigger! You got two minutes to tell me who the fuck you are and what you doin' outside my window."

Devonne blinked through the red haze that covered his eye and took a breath, grimacing at the pain it caused. "You killed my friend."

Jones pulled Devonne's head farther back and slipped the barrel of his weapon tight against the underside of Devonne's chin. "That don't tell me nothin', motherfucker. I killed lotsa folks."

"Big Dog," Devonne said. "You killed Luther."

Jones let go of Devonne's hair and stood. "Well, I got to give you one thing, boy. You are Johnny-on-the-spot. I doubt Luther's blood got cold by now, and here you are."

He picked up a phone from the end table and dialed. After a moment, he said, "Popeye, Slick here. Yeah, I got a dude here that's hot on Big Dog's blood trail. I think you oughta slide on by, see how you think we need to handle this situation. What?" Jones laughed. "Nah, man, he ain't going nowhere, yet."

Eve Campbell paced the floor of the extended-stay motel suite, arms crossed tightly over her chest. It wasn't the first time, nor, she guessed, would it be the last. But tonight, the urge to pick up the phone was stronger than usual.

It had been months since the incident in Mount Clemons— since she'd almost gotten herself killed and since she'd almost gotten Shug Barnes shot or blown to bits as well. Months since she'd felt his touch, tender and warm on her skin—only that once and yet…

She couldn't stop thinking about him, couldn't stop wanting him, this guy she'd known only for a few hours. She was moving on, of course. She had to. But she couldn't forget those precious few minutes before the bomb had gone off. The way it felt to kiss him and the smell of his skin. He stayed with her, not every minute, not even every day. But he was there, a memory she took out every now and then, when she was feeling particularly alone. Sometimes, the memory was comforting; sometimes, it brought pain. Still, she couldn't stop herself from thinking.

That was the problem. Her body and her soul wanted to see him again, but if she did, she would put his life in danger once more.

She stepped over to the phone, looked at the bedside clock. It was after midnight, a weeknight, so the bar would probably be closed. She had the number committed to memory.

Eve lifted the receiver. Her heart was fluttering in her chest like a bird in a too-small cage. After a moment, she dialed the number. It rang, and rang, and rang. Finally, she hung up, disappointed and relieved at the same time.

The twin pipes on Leon's Grand Am sounded like the guttural roar of a jungle cat as he and Shug tore through the Detroit nightscape.

"You might want to back off a little bit," Shug said. "I'd hate for us to get stopped with weapons in the car." His hand crept to the snub-nose, thirty-eight-caliber revolver in the side pocket of his windbreaker.

"I don't know about that," Leon answered. "Part of me wouldn't mind having a couple of boys in blue with us on this mission. What're you carrying, anyway?"

"My father's snub-nose. He kept it for protection. It's never been fired."

"Huh," Leon said. "A Sergeant Joe Friday gun. You'd have to be within three feet of a guy to hit him with that."

"How long's the barrel on yours?"

Leon said nothing for a minute, then, "At least I got twice as many chances to miss."

"Yeah," Shug said. "Nothing like going into battle undergunned." He pulled down the sun visor, flicked on the mirror-light, and unfolded a scrap of paper Leon had given him earlier. "Slow down. I think the street we want is just up on the right."

As they neared the intersection, a dark-colored Chevy Caprice coming from the opposite direction turned left in front of them. When Leon made his turn, the Chevy had just pulled up to the curb on the other side of the street, five houses from the corner.

Shug watched intently as a man got out of the car and eyed their approach. "Keep going," he said. "Then make a left at the next street."

Leon did as instructed, and the first thing they saw was Devonne's Dodge Colt parked halfway down the block, next to an alley.

"How'd you catch this fish?" Popeye asked. He had a cigarette stuffed behind one ear and the grip of a semi-automatic pistol protruding from his waistband.

"He circled the block twice, going so slow I couldn't hardly miss him. Next thing I know, he's outside my bedroom window with this hand chopper." Delbert passed the Beretta to Popeye, who looked it over and raised an eyebrow.

"Nice piece," Popeye said. "Looks fresh outta the package. Kinda makes you wonder where this little fucker's been hangin' out, don't it?" He stepped closer to Devonne and tilted his head to one side to get a better look. "Shit, man, I know this dude. He used to be a King's wannabe, hung around with Big Dog for a while, then disappeared."

Delbert walked over to Devonne and nudged him in the ribs with the toe of his boot. Devonne gasped and grabbed his side, giving out a low groan. Delbert chuckled and said, "You should'a stayed disappeared, bro. Now we got to make it happen for good."

Leon approached the house from the front while Shug made his way silently down the alley, counting houses as he went. At the fifth structure, Shug stopped and surveyed the darkened yard. A one-car garage nestled between the alley and the house. Two metal trash cans framed a small back stoop, with steps leading up to the back door. Shug stepped slowly toward the house, hugging the garage wall. From the corner of the garage, he moved quickly to the left side of the house. A sliver of light spilled out from one of the windows overlooking the driveway. He studied the street, hoping to catch sight of Leon, but it was pitch black.

At the back door, he put his ear to the wood but heard nothing, then tried the knob and found it locked. *Okay*, he thought, *it'll have to be a frontal assault.* He crept cautiously along the right side of the house, keeping his head well below window level. Near the front, light from a half-open window illuminated a section of the side yard. He rose slightly and peeked in.

A worn couch sat just below the window. Across from it, one man squatted on his haunches, leaning back against the wall, while another slouched against the front door. Both were armed with semi-automatics. Shug couldn't see any sign of Devonne, but the men were glancing from each other to the floor in front of the couch. The back of a head, bloodied behind the ear, slowly came into view just above the couch cushions. *Devonne.*

The squatting man spoke. "Where you wanna do it?"

The other shrugged. "I don't know. Let's just throw him in the trunk and drive 'til we find a nice deserted spot. Got to be quick, though; it'll be light before long."

Shug ducked under the window and stuck his head around the side of the house. Leon waited on the far side of the front porch. Shug pointed toward the rear of the house and shook his head. *No rear access.* Then he pointed to the lighted front room, held up two fingers, and tapped the revolver he carried in his other hand. *Two men inside—armed.*

Leon nodded. Shug ducked low again and followed the porch line around to the front steps. Within seconds, both men were poised just to the right of the front door. They looked at each other and nodded. Leon lifted one leg and smashed the door in with his size-thirteen shoe.

Popeye went flying and landed on the floor on his hands and knees. Leon burst through the doorway and kicked out again, connecting with the man's head. As Delbert struggled to yank the gun from his waistband, Shug squeezed off a shot and caught him high in the right shoulder, knocking him back against the wall. The semi-automatic fell to the floor. Shug quickly kicked it away.

Leon turned toward Devonne, lying back against the front of the couch. "Can you walk?"

Devonne shook his head. Dried blood crusted the side of his face. "I don't know. I think I'm busted up inside."

Without a word, Leon knelt, swept the young man up into his arms and backed out of the room onto the porch. Shug swung his revolver back and forth between the two gang bangers, following Leon and Devonne through the door.

Back on the porch a few seconds later, Shug said, "Let's get the hell out of here."

Across the street, Ju-Ju sat in his car, watching as the two men bounded down the steps and raced toward the corner, the big one carrying Devonne like a loose bundle of clothing. He felt a pang of guilt, thinking he should have tried harder to keep Devonne from going. But in the gang world, all the brothers knew they had to get their paybacks. It was an unwritten rule. Maybe Devonne wasn't as far removed from all that as he thought he was.

A light came on in a house two doors down. *Time to move*, Ju-Ju thought. He got out and strode purposefully across the street, up the steps, and into Delbert's house. Delbert lay on his back, trying to staunch the flow of blood from his shoulder with a Kings' gang jacket. Popeye sat on his butt, leaning with his back against the wall. One of his eyes was swollen shut and blood leaked from the side of his mouth. Both men looked up at him when he entered the room.

"Bro!" Delbert said, a glimmer of relief showing through the pain on his face. "I need some help here, man. Glad you came along." Across the room, Popeye merely nodded and mumbled something unintelligible.

Ju-Ju's hand went behind his back to the Glock tucked into his belt. Then he spotted the machine pistol he'd loaned to Devonne lying on the end table. He dropped his hand, sauntered over to the end table and picked up the Beretta.

"Some little motherfucker came after me with that thing tonight. He—"

Ju-Ju turned back to Delbert with a heavy-lidded stare. As he studied the man's face, he saw the slow light of realization dawning there.

Ju-Ju rotated slightly to his left and fired a three-round burst that shredded Popeye's chest. The man listed to his right and slid slowly down the wall, leaving a streaked trail of bright red behind him.

"I should'a known," Delbert said with a resigned smile. "You can't find that kind of piece on the street. I should'a known he got it from you." Delbert nodded slowly. "It was payback, right, for Big Dog?"

It was partly for Big Dog, though Luther had known what he was doing when he went to the cops, and he'd been aware of the potential consequences, too. And it was partly for Devonne, who Ju-Ju hoped would be okay but couldn't know for sure. One thing he did know for sure. Devonne would never be safe if Ju-Ju let these two former gang brothers live. *Nor would he, for that matter.* The Kings wouldn't take it lightly if they knew he'd supplied the weaponry for Devonne's ill-planned revenge. And they'd find out. Of that he was certain.

"Yeah, bro," he said. "For Big Dog."

Ju-Ju stitched another three-round burst into Delbert's midsection, then walked quickly back to his car. More lights were coming on now, up and down the street. Silvery fingers of dawn crept slowly through the trees, and somewhere in the distance, Ju-Ju heard sirens. His car roared around the corner just as the first few of Delbert's neighbors shuffled out onto their porches, sleepy-eyed and wondering what the commotion was all about.

The ride to Harper University Hospital's emergency room was a throbbing, pain-filled blur. Devonne lay as flat as possible on the back seat of his uncle's car and watched the street lights blow by like beacons in the sky. Leon was yelling at him the whole time, telling him how stupid he'd been to try such a damn fool thing, asking how the hell they were supposed to explain things to his momma. Devonne thought maybe he'd responded a few times but wasn't sure. He did know that the words that kept repeating in his brain were *I'm sorry.* And *Thanks, Uncle Leon. Thanks, Shug, for coming to get me.* And, even more often, *Oh shit, I hurt!*

It was only after they'd pulled into the hospital parking lot that Devonne realized Shug wasn't in the car with them. He had followed in Devonne's Colt and screeched into a parking space next to the Grand Am. The two men supported him as they hobbled carefully through the big emergency room outer doors.

Once inside, they eased Devonne into a waiting room chair and huddled briefly, fabricating a feasible explanation for the injuries.

"The way I see it," Shug offered, "is that we were doing inventory at the bar. Devonne was in the back counting cases of beer when a couple of stacks fell over on top of him."

"I don't know," Leon said. "Maybe it ought to be a keg that fell on him."

Shug shook his head. "No, that'd probably have killed him. I like the beer cases."

"Guys," Devonne moaned. "I really appreciate your help, but can we do this quickly? I am in some pain here."

"All right, "Leon said. "Beer cases it is, and you hit your head on a metal desk when you went down."

"Done," the other two said in unison.

Leon checked his watch. "I got to call Roberta before she goes and calls the cops, wondering where this ... this ... moron is."

"I'll talk to the nurse," Shug said.

The two men left Devonne waiting in the chair. He shifted, winced with a fresh round of pain, and watched as Shug spoke animatedly with the duty nurse. Around him were a dozen or more people, some banged up and bloody like himself, others dozing fitfully in their seats. It was his first trip to emergency. He vowed it would be his last.

Within minutes, another nurse and an orderly came out from behind two interior double doors with a gurney. They scanned the room quickly and the orderly called out, "Mister Cole?" Devonne raised a hand, and the two attendants helped him onto the rolling bed.

"You takin' me before all these other people?" Devonne asked. "Am I that bad off?"

The nurse smiled and patted his arm. "It's just a precaution. Mister Barnes thought you might have some internal bleeding."

As they wheeled him toward the doors, Devonne overheard the duty nurse talking to Shug. "Since there's no insurance, I'll need to know who will be responsible for the bill."

He heard the sharp slap of plastic against the top of the reception desk, and, as he disappeared into the inner corridor, he heard Shug say, "Tell me where to sign. Doesn't matter what it costs, put it on the card. The kid's my nephew."

They fussed over him for a while and eventually put him on a drip. Soon, Devonne was floating in a light-gray haze. He heard the buzzing of a fluorescent light above his head one minute, and Big Dog's strained voice the next. *I got me a little girl, almost four years old.* What was her name? He couldn't remember. It was hard to think. *Call Ju-Ju!* Yeah, he would do that. Ju-Ju would remember the little girl's name. But not right now. Maybe when he was feeling better.

There'd been no internal bleeding, just a couple of cracked ribs and a head wound requiring five stitches. Still, they'd kept him for several hours just to ensure there were no complications. Leon and Shug had remained at his bedside the entire time. It was almost two o'clock in the afternoon when one of the nurse's aides finally rolled his wheelchair out through the big doors onto the tiled portico.

Devonne blinked in the warm, early May sunlight, and, with a little help, got cautiously to his feet. All things considered, he felt pretty good. The pain medication had quieted his headache and that, plus being taped up like a mummy under his shirt, had made the dull ache in his side more bearable. If he could just get something to eat, he'd feel like a new man.

"I'll go get the car," Leon told Shug, "if you'll stay here with Devonne."

"Actually, Uncle Leon, I'm starved." Devonne shielded his eyes with his hand and looked up and down the street. "There's a Waffle House over there on the corner. Can we get something to eat?"

"Okay, but it's half a block away," Shug said. "Can you walk that far?"

"I need to stretch my legs some. C'mon, let's do it. I could use a cheeseburger and some hash browns."

The threesome started out, Devonne in the middle, Shug and Leon on either side in case Devonne's body wasn't up to the task. They were just approaching the parking garage exit when a young black man came hurrying out on foot. He glanced at the three men then stopped in his tracks, narrowed his eyes, and pointed a finger at Devonne.

"You!" he shouted. The man balled his fists and dropped into a fighter's stance.

Devonne squinted into the sunlight, finally recognizing the man as James Carver, a former Golden Gloves teammate. They'd fought out of the same local club when they were juniors in high school.

Devonne moved a few steps closer and smiled. "Hello, James. It's been a long time."

Carver straightened from his stance, and his gaze danced back and forth on either side of Devonne's shoulders. "Yeah ... uh, who're these mean-lookin' dudes eye-fuckin' me like I'm some kind of a gang banger?"

Devonne glanced behind him, first right, then left. Leon and Shug were right there, standing lightly on the balls of their feet, ready to pounce.

"Ah, those guys," Devonne said, grinning. "Don't worry about them. They're just my uncles."

The Legacy: Dancing at the Den
September 22, 1955

An aura of tranquility enveloped the City. The economy was good. The Detroit Lions had won NFL Championships in 1952 and again in 1953. Racial tensions had calmed to their lowest levels in over a decade. Dwight D. Eisenhower was President. The country was at peace. The City was at peace with itself.

It was a quiet time, except for the music.

The late 1940s and early 1950s saw Detroit develop as one of America's most important jazz centers, with local musicians such as Milt Jackson, Lucky Thompson, and others achieving international acclaim. In 1954, Hank Ballard and his Midnighters made the jump from R&B to the Pop charts. In '55, another little-known Detroit native, Bill Haley, and his band, The Comets, recorded "Rock Around the Clock" as the opening credits music for a movie called *The Blackboard Jungle*.

Jack Reason's sixteen-year-old son, Mark, stood between the end of the bar closest to the interior wall and the alcove that led into the restrooms. Facing the wall, he stretched his arms out to a width of about four feet. "It could go right here, Dad."

Reason crossed his arms and pursed his lips. "I've gotten along just fine without one for fifteen years. Don't see why I should have one now." Mark walked over and sat down on one of the bar stools. He smiled. *A little condescendingly*, Reason thought with some amusement.

"You're behind the times, Dad. Even the drugstore over by the school has a jukebox. The kids *pour* nickels into it." Mark nodded, looking very much like an authority on the investment of teen allowances. "Trust me; it'll be a money-maker."

Reason studied his son's face, so much like his mother's: those arched eyebrows, that quirky little grin. He figured he'd give in eventually. Really, what was the harm? He planned to retire in another few years, and, if he chose to, Mark would become the new proprietor. The boy had hung around the bar on weekends since he was twelve, helping clean the place after Billy Wilson left to go work for General Motors.

"Those are teenagers at the drugstore, Mark. My customers are older."

"But think of the future," Mark replied. "I mean, a couple of years from now, when I turn eighteen, my friends and I will be your customers."

"But I don't know the music," Reason said, now simply putting off what he knew was inevitable. "Who'll choose the songs?"

"Relax, Dad. I'll take care of that." Mark hopped off the stool and moved quickly to the center of the room. "We could move these tables back and make a dance floor. And you're closed on Sundays; we could start a Teen Night for the kids my age. And then—"

As Mark rambled on, Reason experienced a small twinge of envy for his son's youthful passion. It was more than overshadowed, though, by the pride he felt. He was looking at the passing on of a legacy, such as it was, from one generation to the next, from the old to the new. It was the way of things.

The jukebox was delivered three weeks later, a brand new Wurlitzer with chrome sides that glittered like diamonds in the moonlight. The selection chart was peppered with songs like "Maybelline," "Shake, Rattle, and Roll," "Rock Around the Clock," and "Earth Angel." The over-eighteen crowd packed the house on Fridays and Saturdays, and Sunday's Teen Night had the younger ones lining up at the door. A new dance called

The Bop took over the nation's youth, and set pastors and parents quaking in their shoes.

James Reason didn't put much stock in the growing concern. The Tigers' Den was making more money than it ever had, and the kids who "bopped" their nights away there were having far too great a time to get into trouble.

Over the next few years, the Den's profits soared, enabling James to retire after operating the establishment for almost two decades. Mark Reason took over as the new proprietor, the youngest in the bar's history, in the late fall of 1960. As new, larger dance venues opened throughout the city, patronage at the Tigers' Den gradually returned to the middle-aged workers who had sustained it over the years. During a refurbishing in 1964, the dance floor area gave way once more to tables and chairs. The Wurlitzer, however, remained, the tacit symbol of a young man's independence and a father's love.

Could'a, Would'a, Should'a

Business was slow for a Saturday night, only a dozen or so customers scattered among the booths and tables. The Michigan-Iowa football game was on, and most eyes in the place were glued to the television. Ranked number one at the beginning of the season, the Wolverines were four and one going into the game.

"Heard this might be Coach Schembechler's last season," Leon said, leaning back against the bar, his muscular arms crossed over his chest.

Shug glanced over at his partner. "Twenty years, that's like a dynasty, right? I'd hate to be the next guy."

Leon shrugged. "I don't know. Whoever he is, he'll still have Grbac behind the center. Boy's got an arm on him. Can't deny that." Leon shifted his gaze to the lone patron drinking at the bar. The private detective was the only one in the place who seemed uninterested in the game, staring idly into his third double whiskey on the rocks. Leon pushed off from the bar and went over.

"Get you anything, Rick? Some coffee, maybe?"

Scanlon looked up from his drink, his eyes shot through with tiny veins but keenly focused. "Got anything in a new life?"

One side of Leon's lips curled into a wry grin as he shook his head. "Fresh outta new lives."

"Then I'll have another one of these," Scanlon said, nodding to his glass.

"You sure? That'll be number four."

Scanlon shook a Camel out of the pack lying next to him on the bar top, lit it, and squinted up at Leon through the smoke. "You watchin' my drinks now?"

"Nah, man, I'm just watchin' your back. Don't want you to be messin' up that nice Charger you got parked outside."

"Maybe you're right. Safer for everybody if I drink at home." Scanlon crushed the cigarette out and pulled a money clip from his trouser pocket. He peeled off two twenties and laid them on the bar.

Leon pushed the money back. "Uh-uh. You know you don't pay for your drinks here, leastways when I'm workin' you don't."

Scanlon got up from the barstool, shrugged into his overcoat, and scooped the money and cigarettes off the bar. "Thanks."

Leon watched him leave. A moment later, he heard the sweet rumble of the Charger's pipes as it pulled away from the curb. The detective stopped by Shug's Place every week or two, drank for a few hours, and kept pretty much to himself. Leon never pushed the conversation, figuring the man had his own private demons. But he had saved Leon's niece, Cassie, so he was as much a saint as anyone in Leon's book.

Leon went over to the cash register and rang up Scanlon's tab, then took the money from his own pocket and placed it in the drawer.

Behind him, Shug said, "Gonna cut into your retirement fund, you keep on buying that man's drinks. He can hold some liquor."

"I owe him," Leon said.

"What's his problem?"

"Don't know. He never said, and I never asked. My guess would be a woman."

"Yeah," Shug said, his eyes drifting back to the television. "Lots of us got that."

Scanlon's office was located in the upper Westside of Detroit in an area that had once been a thriving center of commerce. In recent years, the banks and investment firms had developed a contagious craving for greater visibility and had relocated to newer, more architecturally trendy tinted-glass and steel structures within sight of an interstate. The Reardon Building, a former corporate headquarters, had been subdivided by out of state owners and now housed a collection of smaller, service-oriented businesses. Maintenance was spotty at best and provided a frequent topic of complaint for the office dwellers.

Scanlon leaned his forehead against the cool marble façade that framed the twin elevator shafts and jabbed impotently at the lighted buttons. After a few minutes, he cursed under his breath and yanked open the door to the stairwell. Monday morning. Not a good morning for the elevators to be out of service, especially not for Scanlon.

On the fourth floor landing, he waited until his chest stopped heaving, then entered the hallway and stumbled down to his office door. Sunlight penetrated the translucent pebbled glass and sent daggers of pain through Scanlon's bloodshot eyes. He used a handkerchief to wipe the sweat from his face and mumbled his usual Monday morning mantra: "Never again, never again." The telephone jangled on the far side of the door and tripped another pain switch in his whiskey-glazed brain.

Carla picked up the phone as he dragged himself through the door. "Scanlon Investigations." She glanced his way, then swiveled her chair to face the window.

He couldn't blame her. Who'd want to see his ugly mug or catch the whisky-stink that still managed to seep from his pores despite a long, hot shower. He slunk past Carla's desk into his private lair, peeled off his wrinkled overcoat, and flung it at one of the two client chairs facing his desk. It slipped off to the floor. *The hell with it.* For sure, he wasn't going to try bending over to retrieve the goddamn thing.

His own leather swivel chair protested noisily as he collapsed into it. He opened the lower left-hand drawer of his desk and took out a half-full bottle of Canadian Mist. With trembling fingers, he unscrewed the cap and took a long pull. Then he fished out a pack of Camels and lit up. Closing his eyes, he let the alcohol and nicotine work their wonders. Five minutes later, his pulse still pounded between his ears, but he began to think he might live.

When he opened his eyes again, the object of his dreams stood leaning against the doorway to his office. Carla stretched, giving him a profile that almost made him forget his hangover. Her long, dark hair parted down the middle and hung loose, covering one side of her lovely face.

"Good morning, precious." His voice rasped like Linda Blair's demon in *The Exorcist.*

"Want some coffee?"

He started to nod, then thought better of it. "God, yes."

She disappeared and returned a moment later with a steaming mug. Scanlon spiked it with a liberal dose of Canadian Mist and shook out another smoke.

Carla gathered his coat from the floor and placed it neatly on the hook behind the door. "Rough weekend?"

He slurped the coffee, venturing a half smile. "The usual."

She gave him a concerned look. "I wish you'd stop drinking so much."

"Marry me and I will," he said, already knowing the depressing answer to that familiar refrain.

She tried smiling, to make a joke of it, but couldn't pull it off. Her brown eyes went misty. "You're too late, Rick. Sorry."

They'd all been friends in high school: Denny Mancuso, the football team's star quarterback, Scanlon, his favorite receiver, and Carla, captain of the cheerleading squad. After graduation, Scanlon had enlisted in the Army just prior to being drafted. Denny had a football-related knee injury and had scored a 4-F with the local draft board. He started his own print shop and married Carla while Scanlon worked military police duty in Da Nang. Carla's letter had reached him six weeks after the ceremony. That's when it finally dawned on him that he was in love with her. He'd tried to forget about her, had even done a couple of extra hitches in the Army, but nothing had helped. She'd stayed in touch. A letter came every few months, even when he didn't write back.

After his discharge, Scanlon parlayed his military police duty into a private investigator's license and had his name lettered on the door of an office in the Reardon Building.

Denny had turned out to be a better quarterback than businessman, and even with the print shop open seven days a week, Carla had to work to make ends meet. Scanlon had hired her as his secretary two years ago. He thought it would be enough just to have her around.

It wasn't.

Scanlon nodded slowly, his eyes still on Carla's, thinking how, with her hair hanging down like that, she reminded him of an actress he'd had a crush on as a kid, only better-looking. *You're too late, Rick. Sorry.* The last shot of alcohol had numbed the hammering behind his eyes, but hadn't done a damn thing for the hollowness in his chest when he looked at her.

She turned to leave his office and her hair fell away from her face. A purplish-yellow bruise decorated her left cheek.

"Carla?"

She stopped, turned back to him, and stared at the floor.

He went over to her, brushed her hair back, and touched the discolored patch gently. "That son of a bitch," he whispered.

It had started just over a year and a half ago. At first, she'd been able to conceal it with her clothing. A couple of times, though, he'd gotten a little sloppy and left a visible mark. Carla had begged Scanlon to let it go. Said she'd have to quit the agency unless he let her handle it her way—that Denny's business had picked up, and she was sure that's all it was—that he'd been better lately, less angry.

That's when Scanlon had started spending his nights and weekends submerged in a river of whiskey. Now, his jaw tightened and his heart rate doubled. "Leave him." Scanlon said through clenched teeth.

A tear rolled down her damaged cheek. "I tried to. He lost a big contract on Friday and came home drunk. We argued. I called a cab and threw some clothes in a bag and..." Carla leaned her head into Scanlon's chest. "And it was worse than before. He hurt me bad, Rick—said he'd kill me if I ever left him."

Scanlon's breath came out in a low hiss. "Let me see."

"I don't want you to. I—"

"Let me see, damn it!"

She hesitated, then stepped back and pulled the blouse out of her skirt. Her middle was covered with bruises where her husband had pummeled her.

Scanlon's fists clenched and unclenched at his sides. Carla saw the look on his face and shook her head violently.

"No, Rick!" she sobbed. "I know what you're thinking, and I can't take that. You're the only friend I've got now. I can't take a chance on losing you, too."

She melted into his arms, and he felt the wetness of her tears soaking through his shirt. Scanlon willed the tension from his body and stroked her back gently. "All right, Carla. It's okay." He tilted her face up toward his and brushed her cheek lightly with his lips. Her scent filled his nostrils as a cold resolve filled his heart. "Really, it'll be okay. I won't do anything." His eyes found hers and held them. "I promise."

Leon spent most of Monday morning and early afternoon dealing with liquor and beer distributors, signing for deliveries, and stacking cases in the back room of the bar. Shug helped for a while, then decided to get in an early workout and headed for the fitness center. At a quarter past four, Leon stacked the last load of Budweiser and washed up in the restroom. When he came out, Devonne was bent over the phone. The young man glanced up at him, smiled, and spoke softly into the phone before hanging up.

"Momma says tell you hello and wants to know when you're coming for dinner."

"Tell her I'll get by there first chance I get. Between workin' a swing shift at the plant and being a full partner in this place, I ain't got much free time anymore."

"Yeah, it's just that, since Cassie got her own place again, Momma's seemed kind of lonely, you know?" Leon took a cloth from under the counter and began wiping down the bar. "Yeah, I know. Knockin' around in that big old house, you and Cassie out on your own, she got too much time on her hands. She needs something to keep her occupied, make her feel useful again."

Devonne nodded and walked over to the big window beside the bar's front door.

Leon watched as the young man stood there, hands on his hips, staring at nothing. Devonne had been quiet of late, not his usual full-of-ideas, talkative self. Leon decided to keep an eye on the boy.

It was six-thirty that same afternoon when Scanlon entered the bar. He took a stool next to the door, away from the other customers, and nodded to Leon.

The big black man slid a coaster down the bar, grabbing a bottle of Evan Williams and a fresh glass. "Don't see much of you on Mondays. Bad day at the office?"

"Mondays are always bad," Scanlon said. "They arrive right after the weekends."

Leon added ice to the glass and poured the man a double.

Scanlon took a drink and closed his eyes. "How's Cassie doing?"

It was a calculated question, and Scanlon felt a sharp stab of guilt for asking. About eighteen months ago, he had found Leon's missing niece in the clutches of Colombian snuff movie producers. There had been some carnage left at the scene, but Cassie had made it through unscathed, physically, at least. *The emotional and mental aftermath, well, that would take time to heal*, Scanlon thought. He had refused payment for his services, thinking at the time that it was a noble gesture on his part. Now, he'd come to collect his due.

A big smile broke over Leon's face, and Scanlon felt another twinge.

"She's good, really. Working part-time, back in school, got herself a nice little apartment." Leon moved to top off the drink, but Scanlon placed a hand over his glass. "She got engaged a couple of months ago to a senior accounting student, if you can believe that. They're planning to get married after he graduates."

"And your sister, Roberta, wasn't it? She's okay, too?"

"Yeah," Leon said. "Been a little lonely since Cassie moved out again, but she likes the fiancée a lot. She's just happy that Cassie's doin' so well. We all are, thanks to you."

Scanlon, the master manipulator. What a great guy. He looked down into his whiskey, then up at Leon. "I need a favor, Leon, a big one."

"Just say the word, man. I owe you," Leon answered immediately. "I'll always owe you."

"You're closed on Sundays, aren't you?"

"Right, unless the Tigers are playing."

"Good," Scanlon said. "Here's what I need."

The following Sunday afternoon, Scanlon parked down the block from the print shop and waited. Denny came out at five-thirty and bent to lock up. He'd put on a few pounds and needed a haircut. Scanlon fired the ignition, pulled into the street, then to the curb behind Denny just as the other man was about to get into his car. He tapped the horn once. When Denny looked up, Scanlon opened his car door and leaned out.

"Denny! Hey, man, long time no see."

Denny stood frozen, his hand on the car door handle. He watched Scanlon nervously, his eyes wide.

Scanlon figured Denny had to be wondering if he knew about Carla. *You should be afraid, you bastard.* He opened his door the rest of the way and stepped out, smiling. He walked over and extended a hand to his former teammate. "How you been, buddy?"

Denny took Scanlon's hand, his expression relaxing a little. "I'm good, Rick. What about you?"

Scanlon shrugged, trying to keep his smile sincere. "Business could be better, but my money's on crime and greed prevailing. What the hell, we're all just struggling to get by, aren't we?" He put a hand on Denny's shoulder. "Say, you in the mood for a drink? I was just on my way over to a little bar close to the stadium.

I know the owner there, and he'll give us premium brand booze at house brand prices."

"I don't know. I'm pretty beat."

"C'mon," Scanlon urged. "Just one or two and you can be on your way." He faded back a few feet and made a throwing motion with his arm. "We can relive our glory days. Remember the Wheeler game, Denny? You threw for four touchdowns. I had twelve receptions."

"It was five touchdowns. And you never caught twelve balls in your life." Denny's face broke into a grin. "Just one or two drinks, okay? Any more and we'll be doing a play-by-play."

A few minutes later, the Charger pulled up in front of Shug's Place, followed by Denny's ten-year-old Chrysler.

Leon met them at the door. "Sorry, boys, I was just getting ready to close. Haven't had a dozen customers all day."

"C'mon, Leon," Rick said. "You've got two thirsty ones right here. The drinks are on me, and I'll throw in a couple of shots and beer chasers for the proprietor. What do you say?"

The black man's mustache curled wide at the edges as he smiled. "My friend, you've just said the magic words. You and your buddy come on in and have a seat." Leon showed them to a booth in the far corner of the bar, away from casual observation. On his way to get their drinks, he flipped the lock on the front door and unplugged the neon beer signs in the front window. If Denny noticed, he showed no sign of it. Leon brought the pair a good Irish whiskey, and left the bottle and a pitcher of draft beer on the table.

Three hours later, Denny was telling Scanlon for the second time how his knees had kept him from getting a college scholarship. "I could'a been somebody, Ricky. If only…"

Scanlon neglected to tell him he could have been drafted, too, and might never have been lucky enough to marry someone like Carla. Instead, he said, "Yeah, if only. There's a lot of that in life."

Denny shook his head slowly and peered vacantly into his sixth—or was it his seventh?—glass of whiskey. "Could'a been somebody."

They sat there for another ten minutes, neither man saying a word, then Scanlon slid out of the booth. "C'mon, Denny, let's get you home." He helped the other man to his feet, locked an arm around his waist, and dragged him to the door. He nodded to Leon, who waited by the bar.

Leon opened the door and checked the street, then closed and locked the door from inside after the two men left.

Scanlon dug the car keys from Denny's pocket, opened the door to the Chrysler, and poured his former friend into the passenger seat. Behind the wheel, Scanlon said, "I'll drop you off at home and catch a cab back for my car." But he was pretty sure Denny never heard him.

Two days later, a jogger spotted the Chrysler submerged in the shallow waters of Lake St. Clair, near Grosse Pointe Park. The body inside was identified as Dennis Mancuso of 110 Cabot Lane, Detroit. The medical examiner certified death by drowning and called the incident, *another unfortunate alcohol-related accident.* The obituary that appeared in the *Detroit Free Press* later that week listed Denny as a former star quarterback for the Brighton High School Bulldogs.

Leon emerged from the restroom drying his hands on a paper towel.

John Metcalf, one of the retirees who made Shug's Place a home away from home, caught his eye and hoisted an empty beer mug.

"Think I could get another one of these?"

Leon looked over at Devonne behind the bar. The young man had one elbow propped on the bar top, staring idly toward the front window.

Metcalf's eyes followed Leon's. "Boy's been lost in thought, I guess. He got a girlfriend? I'll bet he's thinking about some girl. I always was when I was his age."

Leon smiled down at the man. "Yeah, I imagine that's it, John. Sit tight, I'll get you another draft." He stepped to the bar, filled the mug, and placed it on Metcalf's table. Now the older man seemed lost in thought. *Probably remembering one of those sweet young things from the old days,* Leon figured.

Devonne hadn't moved.

Leon came back around the bar and tapped him on the shoulder.

He turned, blinking twice, as if coming out of a trance. "Yes, sir?"

"I been watchin' you for over a week now." Leon said. "Moving around here like a robot or something, not running off at the mouth like you usually do, ignorin' the customers. What's wrong? And don't tell me it's nothing. I've known you all your life. I know better."

Devonne's eyes dropped to his feet. "I've been thinking, that's all."

"Uh-oh, dangerous territory." Leon put a hand on the younger man's shoulder and squeezed gently. "C'mon, son. What's on your mind?"

"You remember what happened with Big Dog?"

A slight frown creased Leon's brow as he remembered how close he'd come to losing his nephew the night Big Dog was killed. "How could I forget?"

"Yeah, well, there's one thing I never mentioned about that night. Big Dog told me he had a daughter, about four or five years old, stayed with his sister. He wanted me to take her."

Leon's frown deepened. "*Take* her?"

"He wanted me to take care of her, I guess, get her out of the 'hood. I don't know, something."

"Why you?" Leon asked.

"'Cause I got out, which was mostly because of him." Devonne rubbed a hand briskly over his close-cropped hair. "He figured I could return the favor."

They both remained quiet for a moment, then Leon said, "And you been thinking about the little girl."

"I been thinking I've let my friend down."

"So," Leon said, "what you gonna do?"

"I'm not sure. I was thinking of calling Ju-Ju. He knows where the little girl is. Maybe go see her or something. Make sure she's all right."

"What if she isn't?" Leon asked. "What you gonna do then?"

"I don't know," Devonne said. "I'll think of something."

Scanlon got off the elevator and strode purposefully down the corridor toward his office. He unlocked the door and started a pot of coffee. He wanted it ready when Carla got in.

It had been two months since Denny's body was recovered from Lake St. Clair. Carla smiled more these days. She had taken a week off to deal with the funeral and all the official paperwork associated with sudden, accidental death. Then she came back to work with a vengeance, sniffing out half a dozen new clients and talking the building super into new carpeting for the office.

Scanlon was doing better, too. He'd gotten the drinking under control, cleaned up his apartment, even bought a new sport coat and slacks. After work last Friday, he and Carla had had an early dinner at Pepino's and caught a movie. It was a chick flick, but he hadn't minded. Though it was still too early to say for sure, he thought things were beginning to come together for the two of them.

Did he feel a pang of guilt? Not really. A guy could spend his life thinking about what might have been. Or he could go ahead and do something about it. Two lives full of hope and promise, for one miserable, wretched existence? All in all, he believed it hadn't been a bad trade.

That's not to say he didn't think about it once in a while. But then Carla would smile sweetly at him, and he was reminded that he'd never been one to dwell much on moral absolutes.

The Legacy: Billy Wilson Returns
July 26, 1967

The Detroit riot of 1967 began on the evening of July 22 when police raided an illegal after-hours drinking club in Detroit's largest black neighborhood. The rioting continued for five days and spread throughout the city. Seven thousand were arrested, forty-three killed, and over a thousand injured. More than twenty-five hundred buildings were burned.

Mark Reason's wife was distraught and more than a little frightened. "All I'm saying is that you don't have to go. The police will—"

"The police can't stop it, Jenny. Haven't you seen it on TV? They're helpless."

"But it's only a place, a building!" She was crying now. "You can replace it if you have to. I can't replace you."

"You don't understand," Mark said. "It's been in the family for twenty-five years. I have to go."

Mark watched as his wife turned away sharply and rushed from the room. Seconds later, he heard the bedroom door slam. He squeezed his eyes shut and pressed his fingers to his temples. *She didn't understand, couldn't understand.* He went to the front door and looked out. The downtown was haloed in red-orange light. He hurried down the steps and to his car.

Billy Wilson was angry. He was not alone. Like many of his race, Billy and his family lived in an area of Detroit sarcastically referred to as "Paradise Valley," an impoverished hell hole on the east side of the city. At his job, he had been passed over countless times while his white counterparts were promoted. Billy had lost the crooked smile he once had. He'd been misused and abused, and bore the scars to prove it. The rioting that had started a few days earlier was simply the vehicle through which he and his black brothers might vent their growing rage.

Acrid smoke from burning buildings swirled around them, burning their throats, as Billy and his friends wandered through the teeming nighttime streets. They carried clubs and pipes and bricks and cans of gasoline. The sounds of breaking glass, hoarse shouts, and the unmistakable *whump* of fuel-induced fires surrounded them.

A man with his arms full of clothing ran past. "Hey, bros!" he shouted. "Better hurry on down to the sto' while they still got your sizes!"

One of Billy's friends heaved a brick through the darkened window of a dry cleaning store. Another used a pipe to break out the side window of a car parked on the street, then poured gasoline inside and followed it with a flaming book of matches.

The group moved on. Closer to the middle of the block, they stopped outside a bar.

Billy recognized the familiar orange, blue-shaded lettering in the window—*The Tigers' Den*—then thought, *been a long time since I been here. A damn long time.* A couple of years back, he'd read in the paper where James Reason had died. He'd thought briefly about going to the funeral, but something had come up.

"Let's go inside and get us a drink," Billy's neighbor, Linville, said.

"Yeah," said another member of the group. "Let's get us a couple of drinks."

It wasn't like he owed anything to the place itself. Mister Reason was dead. "All right, then," Billy agreed. "Let's go get ourselves a drink."

Linville smashed the lock with a cement block he found lying by the curb and kicked the door open. It was dark inside, the only light coming from a flaming building on the other side of the street. "Shit, man, I need to find a light. Y'all c'mon in and help me look."

Things happened fast after that. The interior lights came on. Somebody shouted, "Stop! Please just go away and leave the bar alone, and nobody will get hurt!"

Billy looked to his left. A man stood just in front of the bar holding a small revolver. Both the man and the gun were shaking visibly.

One member of the group threw a brick that caught the man in the chest and sent him reeling backward to the floor. The gun went flying, and the others were on him in less than a second. One kicked him in the side; another smashed him in the thigh with a wooden club.

"Stop! Please!" the man cried. "I'm sorry. Just take what you want, but please don't—" He stopped in mid-sentence, staring at Billy.

As the man continued to stare, Billy's hand went unconsciously to his face, tracing the length of his jagged scar.

"Billy?" The man said, a faint flicker of hope showing on his face. "Is that you?"

Billy moved further into the room and stared down at the man lying on the floor. *Who the hell…?*

"It is you," the man said. "It's me, Mark, Mark Reason."

It came back to Billy slowly. *The little kid who used to come in and hang around some on the weekends, Mister Reason's son.* "Get off him," Billy said. "I know him."

"Ah, c'mon, man." It was Linville. "I thought we was gonna—"

Billy got up close in his friend's face. "We were gonna do lots of shit, might *still* do lots of shit, just not here." He turned slowly, looking each man in the eye. "That understood?"

The men murmured among themselves as they left, but they'd seen the look on Billy's face, and they *did* understand. This was one honky bar that wouldn't burn tonight.

Billy picked up the revolver and stuck it in his pocket. Then he looked down at Mark Reason again. "You need to go home and stay home 'til this is over." Mark nodded and Billy left, pulling the door closed behind him.

The first pink glow of dawn crept silently through the window of the bar as Mark Reason limped out from the storage area. His side ached badly and his leg was stiff. But nothing appeared broken, *thank God.* He went over to the window. The building across the street, now a gutted shell, was still smoking. Further up the block to his right, a large olive-drab truck pulled to a stop, and soldiers carrying rifles began to emerge. Mark cautiously opened the front door. Billy Wilson sat in the small entrance alcove, hands in his pockets, feet crossed at the ankles.

"I thought I told you to go home," Billy said.

He must have been here all night, Mark realized. "I would've, but I looked out in the alley. Somebody burned my car."

Billy stood and stretched. "Well, better your car than your building." He looked up the street and smiled the crooked half-smile that Mark remembered from years back. "Looks like the Guard is here," he said. "The brothers are all about gone. Guess I'd best be gettin' on back home myself."

"I want to thank you for last night, Billy. I'm not sure what might have happened if it weren't for you."

"I owed your father one, never got around to paying him back. Now you've collected. I reckon that makes us even." Billy nodded once, then turned and started down the street, away from the gathering soldiers.

The '67 riot ended on July 27, following mobilization of the Michigan National Guard and troops from the 82nd Airborne Division.

In early September, Mark Reason put the Tigers' Den up for sale and moved his family to Lansing, where he eventually opened an independent insurance agency. The bar sold just before Christmas to a local businessman named Johnny Lavendar.

Plausible Lies

You sure you wanna do this? Devonne thought to himself. "Nope," he said. "I'm not sure at all, but I guess I need to."

The morning was damp and cold, like Mother Nature wanted to finish up with fall and get an early start on winter. A light rain had started, slicking the streets and clinging like teardrops to the city's bright green, light-reflective street signs. Devonne slowed for the intersection, glanced at the notation scrawled on the small square of paper he held in his hand, and made a left onto Burgess. The address was four houses down from the corner. He pulled in behind a white, rusted-out Chevy Nova.

The house was a low clapboard structure with a tiny concrete porch. Chain-link fencing guarded a hardscrabble yard dotted with clumps of weeds and grass long since gone to seed. A child's tricycle stood next to the porch, its red and blue handlebar streamers providing a wan spot of color in the otherwise monochromatic landscape.

The neighborhood was full of similar houses, a working-class area that had once been kept with pride, boasting manicured lawns and weekend backyard barbeques. But time had moved on, and pride had given way to frustration and, finally, neglect.

Devonne sighed. He'd hoped for better. He glanced at the dashboard clock. An hour and a half before he was scheduled to open the bar. He took a deep breath, then stepped out into the rain and headed toward the house.

He knocked three times and was about to leave when he heard a muffled voice from inside. It might have been a child's voice.

Not sure if he was relieved or disappointed, he waited a few seconds more and knocked again. There was another long, silent pause before the bolt slid back. Part of a woman's face appeared in the three-inch slot afforded by the chain lock.

She stared at him, looking him quickly up and down, but said nothing.

"Good morning, ma'am. My name is Devonne Cole. I was a friend of Luther's."

"Luther's dead," she said.

"I know. He and I talked not long before he was … before he passed. He said he had a daughter, Necie, and that she was staying with you. Uh, you are Miss Juanita Reeves, aren't you?"

The woman studied him again for several seconds. "Uh-huh."

"Luther asked me to stop by," Devonne said. "He thought maybe I could help."

For just a second, something other than suspicion crept across the face behind the door. "Help how? Like with money, you mean?"

Devonne paused briefly, unsure himself what he'd meant. "Maybe."

The door closed then opened again, and the woman stepped to one side. He crossed through the doorway into a small hallway. On the floor in one corner, a dark-skinned Barbie sat next to a small, stuffed elephant. A bedroom opened off the hall directly across from him. A living room lay to the left, and what appeared to be a dining area beyond it.

The woman shut the door, and he followed her into the living room. It was cluttered with stray articles of clothing, fast food sacks, and empty beer bottles. A child's coloring book and an open box of Crayolas rested on one end of a coffee table crosshatched with scars from old cigarette burns.

Luther's sister took a seat in the middle of a worn, flower-patterned sofa. Greasy-looking throw pillows were propped in the corners on either side. Devonne sat in the only other chair in the room, a stained, sagging relic from the 1950s. He guessed the woman to be in her late thirties, thin, short, with caramel skin tones.

She wore a chenille bathrobe belted at the waist and hugged herself like she was cold.

"How'd you know Luther?"

"We met when I was in school. Used to hang out together before I went into the Navy."

"Big brother was in the Kings," she said. "You part of that?"

Big brother? That would put her somewhere in her twenties. "Sort of, for a while. Luther was the one encouraged me to join the Navy, got me away from all that."

"You in the Navy? You ain't got on no uniform."

"Nah," Devonne said. "I got discharged. I work for my uncle and another guy now. A bar over on Labrosse—Shug's Place." He shifted in the chair. "Is Necie here? I'd like to say hello."

The woman smiled a little for the first time and turned toward the dining area. "Necie, c'mon out here. Somebody want to see you."

A moment later, the little girl appeared from the rear of the house. A tattered pink-and-white-striped blanket lay draped over her left shoulder. She stopped when she saw Devonne and stuck her thumb between her teeth, staring at him with big hazel eyes.

"C'mon in here," the woman said. "This man was a friend of your daddy."

The girl walked slowly through the dining area and stopped next to the sofa. She wore a flimsy cotton dress that had what looked like mustard stains down the front, and she was barefooted. Her smooth skin was slightly lighter than her aunt's and much lighter than Luther's had been. Her hair was a soft mass of dark curls.

"Her momma was white," the woman said. "That's where them hazel eyes come from."

Devonne smiled, leaning forward in the chair. "Hey there, Necie." The girl continued to stare at him silently.

"She don't say much," the woman said, brushing at the discolorations on the girl's dress. "Mostly just plays with her dolls and watches cartoons on television." Her eyes flicked back to

Devonne. "Uh ... you said something about helping. We could sure—"

There was a noise like a door lock turning, and the girl and her aunt looked up sharply. Devonne felt a rush of cold, damp air on his neck. As he turned to look, an angry voice boomed in his ear.

"Who the fuck is this?"

A twenty-something black man stood in the hall. He wore jeans, boots, and a faded wool jacket. Devonne started to rise. "I was a friend of—"

The man stepped forward quickly and stuck a finger in Devonne's face. "I didn't ask *you* nothin', motherfucker!"

"He ain't nobody, Tyrell. He's just—"

"Where's my stuff, bitch?"

"What?"

"I said, where's my stuff, bitch?" The man swept past Devonne, looming over the woman who clutched frantically at the top of her robe. "What you *done* with my *stuff?*"

The little girl began to wail, and the man grabbed her by the hair and dragged her in close to his body. His left hand dipped into the pocket of his jacket and came out holding a knife. There was a soft *snick* and a six-inch blade gleamed dangerously in the room's dim light.

Devonne sprang from the chair without thinking, grabbing the man's wrist with one hand and driving an elbow into the side of his head. The man grunted and the knife dropped to the floor.

The woman grasped Necie's hand and scrambled back toward the dining area just as the man lashed out at Devonne with a fist. Devonne jerked back, catching only a glancing blow on the chin. Then his instincts took over. He was no longer Devonne Cole, the responsibly employed business admin student; he was the rangy kid who had compiled an impressive eighteen-two-and-two Golden Gloves record during his junior and senior years in high school.

He jabbed twice with his left. The first blow broke his opponent's nose. The second split his lip. He followed with a vicious right cross that sent a spray of blood and saliva into the air. The man dropped like a stone onto the green shag carpet.

Devonne's chest heaved with adrenaline. He looked around the room. Necie and her aunt were nowhere to be seen. He knelt and checked the pulse at the base of the unconscious man's neck. Still there, still healthy enough, but the guy was definitely down for the count.

As Devonne rose, a glint of glass from the sofa caught his eye. Behind one of the throw pillows, he found a clear syringe and a two-foot length of hollow rubber tubing. He checked further, pulling out one of the seat cushions. Wedged into the crease where the arm rest disappeared into the base of the sofa, he found a bent metal spoon. His thoughts went back six months to the night when Big Dog was gunned down. Ju-Ju had spoken about Necie's momma having OD'd on smack, then about Luther's sister taking the girl in. "I ain't sure she's much better," he'd said, "if you know what I mean."

Devonne called out: "Miss Reeves? Necie?" No answer. The house was quiet. He stepped into the dining area and called out once more. Still no answer. Beyond the dining area, he found another hallway: bathroom on the right, closet on the left. Across the hall was a kitchen, then another closed door. He glanced back at the unconscious man and quickly tried the knob. Locked.

He should do something about Necie. He could call the police, but what would he tell them? That he'd come to call on a murdered gang member's daughter? That he'd gotten into a fight with another man who was ... what? Friend? Husband? Some relative of the girl's aunt? He didn't know. That he'd found drug paraphernalia on the premises? Whose was it? The aunt's? The guy lying on the living room floor? Could be. He heard again in his mind, *"Where's my stuff, bitch?"*

He knocked on the locked door. "Miss Reeves, are you in there?" Nothing. Maybe they'd gone out a back door. He *hoped* they'd gone out a back door, and that they'd stay away until it was safe to return. As his adrenalin rush faded, he felt sure he should do something; he just wasn't sure what. Better to give it some thought, not act in haste. He was sure he didn't want to be there when the man on the floor woke up. With a nervous glance at the still unconscious man, he left through the front door.

It was close to noon when Shug found a parking spot between the bar and Mack's Grill and eased the Olds 442 to the curb. He was glad he hadn't been scheduled to open up. The telephone had awakened him in the middle of the night. No one was on the line, but he hadn't slept well afterward.

Devonne was behind the bar, stocking the beer cooler, as Shug pushed through the door. Otherwise, the place was empty.

"Morning," Shug said.

"Is it still morning?" Devonne said. "Seems like it ought to be later."

"Eleven-fifty," Shug said. He shrugged out of his jacket and hung it on a hook in the back room before returning. "I overslept."

"You're the boss. I guess you can oversleep whenever it strikes you." Devonne flattened an empty cardboard beer case and stuffed it into the recycling bin. "Say, Shug, a weird thing happened to me this morning. I went—"

Both men turned as the front door swung open. A burly man in a brown suit stepped into the bar followed by two uniformed police officers.

Shug stepped over to the bar. "Help you, fellas?"

The burly man didn't answer, his gaze focused over Shug's left shoulder. "Are you Devonne Cole?"

"Yes, sir, that's me."

The man extracted a folded sheet of paper from his inside coat pocket and placed it on the bar. "Mister Cole, I am Detective John Stamey, with the Detroit Police Department. I'm here to arrest you for the murder of Tyrell Lee Burton."

Shug glanced sharply back at Devonne, who stood frozen in place for a moment, then turned a sickly shade of ash-gray. "Sir?"

"What the hell's going on here, detective?" Shug asked. "Devonne hasn't murdered anyone. That's ridiculous."

Stamey nodded at the officer nearest the end of the bar, who produced a set of handcuffs and moved toward Devonne.

Shug stepped between the officer and his young employee and held up a hand. "Whoa, wait just a minute. I'd like to know—"

The officer stopped where he was, his hand going to his sidearm. In a voice louder than necessary, Stamey said, "Sir! Back off, please."

Shug's gaze shifted to the detective. Both he and the second police officer were in defensive postures, tensed, eyes bright. Shug raised his other hand and approached the bar again. "Okay. Okay. I'm not trying to be a problem here. I'd just like to know what's going on."

Stamey relaxed a little. "Who are you, sir?"

"Shug Barnes." Behind him, he heard the snap of the cuffs as they closed on Devonne's wrists. "My partner and I own this place. Devonne works for us. He's my partner's nephew."

Stamey looked at the first cop and jerked his head toward the door. Devonne was escorted around the bar, hands locked behind him—shock, confusion, and fear showing in his eyes.

"Shug … I … I didn't—"

"I know, Devonne. I know. Don't worry. We'll get this straightened out. It's a mistake. I'll call Leon." Shug watched as Devonne and the officer disappeared through the doorway.

"Give me a minute," Stamey told the other cop, who nodded, then joined his partner outside. The detective pulled a card from his shirt pocket and placed it on the bar next to the arrest warrant. "There's a number there if you want to call the lieutenant later."

"Can't you tell me what happened?" Shug asked.

Stamey shrugged. "Can you tell me where Cole was this morning?"

"I came in just a few minutes ago. Devonne was here. He opened this morning at eleven."

"Well, we got a witness says he killed a guy in her house around ten, ten-thirty. I was you, I'd be getting the kid a lawyer."

After Stamey left, Shug called Leon at the BOP plant in Southfield, waiting ten minutes for him to get off the production line and to a phone.

"What's up, partner?" Leon asked.

"Devonne's been arrested for murder. The cops just left with him."

Leon arrived at Detroit Police Headquarters shortly after one o'clock and spoke to a civilian employee seated behind a large, curved reception desk in the lobby. He was told he'd have to speak with a detective, none of whom were available at the moment, and asked to take a seat.

He sat.

Gray-tinted rectangular slabs of glass ran floor to ceiling in the lobby area, further weakening what little sun had broken through the mostly cloudy sky. It had stopped raining, but small beads of moisture still dotted the exterior of the glass walls. An array of the city's populace sat scattered about on upholstered, chrome-trimmed chairs or paced impatiently across the polished tile floor: mothers with small children, men and women in business suits, one old man with his face buried in his hands.

The reception desk sat in the middle of the large space, a buffer between the bank of elevators in the rear and the steady stream of visitors and workers in the front. The continuous low hum of muted voices and constant movement reminded Leon of a bee hive.

One of the elevator doors slid open, and a stocky, dog-faced man in his late forties lumbered over to the receptionist. He leaned sideways against the desk as he spoke, his eyes darting around the packed room. The receptionist looked Leon's way and nodded once. The man started across the floor. Leon stood and met him halfway.

"Mister Tweed, I'm Detective John Stamey. You're here about your nephew?"

Leon nodded. "Gotta be some mistake, detective. Devonne wouldn't kill anyone."

"Let's go upstairs," Stamey said, turning toward the elevators.

Leon followed, and the two men rode up three floors in silence. When the doors opened, Stamey led Leon to a small interview room away from the rows of desks and offices. They sat down on opposite sides of a green metal table.

"What can you tell me?" Leon asked.

The detective sat quietly for a moment, breathing heavily through his nose before he spoke. "According to our witness, Mister Cole came to her house this morning around ten o'clock, claiming to be a friend of her brother's. A few minutes later, the witness's boyfriend came in, an argument ensued, and the two men fought. Our witness and her niece retreated to a back bedroom. When things quieted down, she went back out and found the boyfriend lying dead on the living room floor, a switchblade knife protruding from his chest. She called nine-one-one."

Leon sat in stunned silence, his neck and shoulder muscles tightening up like they'd been popped with a bull prod. After a moment, he spoke. "Can I see him?"

Stamey levered himself up out of his chair. "Let me check." He came back minutes later and stuck his head into the room. "He's been processed and is in a holding cell. You can have ten minutes."

The holding cell was a five-by-five room with a small, wire-protected window cut into the wall. Devonne sat inside on the room's only piece of furniture, a straight-back chair. He was bent forward, his face resting in his hands. Leon spoke to him through the window.

"Tell me you ain't done this thing, son."

Devonne looked up quickly. A mixture of relief and anxiety flooded his sallow features. "Uncle Leon! I... I..." He shook his head and moisture filled his eyes. "I didn't kill anybody! I just went there to see Luther's daughter."

As Devonne wiped at his gathering tears, Leon noted the angry abrasions on both sets of knuckles. "How'd you hurt your hands?"

The young man dropped his hands to his lap and studied them for a moment. "Let me start at the beginning."

Leon sat thumbing through the yellow pages while Shug drew a fresh draft beer for one of the bar's regulars. He kept picturing Devonne's face looking out through the small holding cell window.

Shug hurried back over. "What have you told Roberta?"

"Nothin' yet. I dread talkin' to her. She's gonna have a stroke when she hears about this."

Leon had come straight back to the bar after leaving police headquarters and told Shug his nephew's version of everything that happened that morning. Both men were firmly convinced that Devonne was telling the truth. Unfortunately, the police thought otherwise. Devonne's initial appearance before a judge was scheduled for later that afternoon.

"I got to find a lawyer," Leon said, running his finger down a list of attorneys.

"What, you're just going to pick one out of the phone book?"

"You got a better idea?" His tone was clipped, a little edgier than he meant for it to be. "I mean, you know somebody?"

"There's the guy who did our partnership papers. Something, something and Mullins, wasn't it?"

Leon shook his head. "Uh-uh. I need somebody with criminal defense experience."

"Call your buddy, Scanlon," Shug said. "P.I. like that, he's bound to know a defense lawyer."

Leon smiled for the first time in hours and flipped to another section of the directory. "Good thought, partner. Good thought."

"Sure, I know a guy," Scanlon said. "Everett Fish, has an office not far from your place. It's a no-frills operation, but the guy's got smarts. The people in the prosecutor's office even respect him. They just don't like to go up against him."

"I need him in a hurry," Leon said. "Like right now."

"Hold on a minute," Scanlon said.

In the background, Leon heard Scanlon ask his secretary to get Fish's office on the other line. A minute later, the detective was back and rattled off a street address a few blocks from the bar.

"Go straight over there. He's just leaving the courthouse now, should be back in the office about the time you get there."

"Thanks, Rick. I appreciate your help, owe you another one."

"Actually, we're even, friend. Call me if I can help with anything else."

Leon lucked out, finding a parking spot right in front of the attorney's office. A small black-lettered sign identified the inconspicuous second floor walk-up sandwiched between a used bookstore and a Greek pastry shop. He got out of the car and took the stairs two at a time. The door was located directly at the top of the stairwell. He opened it and stepped inside. An attractive black woman sat perched on the edge of a swivel chair, behind a beige metal desk in the outer office. A thick legal file rested on top of the desk. She looked up as Leon came in.

"Good afternoon," she said. "May I help you?"

"Yeah, I'm here to see your boss, Mister Fish." The woman sat up a little straighter in her chair, an amused look on her face. Leon wondered if he'd gotten the name wrong. *It was Fish, wasn't it?*

"And you would be..." She placed her elbows on the file, steepled her fingers, and touched them to her lips. They were, Leon couldn't help noticing, extremely nice lips.

"Leon Tweed. Rick Scanlon called and made the appointment for me. Probably talked to you."

She smiled. "Right." It came out slow and with just a hint of a mid-western drawl. "Have a seat, Mister Tweed. The *boss* will be here shortly."

Leon chose a chair next to the room's only window as the woman returned to her file. He watched as she flipped through the papers and made notes on a yellow legal pad. Her eye color and skin matched perfectly, a kind of smoky taupe. She wore her hair short and feathered toward the back. It made Leon think of a photograph he'd seen in one of his dad's magazines as a kid: *Lena Horne*. She reminded him of Lena Horne. He was about to tell her so when the door banged open and a short, thin man burst in.

"Will they *ever* stop tearing up the goddamn streets around the courthouse?" He spoke in a booming voice that belied his diminutive size. "No wonder they can't keep their assistant prosecutors. Who'd want to fight that shit every day of the week?"

The woman didn't answer, nodding instead in Leon's direction.

The man dropped his overstuffed briefcase on the desk with a loud *thump* and came at Leon with an outstretched hand. "Ah, Mister Tweed, I presume. Rick Scanlon called, and Janelle here got the message to me. I suppose you've introduced yourselves?"

"Not entirely," the woman said.

Fish glanced at her and raised his eyebrows. "Well, then, Mister Tweed, meet Janelle Williams, my partner and colleague in our noble fight against fascism."

Leon's face felt hot. "Sorry, Ms. Williams, I thought—"

Janelle smiled and held out her hand. "That's all right, Mister Tweed. I was a secretary once. Nothing wrong with that."

Leon took her hand. It was cool and smooth, with sensible, clear-lacquered nails, a firm but friendly grip. He looked her in the eyes, said, "Good to meet you." Then he thought again of the fear and shock he had seen in Devonne's eyes and turned back to Fish.

"I need your help," Leon said. "Right away, if you can."

Fish pointed to one of the two office doors that flanked the reception area. "Let's all go into my office."

Fish's office was small, containing only his desk and chair and two visitors' chairs. The walls were lined with leather-bound law books. Stacks of documents rose up from the carpeted floor like miniature skyscrapers. The desk itself was empty except for a telephone and a legal pad. Leon took one of the visitors' chairs while Fish threaded his way through the stacks to his own seat.

"We're a small firm, Mister Tweed, and Janelle and I share most duties. She will sit in with us, if you have no objections."

"None at all," Leon said. Janelle slid into the seat next to him, and he caught a hint of sandalwood cologne.

"All right," Fish said. "Tell us the story."

Leon did, beginning with his receiving Shug's telephone call on through Devonne's account of his visit to the Reeves woman's house. He ended with a brief summary of his nephew's accomplishments, both work and education-related, since he'd left the Navy.

"Any prints on the knife?" Fish asked.

"Don't know," Leon said.

"What about the woman?" Janelle asked. "Or the guy who was killed?"

Leon shook his head. "Don't know anything about either one of 'em. When Devonne was a kid in high school, he ran with some members of a street gang. Wasn't really part of the gang, at least I don't think he was. But this little girl was the daughter of one of Devonne's gang member buddies. The guy was killed several months ago, and the little girl's been living with the Reeves woman, her aunt."

Leon looked from Janelle to Fish and leaned forward in his seat. "That's the only reason he went there, to check on the little girl. She'd been on his mind for a while."

"And your nephew's initial appearance is this afternoon?" Fish asked.

"Right." Leon said, glancing at his watch. "About an hour and a half from now."

Fish turned to Janelle. "Call down to the county prosecutor's office. See what you can find out about the evidence, the woman and the dead guy, too. I'll call you later." He stood and sighed loudly. "Looks like I'll be fighting that goddamned courthouse traffic again."

Shug was working the bar and the tables, taking deliveries, and keeping an ear out for the phone. He'd already tried to reach Frank Owens three times at the Homicide Division and held off only after he realized the man catching calls was getting pissed.

When the telephone finally rang, he was on it in less than three seconds.

"Shug's Place."

"It's Frank Owens. I just got in. What's up? I got a guy here says you've been a real pain in the ass."

"You remember Leon's nephew, Devonne?"

"Sure," Owens said. "Nice-looking kid. Used to be in the Navy, right?"

"He was arrested this morning for murder."

There was silence on the line. *Owens, running through all the possibilities*, Shug guessed, *wondering what was coming next.*

Finally, Owens said, "Okay."

"He didn't do it," Shug said. "He's a good kid; he's—"

"Who made the arrest?"

"One of your guys, Homicide Detective name of John Stamey."

"What are you looking for?" Owens asked.

"I'm not sure exactly. More information? Anything, I guess. I'm worried about Devonne, and you're the only cop I know down there."

"All right, I'll talk to Stamey and see what he'll give me. Call you back when I know something."

"Thanks, Frank."

"Don't expect much," Owens said. "Stamey's not the easiest guy to work with."

After Fish left, Leon and Janelle Williams moved into her office, where she jotted down his contact information and filled out a receipt for his retainer check. Her office mirrored none of the clutter of Fish's. Instead, she had neat stacks of files on the desk, along with a color photo of two small children. An IBM personal computer sat on her credenza. Lush green plants caught intermittent afternoon sunlight in front of the window.

Leon sat in one of the visitors' chairs, full of nervous energy, knees bouncing, fingers drumming on his thighs.

Janelle looked up from her desk. "Try not to worry, Mister Tweed. We'll do everything we can for Devonne."

"Will he have to stay in jail? I can talk to a bondsman if you think—"

"Hmmm, I doubt the judge will allow a release on bond in a capital case."

Capital case. The words sent a chill down Leon's spine. "I just feel like I need to be doin' somethin', you know?"

Janelle smiled. "Well, I can think of two things. First, you said Devonne's mother doesn't know about any of this yet, right?"

Leon nodded. That was the one thing he *didn't* want to do—talk to Roberta.

"You should probably talk to her."

"And the other?" Leon said.

"I believe if I were your nephew, I'd like to see a friendly face in the courtroom when I went before the judge this afternoon."

He could do that, plus it would mean postponing his discussion with Roberta for a few hours more. "Good idea," he said, trying for a smile but not quite making it. "Right now, I'd fight anything or anybody to help Devonne. If the traffic's all I got to work with, I'll fight that."

"It's not really all that bad," Janelle said. "Everett just enjoys complaining."

Fish studied the young man sitting across from him in the interview room—pleasant, polite, intelligent-looking, and scared to death. "What have you told the police?"

"Nothing," Devonne said.

Good, Fish thought. He not only looked intelligent, he was.

"When can I get out of here?"

"That depends on a lot of things," Fish said. "Your uncle gave me what information he knew. Now, I need to hear it all from you. Start from the beginning. Tell me about your friend. Tell me about Luther."

Fish made notes while Devonne talked, comparing the young man's version of what had happened with what he had learned from the assistant prosecutor who'd been assigned the case. The two stories meshed well enough up until the man identified as Miss Reeves' boyfriend, Tyrell Lee Burton, entered the scene. According to Reeves, the fight had started as a result of Burton's mistaken perception that Devonne was an old boyfriend. His client's account was decidedly different, of course, up to and through his leaving the house with the still unconscious but very much alive man lying on the living room floor.

One person's word against the other's. If it came to that, who would a jury believe? The state's case was helped by two factors. The woman had picked Devonne out of a line-up as the man who came to her house that morning, and he had abrasions on his knuckles from the fight.

On the defendant's side, he had never been in trouble with the police, had served honorably in the Navy, and held down a responsible job. Better still, there were no fingerprints on the weapon. Fish had dealt with far worse situations, but that wouldn't help Devonne get out of jail. There was enough on the state's end to hold the kid over for a preliminary hearing. And that would mean no bail.

"The drug stuff," Fish said. "You think it was the woman's or her boyfriend's?"

Devonne shrugged. "Don't know. Could have been hers. A friend of mine once implied she might be a user. But the guy, he said, 'Where's my stuff?' He was pretty pissed off so it might have been his, too."

"Or maybe he was referring to a stash," Fish suggested.

"Could be, I guess. What worried me was the little girl, her being around that kind of thing."

There was a knock on the interview room door, and a uniformed cop leaned in. He spoke to Fish, motioning with his head in Devonne's direction. "He's due in the courtroom in fifteen."

Fish waited until the cop withdrew. "We need to find out more about Miss Reeves," he said.

"The guy, too," Devonne added.

Fish nodded. "Yeah, the guy, too."

Shug stared absently across the bar at a handful of mid-afternoon customers, his fingers still resting on the telephone. Frank had called back within thirty minutes and shared the information he'd gotten from Detective Stamey. The evidence was circumstantial, yes, but Juanita Reeve's positive identification and statement were damning. Period. End of story as far as the police were concerned, but not for Shug. He picked up the receiver and punched in Owens' number once more.

"Hello again, Shug," Owens said.

"How'd you know it was me?"

"ESPI," Owens said.

"I've heard of Extra Sensory Perception, but what's the I for?"

"It's Extra Sensory Police Intuition. I could tell from your voice you weren't satisfied with the information I gave you." Owens paused for a second, then sighed loud enough to be heard over the phone. "Just like I can tell you're gonna continue to bug the shit out of me until you get whatever it is you want."

"So, are you going to help me?"

"Do I have a choice?" Owens said.

Owens pulled up what information there was in the files about Tyrell Lee Burton and Juanita Reeves. Burton had been arrested twice for possession of illegal drugs, one of those for possession with intent to distribute, and had spent eleven months in the Wayne County Detention Facility. Information on Juanita Reeves proved more difficult. She had no police record, but Owens put Shug on hold while he called a friend at the Wayne County administrative offices. County records showed only that Reeves was collecting welfare and aid to families with dependent children. Nothing that could be used to impugn her credibility.

"Sorry there isn't more," Owens said. "Devonne always seemed like a nice kid."

"I appreciate your help, Frank."

"Yeah, well, I guess now I can spend what's left of the day protecting and serving the other million people that live in this city."

Shug hung up the phone, came out from behind the bar, and did something he'd not done in the eight years he'd owned the place. "Guys," he said. "I'm sorry, but I have to close up for a while. Nobody has a tab today; the drinks are on the house. But I have to ask you to leave." When the last of the customers had gone, he placed the *Closed* sign in the window and locked the door behind him. Then he cranked up the Olds and turned out into the traffic.

Twenty minutes later, he pulled in thirty yards away and on the opposite side of the street from Juanita Reeves' house and killed the engine. He'd driven there only because he didn't know what else to do. Burton was dead; Reeves was alive. And here he was, watching her house. *For what? What did he hope to accomplish?* He didn't know. Only that he had to do something. He sat in the car for almost an hour and was about to give up and go back to the bar when the front door to Reeves' house opened. He sat up straighter in the seat.

A black woman came out, looked casually up and down the street, then pulled the door shut and got into a battered Chevy Nova with rusted-out quarter panels. Shug started his car and waited until the Nova was making a left at the end of the block, then gunned the Olds forward to keep her in sight. He stayed half a block behind her until she turned onto a major through-street, then he fell in a few cars back.

He wasn't even sure it was the Reeves woman, but it was all he had at the moment, so he stayed with her. When she turned into the parking lot at the Greyhound terminal, he coasted on by and parked on the street. After a minute, she got out of her car and headed for the terminal.

Shug followed, thinking *where was the kid?* He stopped outside the entranceway and peered inside the terminal, putting his hands up against the glass doors to block out the light. The woman went directly to a bank of lockers on the far wall. She opened one of the lockers, extracted a duffle bag roughly the size of an airline carry-on, and headed back toward the entrance. Shug ran back to his car, and, when the woman pulled back out onto the street, followed her home.

Got to be drugs, he thought. *What else would she stash in a locker at the bus station when she had a house?* As the woman reentered her home, he caught a brief glimpse of a small girl before the door closed. *Left by herself?* How old had Devonne said the girl was? Four? Five? Way too young to be left in the house alone. Shug slammed the gear shift lever into first and disengaged the clutch. He needed to talk with Leon.

Leon was standing on the sidewalk staring at the *Closed* sign when Shug slipped into a space on the opposite side of the street. Shug waited for a car to pass, then sprinted across the pavement.

"What the hell's this?" Leon asked.

"I closed the bar to follow the Reeves woman."

Leon lowered his head and looked at Shug over the top of his sunglasses. "You what?"

Shug dug in his pocket for his keys. "C'mon inside. I'll explain." As the two men entered, Shug asked, "How's Devonne?"

"Not good. He was held over for a preliminary hearing without bail." Leon slammed his softball-sized fist down on top of the bar. "I couldn't do a goddamned thing!"

Both men were silent for a moment, then Shug said, "I followed the Reeves woman to the bus station. She got a bag from one of the lockers and took it back to her house. I think it was full of drugs." Adding, a second later, "She left the kid at home by herself."

"Who knows about this?" Leon asked.

"Me. Now you."

"Well, we gotta tell somebody."

Shug stepped over to the phone, shaking his head, already hearing the detective's sarcastic response in his mind. "I'll call Frank Owens."

Shug talked for a while, then listened, then talked some more. Leon paced the whole time. Shug hung up the phone. "Owens says it's not enough for a search warrant. Besides, he'd have to convince Stamey to pursue it, and Stamey's happy with what they got."

"Meaning Devonne," Leon said.

Shug nodded. "Meaning Devonne."

Leon paced some more, then checked his watch and grabbed the telephone. "Maybe I can catch Janelle before she leaves the office."

"Who?" Shug asked.

Punching in the numbers, Leon said, "One of Devonne's lawyers."

"Fish and Williams." In spite of the moment's urgency, that soft mid-western drawl caused Leon to picture Janelle in his mind.

"Janelle," he said, "this is Leon Tweed. There've been some new developments." He spent three minutes telling her about Shug's surveillance efforts, adding, "We tried the police but got no help there. They say it's not enough for a search warrant."

"What you need," she said, "isn't a search warrant. All you need is to get inside the house, see what's going on."

"Can you do that, get us inside?"

"Probably not, but hold on a minute. What time is it?"

"Five minutes to five."

"Stay on the line, Mister Tweed. I'll be back."

There was a click and Leon's ear filled with an elevator-music version of "Stairway to Heaven." Janelle was back before the song ended.

"Here's the deal," she said. "In twenty minutes, Miss Reeves will get a visit from Thelma Sayer of Wayne County Child Protective Services. She'll be investigating a report that the child has been left alone in the house for extended periods. Can't guarantee she'll find a thing, but she knows what to look for. Maybe she'll get lucky."

"Great," Leon said. "I don't know how to thank you."

"Don't thank me. Thank God I know a public servant who's more interested in a kid's welfare than in going home on time."

"I think we'll go over there," Leon said, "to the Reeves woman's house, see what happens."

"You won't be able to go in," Janelle said.

"Yeah, but it'll feel like we're doing something at least."

"Tell you what," Janelle said, "I'll be down on the sidewalk in two minutes flat. Pick me up."

A smile broke over Leon's face. "Look for an Olds 442, black vinyl over bronze. Two minutes."

The three of them pulled into the same spot where Shug had parked earlier.

"I had thought there'd be crime scene tape all over the place," Shug said.

"Not necessarily," Janelle said. "They're in and out pretty quickly, and when they have an eye witness account and a solid suspect, there's no reason to keep the scene preserved for an extended period of time."

They'd been there less than five minutes when a gray Taurus sedan slowed and stopped in front of Reeves' house. The woman who got out looked to be in her early thirties, stout, with serious glasses and a black bag that could have been either a briefcase or a purse.

"Thelma and I were roommates in college," Janelle said.

The woman went up and knocked on the door to the house. She waited briefly, then knocked again. A minute passed. She knocked a third time. Nothing happened. Another minute passed. Sayer stepped off the small porch and retraced her steps along the walkway.

"She's leaving," Shug said. "Isn't there something else—"

Then, before anyone could reply, the woman paused at the fence gate, turned and started across the weed-filled yard. Seconds later, she disappeared around the side of the house.

They waited.

After a few minutes, Leon looked at Janelle, sitting in the back seat. "Should we go check on her?"

"Give her a while," Janelle said, adding, "She knows how to take care of herself. We took karate together."

Leon and Shug exchanged glances. Leon raised his eyebrows. He thought of the photo of the kids on her desk and wondered if they were hers.

There was nothing else to do while they waited, so they talked. Janelle told them she'd done her undergraduate studies at the University of Indiana, where she majored in political science. She'd applied for law schools in Chicago and Detroit because she was tired of living in "corn country," and she was accepted at both Loyola and Wayne State Universities.

Leon sat with his back against the passenger side door, his left arm resting on the top of the Olds' bucket seat. "So, why'd you choose Detroit? Loyola's supposed to be a great school."

She reached up and touched his arm. "Motown, baby. I love that sound."

He grinned at her, then felt guilty for doing so; Devonne was still in jail, and here he was staring at this beautiful woman, thinking now she looked even better than Lena Horne.

He was about to tell her about his collection of Motown albums when he heard the first wail of the siren and saw the orange and white ambulance make the turn at the end of the block. It howled to a stop in front of Reeves' house and two paramedics ran toward the front door.

Leon and Shug were halfway out of the car when Janelle yelled, "No! Wait!" She pointed at the house. "Look, there."

Thelma opened the front door, holding Necie's hand, and the paramedics disappeared inside. Moments later, one of the men came out and retrieved a gurney from the back of the truck. Five minutes after that, they wheeled the Reeves woman out, oxygen and IVs going, and slid her into the vehicle.

"That's Reeves," Shug said. "I recognize her from earlier."

The ambulance sped away and was replaced less than two minutes later by an unmarked Crown Vic. A bulky figure emerged from the car.

"That's Stamey," Leon said, watching as the man made his way across the yard and into the house. "Should we go over, try to find out what's happening?"

"I think not," Janelle said. "I'll try Thelma later and see what she can tell us. Frankly, right now, guys, I could use a drink."

"You got it," Leon said as Shug turned over the big engine. "And it's on the house."

Shug and Leon reopened the bar. An hour and a half later, Janelle sat on one of the four-legged stools, phone to her ear, getting the details from Thelma Sayer. Leon and Shug sat across from her behind the bar, trying to make sense of the one-sided conversation.

"Thanks, Thelma," Janelle said. "I owe you a favor." She replaced the receiver and took a delicate sip of her beer. "Okay, here's the story. When she didn't get a response to her knock, she went to the back door and tried it. It was locked, but she kept knocking, and finally the little girl came into the kitchen and was able to let Thelma in." Janelle took another small sip of her beer. "Apparently, the front door was dead-bolted, but the back door wasn't. Thelma found Miss Reeves unconscious on the sofa, OD'd, the tubing still draped around her arm. Thelma called nine-one-one, got an ambulance moving, then notified the police. Reeves was still breathing when they carted her off, but Thelma doesn't know anything more about her condition. She waited until the detective arrived, gave her story, and then left."

"What about Necie?" Shug asked.

"She'll be placed in a Child Protective Services facility tomorrow and then in foster care as soon as possible. For tonight, she's staying over with Thelma."

"Devonne would be glad to know she's out of there," Leon said, thinking about his nephew having to spend the night in a jail cell. "Wish I could tell him."

"Tomorrow," Janelle said. "You can tell him about it tomorrow." She finished her beer and blotted her lips with a napkin. "Speaking of tomorrow, I have an early appointment in the office. I should probably go."

"You have to leave right now?" Leon asked. "The office workers'll clear out of here in another half an hour, then Shug can handle the place by himself for a few minutes. I'll walk you back to your car." He glanced at Shug, who was studying record selections on the juke box over near the restrooms. "That okay with you, Shug?"

"Uh-huh, sure," Shug said, rummaging in his pocket for change.

"Well," Janelle said, "I suppose I could stay for—"

Janelle was interrupted by the first strains of Marvin Gaye's "Pride and Joy" pumping through the Rock-Ola's speakers. She turned to look at Shug and smiled.

"Motown, baby," he said, his face reflecting the soft reds and yellows of the jukebox lights. "We got dozens of 'em."

The office workers hung around longer than usual that evening. It was nearly nine when Janelle started gathering her things for the walk back to her car. Leon wiped his hands on a bar towel and had just grabbed a light jacket when the front door opened and his nephew walked in, followed by Detective John Stamey.

"Devonne!" Leon exclaimed. He tossed the jacket aside and hugged the young man tightly. "What's happened? How'd you get outta jail?"

Stamey, hovering close by, cleared his throat and said, "I can explain, Mister Tweed, if you'll permit me."

Leon glanced at Janelle, asked, "Can you wait while I—"

"Are you kidding? I'd wait all night to hear this. Please go ahead, Detective Stamey."

They all settled around one of the tables, Stamey seeming a little awkward but sounding professional as he laid out the sequence of events.

"I found drug paraphernalia on the coffee table, which provided me with probable cause to look around. In one of the closets, I found a duffle bag with over a kilo of heroin in it. The bag had been opened, and the Reeves woman had used some of it to shoot up. Turns out it was the pure stuff, uncut, and that's what caused her to OD."

Leon sighed. "And she did this in front of the little girl."

Stamey nodded. "Yeah, the kid referred to it as 'Auntie Juanita's medicine.' Apparently it was a regular thing. Anyway, I saw Miss Reeves in the emergency room after she'd come around." He looked at Janelle. "By the way, miss, if your friend hadn't gone over to check on the little girl, Reeves would be dead by now."

"And I'd still be in jail," Devonne added.

"Yeah," Stamey agreed. He cleared his throat again. "Uh, you think I could get a beer or something? It's been a long day."

"For us, too," Shug said, but he went to the bar, drew a tall draft, and brought it back for the detective.

Stamey took a long drink, wiped his mouth with a hand, and continued. "When I confronted her about the smack, she broke down and told me everything. She and Burton had a history, lived together off and on. He used her to pick up drugs coming in from out of state, which he cut and sold to street-level dealers. To make a long story short, she ripped him off. Took possession of an incoming shipment and put it in a locker she'd rented at the bus station, but not the one he had a key for."

Stamey gave Devonne a guilty look. "After Devonne left the house, she came out of the bedroom and found Burton unconscious on the floor. She was frightened for her life, she said, got the knife from under the sofa, and, well, I guess you can figure out the rest."

The table was silent for a moment, then Janelle asked, "What about Necie? Did she see any of this?"

"Nah," Stamey answered. "She stayed in the bedroom the whole time, didn't see anything."

Another long silence settled over the table. Stamey drained the rest of his beer and looked from one person to the other, resting his gaze finally on Devonne. "I hope you can understand. It all seemed very plausible at the time, the abrasions on your hands, her account of the fight. I really had no choice."

Devonne nodded. "I'm just glad to be out and back here with my friends."

Stamey looked at his watch. "Yeah, well, like I said, it's been a long day." He pulled a wallet from his inside coat pocket. "How much for the beer?"

"There's no charge for the beer, detective," Leon said. "We appreciate your bringing Devonne back."

Stamey got out of his chair. "Well…" He seemed about to say more, then changed his mind and went out the front door.

Devonne looked around the table, grinning now. He stopped when he got to Janelle. "Don't believe we've met."

Janelle extended her hand. "Janelle Williams, of Fish and Williams, one of your attorneys for a few hours this afternoon."

Leon left to walk Janelle back to her car, and Shug filled Devonne in on everything that had happened since his arrest earlier that morning. The television played softly in the background, and Shug wondered if Burton's murder might make the ten o'clock news, but doubted it. Drug-related murders were a dime a dozen in Detroit.

"I don't know what I would have done," Devonne said, "if it wasn't for you guys."

"There are a whole lot of people we can thank for the way things turned out," Shug said, thinking he owed Owens more than just a couple of free beers.

"I never thought I'd end up in jail when I started out to check on Necie this morning. It's hard to imagine her living like that, drugs in the house and all."

"Yeah," Shug said, "but she'll probably be all right now, maybe end up with a nice foster family, out of the bad neighborhoods."

Devonne leaned in closer. "Say, Shug, speaking of foster homes, I was wondering ... do you know what the requirements are for becoming a foster parent?"

Shug looked at the young man with new interest. "Why?"

Devonne shrugged. "I don't know. I was just thinking about Luther, all he did for me. I guess I was—"

Thinking he knew where this was going, Shug said, "I don't think single young men qualify as foster parents."

Devonne frowned and his shoulders sagged. "Yeah, that's what I figured."

"On the other hand, I've heard you remark about your mother, how lonely she's been since you and Cassie moved out, got your own places."

The beginnings of a smile played at the corners of Devonne's mouth.

"If it were up to me," Shug said, "I'd say Roberta would make a fine foster parent, especially if she had a bright young man around the house to help her out with things."

"You're right," Devonne said, his face beaming. He walked over and picked up the phone. "I'm going to call her, see if she'll arrange to meet with Miss Sayer and Necie."

"Uh, Devonne?" Shug said.

"Uh-huh?"

"If I were you, I wouldn't mention anything about today."

They had said little on the fifteen-minute walk back to Janelle's car, each perhaps recalling the day's almost surreal turn of events.

"That's it over there," Janelle said, pointing to a blue Firebird.

Leon walked over and ran a hand along the car's sleek, smooth front fender. "Nice. I wouldn't have picked you for a muscle car."

She walked over and stood next to him. "I like a little muscle. It enhances my self-esteem."

"Like you'd need that," he said, grinning at her in the glow from a mercury vapor streetlight.

She grinned back at him. "Well, it's been quite a day, hasn't it?"

He nodded.

"The way things worked out," Janelle said, "I guess you won't be needing our services any longer."

"I guess not. Professionally speaking, I mean."

"Professionally speaking?" Her eyebrows arched inquisitively.

"I meant to ask you, the photo of the kids on your desk. Are they—"

"They're my nephews," She smiled at him. "I'm not married."

Leon smiled back. "Say, I was wonderin'—there's this little R&B club I know of over on the Westside. Aretha Franklin used to stop in there sometimes and do a number or two with the boys. I was wonderin' if you'd like to go there with me sometime."

"Why, Mister Tweed," she said, looking up at him now, her eyes twinkling. "I was beginning to think you'd never ask."

"Call me Leon."

The Legacy: Long Time Gone
February 15, 1973

When he was young, Johnny Lavender had taken a lot of crap because of his name. Not now, though. At six-foot-three and two hundred seventy pounds, he was a bear of a man. Rough-looking, with shaggy hair and a scruffy beard, he wasn't the kind of guy who'd be approached for a handout, or anything else, for that matter—maybe even make a person want to cross the street.

He sat behind the bar, studying his accountant's quarterly report and having a post-closing Irish whiskey. Late like this, the place was unnaturally quiet.

"Hey, Johnny?"

Looking up from the numbers, the bar owner let his eyes rest on the dark-haired girl sitting at the nearest table. His scowl softened, and his gruff voice rumbled out low and slow, like distant thunder. "What is it, sweetheart?"

"Where is Hue, anyway?"

"Say that again, please?"

"Hue. In Viet Nam. Where's it at?"

"I don't know. Somewhere in the middle of the country, I think. Why?"

"I was just wondering." Her gaze returned to the creased sheet of paper in her hand.

Johnny had hired Bonnie Hall eighteen months before as a combination waitress and cage dancer. He'd pulled out the juke box, replaced it with a sound system, and renamed the bar Disco

Labrosse. The cage dancing thing had seemed like a good idea at the time but hadn't worked out like he'd planned. Bonnie was a great dancer, but he hadn't liked the way the customers looked at her.

Bonnie got up and moved onto the stool opposite him. "That'd be pretty safe, wouldn't it, being in the middle of the country?"

"Yeah," he said. "I guess that would be one of the safer places." *Over there*, he thought but would never say, *no place is safe*.

She'd met her soldier, Tom, over a year ago when he stopped for a drink on his way to the train station. Since then, the letters came like clockwork, two or three a month. First from California, then Viet Nam. She'd read them to Johnny, at least *parts* of them. He figured she left out some of the personal stuff. But the letter she held now had been the last one she'd received, well over a month ago. She didn't have to tell Johnny she was worried. He could see it in her eyes.

"I'm sure he's all right," Bonnie said. "I mean, letters get lost all the time, don't they?" She looked down at the stapled sheaf of papers on the bar. "What's that you're looking at?"

A small furrow creased Johnny's brow. "Quarterly report from my accountant."

"Oh yeah?" She gave him that cute little smile, the one that showed her dimples. "How're we doing?"

The furrow smoothed out. He couldn't help smiling back at her. Never could. "We're doing just fine." *She didn't need anything else to worry about.* "Disco's alive and well."

"Good. Well, I guess I should be going now."

She shrugged into her coat and fluffed her hair over the fake fur collar. She'd been wearing her hair in a gypsy cut that Johnny liked a lot. It gave her face a slightly exotic look.

"See you tomorrow," she said.

"G'night, Bonnie. Be careful going—"

The jangle of the telephone surprised both of them. Johnny picked up. "Disco Labrosse." A moment later, he handed her the phone. "It's for you." As she said hello, Johnny picked up his

Shug's Place

papers and disappeared into the darkened back room. He heard a small yelp, like that of a startled puppy, and sneaked a look. Bonnie was crying, then laughing, then dancing in a little circle. He retreated to the dark and waited. It seemed like forever. Then she called out.

"Johnny?"

He went to the doorway.

"He's back! In the states! In California! He wants me to come out there. He's wiring money for a bus ticket."

Johnny walked slowly back out into the bar area. "That's just great, sweetheart, just great."

She ran around behind the bar and hugged him. He let his hands slide over her back, feeling her shoulder blades, the delicate ridges along her spine.

"I've got to get some new clothes," she said, pulling away. "Can I get an advance on my paycheck, Johnny? Just a small one? Should I get my hair cut? They say it's warm all year round out there. I could—"

"Don't cut your hair," he said, swallowing hard. "It's fine. It's ... beautiful. You look beautiful." Johnny took out his money clip and peeled off five twenties. "Take this, my gift to you. I'll send your check to wherever. Just let me know."

"Thanks, Johnny!" The door slammed behind her and the bar again took on an eerie quiet. Johnny took a deep breath and let it out slowly. He looked over at the dance cage mounted in the corner next to the back bar. He'd taken her out of the cage months ago. Now, she'd flown away.

He wished he'd said something, done something. He downed the last of the Irish whiskey. It was cold and bitter on his tongue. But, anyway, what could he have done? She'd been his to look at, to talk to and share a drink with—but in her heart, she'd been a long time gone.

Over the next few months, Johnny Lavender remade himself. He permed his hair, bought several leisure suits, and had the dance cage removed and replaced with a disc jockey's booth. On weekends, he often sat in during DJ breaks, spinning records and calling himself the "Disco Bear."

The investment paid off. Profits improved and so did Johnny's spirits. In 1977, Disco Labrosse was selected as one of the location scenes for an independent movie production. If one listened closely, one could hear Johnny's voice in the background, introducing Thelma Houston's "Don't Leave Me This Way."

Bird with a Wing Down

The telephone jangled, and Shug's heart leapt in his chest even before his eyes snapped open. He didn't need the shroud of darkness covering him to know it was very early morning. The phone rang again. He threw the covers back and groped for the switch on the table lamp. He blinked in the light, checked the bedside clock: two-thirty. The phone rang a third time. He rubbed his face with his hands, then reached beyond the lamp and picked up the receiver.

"Hello," he said, his voice husky with sleep.

Nothing.

He waited.

Still nothing.

After a few seconds, he placed the instrument gently back in its cradle.

How many was that? He couldn't remember. It had taken a while for him to recognize the pattern, although he could hardly call it that. It was days, sometimes weeks between calls, but always between midnight and three.

He thought it simply a nuisance caller in the beginning and considered having his number changed. But then he wondered, or maybe hoped, *what if it was Darcy?* Darcy, trying to work up the courage to tell him she'd been wrong to refuse his help, to ask if they could forget all that and start fresh. Several times, he'd almost whispered her name into the phone. But he hadn't. Maybe he was the one running low on courage.

Shug got up and slipped into his sweats and running shoes. There'd be no sleep now, so he might as well do a few miles around the neighborhood. He actually liked running in the middle of the night. He liked the exertion and sweat and exhaustion that overtook him afterward and sent him back into a deep, untroubled sleep, *almost* always.

Darcy Rainwater placed the telephone receiver gently back in its cradle. How many times had she done it? Picked it up, held it for minutes on end, replacing it only when it began its obnoxious warble. What was she afraid of? *And that, Darcy, is the problem.* Not only did she not know what she was afraid of, she was afraid of finding out. That would require self-analysis, a laborious and painful process. *Hadn't she had enough pain already?*

She had convinced herself she'd come home to heal. What better place to forget about the nightmare she'd gone through than a comfortable home with her caring, loving mother? Someone who'd quell her fears, place a cool, smooth hand on her forehead, tuck her in at night with a kiss on her cheek. It had worked—for a while.

After more than a year, though, she'd grown restless, walking from window to window of her mother's two-story Victorian, looking out through the glass as if she expected to find answers in the occasional passing car or the boxwood hedges that ran along either side of the house.

Now, watching from the upstairs bedroom window as her mother worked in the garden, Darcy envied the woman's perpetual sense of tranquility. Darcy wasn't like that, never had been. She was her father's child.

Her mother looked up from where she knelt beside a patch of peonies and smiled, gesturing for Darcy to open the window. She did.

"Are you ready for lunch, dear?"

"I'm not very hungry."

"Nonsense," her mother said, still smiling, "you need to keep up your strength. I'll be right in and fix you some soup and a grilled cheese sandwich."

"Really, Mom, I'm—"

But her mother was already up and moving toward the back door. Darcy sighed, closed the window, and headed for the stairs.

Darcy took another small bite of the sandwich. The lump of cheese and skillet-grilled bread seemed to grow as she chewed. She choked it down with a swallow of freshly made lemonade and placed her napkin on the table.

"You've hardly eaten anything at all," her mother said.

"I just don't feel like eating."

Her mother rose and took their plates to the sink. "You'll need some fuel for your physical therapy session this afternoon."

The thought of another grueling two hours of pain and mind-numbing repetitions rested as a heavy weight on Darcy's shoulders. She'd been at it for months but still walked with a limp.

"I don't even know why I go," she said. "It's not doing any good."

Her mother came around behind the chair and massaged the tight cords of muscle in her daughter's neck. "Oh, Darcy, you're like a bird with a wing down. You have to heal before you can fly. It'll take time and patience, but it will all work out. You'll see."

How much time? How much more patience do I have? Darcy thought. *How long can I live here, sheltered from the world. How long can I hide?*

"You'll see," her mother said again.

The therapy session left Darcy sweaty and exhausted, depressed, too, despite the perky therapist's constant reassurances. She walked down the long corridor of the clinic, eyeing the all-too-familiar parade of infirm, trying with all her might not to favor her weak leg. *She wasn't like them, with their walkers, their crutches and canes, their wheelchairs and prosthetics. She was ... she was—*

The corridor floor seemed to shift beneath her, and, for a moment, she felt as though she were in one of the carnival fun-houses she had adored as a child. A prickly crawling sensation moved up along her spine and over her shoulders and lodged itself at the base of her skull. Then a red haze crowded the corners of her vision, and she put a hand out for support.

A strong arm encircled her waist, and the next thing she knew she was sitting in a chair with her head between her knees.

"Are you feeling better?"

Darcy took a deep breath and slowly raised her head. Her vision began to clear, and she became aware of a woman kneeling at her side. They were in an office reception area. The woman rubbed her back gently.

"You nearly fainted," the woman said.

"I just left a therapy session. Forgot to drink the juice. I guess I—"

"You're dehydrated," the woman said. "Let me get you a glass of water."

Darcy was aware of the woman leaving then coming back a few seconds later.

"Here, drink this."

Darcy took small sips of the water and gradually began to feel better. "Thanks, I owe you one."

The woman smiled. She was in her early forties, with prematurely graying hair pulled back into a French Twist. Not pretty, but pleasant, with a confident look about her.

"I'm Elaine Hurst. This is my office. I was just on my way out for a late lunch when you happened by."

"You're a doctor?" Darcy asked.

"Psychologist," the woman said, nodding.

"Well, I'm feeling better now. I suppose I should let you be on your way." Darcy tried to rise, but the red haze invaded her vision once more. She sat back down heavily.

"When did you eat last?" Doctor Hurst asked.

"Sometime late this morning, a little soup and a few bites of a sandwich."

"Stay right in this chair and don't move. I'll bring us both something from the cafeteria."

Darcy drained the last of her orange juice and folded the wrappings of her club sandwich into a neat package. "I don't know how to thank you, Doctor Hurst."

"Call me Elaine, please. It's a pleasure to meet you, Darcy."

"You know, while you were in the cafeteria, I was thinking how odd it was that I should just, out of the blue, fall into the arms of a psychologist."

Elaine raised her eyebrows. "Oh?"

It seemed to Darcy the classic clinical response. She smiled. Half an hour ago, talking to a psychologist was the last thing she would have considered. Now, although they'd spoken only of very non-clinical topics, Darcy felt comfortable and relaxed in Elaine's presence. It was different from what she felt talking to her mother, who, whatever else she was, would always be her mother.

"I was wondering," Darcy said, "if I wanted to see you professionally, would I need a referral?"

Elaine folded her hands one on the other and sat back in her chair. "I feel sure that can all be worked out. Have you seen a psychologist before?"

"No, never."

"It can be a rewarding experience," Elaine said, "but it's not always a walk in the park."

"I'm strong, Elaine. I can handle it."

Elaine nodded. "Yes, I can see that." She shuffled through the items on the desk and located a calendar. "Let's set you up with an appointment."

Three days later, Darcy entered Elaine's office for the second time. A middle-aged receptionist now sat at the desk where she and the doctor had previously shared lunch.

"I'm Darcy Raintree," she said. "Here for a one o'clock appointment."

The receptionist smiled. "Yes, Doctor Hurst is expecting you. Please go right in."

Darcy knocked lightly on the door and pushed it open. The doctor sat behind a dark-cherry desk. She rose from her chair and extended her hand.

"Hello, Darcy."

Darcy grasped the offered hand. It was warm and dry. "Good afternoon, Elaine." She took a few seconds to glance around the office. Recessed overhead lighting bathed the room in a cozy glow, and the air was tinged with a hint of cinnamon. The wall on her right was lined with book-filled shelving in the same finish as the desk. On the other wall, the less noticeable one, was a scattering of framed diplomas and certificates. They were put out of the way, almost as if to say, "I need to put them up, but I'm not trying to impress anyone." The rest of the office was personal. Elaine had photographs of what Darcy assumed were her husband and her children, all of whom appeared well-adjusted and happy.

"Please," Elaine said, "have a seat."

Darcy took one of the two visitors' chairs. "No therapy couch, huh?"

Still smiling, the doctor shook her head. "I hope you can be comfortable and relaxed without one."

"I guess we'll see," Darcy said. "So, how do we start?"

"With something easy," Elaine said. "Tell me about your childhood."

"It was normal. We had a nice house. I loved my parents and they loved me. I had everything a young girl could want."

"You were entirely happy?"

Darcy nodded. "Yes, I was until..."

"Until?"

Darcy looked down at her hands. "Until my father died."

"How old were you when that happened?"

"Fourteen," Darcy said. "He had a heart attack."

"That must have been hard on you," Elaine said. She got up, closed the blinds on the office's one window, and returned to her seat.

Darcy nodded again, still looking at her hands clasped together in her lap.

Doctor Hurst leaned back in her chair. "Why don't you tell me about your father? Anything that comes to mind."

"All right. I'll tell you what I remember most." She closed her eyes and began.

She remembered how her heart had thrummed in her chest as her father had taken a wrench and loosened the bolts that held the training wheels in place, twisting them up several inches off the ground and tightening them in place.

"Are you ready, Angel?"

She looked up at him. He was smiling down at her as she held the bicycle, one foot on the pedal, the other on the sidewalk. "I'm ready, Daddy."

He had steadied her as she started off, jogging along beside her for a few steps with his strong hand on her back. Then she began to get the hang of it, feeling more confident as she picked up speed and the two-wheeler stabilized as though it had a will of its own. She felt the wind in her hair and the *whump, whump, whump* as the tires bumped over the concrete sections of the sidewalk. *She was doing it! She was flying and the world had become her own.* She was halfway down the block when a black and white blur shot across one of the yards to her left.

A furious barking exploded in her ears. The creature—a huge and wild-eyed, ferocious thing—snapped angrily at her leg, spittle flying from its fanged mouth. She screamed and looked back over her shoulder for her father, and then came the awful screeching sound of metal grinding on concrete and she felt the skin being flayed from her hands, arms, and legs. And the thing was on her, snapping and barking. She could smell its rancid breath in her face.

It had all been so wonderful, but now she was going to die.

The barking changed abruptly to a strangled yelp. She opened her eyes. Her father had the dog by his collar, struggling to haul it off her.

One of the neighbors was running toward them yelling. "Max! Max! Stop that—stop that barking! Easy, boy, easy!" The man grabbed the dog and dragged it back into the yard while the animal growled, gnashed its teeth, and tried frantically to free itself.

Her father bent down and brushed the hair out of her face. "Are you all right, Angel? How bad does it hurt?"

Darcy began to cry. Her father picked her up and cradled her in one arm. He scooped the mangled bicycle up with his other hand and started back down the sidewalk toward their house.

"I'm real sorry about that, Mister Raintree," the neighbor called after them. "Max don't like bicycles."

Her father said nothing, just kept walking. Darcy heard the neighbor's voice again over her muffled sobs. "Probably shouldn't be riding on the sidewalk anyway. They're made for walkin'."

She felt her father's body stiffen, felt a slight shift in his gait, and then he continued on, finally delivering her into her mother's arms for cleaning and medicating.

Darcy had come out onto the front porch later, arms and legs stained orange with mercurochrome and spotted with Band-Aids and gauze bandages. Her father sat quietly in a metal porch chair, staring off into the distance. He smiled when he saw her.

"I'll have your bicycle fixed tomorrow."

"I don't want to ride it again, Daddy. I'm afraid of the dog."

"The dog won't bother you again, Angel."

"But how can you know that?"

"What did your father say then?" Elaine asked.

Darcy had been so caught up in the memory, it took her a moment to refocus on her surroundings. "He just looked me in the eyes and said, 'I'll take care of it.'"

"And did he?"

Darcy shrugged. "I never saw the dog again."

"What do you think happened to it?"

"I don't know. I just never saw him again. Maybe my father spoke to the animal control people. Maybe the neighbor got rid of him. It didn't matter what happened to the dog, anyway, as long as he didn't chase me anymore."

Elaine leaned forward in her chair and tapped a yellow pencil on the legal pad centered on her desktop. Darcy took the gesture as a signal that their session was over.

"Well, I think that's enough for today." Elaine stood, walked over to the office's window, and twisted the rod that opened the blinds.

Darcy blinked in the new light and stretched, feeling oddly relaxed. She'd been reluctant to attempt analyzing herself. Or maybe she'd just been lazy. But if someone else wanted to take a shot at figuring her out, well, that was a different story. *Have at it*, she thought. *Tell me something like "Darcy, you're a little bit neurotic, but then almost everyone is, so here's a prescription for what ails you. Take it and live happily ever after."* Therapy wasn't so bad. In a way, it was kind of fun.

Darcy dreamed that night. The dream started with her lying in her bed, the same bed, in fact, where she now lay. Only in the dream, she was six years old again and still sporting antiseptic stains and Band-Aids. She heard panting outside her open window and thought surely the neighbor's evil dog had come back for her. Even as she lay pretending to be asleep, she knew the monster was preparing to leap, red-eyed and snarling, through her window and finish its intended meal.

But the raspy panting diminished in her ears, and she thought maybe the creature had been distracted by some more fascinating repast—perhaps the pudgy five-year-old who lived across the alleyway that ran along the rear of their property. Then she heard a *chink*, a couple of seconds pause, and another *chink*, and another pause, and the noises continued on for several minutes. In her dream, the rhythm of the sounds lulled her back to sleep, and when she dreamed, a dream within a dream, it was of herself flying down the sidewalk on her bicycle.

"I suppose we should talk about the accident," Darcy said at a later appointment.

"The accident; is that how you refer to it?" Doctor Hurst asked.

"Well, I guess you could call it the incident, the event, or any other damn thing you want to. I prefer to call it the accident. Whatever you call it, it was what got me here."

"What do you mean by here?"

"Grand Rapids, my mother's house, physical therapy." Darcy shifted in her chair and glanced around the dimly lit room. "Your office, too, I guess."

Doctor Hurst nodded. "Go on, tell me about the accident."

Darcy did, beginning with the series of shotgun slayings, then the murder of Mike Connolly, the man who'd become a surrogate father to her, and ending with her own pursuit of the killer known as Smoothbore.

"I caught up with the guy as he was about to exit the alley. He fired one shot at me and made a run for his van. I was still in the mouth of the alley when he turned into it. I got off one shot, or maybe two, before he hit me with the vehicle." Darcy went silent for a moment, remembering that split second of panic just before she went careening against the brick wall of the alleyway. "I was in the hospital for just over a week."

"Why did you decide to come back to Grand Rapids?"

"I ... I'm not sure."

"Did your mother ask you to come back?"

"She said I'd be welcome and she'd help take care of me."

"Did you want to be taken care of?"

"I'm not sure what I wanted," Darcy said.

"And the man you had been seeing?"

"Shug."

"Did Shug offer to take care of you?" Doctor Hurst asked.

Darcy nodded. "He asked me to stay with him."

"But you chose not to do that. Any idea why?"

"No," Darcy said, looking down at her hands folded in her lap.

Doctor Hurst tapped her pencil on the pad. The session was over. Then she leaned back in her chair and said, "And the killer you were pursuing, he was never caught?"

Darcy looked up, felt her jaws tighten. "No."

The doctor rose and went over to open the blinds. For a moment, she stood with her back to the room, looking out into the clinic parking lot. Then she asked, "Do you still think about him?"

"Which one?"

"Either one," Doctor Hurst said.

"Yes, both of them. All the time," Darcy said.

Darcy knelt in the backyard and dug her trowel into the rich earth. Her left leg hurt, but working in the soil and the cool fall air lifted her spirits. And her mother was delighted that she was out of the house, getting some sunshine for a change. She pried a small rectangle of chrysanthemums from a black plastic casing and centered it in the freshly dug opening, molding the dirt up around the base of the planting.

"Do you still miss Daddy?" Darcy asked her mother, who was pulling weeds from a nearby row of monkey grass.

Her mother turned to her, smiling. "Every day. I've missed him every day for almost twenty years now. He was a good man, a good husband, a good father." She yanked out another patch of weeds. "Not much of a gardener, though. That was my bailiwick."

Her mother stood and walked over to a head-high plant virtually exploding with white trumpet-shaped blooms. "This Angel Trumpet was the only thing he ever planted in his life. Strangest thing it was, too."

Darcy got up, wincing slightly as she put weight on her leg, and joined her mother. "That's what he used to call me. I never knew he planted this."

Her mother nodded. "It was right after that dog chased you and made you fall off your bike. I came downstairs the next morning, and he was at the kitchen table, his hands and knees filthy with dirt. I said, 'Good Lord, Lester, what on earth have you been doing?' He looked up from his coffee and said, 'I've planted a flower, Mary. It's called an Angel Trumpet.'"

"I sat down at the table and asked him when and where he'd gotten a flower to plant, and he told me he'd gone to the nursery first thing that morning and picked it out. I was about to ask him why he'd do such a thing—he'd never taken an interest in flowers before—when he popped up from his chair and said, 'Come out and I'll show it to you.'"

Darcy gently touched one of the bright white blooms and leaned forward to catch its fragrance. "It smells wonderful."

"Yes," her mother said. "It was truly a beautiful plant from the very first, about three feet high then, and as full as you'd ever want. I was so impressed by its beauty, I forgot all about asking why your father had suddenly decided to take up gardening."

"Did he plant anything else?" Darcy asked.

Her mother turned and went back to the row of monkey grass. "No, that was the only thing." She shielded her eyes from the sun and looked back at the lush blooms. "It's a shame, though. I've never had a plant do so well as that one."

"Beginner's luck," Darcy offered.

"It's just as well, I suppose," her mother said. "Otherwise, he might have eaten us out of house and home."

"What do you mean?"

"When I went to fix lunch that day, most of the leftover roast I'd fixed the night before was gone. I asked about it and he just said, 'Planting's a hungry business.'"

A few days later, Elaine said, "Tell me about Mike Connolly."

"He was like a father to me."

"In what way?"

Darcy closed her eyes, remembering the sergeant's big, florid-cheeked face. "He watched out for me, taught me to be strong. He was like a rock, always there to hang onto when the waters got rough."

"Like your own father?"

"Yes, like my father was."

"But then," the doctor said, "like your father, he was gone, too."

Darcy nodded and remained silent.

"And when the waters got rough, the accident..." Doctor Hurst let the thought hang there, suspended in the air over Darcy like the Sword of Damocles.

Darcy sighed. "I came home. I ran. I hid."

They were quiet for a minute, then the doctor asked, "What were you thinking about Shug Barnes when you left Detroit?"

"I don't know. I've already told you that. I—" Her shoulders began to shake, and she felt the moisture welling up in her eyes. "I'm supposed to be *strong*. Not go running to a man every time something goes wrong." She snatched a tissue from the ever-present box on Elaine's desk and used it to wipe her eyes and nose.

"I can see where you're going with this," Darcy said. "You think I have some kind of father issues going on. Well, let me tell you one thing. I never thought of Shug as a father figure; that's for damn sure."

The doctor shrugged and smiled. "But you left him."

Darcy's cheeks grew hot, and she began to tremble with an irrational rage. She tried briefly to control it. "Yes, so?"

"I don't know," Doctor Hurst said. "You tell me."

Darcy pictured Shug in her mind, thought of his touch on her skin, so tender and soothing. She actually felt her anger ebbing away. That's what Shug did, calmed and relaxed her, like balm on an open wound. He was compassionate, gentle, and innocent. Not like her father, whom she now realized, had made absolutely certain the dog would never bother her or anyone else again. Not like Mike Connolly, either, who'd gone after the vigilante killer on his own. Both of the premier men in her life had suffered no restrictive moral compunctions. They'd simply taken care of business.

She recalled her conversation with Joel Melton in the hospital, when she'd worried that Shug might try to find Smoothbore. It must have been the medication she was on. Shug wasn't like that. He wouldn't hurt a fly.

So, why was she attracted to him? And why had she left? Her thoughts raced around in her head like a carousel—spinning, going nowhere.

"Darcy?" Elaine asked.

Darcy opened her eyes. "My leg is hurting. I'd better go." She got up from her seat and left the office.

When Darcy arrived home, she immediately picked up the telephone and dialed the number for the Detroit Police Department. She asked for Frank Owens and heard the *thunk* of the telephone receiver being placed on a desktop. In the background, the muted buzz of the Homicide Division squad room filled the dead air.

"Frank Owens," the voice said.

"Frank, it's Darcy Raintree."

"Darcy! How long has it been since we talked?"

"Almost a year," she said.

"Doesn't seem that long."

"It does when you're sweating in rehab three times a week."

"Oh, yeah, how's the leg coming along?"

"It's okay." *If I don't think about it.* "Say, Frank, I've decided to come back to work. Is Lieutenant Whitman still in charge?"

"Sure, who else? After seventeen years, his ass has become permanently attached to his desk chair. But, Darcy..."

"Yes?"

"We've got a full complement in the division right now. I'm not sure what's available."

"It doesn't matter," she said. "I've *got* to get back to work."

Two weeks later, Darcy was back on duty, assigned temporarily to the Detroit PD Fugitive Squad, an invention of the new police commissioner. The squad's sole task was to find and arrest known violent felons.

It hadn't been easy. She'd been away for a long time. But Whitman had gone to bat for her, and it hadn't hurt that she'd been Mike Connolly's protégé. *Even now*, she thought, *he's still helping.*

The assignment couldn't have been better, though she would've taken almost anything. As it was, she had a desk, a service weapon, and a degree of autonomy. It was made to order for her purpose.

Darcy read the Smoothbore file a second time, studying her notes and reports along with those Mike had contributed. It was still an open case after all these months, but there'd been no investigative activity for the past year. That was about to change.

He was hiding somewhere, biding his time, lying low. But sooner or later, he'd be driven to kill again. And when he did, she'd find him and kill him just as coldly as he'd killed Mike Connolly—as he'd tried to kill her. She closed the file and plucked her suit jacket from the coat rack. She was through for the day, officially. It would be dark in a couple of hours, though. She'd prowled Detroit's streets before. She could do it again.

The cold was getting to Darcy's leg. She switched the ignition on and cranked the motor of her car. A few minutes later, the heater kicked in, which helped a little. It had been three weeks since she'd reported for duty, and she'd spent most of her evenings doing exactly what she was doing now, cruising the back streets and alleyways of downtown. Stopping periodically and sitting, then picking another spot and repeating the procedure over and over until her eyes were so tired and her leg was so stiff she could do it no longer.

She had begged off her mother's invitation to come home for Thanksgiving, citing an arduous work schedule—which was the truth, really. The squad was under pressure to produce results. She and the unit's other three detectives had worked tirelessly to do just that. It had paid off. They'd brought in eleven felons with outstanding warrants. She'd been in on four of the arrests. It felt good to be back on the job, but the hollow place in her gut still gnawed at her. *He was here, somewhere. You don't just blow away five people and say, Well, I'm done with that.*

Darcy pressed a button on her watch, and the illuminated blue screen showed that it was a few minutes after eleven. The warm air from the heater was making her drowsy. She put the car in gear and pulled away from the curb. There was an alley halfway up the block. She cut her lights and turned into it, using the small yellow rectangle of light at the far end as her guide. Except for the rats, which she couldn't see but knew would brave any weather to ravage the dumpsters, the dark stretch was empty.

At the mouth of the alley, she paused and eased her car out to the edge of the street. Only a few people were out, bundled against the cold. She turned left and stopped again at the intersection. She glanced at the street signs glowing yellowish-green in the mercury vapor lights: Pine and Trumbull.

And thought of Shug.

Seven blocks south, she would find the familiar, cozy bar smelling of cigarettes, popcorn, and beer, and the soft glow of the lights reflected in the ebony bar top. Maybe an oldie would be playing low on the juke box. And Shug, with his boyish grin and hair pulled back in a ponytail, would be serving another round.

For the past few weeks, Shug had always been somewhere in the back of her mind. She'd kept him trapped there by working until she was totally exhausted and falling into bed practically asleep on her feet. Like a letter from a faraway lover, she had held his image in her head—loath to open the envelope for fear of the pain the message might bring but unwilling to toss it away for the promise it might hold.

Darcy looked to her left. She could be home in fifteen minutes and asleep in twenty-five. Her shoulders ached; her eyes burned. She rested her head on the steering wheel. After what seemed a long time, but probably was less than a minute, she turned south on Trumbrell. By the time she pulled up in front of the bar, her heart was beating at twice its normal rate.

Darcy got out and stepped to the bar's front window. Shug was behind the bar, head down, counting out money. He glanced in her direction, and she jumped back, her heart in her throat. The last thing she wanted was for him to see her staring through the window like a puppy waiting to be adopted. She almost ran back to her car. Then she steeled herself and pushed on the door. A young black man saw her and hurried over.

"We're about to close, ma'am, but—"

She gave him a tight smile and stepped inside. Shug looked up. As she watched, the color drained from his face. There was a subtle difference about him. His hair was shorter, neatly trimmed, and he'd gotten thinner. He looked good. She walked slowly over to the bar.

"Hello, Shug," she said. It was almost a whisper. Her hands were trembling.

A wide grin spread over his face. "Hello, Darcy."

She held her coat together as she slid onto a bar stool. "Mind if I sit down?"

He didn't answer right away, just kept staring at her like he couldn't believe she was there.

The last of the customers had gone, and they sat together in one of the booths. Shug had poured coffee for them. The young man, Leon's nephew she came to find out, turned off most of the lights and locked the front door behind him as he left.

Shug rotated the cup in its saucer, pushing it around with his forefinger so that the handle pointed at Darcy. "So ... how've you been?"

"It's hard to say," she answered. "Depends on your perspective, I guess." *Just ask my former head doctor.*

"From your perspective, then, how are you?"

"I've been pretty messed up for a long time, but I think I'm getting better. I'm back at work."

"Back with Homicide?"

"No, it's a special squad. We track down and arrest people with outstanding warrants, especially those wanted for violent crimes." She took a sip of the coffee. "It works well for me. On my own time, I've taken on one of the department's cooler cases. I'm sure you'll remember it—Smoothbore."

Something flickered behind his eyes when she said it. She wasn't sure what. It was something she couldn't read. *It's been a long time, Darcy. Maybe you never really knew him that well. Or maybe you've just forgotten.*

"I'm going to find him, Shug, sooner or later."

Shug rotated the coffee cup again, then picked it up, started to take a sip, and put it back down. He looked out across the bar. "How long have you been back?"

She'd known he'd ask the question. It had been part of the reason she'd put off seeing him. And the longer she'd put it off, the harder the question was to answer.

"A few weeks," she said.

He nodded slowly, but he still wasn't looking at her. *This is too hard*, she thought. She wanted to get up and run for the door.

"I thought about you lots," she said. "I almost called you dozens of times. I just..."

He turned to look at her then, and she saw something else in his eyes.

"I hoped that you would," he said. "I often thought..."

The look on his face made her heart feel as though something had grabbed hold and was squeezing the life out of her. *She couldn't do this!* She bumped out of her seat, sloshing coffee across the top of the table.

"I'm sorry, Shug." *Goddamn it!* She was starting to cry. "I shouldn't have come. This is not going well. I—"

Then he was up out of his seat and wrapping his arms around her, not letting her go. She stiffened for just a moment, then let herself fold into him. *Oh, God, it felt so good.*

Shug lay beside Darcy in his bed, twisting a strand of her dark hair between his fingers, her breath slow and regular against his chest. He stared at the ceiling, wondering if he might wake up and find it all a dream.

Standing beside the booth earlier, he had kissed the tears from her cheeks, holding her tight enough to feel her heart pounding. Then she'd lifted her face and he kissed her lips. She'd told him how sorry she was for everything. He'd been unable to say anything. He'd simply held her until she whispered in his ear, *I want you.*

He'd driven to his house with her car headlights in his rearview mirror. Thinking that, at any moment, the lights would fade or suddenly disappear. But they hadn't, and once inside, the two of them barely made it to the bedroom.

It was still hard for him to believe that Darcy was there, warm and soft against his body. He had lots of questions, but there would be time for that later. For now, he would sleep.

The ringing phone woke him a little after three a.m., Darcy still curled up by his side. He frowned in the dark. *If it hadn't been Darcy calling him in the middle of the night, then who?* He snagged the receiver from its cradle on the nightstand. But the phone kept on ringing.

Beside him, Darcy sat up in the bed. Shug flicked on the table lamp as Darcy leaned over and retrieved her purse from the floor. She pulled out what looked like a black brick and put it to her ear. "Raintree," she said.

She listened for a minute, said, "I'm on my way," and scrambled for her clothes.

"What's that?" Shug said, pointing at the black brick.

"Portable phone. The whole squad carries them now." She zippered her skirt and began buttoning her blouse.

"Where are you going?"

"One of our guys on a stakeout says he saw a man coming out of a house carrying what looked like a shotgun. He knew I'd be interested."

"But it's not Smoothbore. It can't be."

Darcy paused with her coat half on and stared at him. "Why can't it?"

"Because it's been too long. He's gone, Darcy, or ... dead, maybe."

"I don't think so," Darcy said. "He's out there, and I'll find him." She started for the door, then turned and came back and kissed him briefly on the lips. "I'll call you later."

Shug watched her disappear through the bedroom door and heard the front door close a moment later. *Déjà vu*, he thought, recalling a similar night months ago. This was a hell of a situation. He knew he should just tell Darcy what happened to Smoothbore, and who he really was—the current attorney general's son.

But, it wasn't just Shug involved. He had to consider Leon and Devonne, and Devonne's buddies, Faro and Ju-Ju. He didn't want those two ticking off a list of possible names, wondering who'd dropped the dime on them. But it was more than that, too. Something he'd learned when he was young.

Shug's great uncle had been employed by the United Auto Workers Union back in the '30s and '40s. He'd been in his seventies, and suffering from Alzheimer's when he'd taken a teenaged Shug aside. The man's eyes narrowed as he glanced around to make sure no one was listening, and then gleamed with a devilish light. *If you ever, ever, ever have to kill a man*—he winked at Shug conspiratorially—*don't never tell a living soul about it, no matter how great the temptation.* At the time Shug had dismissed the incident as senility. Then, at the old man's funeral, he'd overheard two union members talking and wasn't so sure.

Shug had never killed anyone outside of combat, but he'd been tightening the trigger on Smoothbore's back before Faro stopped him. It was close enough, he figured, and he couldn't shake his great uncle's caution.

The black man sitting cuffed to the chair across from her was giving Darcy a baleful stare. He fixed her with flat, expressionless eyes, unblinking, trying hard to maintain an air of casual indifference to his current situation.

Darcy might have stared back with a cop's practiced smugness, but she didn't. In fact, she didn't give a rat's ass that the guy had tried to blow another guy to kingdom come. She was deflated.

A domestic disturbance, that's all it had amounted to, *a goddamned domestic disturbance.*

She'd arrived at the scene scant minutes after she had gotten the call, stoked and ready for action. Two patrol units were already there, light bars blazing. Turned out the guy's wife had placed a call to nine-one-one and given them an address. Darcy had followed the uniforms up a flight of stairs and found the poor dumb fuck of a husband trying to bust another guy's door in with the butt of a shotgun. Fortunately for everyone involved, the husband had given up peacefully.

Darcy thought the man's anger was rekindling itself, though, now that he'd had a chance to stew for a while. She glanced over at him as he lifted his chin and looked at her through hooded eyes.

"Dude was messin' with my wife," he said.

Darcy said nothing.

"Dude be messin' with *your* wife, you'da done the same thing."

She could have argued the finer points of what was wrong with that statement, but instead she said, "No, I wouldn't; I'd have used something that wouldn't buy me as much jail time as a twelve-gauge. Like, say, a baseball bat."

The man blinked. Then he looked off to one side, and the corner of his mouth curled into a small grin. He turned back to her and nodded.

"Yeah, I like that," he said, grinning wider now, "a baseball bat."

The door opened on her left, and one of the two uniforms she'd been with earlier in the evening stepped in. "We're ready to take him for processing now. Thanks for babysitting."

Darcy got up. "Too bad," she said, passing the cop. "We were just beginning to build a rapport."

A moment later, Darcy pulled the portable phone from her purse and dialed Shug's home number, moving to a quiet corner as she did so. The clock on the wall behind the night sergeant's desk read twenty minutes to four.

"It's me," she said. "Did I wake you?"

"No, I was awake. Are you okay?"

"I'm fine. It was nothing, really, a false alarm, a simple domestic problem, suspect in custody."

"What now, are you coming back here?"

Suddenly, Darcy had never felt so tired. "No. I'd better get some sleep. I've got a full day tomorrow."

"All right, then," Shug said. "Talk to you tomorrow?"

"Yes, tomorrow," she said and ended the call.

Shug sat on the side of his bed with the silent telephone receiver in his hand, staring at it as if it were a mysterious foreign object that had affixed itself to his body. He dropped it back into its bedside cradle and got up and walked into the kitchen for a drink of water.

He'd gone most of the evening halfway wondering if he'd wake up and find himself coming up from a dream. Then, after they'd made love, with Darcy lying beside him in the dark, he'd begun to think it was for real. But then she'd raced out of the house after the phone call, *and the look on her face...*

He heard a soft *meow* behind him and turned to find Midnight sitting in the kitchen doorway. Framed in a shaft of light coming from the bedroom, the cat was watching him solemnly, questioningly, it almost seemed.

"I don't know, buddy. What do *you* think?"

The cat said nothing.

Shug opened a cabinet, got down a box of dry food, and poured some into the cat's bowl. Then he sat down on a kitchen chair and listened in the darkness to Midnight's methodical crunching.

He didn't know what else to do.

Alone in the car, winding her way back to her small apartment, Darcy replayed the last five hours. The almost paralyzing fear of seeing Shug again, then the relief she'd felt when he'd taken her into his arms. And the sex—it had been a long time for her and she'd been more than ready, even if she hadn't thought much about it—the sex had been great.

Then she'd gotten the telephone call and had morphed into Darcy the Avenger again, running on a dangerous mixture of hot adrenalin and the cold desire for revenge. And, just like with a drug, the inevitable crash came afterward.

She wondered how the sage Doctor Hurst might have analyzed her actions with regard to each set of circumstances. She smiled, musing on that for a while. *So, what do you think, Darcy?* "Well, Elaine," she said aloud, "I think being with Shug was a reactive response on my part. The other, when I thought I might find Smoothbore, and tore out of Shug's house with blood in my eye, I'd call that proactive, wouldn't you?"

Eve Campbell took another bite of the energy bar and a small sip of the soda she'd packed earlier that morning. Her butt was sore, her back was stiff, and she had to pee, but she couldn't afford to leave the car and risk missing her target, not after spending the better part of a day watching the house.

Over the past few weeks, she'd done a lot of calling, a lot of networking with sources she never thought she'd use again. All for one reason—to find Eric Farber. She was the prey turned hunter, forced into a corner by overwhelming circumstances, fighting against all odds for life itself.

That's exactly what she was doing, she thought, fighting for her life—the life before she'd started running, always looking over her shoulder and masquerading as someone else. She just wanted to be Eve Campbell again, to sign her real name to a check, or to a lease, or to a painting. There was something else, too. There was Shug Barnes. It was ridiculous, she recognized, to expect anything from a man she'd known for only a few hours over two years ago. But it was her way of escaping the blandness of her existence. She wanted love, or at least affection, and companionship. Someone to watch TV with, or go for ice cream with, or feel the weight of beside her in bed. If nothing else, Shug had reawakened some suppressed longing inside Eve, had made her want more. And she realized she could never have Shug, or anyone else, as long as Eric Farber remained free.

So, here she was, camped out in her car a hundred yards from a small, wood-frame house on the outskirts of Seattle, waiting for a glimpse of the man who had made her life a living hell for so many years. Over the last six hours, not so much as a door had opened nor a window shade been raised. *Was her information wrong?* She wondered.

A flash of light in the side mirror of her car caught Eve's attention. A USPS truck made its way down the rural road, leaving a red-clay dust plume in its wake. Eve ducked below the dashboard as the truck passed and sat up again just as it stopped at the mailbox of the house she'd been watching.

A moment later, her patience was rewarded. The front door of the house opened, and a man emerged. Eve lifted the binoculars to her eyes. The figure strode to the mailbox. Her heart soared.

It was him!

She noted the slight limp as he walked, and a grim smile stretched her lips. She was glad now she hadn't killed him that night outside Atlanta. That would have solved one problem but created another: the specter of her old life brought into the light of day. This was better—an anonymous telephone call to the local authorities, pinpointing the location of a man who'd been on the FBI's list of wanted criminals for more than a decade.

Eve waited until Farber had returned to the house, then started her car and headed for the nearest pay phone.

Shug glanced at the bar's television screen as the Channel 4 news crew lapsed into their usual cheery banter in the last half-minute of the show. "So, Mary, got your Christmas shopping done?" The anchor showed a perfect set of blindingly white teeth.

The co-anchor flashed back with her own glistening smile. "Almost there, Chuck, but I'm kind of a last-minute shopper. I love getting out on Christmas Eve."

Chuck nodded and turned back to the camera. "Well, for those of you who prefer less chaotic shopping, don't forget, there're only six days left before the big day." He picked up a thin sheaf of papers from the anchor desk and tapped them into a neat package. "And that's it for now. We'll be back at eleven. Stay tuned for the NBC evening news."

Shug picked up the remote and lowered the volume. "So, Leon, got your Christmas shopping done?"

Leon gave him a smile that was more scary than cheerful. "Not yet, but I'm out every night now, breaking into people's cars and takin' their stuff. It's kind of like having some of them, what you call 'em, personal shoppers."

"That's my man," Shug said, "filled with the holiday spirit."

"Yeah," Leon said. "Speaking of the holiday spirit, how you and the lovely Miss Raintree doin' these days? Seems to me like you up one day and down the next. After the pining you did when she left, seems like you ought to be happy, now she's back."

"I am. Happy, I mean. We're fine when we're together. It's just that Darcy's got a heavy workload right now."

"Preoccupied, huh?"

"Who, me or her?"

"One of you, for sure," Leon said.

"What are you talking—"

A muffled explosion came from the TV, and both men turned to look. The picture was filled with smoke and flames. Burning debris shot skyward, then arced down to the ground like Fourth of July fireworks.

"That was earlier today," the NBC anchor said. "Now, let's go live to the scene, Seattle's King 5 TV affiliate, Raymond Lewis, reporting."

The on-location reporter appeared on the screen. Behind him were police and fire vehicles with light bars flashing and, beyond that, the smoldering ruin of a house. As he began his lead-in, a smaller window appeared showing the photo of a man in his early twenties, long hair and beard, dressed in a fatigue jacket and jeans. The caption under the photograph read: Eric Farber.

Shug grabbed the remote again and increased the volume.

"And so, John, according to the Seattle Police Department, the body found in the ruins of this modest rural home is reportedly that of Eric Farber, a long-sought former member of the Weatherman activist group which claimed responsibility for several politically motivated bombings in the early 1970s. Farber, in particular, was alleged to have been involved in a car bombing in Illinois that resulted in the death of police officer James..."

Leon moved closer to the TV. "That's a hell of a—"

"Wait," Shug said. "Let me hear this."

The reporter went on to tell of the police surrounding the house based on an anonymous tip, and the standoff that ensued— a standoff that ended with the earlier explosion and the house being engulfed in flames.

"Police officials speculate that Farber blew up the house, and himself, to avoid capture. A violent life, ended violently." The serious-faced reporter gave a brief nod to the camera. "Back to you, John."

Leon was speaking again, but Shug's mind was somewhere else, thinking back over two years ago to a secluded house near Mount Clemons where his own world had nearly exploded— and to a chestnut-haired girl named Eve.

It was near dark when Darcy left the police headquarters building and found her car in the parking lot. She was about to slide inside when she heard footsteps behind her, and a familiar voice called her name.

"Darcy."

She turned and managed a tired smile. "Hello, Frank."

Frank Owens walked over and leaned an elbow on the roof of her car. "For someone working in the same building, I haven't seen much of you lately. How's it going?"

"Busy," she said. "We're experimental, you know? Have to prove ourselves every day."

Frank nodded. "Well, from what I hear, the squad's doing a great job. Almost too good, if you know what I mean."

"What?"

"Oh, just the usual department politics, some insecure lieutenants and captains jealous about you guys stealing their collars, that's all. It's nothing, really."

Darcy bristled. "If they'd made their collars in the first place, those scumbags wouldn't be on the streets."

Owens held up his hands in a gesture of surrender. "Hey, it's not me. I'm all for you guys. The more arrests you make, the better my chances of living to collect my pension."

"I'm sorry. I'm just tired. Forgive me?"

"Sure." Owens started away, then paused and said, "I hear you and Shug Barnes are seeing each other again."

"Yeah, for a couple of weeks now."

"Good. He's a decent guy."

"Yeah," Darcy said and watched as Owens waved and disappeared among the rows of parked cars. She got in, cranked the engine, and sat for a minute. Her left leg was aching badly. She massaged it, digging her fingers into the damaged muscle. *Frank's right*, she thought, *Shug is a decent guy. Maybe too decent.*

"Get over it, Darcy," she said aloud. "Self-analysis is not your strong suit." She pulled out into the street, thinking it would be nice seeing Shug later, curling up beside him in his bed, feeling his warmth as she drifted off into some much-needed sleep. But for the next few hours, she had work to do.

It was full dark now. He was out there somewhere. She knew it in her heart. She would find him. And when she did, she would kill him.

The Legacy: Feels Like Home
October 18, 1981

So, we thought we'd stop by the bar and say hello, if that's all right. The funeral is on Friday, so it'll probably be Saturday afternoon. Can't wait to see you (and the old place). Hey, you still have the dance cage?
Affectionately,
Bonnie

"Who's the letter from?"

Johnny Lavender slipped the folded note back into its envelope and tucked it into his shirt pocket. "Just a woman who used to work here back in the early seventies. She's flying in for her grandfather's funeral later this week and planning to come by here on Saturday."

"Hmmm. An old flame, maybe?"

Johnny walked over and slid his arms around his wife's trim waist. "Nah, she was way too young for me. Anyway, she's bringing her husband and little girl with her."

Carol Lavender smiled coquettishly. "You sure?"

He kissed the tip of her perfect nose, wondering how in the world he'd ever gotten so lucky. Then he gave her a rakish grin. "Well..."

"Okay, big guy. That settles it. I'll make sure *I'm* here on Saturday afternoon." Carol shouldered her purse and turned toward the door, then paused. "Oh, and don't forget, you need to make sure the bank wired the funds to the Florida mortgage company."

"I'll do it this afternoon," Johnny said. "Love you, babe. See you tonight."

After his wife left, Johnny turned slowly, studying the bar's interior. He'd miss the place. He'd had some fun times and made a comfortable living, but he wouldn't miss the winters. He was looking forward to a warmer climate.

Johnny's hand went absently to the letter in his pocket. He wondered if Bonnie had changed much in eight years. He'd stopped missing her a long time ago, but he wouldn't mind seeing her again. Maybe he'd get a haircut.

The bar wasn't busy on Saturday afternoon, and, for once, Johnny was glad. True to her word, his wife Carol had come in just after noon. "To help out at the bar and give you more time to visit," she'd said. It made him smile. She wasn't the jealous type, nor did she have any reason to be, but he noticed that she'd gone to a few extra pains to look good.

Bonnie, along with her husband, Tom, and daughter, Carrie, arrived promptly at two o'clock. Bonnie still looked great—and happy. She gave Johnny a big hug, and they all sat down at one of the tables for beers and a coke for Carrie. Bonnie glanced quickly around the room. "Gosh, this feels almost like home."

"I hope you don't mind," Tom said, "but I asked a friend of mine to meet us here. We were together in Nam, and I haven't seen him since I came back to the States in seventy-three."

"Not at all," Johnny said. "We can always use a new customer." He swept an arm around at the elaborate sound system speakers, the immobile disco ball over the dance floor, and the nearly empty bar. "Business has been slow. Disco's out, you know. I could renovate, I suppose, but we've decided to hang it up and move to Florida."

Bonnie touched Carol's arm. "You'll love the warmer weather. That's why we decided to stay in California. And *everything* grows there. I can't even kill a houseplant."

"Oh? Do you have a flower garden?" Carol gushed. "Maybe you could help me figure out what kinds of plants and flowers I'll want."

Johnny glanced at Tom and rolled his eyes. Tom smiled, nodded, and took another sip of beer.

Shug's Place

Jeffery Barnes pulled in at the curb in front of Disco Labrosse. He sat there for a moment, listening to the tick of the engine cooling and inhaling the new-car smell of his one post-discharge indulgence, a new Chevy Sport Coupe. He remembered this part of town well. His grandmother had lived in the next block, and they'd come to Mack's Grill for hamburgers when he was a kid. He thought he remembered the bar, too, but it was called something else back then.

He'd been both pleased and surprised when Tom Samuels called earlier in the week and asked if they could meet for drinks. Best buddies in Viet Nam, they had fallen out of touch over the years. It would be good to see him again.

Barnes got out of the car and opened the door to the bar. The inside lighting was subdued, and it took a moment for his eyes to adjust.

"Shug!" a voice called out. "Over here."

To his right, he saw his friend, Tom, at a table near the wall, sitting with his wife and kid—he assumed—and an older man and woman. "Tom," he said, walking over. "Great to see you, man."

Tom stood and extended his hand. "Shug, great to see you, too."

They went through hugs and introductions, and Carol, who turned out to be the bar owner's wife, brought everyone fresh drinks. After an hour's worth of reminiscing, Carrie became hungry, and the three females went down the street to Mack's.

"So," Tom said, "you did two more hitches after Nam, huh?"

"Yeah, I thought I'd give the Army a chance, but it got old after a while."

"What are you doing now?" Johnny asked.

Shug leaned back in his chair and sighed. "Well, so far, not much. I'm a month into civilian life, and the only thing I've done is buy a new car."

"You could always try the auto industry," Tom suggested. "I've heard it pays well."

Shug nodded. "I put in an application at the BOP plant in Southfield, but I don't know. I'd like to find something a little more ... interesting? Maybe something where I could be my own boss for a change."

Johnny Lavender cleared his throat. "'Ever think about running a bar? Mine's up for sale. Carol and I are moving to Florida."

Shug laughed. "All my experience is from *this* side of the bar, not operating one."

"It's not a bad life," Johnny said. "You are your own boss, and you meet lots of interesting people." He smiled. "I met Carol here."

"And I met Bonnie here," Tom said.

"Yeah?" Shug said. "Well, I'd say you both got really lucky."

When he arrived back at his apartment a couple of hours later, Shug noticed the little red light blinking on his answering machine. He pressed the playback button, listened for a minute, and then replaced the receiver. His application at the Southfield plant had been accepted. He was to report to personnel on Monday for paperwork processing and training, and start third shift later that evening.

So much for being my own boss, he thought. He kicked off his shoes and turned on the television. Michigan was playing Penn State. He thought, *third shift—I'll have to get used to sleeping days.*

During the third quarter, he went on a halfhearted pantry search, then decided he was still full from the burgers the women had brought back from Mack's Grill. They tasted just like the ones he'd had as a kid. *And those onion rings...*

He sat back down and tried to imagine himself behind the bar at Disco Labrosse. First thing, he'd have to change the name. Disco was deader than dead. The bar would probably cost a fortune anyway. All he had was a small savings account and his Apple Computer stock. *Of course, the stock had done well.*

But the pay at the BOP plant would be awfully good, even if it was working third shift. He could buy more Apple stock, maybe start a retirement account. *God, he was sounding like his father now.* He toyed with names he might use for the bar. Of course, he'd have to replace that old sound system. *But there was that space between the bar and the restrooms.* He wondered if a Wurlitzer or a Rock-Ola might fit in there.

Kill Me Softly

The bar crowd, lively and full of holiday cheer at six o'clock, had dwindled steadily since eight. Now there were less than a dozen customers left. It was always like that on Christmas Eve. Seemed everyone had someplace to be. Shug didn't mind. He was closing early tonight. For the first time in a long time, he had someplace to be.

The front door banged open, and Leon blew in with Janelle Williams right behind him. Both were laden with shopping bags and festively wrapped packages they piled on the far end of the bar.

Leon turned and waved to the few remaining patrons. "Merry Christmas, folks!"

A chorus of hearty replies greeted him, Janelle, too. Since the two had started dating, Janelle often stopped by for a glass of wine after work. It hadn't taken long for her to become friendly with most of the regulars.

Several of the shopping bags had logos that said *Just Toys* and *Small World*. Shug walked over and looked inside. "Well, I don't have to guess who most of this is for."

Leon beamed, something he'd been doing a lot of lately.

Janelle jerked a thumb in his direction. "Don't be too sure, Shug. I thought I'd never get this big lug out of the toy store. Of course, his tastes run more to basketballs and light sabers than toys suitable for Necie."

"Nothin' wrong with that," Leon said, grinning. "Little girls got to be prepared for sports and space travel, just like little boys."

Two months previously, Janelle, a lawyer, had helped guide Leon's sister, Roberta, through the bureaucracy of becoming a foster parent to the daughter of Devonne's late friend, Luther Johnson. Devonne moved back in with his mother to help out, and five-year-old Necie had become the darling of the entire family. Leon glanced around the bar. "Where's my nephew?"

"I sent him home early," Shug said. "He was going to help Roberta get Necie's Santa Claus stuff ready."

"It'll be a new kind of Christmas for the three of them, 'specially Necie," Leon said.

Janelle looked up at Leon and smiled. "For all of us." She turned back to Shug. "We're going over to Roberta's later. You're welcome to join us if you'd like."

"Thanks, but Darcy's coming over for a late dinner. I'm stopping by Russo's for Italian takeout on the way home."

"I can stay if you want and help close up," Leon offered.

Shug shook his head. "No, you guys go on to Roberta's." He checked his watch. "I'll be out of here in half an hour."

Shug lay in bed listening to the sound of Darcy's breathing. She had arrived late, almost eleven-thirty. The veal parmesan, languishing in a warm oven for over an hour, had become rubbery, and the salad had wilted. After a quick meal—Darcy seemed barely able to keep her eyes open—they'd gone straight to bed.

They did make love. It was Christmas Eve, after all. But Shug couldn't shake the feeling that it had been a bit mechanical on Darcy's part—like brushing her teeth before going to sleep. Then he chided himself for being selfish. She had been working so hard. The Squad was under a microscope, more from within the Department than without. Twelve-hour shifts had become routine, some days even longer. And it wasn't like he was sitting around waiting for her; most nights, he got home after midnight.

Darcy shifted beside him and threw her arm across his chest. He felt her warm breath on his neck. *It'll be all right*, he thought. *We're doing fine. Tomorrow's Christmas, and we'll have the whole day together.*

Shug's Place

Eve took a last look around the small California bungalow that had been her refuge for the past six months. The rent was paid through the end of December, but she saw no reason to spend any more time there. Her paintings and art supplies had been crated up weeks ago and shipped to the gallery in New York. The car had been serviced and packed with her few belongings. She was ready to start her new life—one without the shadow of her past hanging over her like a malevolent black cloud. She'd watched the news coverage from Seattle with tears of relief in her eyes. And for the first time in years, she had slept without a nagging twinge of fear.

The telephone rang in the quiet house and startled her, despite her newfound sense of calm. She'd called that morning to have the phone service discontinued, but apparently the order hadn't taken effect yet. She stepped into what had been her painting studio and picked up the receiver. "Hello?"

"Eve?" It was Stacy, the owner of the gallery that displayed her work.

"Stacy," Eve said, glad to hear her friend's voice. "I was just about to leave."

"Huh. Driving across the country is one heck of a way to spend Christmas Day, if you ask me. I keep telling you to sell the damn car and fly here. You won't need a car in the city, anyway."

"I know. It's just that, well, there's a stop I want to make along the way."

"Okay, whatever. When do you think you'll be here? I've made room for you at my place until you can find an apartment."

"I'm not sure, a week maybe. I'll call you from the road and let you know for sure."

"That's fine; I'm not going anywhere, and Eve, be careful on the road."

"You know me; I'm always careful." It was a familiar refrain, one she had lived by, but now she said it with a smile. "See you in the city."

By six o'clock that evening, the holiday lights strung on the houses along the block were glowing festively. Farber sat in his car for over two hours, watching patiently as excited, package-laden families trundled in and out of the various dwellings. The car was a ten-year-old Taurus sedan, gunmetal gray, virtually indistinguishable from the dozen or more other vehicles parked along this normally quiet street in El Cerrito.

He thought it ironic she had chosen to hide here, less than an hour's drive from Cal-Berkeley, the hotbed of civil unrest during the war years. But then, she had always been smart as well as elusive. Not as smart as him, though. He'd always been able to track her down, sooner or later. And this time her guard would be down.

He'd seen no movement or lights on in the bungalow a few spaces down from where he'd parked, and there was no car in the driveway. If she was in there, which didn't appear likely, he'd deal with it. If she wasn't, he'd wait. He got out of the Taurus, moved quickly down the sidewalk, and then to the back of the house. He listened at the door for several minutes and heard nothing. Satisfied Eve wasn't home, he used the butt of his nine-millimeter automatic to break out the back door glass and slipped his hand inside to free the lock.

There was a stillness to the house he didn't like. Moving quickly in the fading light, he checked the closets and drawers. Her clothes and personal papers were gone. The refrigerator was empty. *She'd run again! But no, think, damn it!* There was no way she would know. *How could she?*

He checked the house once more and again found nothing that might give a clue to her whereabouts. He stood looking out through the front window, cursing himself for being too late. Then he saw the green plastic waste container sitting at the curb, City of El Cerrito stamped in white letters on its side, and he smiled. Moments later, he was on the street carrying a black Hefty bag over his shoulder like a shadowy Santa Claus—just another Christmas turkey-sated family member lugging his cache of presents to the car for the ride home.

Across the street, a young family loaded Christmas treasures into the trunk of a Buick Le Sabre. They smiled and waved. "Merry Christmas," shouted the younger of the two children.

He waved in return and shoved the bag into the rear of the Taurus. Minutes later, he sat in the empty parking lot of a major discount store, using a flashlight to ferret through the trash. He found two things of interest: a paid receipt for the recent servicing of an older model Dodge sedan, and three months' worth of telephone bills. There were only a few long distance calls, but they were primarily to two numbers: one with a New York City area code, and one, accounting for most of the calls, to Detroit. The calls to Detroit were all minimum charges, all less than two minutes in duration. He thought that odd but was too excited to give it much importance. He had what he wanted—locations. He had found her before with less. As he shoved the bag out of the car onto the asphalt, he thought he had a pretty good idea where the Detroit number would lead.

He pulled out of the parking lot and turned north. In half an hour, he'd be on Interstate 80 East, heading toward Detroit. New York, too, if necessary, but he doubted it would be. He smiled at the thought and allowed himself a little chuckle.

"Merry Christmas, indeed."

Darcy was restless. She and Shug had slept until almost noon, ate a late breakfast, and watched a couple of saccharine-sweet Christmas classics on television. It was nearly five now, and Shug had clicked through the channels until he'd found a pro football game in progress.

She got up from the sofa and walked into the kitchen. Outside, the light was just beginning to fade. She looked in the refrigerator absently then closed the door and went and stood in the doorway that led into the living room.

"What do you want to do for dinner?"

"I don't know. We can go out if you want."

"It's Christmas," she said. "Everything's closed."

"There're eggs left. I can make omelets."

She leaned against the doorframe and crossed her arms. "I don't think so. I think I'll go out and see if I can find a grocery that's open. Maybe go by my apartment to shower and get a change of clothes."

Shug looked up from the game, his face registering disappointment. "Really? You can always shower here."

"I could use a little fresh air," she said, heading for the closet. "Enjoy the game. I'll be back in an hour or so."

She shrugged into her coat and shut the door behind her. The cold air felt good on her face as she walked to her car. Streetlights were coming on up and down the block, and traffic was sparse. Darcy started the car and pulled away from the curb. She wasn't feeling so restless now. *Why was that?*

At her apartment, she showered and changed, then put her work clothes in a garment bag and took them out to her car. It was after six o'clock. *Good luck finding a grocery store*, she thought, swinging back out onto the asphalt. They'd probably end up with an omelet anyway. But it felt good being out, the streets virtually deserted. It was a proprietary feeling. The city was hers.

Darcy cruised by several closed supermarkets and then turned back in the direction of Shug's house. As she did, the downtown opened up before her like an ocean of sparkling lights and tinsel. She wondered where *he* was tonight. Cozied up in front of a fire somewhere? Or maybe he liked the night air, too, the mostly empty streets. The thought was a siren song in Darcy's head.

She turned right at the next intersection and began a zigzag pattern through the central business district, cruising slowly, and turning up the occasional alley. She'd be late getting back, but it would be all right. Shug was watching football.

Three days after Christmas, Eve checked into The Grove, a residence motel just off Interstate 75, near Detroit's Eastern Market. She might stay only one night, but she might as well be comfortable. Eve gave the clerk a credit card and registered under her own name. She smiled as she did. Using an assumed name had become second nature. Her real name sounded almost foreign when she said it aloud.

It was going on six when she finished showering and dressed in jeans and a long-sleeved, knit sweater that matched her hair. It was only then she allowed herself to look in the telephone directory from her nightstand. It was still there, of course, under "Bars and Lounges"—Shug's Place.

Was she crazy? Maybe. She'd pictured it many times. She'd walk into the bar and he'd be there, and then he'd look up and see her and a smile would break across his face as he said her name.

"Get a grip, Eve," she said, shaking her head. "He may not even recognize you." *And what then? On to New York*, she guessed. She'd had so little control of her life for so many years, and now she had so much. Perhaps it was wrong to want even more. Even so, she did want it, all of it. She checked her face in the bathroom mirror once more, grabbed a jacket, and headed for her car.

Ten minutes later, she found herself hesitating once again, outside the bar. Eve took a deep breath, steeled herself for whatever might lie ahead, and opened the door.

Eric Farber arrived in Detroit a little past noon on Tuesday. He'd taken Interstate 80 out of California and picked up I-94 in Toledo. He got off at the exit for the baseball stadium and cruised by the bar where Eve had found refuge before. The Olds 442 he'd followed to Mount Clemons so many months ago was parked at the curb in front. *Good.* The bait for the trap was in place. He could just sit and wait. He knew in his heart she'd show up there sooner or later. On the other hand, he didn't particularly want to deal with the guy who'd been with Eve that night if he didn't have to. He decided to check the hotels and motels close by. If he could find her alone, he'd have more time to enjoy what he'd planned all these years.

The bar wasn't that crowded. Shug sat at his small desk in back, studying a work schedule for the next week while Devonne filled drink orders out front. With Leon working a swing shift at the plant, it required constant shuffling to keep two people on hand when the bar was open. He was spending more time there than he liked, but with Darcy working like she was, well, what else was he going to do?

He stood and stretched, thinking he might run out for some dinner. A new Thai restaurant had opened a couple of blocks from the bar. Pad Thai would be good, or maybe a curry dish. He stepped out into the area behind the bar where Devonne was serving a customer. "Say, Devonne, you want some—"

As the young man turned, the customer's face was revealed. For a split second, Shug couldn't believe what he saw. He stood frozen, mouth agape. He remembered the television newscast from the week before, the burning house in Seattle. *No*, he thought. *Couldn't be.* But there she was. He frowned slightly and tilted his head to one side as though that might alter the perception of what he was seeing.

"You okay, Shug?" Devonne asked, his gaze drifting from Shug to the woman, then back again to Shug.

"Hello, Shug," she said and smiled. A glass of ale sat on the bar in front of her. The liquid matched the color of her hair and the top she wore. Emerald green eyes looked at him expectantly.

He moved across the floor robotically then stood looking down at her. "Eve?"

"I didn't know if you'd remember."

Shug glanced once at Devonne, who quickly found something to do at the other end of the bar.

"Some things you don't forget," Shug said.

"No, you don't," she replied.

They sat together in one of the corner booths, away from the other customers, while Devonne handled the bar. Shug had gone down the street to Mack's Grill and brought back cheeseburgers and onion rings. Eve bit into one of the rings and licked her lips.

"Tastes like old times," she said.

"Old *time*, you mean. It was just the one night, although it was one of the craziest of my life." As he spoke, the remembered image of her naked body drifted lazily through his head and then dissipated. *Like smoke in the wind*, he thought.

She nodded. "Mine, too. I searched for him, you know? For days afterward, I looked in the newspapers, hoping to see a report where the police had found his body and identified him. There was nothing, though." She took a bite of the cheeseburger and chewed slowly.

Shug watched her.

"So, I knew he was still out there somewhere. I drove to California and went underground again. It was about as far away as I could get. But it wasn't far enough. He came close twice more, and I moved twice more. It drove me crazy, living like that, always looking over my shoulder, always fearful."

"You gave me the impression you'd almost gotten used to it," he said.

"I had, or at least I thought I had ... until..."

"Until what?"

"That night, when we were together, before the bomb, it was so ... it felt so good, so right." Color rose in her cheeks as she took a sip of the ale. "I'm sure I made something from nothing. I mean, we'd just met, and not under the greatest circumstances at that." She shrugged and looked away. "Anyway, after that evening, I felt really alone for the first time."

They were quiet. Shug sipped his beer. His food lay untouched in front of him. Eve ate another onion ring.

"I finally realized," she said, "I could never have a complete life, never have a normal relationship with a man, never have a family, as long as he was after me. I couldn't go to the police, so I had only one other choice. I went after him."

"How?" Shug asked.

"I still have friends, people like me who realize what we were doing back then was wrong, and we're all trying to make amends. We stay in touch and look out for each other when we can. Farber was always cagey, but he thought he was better than he was. People who spent time underground know where to go and what to look for. He did it to me, then I did it to him. Once I started, it took me three months to track him to Seattle."

Shug's eyes widened. "You bombed his house?"

Eve smiled. "No, I called the police anonymously and gave them his location. They were only too happy to check it out. They say he set the explosives off rather than be captured."

"Well, whatever happened," Shug said, raising his glass to her, "it's over now."

Farber had already checked over a dozen hotels and motels when he turned into the residence inn parking lot near the Eastern Market. He parked outside the office and went in. The desk clerk was a dour-looking man in his middle-fifties.

"May I help you, sir?"

Farber smiled. "Yes, I'm meeting my sister here. She's coming in from the West Coast, so I'm not sure if she's arrived yet."

"May I have her name, please?"

"Eve Campbell," he said, confident she felt safe enough to use her real name now that she thought he was dead.

The clerk consulted his computer. "Yes, sir, she checked in a bit before six o'clock."

Now Farber beamed at the man. "Great! Can you give me her room number?"

"No, sir, but I'll be glad to call and let her know you're here."

"On second thought," Farber said, "I think I'll pick up a bottle of wine first. You know, to celebrate her arrival. I'll be back later. You can call her then."

He went back, got in his car, and drove slowly through the parking lot looking for the Dodge sedan he knew belonged to her. When he found nothing, he backed into a space out of sight from the office but where he could see the entrance. He'd followed the bitch this far; waiting a few more minutes, or even a few hours, wouldn't present a problem.

He chuckled softly, thinking of how easily she'd shed her cloak of secrecy and caution in her elation over his apparent demise. He had sensed her on his trail and had hoped to lure her to the house in Seattle. He hadn't expected she'd call in the cops, though, and that had proven unfortunate for his housemate, Roy, another former member of Weatherman. Roy had panicked, wanting them to give themselves up, and Farber knocked him unconscious. The house had been pre-set with explosives and remote detonation capability. Farber had set off a small charge in the front part of the house and escaped during the confusion resulting from that blast. He'd been a block away when the second, larger explosion went off. That Roy's charred body had been mistaken for his was a development he hadn't anticipated, but a welcome one. The misconception probably wouldn't last, but it had bought him time.

Farber popped the trunk latch on his car and went back to inspect his cache of weaponry: an assortment of guns and explosives retrieved from a commercial storage unit near the Seattle house. He finally settled on one and got back in the car. His revenge had been a long time coming. He could already taste its sweetness.

Shug and Eve finished their meal and were sipping coffee in the corner booth. He'd asked about her painting, and they'd made small talk about the bar. He'd told her of his hiring Devonne, and an abbreviated version of how Necie had come to be a part of that family. He hadn't mentioned Darcy at all, and now was wondering why he'd hesitated.

She was quiet while he talked, mostly watching his face. Finally, she slid her hand across the table and let it rest on his. Her touch was electric, and the feeling surprised him.

"I called you, you know?" She shifted her gaze down to their two hands. "I'd lie awake in bed at night, waiting for sleep, and I'd start thinking of you, and I'd call. I'd want to talk to you, but I was afraid to, afraid to let you get involved with me in any way. It was too dangerous." Her eyes flicked up to his again. "Sometimes, just hearing your voice was enough, though, and I could go to sleep."

"That was you?" Shug asked. "I thought ... uh ... I'm not sure what I thought."

Eve nodded. "You were my white knight, the one who saved me from the dragon. It was a fantasy, I know, but it kept me going. It helped make me strong again, strong enough to finally try and take back my life." She pulled her hand back and gave him a shrug. "So, here I am, still wrapped up in a fairy tale, waiting to see how it will all end."

Shug's mind was a jumble of mixed emotions. Sitting across from him, smiling a little half-smile, she *could* play the part of a fairy tale princess. He thought again of the night near Mount Clemons, her trim athlete's body, the way she'd looked at him when he'd pulled her down to him, those eyes. Then the picture faded as Darcy's image popped into his head.

He sighed and leaned back against the wall of the booth. "Yeah, I'm kind of waiting, myself, to see how this whole life thing is going to resolve itself."

Her smile thinned a little, but otherwise her face remained unchanged. "Don't worry, Shug, I'm a grown woman. You're not any more responsible for my happiness than I am for yours." She got up from the booth and stood beside him. "But do me one more favor. I've got something for you back at my motel. Ride with me to pick it up, and I'll drop you off back here afterward."

A hint of her fragrance—she smelled like taffy—reached his nostrils, and he could feel the warmth her body gave off.

"Yeah," he said. "I can do that."

Darcy parked across the street from the bar and shut off the engine. She leaned back against the headrest and closed her eyes. It had been a long day. She and her partners had received a tip from an informant and had apprehended two known felons, armed robbery suspects, in a car parked outside a downtown liquor store. She'd been psyched afterward, full of adrenalin. When she got off work, she started her own personal patrol with a vengeance. It had again proven fruitless, and now, though it was only nine o'clock, she was tired and deflated. To top it off, she hadn't seen or spoken to Shug in nearly three days and was feeling guilty about it.

In fact, she'd been feeling guilty a lot during the past few weeks. Her work and self-imposed routines kept her busy all day and well into the evenings. Two or three times a week, she'd spend the night with Shug. They'd make love, and then she was up and gone in the morning before he woke. He had become a kind of release, a way of distracting her from the frustration that was becoming more and more the biggest part of her waking hours. *Go on, say it ... your obsession.*

She didn't like feeling guilty. It irritated her. But she did like Shug. He was a really nice guy, and he deserved more than she was giving. *How much was she capable of giving?* Darcy pressed the heels of her hands against her eyes. She was too tired for this. A glass of wine would help, and she could spend a little time with Shug. She had her hand on the car handle when the bar door opened and Shug and another woman walked out. Darcy watched as they got into a dark Dodge sedan and drove away.

She hesitated for a moment, confused but curious as well. Then she started her car, did a u-turn in the street, and fell in behind the two of them as they headed toward the interstate.

Eve drove with quiet efficiency, her outward calm belying the fluttery feeling in her stomach. *What had she expected?* That Shug, after all these months, would have harbored some similar version of the far-fetched fantasy she had created? *Grown-up woman, my ass*, she thought. Still, she clung to the hope. *As long as she kept driving, as long as he was with her...*

They arrived at The Grove and turned into the parking lot. "Here we are," she said.

The motel was laid out simply: a low-slung office fronted by a columned portico. The rooms, some constructed like garden apartments, others like townhouses, formed a rectangular pattern around an interior courtyard where the pool was located.

"My room is on the side," Eve said. She drove past the office, made a left turn, and found a space near the end of the long row.

She cut the engine and looked over at Shug. He sat with his back angled against the door, watching her.

"We won't be long," she said. "I promise."

"It's okay. We don't have to hurry. The crowd's small tonight. Devonne can handle it."

Shug's face was bathed in shadow. She tried to read it but couldn't. Was there a message in his words? *Probably not*, she thought. But she couldn't help hoping.

Shug got out of the car and followed Eve to the door. During the drive to the motel, he'd kept asking himself what the hell he was doing. He still hadn't gotten an answer. What he had gotten was a jittery feeling somewhere deep inside, the kind he used to get in high school when he was taking a girl home from a date, wondering whether he'd get a goodnight kiss.

At the entrance to her room, Eve slid a large brass key from its paper sleeve and opened the door. They went inside, and Shug pushed the door closed behind them. Eve flipped a wall switch, and the room was bathed in soft orange hues. A kitchenette lay on Shug's right, separated from the foyer by a counter that could be used for dining. To the left, a sitting area housed a sofa, desk, and television. Across the foyer and directly opposite the door, steps led up to a sleeping loft.

Eve set her purse down on the bar. "It's upstairs," she said. "Come up with me?"

"Sure," he said. The jittery feeling ratcheted itself up to the hum of a high-tension wire.

At the top of the stairs, she flipped another switch, and the same soft, warm glow illuminated the loft. The bed was turned down, and a colorful breakfast menu lay on top of the pillow. Eve went to the closet and returned with a flat package wrapped in brown paper. "Here," she said, holding it out to him.

He peeled a strip of masking tape from one edge, slid the canvas out, and laid it on the bed. Glowing tans and rich sables defined vague shapes that might have been rolling hills and pastureland. Scattered dabs of muted yellows and oranges decorated the mid-ground of the canvas like wildflowers. He stood looking at the painting for several moments.

Eve brushed his arm with her shoulder. "It's a—"

"I know what it is," he said, finally pulling his eyes away from the beauty of her work and turning to look at her. "It's a companion piece to the other one, the one you left in my car."

She nodded. "I started it as soon as I got my studio set up again. You've been on my mind for quite a while, Shug."

"I never knew," he said. His face was inches from hers now, his body humming with the need to reach out and touch her even as the image of Darcy began to form again somewhere in the back of his mind. Eve's hand slid behind his neck, and she kissed him gently with lips that were soft and moist.

"I've been seeing someone," he made himself say. Then he waited for Eve to back away from him, waited to see the hurt look of rejection in those oh-so-green eyes.

She did back away, and he was suddenly filled with self-loathing and regret. Then she grasped the hem of her sweater with both hands and pulled it up over her head in one fluid motion. Standing before him in a lacy white bra and jeans, she said, "That's all right, Shug. I'm shameless when I want something." She slipped her arms around his waist and pressed herself into him. "So, what do you think?"

"I think I feel my resolve weakening," he said and bent down to her.

Farber watched as the Dodge made the turn into the parking lot. He ducked below the dash as the headlights washed across his windshield then smiled as the car eased into a space not fifty yards from where he sat. The smile faded a little when the man got out and followed Farber's intended prey to the door. But then he remembered the fiasco that night near Mount Clemons. *It was the same guy, had to be,* he thought. Well, that wouldn't be so bad. He had a score to settle there, too. The downstairs lights came on in the motel room, and shortly afterward, the lights in the upper level.

His heart rate climbed as he pictured the coming scene in his mind. It would've been nice to toy with her, make her beg for her life, but the unexpected guest would make that scenario difficult. He'd have to be neutralized first, and then there wouldn't be time to drag things out. Gradually, another mental picture formed in Farber's head: the two of them in bed, making enough noise that they wouldn't hear him forcing the door. He reached under the seat and pulled out a two-foot-long steel pry bar. Then he checked the quiet parking lot and opened the car door.

Darcy slowed as the Dodge sedan made a right into the parking lot of a residence motel just off the interstate. It would have been too obvious for her to make the turn as well, so she stopped her car on the street and watched as the sedan found a parking space on the side.

She'd done a lot of thinking as she followed the pair: shocked at first, then angry, then, little by little, coming to realize that she was actually relieved. When she let herself think about it, she knew she'd been using Shug. Giving just enough to ensure he was there for her when she needed him but keeping him at arm's length emotionally. She saw it in his eyes sometimes, and it stoked her feelings of guilt. She didn't have time for guilt.

She had her hand on the gear selector, ready to leave, when she saw the flash of an interior light from a car parked in the corner of the motel lot. A man got out of the vehicle, and when he did, she saw in his hand what appeared to be the profile of a long-barreled weapon. Her fingers found a button on the console, and the car's passenger-side window hummed down quietly. She heard the car door slam shut, and then another sound she knew quite well, one that made her heart leap in her chest: the ratchet of a pump shotgun—locked and loaded.

She cut the ignition and pulled her service weapon from its holster. Then, quickly and quietly, she slipped out of the car and followed the man as he made his way through the dark parking lot.

Farber crept along the back side of the row of cars parked farthest from the buildings until he was directly opposite the door to Eve's room. He checked the lot again. Satisfied he was alone, he ran in a crouch across the width of the lot and knelt beside Eve's car. After a few seconds, he went to the door, and, just for the hell of it, tried the knob. It was unlocked. *Oh my, Eve, how careless you've become.* He listened at the door for a moment then gently pushed it open.

The downstairs was empty, just as he had imagined it would be. He eased the door closed behind him and stopped at the foot of the stairs. From above came sounds of vague movements, whispers, and the rustle of clothing.

He smiled grimly and started up the stairs, the shotgun held ready.

Shug tried to convince himself there was nothing wrong with what he was doing. After all, he thought, he and Darcy had made no commitments to each other. At least, she'd made no visible commitment to him. *Hell, she hadn't even called him in the last three days.*

At the moment, though, it was very hard to think of anything. He was lying on his back on the bed, still clothed, but working on his shirt buttons. Eve straddled him, kissing his eyelids, his nose, his lips. Her hair tickled the sides of his face. His hands went to her slender waist, slid up along her ribcage, then around to the fastener on the lacy white bra.

He found it, released the catch, and let his hands trail up her back to her shoulders. As Eve straightened to slip off the bra, Shug's peripheral vision registered movement to his left. He snapped his head in that direction. Rising, almost floating up from the stairwell, it seemed, the dark shape of a man materialized. At first, Shug saw only the man's eyes, glinting brightly in the soft light, burning with intensity. Then he spotted the gun, saw it swinging around as the figure cleared the low wall of the stairwell.

Shug tried to defeat time. He tried to move faster than the awful slow motion of panic would allow. He grabbed Eve's shoulder and pushed as hard as he could to his right. Her eyes widened in surprise as she went flying across the bed, arms and legs flailing futilely in the air. Her mouth opened in a silent scream, or maybe it wasn't silent, but for Shug it went unheard as the room exploded in violent sound.

Eve spun in slow motion, chestnut-colored hair flying wildly about her face. Her left hip hit the edge of the bed, and she bounced, twisting in mid-air, as the buckshot slammed into her soft flesh. A vivid spray of blood filled the air, as fine as mist. It hung there for a moment, like vapor, pink and iridescent in the soft light as she fell to the floor.

Shug's lungs filled, and desperate words formed in his throat. He thought he shouted, "No!" but couldn't be sure. He struggled into a sitting position, moving slowly and laboriously, like a man underwater. The barrel of the shotgun moved again, this time in his direction. An ejected shell casing arced through the air. Shug's hand found the edge of the painting, and he slung it at the gunman with all his strength. The painting sailed across the room like a misshapen Frisbee. Another concussive blast caught it at the last second, and sent tatters of canvas and chunks of wood flying back into Shug's face.

Then time restarted. A dozen things happened at once. Shug rolled up into a crouch and launched himself at the intruder. The gunman pumped the shotgun. Another casing went flying. Shug saw the orange-red flame from the muzzle blast. He felt himself lifted, tossed back onto the bed. Then he rolled off onto the floor beside Eve's inert form. A barrage of muffled explosions followed: one, two—a pause—then three, four, five. The sounds rang in his ears like rolling thunder. Finally, the salvo was drowned out by the roar of blood rushing through his head. He closed his eyes. A feeling of calm washed over him. He was drifting backward in time to a bar in Barstow, California. He was sitting alone at a table, having a beer, waiting to be shipped out to Viet Nam.

Across from him, lined up at the bar, a group of paratroopers just back from jungle country clinked beer mugs and sang. *If I die in a combat zone, well, box me up and send me home.* He smiled and took a shallow breath as the blackness overtook him.

Darcy ran across the parking lot with the Glock held down at her side. The man had gone inside the same room Shug and the woman had entered only moments before. Her heart rattled inside her ribcage like a snare drum. She went to the motel room door, listened intently, heard nothing. She tried the knob and found it unlocked just as the first gunshot sounded.

She hit the door with her shoulder, sending it banging back against the interior wall as a second discharge boomed in her ears. Above her, the silhouette of the man she had seen stood framed in the light at the top of the stairwell. She raised her weapon and fired just as a third shattering report issued from the shotgun.

In her mind, Darcy saw the pale, moon face of Smoothbore in the windshield of his van, bearing down on her in the alley, grinning like a maniac. She felt the impact from the van then the second impact as she bounced off the cold brick wall. She saw Mike Connelly's florid Irish face and heard his sweet, lilting voice. *I was waitin' for the angels, darlin' ... then there you were—my own special angel, come to take me home.*

At the top of the stairs, the shooter turned, ejected a shell casing, and swung the muzzle of the shotgun downward toward Darcy. She squeezed the trigger—once, twice. The man straightened, took a half-step backward, grasping at the stairwell railing, then toppled forward, tumbling head over heels and coming to rest at the bottom. Darcy walked over and stood looking down at him. Then she raised her weapon again and kept pulling the trigger until the gun was empty.

It had all taken less than a minute. The room was silent. Then somewhere in the distance, sirens began to howl like banshees.

Deep in the bowels of the police headquarters building, Jason Reed, a young civilian computer technician, sipped at his coffee and stared absently at the flickering lines of data on his computer screen. It was bad enough that he'd been called in from a warm bed and the warm girl he'd picked up at a local singles bar. He also had a hangover from hell. After all, the stiff—the *deceased*, if he was into being politically correct, which he wasn't particularly—would still be there during regular work hours. He'd been told it was a cop-involved shooting. *Must have been a real humdinger to have to get him up in the middle of the night.*

But that was the price of being the head geek, he lamented. No one else on staff, not the uniforms and certainly not the detectives, whom he often referred to as the dinosaurs, could run NCIC fingerprint searches like he could. Still, he wondered if the girl—he thought her name was Shirley, or maybe Shelly—would still be there when he got back home.

The computer dinged, and a still image appeared on the monitor. He leaned forward and began to read. Half a minute later he said, "Oh shit!" His hangover was forgotten, as was Shirley, or Shelly, or whomever she might be. He picked up the telephone and punched in the number for his supervisor.

Someone else would be getting out of a warm bed.

Later that morning, three men—Jack Smiley, the Chief of Police; Captain Randolph Todd, Chief of Detectives; and Lieutenant Hank Caldwell, who had oversight responsibility for the fugitive squad—sat around the chief's conference table, waiting silently as his secretary served coffee.

When she closed the door behind her, it was Todd who broke the silence. "How do you want to handle this, Chief?"

"Like nitroglycerin," the chief growled. He glared at Caldwell, who shifted uncomfortably and looked down, avoiding the man's angry gaze. "Christ almighty! How many times did she shoot him?"

"Sixteen times. Missed once," Todd said. "Emptied the magazine. They practically had to scoop the guy into the body bag with a shovel."

Chief Smiley closed his eyes and shook his head as if to clear the image from his brain. "How'd she happen to be there when all this went down?"

"A love triangle," Todd said. "She was following her boyfriend and another woman, and so on and so on."

The chief let out a long breath and lowered his chin to his chest. "Christ almighty," he said again.

"Uh, Chief…" began Hank Caldwell.

"What?"

"Maybe we can spin this thing to our advantage." He glanced at Todd, then back to the chief. "All the press knows for sure is that shots were fired."

"Shots?" Smiley bellowed. "It was a goddamned fusillade in there. We're lucky no one in the adjoining rooms was exploded like a fucking Halloween pumpkin!"

"I know, sir," Caldwell said. "But we also have an opportunity here. Farber was still wanted by the FBI. He killed a cop. All I'm saying is that we should, you know, play up the positive aspects of the incident." He paused briefly and licked his lips. "I mean, we did what the FBI's been trying to do for nearly two decades."

Chief Smiley drummed his fingers on the table top for a moment, then looked at Todd, who simply shrugged and said, "Sure, why not?"

The chief sighed and ran a hand through his bristly salt-and-pepper hair. "This whole fugitive squad was the commissioner's idea in the first place. The son of a bitch will be here in fifteen minutes. We'll let him decide."

D arcy paced outside the police commissioner's office. He was on the telephone, the receptionist had said, but would be with her as soon as he was through.

Lieutenant Caldwell had shown up at The Grove shortly after the first uniforms arrived. Following an intense ten-minute interrogation, she was instructed to go home, stay home, and speak to no one about what had happened. She'd spent that night and most of the next day in and out of periods of fitful sleep. Calls and messages left for the lieutenant went unanswered. She'd tried phoning the hospital several times only to be informed that no information was available on the status of either Jeffery Barnes or the woman who had been brought in with him.

The door to the commissioner's office opened. "Detective Raintree?"

She followed the commissioner into his office. He sat down behind his desk and gestured for her to take one of several gleaming leather guest chairs. The commissioner was a fit man in his early sixties, with a tan face that suggested an active outdoor life. He stared at her for a moment, *not unkindly*, she thought, before he spoke.

"Have you seen the morning newspapers?"

"No, sir. I don't take the paper." She shrugged to hide her nervousness and tried to smile. "Not much time for reading these days."

"Well, then, you should take a look at this." He slid a copy of the *Detroit Free Press* across the desk. She picked it up and scanned the first page. Just above the fold, she found a four-column spread with a subhead that read: *Detroit Police Bag Suspected 70s Bomber.* There was a file photo of Eric Farber taken in 1969 when he was arrested at an anti-war demonstration, and a smaller recent photo of Commissioner Sinclair himself.

Darcy looked up over the top of the newspaper at the man sitting behind the desk. He was smiling. She lowered her gaze and read on: *Eric Farber, a former member of the Weatherman radical organization, and a suspect in the killing of a police officer in Chicago in 1970, was shot to death Wednesday evening by an alert member of Police Commissioner Lyle Sinclair's newly formed Fugitive Squad. Detective Darcy Raintree spotted Farber, who was on the FBI's Most Wanted List, outside a bar in the downtown area and followed him...* She finished the article, which was accompanied by a two-column sidebar describing the Weatherman organization and Farber's suspected involvement in the Chicago killing. Darcy put the paper down on her lap and shook her head.

"What it says here, this is not exactly the way—"

"What it says there," Commissioner Sinclair interrupted, "is the official police account of the incident. It is, in fact, the way it was reported to me by the chief of police, and the way I reported it to the news media." He smiled again. "Therefore, it must be true."

Darcy remained silent, trying to work through the implications of the commissioner's words.

Sinclair continued. "You, Detective Raintree, I should say Detective *Sergeant* Raintree, are a hero." He got up from his chair and came around to sit on the edge of the big mahogany-paneled desk. "And you are now the tactical leader of the fugitive squad."

"Sir?" Darcy said.

"That's right, tactical leader. A new position I just created. But don't think it's going to be easy." The commissioner's brow furrowed slightly. "As you may know, there's been an undercurrent of jealousy within the department about the arrests you and your fellow squad members have been piling up." He reached down and picked the newspaper up from Darcy's lap. "But this," he said, holding the paper aloft, "this makes it all different. This makes us all look good. Why, I'm even thinking of expanding the squad. You'll be picking the new men, of course, or women, as the case may be."

Is this for real? Darcy wondered, *or some kind of cruel joke?* But it must be true, because the commissioner was looking at her expectantly, his eyebrows arched.

"So, Darcy, what do you think? Are you up for this?"

She nodded, licking her lips. "Yes, sir, I just ... I'm surprised, that's all."

"Nonsense," he said, extending his hand. "You deserve it."

Darcy was still dazed from the meeting as she rode the elevator down to her floor. Dazed, but excited, too. There was so much to think about. It occurred to her that she wouldn't have as much time to spend working the old case, the one that had brought her back to Detroit and to the police department, but it didn't seem as important now.

Something had happened to her at The Grove. Some kind of bubble had popped and released all the pent-up frustration that had been building inside her over the past couple of years. She knew she'd keep the Smoothbore file on her desk, there for her when she could afford the time and energy, but now there was a whole new world out there—hers alone to conquer.

Shug had died, but he was still thinking. *Was that right? Could you be dead and still think?* He'd often wondered about death, especially when he was in the jungle. One of his buddies, a private named Armbruster whom they'd called "Melon" because of his big round head, was a born-again Christian and had argued vociferously for the existence of an afterlife. Others had argued, just as vehemently, that there was no such thing, just *zip* and gone. Shug had stayed on the periphery, saying he was just trying to keep an open mind about all of it.

"No you ain't," a skinny kid from Nebraska informed him. "What you're doin,' my man, is hedgin' your bet."

He wondered.

He saw Eve hovering ghostlike above him in the gloom, and he knew then that he was dead, for surely she was dead. He'd seen the spray of blood as the buckshot tore through her back. He tried to speak. It took great concentration, and still the words wouldn't come.

"Hello, Shug," she said.

So, it was true. She was dead. He *was* dead. Only a dead person could hear another dead person speak to him. So be it. He slipped back into the soft, feathery fog.

The room swam back into focus, and he could feel his heart thumping with a steady rhythm. From somewhere behind him, he heard an insectile buzzing he recognized as the sputtering last stage of a failing fluorescent bulb. The unmistakable hospital décor and the pain in his neck and shoulder finally added up.

So, he wasn't dead, at least not yet.

SHUG'S PLACE

The room glittered with sunlight. Sitting next to the window, reading a magazine, was Eve. She wore jeans and a light-blue chambray work shirt, and her left arm was in a sling. Her hair gleamed with copper-blonde highlights and she looked like an angel. But angels had wings, not slings.

"Eve?"

She looked over at him, searching for something in his eyes and apparently finding it. "Hello, handsome. I wondered when you were going to come around again." She placed the book in her chair and came over to stand by the bed.

"What happened?"

"It's a long story," she said, giving him a wry grin. "You sure you have the time for it?"

He looked around the room, noticing for the first time the IV tube taped to his wrist and the bandages covering the upper part of his body. "It would appear that I do."

"Okay," she said, sliding the chair over and sitting down. "When you said you'd been seeing someone, you should have told me she carried a gun."

Eve had been conscious when Darcy came up the stairs. The woman had seemed shell-shocked, holding an automatic weapon loosely at her side as she surveyed the room. Blood spatters decorated the wall and bed linens, and the room stank heavily of cordite.

"Help us," Eve had said.

The woman had turned slowly and looked first at Eve, who lay propped against the wall, her blood-soaked brassiere still hanging loosely from one shoulder. Then at Shug, who lay on his back, the left side of his torso covered in dark red blood. She dropped the weapon and sank to her knees on the carpet. In a voice so low Eve could barely hear, the woman said, "Shug?" A single tear made its way slowly down her cheek.

"Help us!" Eve repeated. "He's still alive. Get help!"

Eve might have told him of the look that passed between her and the policewoman as Eve was being carried out and placed into the ambulance alongside Shug. But she did not. What she did say was more along the lines of what she had read in the newspaper and heard on TV.

A nurse came and checked Shug's vital signs, pleased that he was awake. She informed him that lunch would be served around eleven and asked if he would like beef or chicken. He opted for the beef, thanked the nurse, and waited for Eve to continue.

Her injury was not as bad as it had first appeared. Thanks to his quick action, she said, only a few pellets had impacted her upper arm and shoulder. One had nicked a bone and hurt like hell, but the rest were flesh wounds. She'd spent two nights and one day in the hospital, then was released.

"You saved my life," she said, squeezing his hand. "And we were both lucky that Farber's real expertise was in explosives—not shooting. He was either distracted when Detective Raintree fired her first shot, or she might have winged him. There was no way to know for sure."

Shug had taken pellets in the neck, upper chest, and shoulder. He'd been in surgery for three hours. He would fully recover, they'd said, but it would take time and patience.

"They kept you sedated," Eve told him. "One of the slugs was lodged next to the carotid artery. They didn't want you moving around after the surgery, tearing anything loose."

"How long have I been out?"

"Four days and…" She looked at her watch. "…nine hours."

Shug closed his eyes. Then they popped open again. "Oh my God, the cat! He'll starve."

"Relax," Eve said. "I've been feeding Midnight. I think we've established a relationship of sorts. He's been sleeping with me in your bed."

"You've been staying at my house?"

"Uh-huh. Your partner had a spare key. Under the circumstances, we didn't think you'd mind. I mean, well, I'd sort of worn out my welcome at The Grove."

Shug's Place

After she received treatment, Eve had been questioned by the police and shown photographs of Eric Farber. She told them she had no idea who he was or why he had attacked them. A robbery attempt, perhaps. They said they'd be back to speak to her again. But they hadn't come back, and the following day, after she'd seen the story in the paper, she didn't think they would.

"Leon and his nephew have been here every day to look in on you." Eve sat down carefully on the side of the bed and rested a hand on Shug's thigh. "They tell me you're quite a fellow. I think so, too."

"I'm not so sure about that." He realized then that Eve must have been there with him practically the whole time. "Anyone else drop by?"

"I wondered when you'd ask," she said. "As a matter of fact, Detective Raintree came by for a few minutes the day before yesterday. She was very relieved to know you'll recover."

And that's all there is to that, folks, Shug thought. *Shit happens.*

"Are you in love with her?" Eve asked.

Shug was quiet for a moment. "I thought I was. Now…" He remembered how he'd felt in the motel room, with Eve, what seemed a long time ago. "…now, I'm not so sure."

"Hmmm," Eve said. "I think I can live with that for the time being." She gave his thigh a gentle squeeze. "You know what, Shug? I've lived for so long always looking over my shoulder, I'm ready to take some time and enjoy life. I want to see sunsets on the ocean, feel warm breezes in my hair, and sip chilled wine in the moonlight."

"You want to go to Florida?"

Eve shook her head and smiled. "I was thinking of the Greek Isles."

A dull ache began in Shug's chest, one he didn't think was from his injury. It registered in his brain that he didn't want her to leave.

"I've done well selling my work," she said, "made a small fortune, really. I can go anywhere I want, stay as long as I like. I can paint anywhere."

He thought of asking if she'd consider Detroit again but didn't. He didn't want to seem pathetic.

Then she said, "It'd be nice if you'd go with me when you're well enough to travel."

"Me?" He couldn't help grinning. "You want me to go with you to the Greek Islands?"

"Uh-huh."

"What about the cat?" He would wonder later why he hadn't thought of the bar. Only then would he realize how one moment in time could change a person's sense of values forever.

"Oh, I know of a certain extended family of yours who'd probably be willing to take care of Midnight."

He had to laugh at the thought of Leon or Devonne dealing with his aloof feline, even though it hurt a little. He liked this woman. She had a sense of humor; she was beautiful. He'd never been to the Greek Islands, but he thought it could be interesting.

"Yeah," he said. "I could do that."

Eve leaned down and brushed his lips with hers, and he felt a flood of warmth fill his belly. "Besides," she whispered, "I'm determined to make love with you. Or, at least, die trying."

All's Well

The weather was hot, eight straight days of ninety degrees or better, but the Tigers were cold, having lost thirty-three of their last fifty-five games. *Nothin' new in the Motor City*, Leon mused. The team was presently in the middle of a three-day road trip to Toronto, offering one of those rare summer Sundays when Shug's Place was closed.

Leon and Janelle were having lunch at Roberta's, a frequent occurrence since Necie had become part of the picture. Devonne, whom Necie and everyone else in the family now referred to as Uncle Devonne, lay sprawled on the living room floor between the furry black cat and the five-year-old. The little girl's pink tongue peeked from between her lips as she concentrated intently on her coloring book.

"That's it," Devonne said. "You're doing really great."

She held the book up so Leon could also see her work. "Look, Uncle Leon. I'm staying inside the lines."

"That's just fine, honey," Leon said, grinning. *Girl had more uncles than she knew what to do with.*

The doorbell rang, and Roberta shouted from the kitchen, "Can you get that, Leon? It's probably Cassie and Rodney."

Leon opened the door. Cassie was there with her soon-to-be husband and a big smile. "Hey, Uncle Leon." She hugged him hard, brushed his cheek with her lips, and disappeared into the kitchen where Roberta and Janelle were busy preparing the meal.

Rodney extended his hand. "Afternoon, Mister Tweed."

Leon took the offered hand and gave it a brief shake. "Just call me Leon, son." He had suggested this more times than he could count, but the young man seemed to have a thing for formality. Leon figured it went with his training as an accountant.

The two men sat down on the sofa. Rodney scooped up the TV remote and found a baseball game on TBS. *At least the boy likes sports.* Leon picked up the Sunday paper, then changed his mind, put it down, and pulled an envelope from his pocket. It bore a colorful foreign stamp and a return address from Psara, which he knew was somewhere in the Aegean Sea.

The letters, some were actually little more than notes, came once a month, on average. The first few had detailed a mélange of exotic places and awesome sights, the hurried scribble of someone intent on making the most of an extended vacation. Of late, though, they had become more relaxed, written in the hand of a man who appeared fully comfortable with his surroundings and himself.

Leon ripped the edge of the envelope and slipped the folded paper out. He began to read.

"That another letter from Shug?" Devonne asked.

"Uh-huh," Leon said, his eyes moving slowly over the lazily inked lines.

"He say when he's coming back?"

"Haven't got that far yet. Don't worry, I'll read the letter for everyone to hear after we finish lunch."

Necie paused in her work and turned to Leon. A tiny furrow had creased the junction between her dark eyebrows. "Are we ever gonna see Uncle Shug again?"

Yet another uncle, Leon thought. *But she's got the question right.* He grinned at the little girl and shrugged. "Maybe so, honey, maybe one of these days."

Gentle waves lapped at the shoreline, lulling him into a luxurious, semi-conscious state that he thought of as *floating.* He wasn't truly asleep, yet he couldn't feel the lounge chair beneath him. He couldn't feel the weight of his body or any particular sensation in his arms and legs. The late afternoon sun shown orange-red through his closed eyelids and cradled him hammock-like in its warmth. Palm fronds did a rustling slow dance in his ears, and the sea breezes whispered over his chest like a lover's caress.

The orange-red glow faded. *A passing cloud*, he thought. Then he heard her voice.

"Say, handsome, you planning to sleep all afternoon?"

He opened his eyes. She stood over him, tanned and beautiful. The sun had bleached her hair almost blonde, and light shimmered around its edges like a golden halo. Closer to the water, a half-finished landscape rested on a wooden easel. Next to that, a folding table held her paints and brushes.

"I might," he said, "unless you can offer a more attractive alternative."

She knelt beside him and slowly twirled her finger through the fine curls of hair that surrounded his belly button. "Oh, I imagine I can think of something." Then she squinted up at the sun and gave him an impish grin. "The light's going bad anyway. I'll be through soon."

He watched her walk away and interlaced his fingers behind his head. It had been almost five months since they'd boarded a plane for New York, and then, a few days later, for Athens, Greece. Sometimes, it seemed ages ago, the memories of Detroit fading like those of his childhood, and the war. It was the same with the bar. He had become a silent partner in Shug's Place—*the name even sounded strange now*—relegating its operation to Leon and taking only a small percentage of the profits.

A letter he'd started but hadn't finished lay beside him in a beach bag made from woven grapevines. He fished it out and had penned a few more lines when her shadow blocked the sun again.

"Another letter to Leon? We can wait until you're through, if you want. There's no hurry."

He dropped the pen and paper back into the bag. "No, I think I'd like a glass of chilled wine—we can skip the loaf of bread—and thou."

"You're such a poet."

"And quite a romantic," he added.

"Uh-huh, that, too, especially in the afternoon." She took the beach bag and the half-finished canvas while he gathered up the easel and the rest of her supplies. "I think the islands have been good for you. Think you'll ever want to go back?"

He thought about it for a minute as they strolled barefooted along the water's edge. Somewhere, off in the distance, he heard music. From overhead came the raucous cries of seabirds. "I don't know, maybe one of these days." *For now, though, he had no interest in making plans.*